THE SALT ROAD

THE SALT ROAD

Jane Johnson

WINDSOR
PARAGON

First published 2010
by Viking
This Large Print edition published 2010
by AudioGO Ltd
by arrangement with
Penguin Books Ltd

Hardcover ISBN: 978 1 408 48830 0
Softcover   ISBN: 978 1 408 48831 7

British Library Cataloguing in Publication Data available

Printed and bound in Great Britain by
CPI Antony Rowe, Chippenham and Eastbourne

This is the dead land
This is cactus land
Here the stone images
Are raised, here they receive
The supplication of a dead man's hand . . .

T.S. Eliot, *The Hollow Land*

Salt is the soul of the desert.

Sahrawi proverb

Must a people disappear for us to know they exist?

Mano Dayak, freedom fighter
and negotiator (d. 1995)

CHAPTER ONE

When I was a child, I had a wigwam in our back garden: a circle of thin yellow cotton draped over a bamboo pole and pegged to the lawn. Every time my parents argued, that was where I went. I would lie on my stomach with my fingers in my ears and stare so hard at the red animals printed on its bright decorative border that after a while they began to dance and run, until I wasn't in the garden any more but out on the plains, wearing a fringed deerskin tunic and feathers in my hair, just like the braves in the films I watched every Saturday morning in the cinema down the road.

Even at an early age I found it preferable to be outside in my little tent rather than inside the house. The tent was my space. It was as large as my imagination, which was infinite. But the house, for all its grandeur and Georgian spaciousness, felt small and suffocating. It was stuffed with *things*, as well as with my mother and father's bitterness. They were both archaeologists, my parents: lovers of the past, they had surrounded themselves with boxes of yellowed papers, ancient artefacts, dusty objects; the fragile, friable husks of lost civilizations. I never understood why they decided to have me: even the quietest baby, the most house-trained toddler, the most studious child, would have disrupted the artificial, museum-like calm they had wrapped around themselves. In that house they lived separated from the rest of the world, in a bubble in which dust motes floated silently like the fake snow in a snow-globe. I was

1

not the child to complement such a life, being a wild little creature, loud and messy and unbiddable. I liked to play rough games with the boys instead of engaging in the sedate, codified exchanges of the other girls. I had dolls, but more often than not I beheaded or scalped them, or buried them in the garden and forgot where they were. I had no interest in making fashionable outfits for the oddly attenuated pink plastic mannequins with their insectile torsos and brassy hair that the other girls so worshipped and adorned. I had little interest even in my own clothes: I preferred making mud missiles and catapults and chasing my playmates till my sides hurt from a combination of laughing and stitches, building hides and running around half naked, even in the winter.

'You little savage!' my mother would admonish, accompanying the words with a sharp smack on the backside. 'For God's sake put some clothes on, Isabelle.' She would say this with all the severity her clipped French accent could deliver, as if she thought she could imprint civilized behaviour on me by the use of the full version of my old-fashioned name. But it never really worked.

My friends called me Izzy: it fitted the chaos of me, always buzzing, always noisy—such a trial.

In the garden behind our house my friends and I played at being cowboys and Indians, Zulus, King Arthur and Robin Hood, armed with swords and spears in the form of bamboo canes robbed from the vegetable patch, and make-believe bows and arrows. When it came to the Robin Hood game I always insisted on playing a merry man, or even the Sheriff of Nottingham—anything other than Maid

2

Marian. In all the versions of the legend I'd come across Maid Marian didn't do very much except get imprisoned and/or rescued, which didn't greatly appeal to me. I had no interest in being the swooning prisoner: I wanted to wrestle and hit people with sticks, like the rough little tomboy I was. This was in the late sixties and early seventies: girlpower hadn't yet turned Maid Marian, Guinevere, Arwen or any of the other complaisant heroines of legend into feisty, all-action go-getters. Besides, in comparison with the pale, pretty girls who were my friends, I was too ugly to play the heroine. I didn't care: I liked being ugly. I had thick, black hair and dirty skin and earth under my nails and calluses on my feet, and that was how I preferred it. How I howled when my mother made me take a bath, when she attacked me with Wright's coal tar soap, or tried to untangle my hair. If guests were staying at the house, as they occasionally did, she had to warn them, 'Take no notice of the screaming: it's only Isabelle. She hates having her hair washed.'

You'd never have recognized me three decades later.

The day I went to the solicitor's office to take charge of the letter my father had left me in his will I wore a classic Armani trouser suit and Prada heels. My unruly hair was cut and straightened into a neat shoulder-length bob; my make-up was discreet and expertly applied. The dirt under my nails had been replaced with a practical square-cut French manicure. Ironic, really: I now presented myself in a manner of which my mother would have thoroughly approved, had she still been alive. It was hard even for me, who had travelled every

3

step of the long path between the grubby little hooligan I had once been and the carefully turned-out businesswoman I had become, to reconcile the two.

*　　　*　　　*

The letter he left for me was short and cryptic, which was apposite: my father was a short and cryptic sort of man. It said:

My dear Isabelle
　　I know I have been a great disappointment to you, as a father and as a man. I do not ask for forgiveness, or even understanding. What I did was wrong: I knew it then, and I know it now. One bad decision leads to another and another and another; a chain of events leading to catastrophe. There is a story behind this catastrophe to be told, but I am not the one to tell it. It is something you need to piece together for yourself, for it belongs to you and I do not want to reinterpret it for you, or to spoil it as I have spoiled everything else. So I am leaving you the house: and something else besides. In the attic you will find a box with your name on it. Inside that box are what you might call 'waymarkers' for your life. I know you have always felt at odds with the world in which you found yourself, and I must take at least half of the blame for that; but perhaps by now you have come to terms with it. If that is indeed the case, forget this letter. Do not open the box. Sell the house and everything in it. Let sleeping beasts lie.

Go in peace, Isabelle, and with my love. For the little it is worth.

Anthony Treslove-Fawcett

I read this in the lawyer's office in Holborn, a brisk ten-minute walk away from the office where I worked as a highly paid tax accountant, with the solicitor and his clerk watching on curiously. Also in the envelope, a set of house keys on a battered leather fob.

'All well?' the solicitor asked brightly. A strange question to ask someone whose father has just died; though maybe he was not to know that I had not seen that father in the best part of thirty years; not in person, at least.

I was shaking so much I could hardly speak. 'Yes, thank you,' I replied, stowing the letter and keys clumsily into my handbag. Summoning every ounce of resolve, I gave him a smile so bright it would have dazzled blind Justice herself.

The senior partner tried not to show his disappointment at my failure to disclose the contents. Then he passed me a folder of papers and started to talk very fast.

All I wanted was to be outside now. I needed sunlight on me; I needed outdoor space. I could feel the walls of the office—its stacked shelves and massive filing cabinets—closing in on me. The words 'probate' and 'frozen accounts' and 'legal process' came at me thick and fast, a maddening buzz of flies in the back of my skull. While he was still in mid-sentence, I wrenched open the door, stepped out into the corridor and fled down the stairs.

5

When my father left us, I was fourteen. I had not cried, not one tear. I had mixed feelings about his absence: I hated him for walking out, despised him for running away and abandoning us; but from time to time I suffered flashes of mourning for the father he had occasionally shown himself to be and also felt a considerable relief that he was not there any more. It made life easier, if colder and poorer. My mother did not show the distress his disappearance must have caused her. She was not a demonstrative woman, my mother, and I didn't understand her: she remained a mystery to me throughout my life. My father, with his volcanic temper and choleric disposition, seemed more like me; but my mother was a perfect Ice Queen, chilly and polite, interested only in the outward face one turned to the world. When it came to child-rearing she made it her business to monitor my progress at school, my appearance, my manners. She found emotional display vulgar, and I must have been a terrible disappointment to her with my exuberance and rages. She treated me with a sort of cool impatience, a repressed exasperation, forever repeating her corrections and strictures as if I were an espaliered pear tree that constantly needed lopping in order to make it grow along the correct lines. For most of my life I thought all mothers were like this.

But one day when I returned from school there was something different in the atmosphere of the house, something charged and threatening, as if an electric storm was lurking inside. I found my mother sitting in the half-dark with the curtains drawn. 'Are you OK?' I asked, scared suddenly by the idea of losing a second parent.

I pulled the curtains back and the harsh late-afternoon sunlight obliterated her features, making her face a flat white Kabuki mask, turning her into a foreign, disturbing presence. For a moment this faceless woman sat staring at me as if I were a stranger. Then at last she said, 'Everything was wonderful between us until you came along. I knew you would ruin everything from the first moment I held you in my hands.' She paused. 'Sometimes you just know these things. I told him that I never wanted children; but he was so determined.' She fixed me with her dark eyes and I was appalled by the quiet malevolence I glimpsed there.

Long moments passed and I felt my heart beating wildly. Then she smiled at me and started to talk about the rhododendrons in the garden.

The next day she was just the same as usual. She clicked her tongue over the state of my uniform (I had fallen asleep in it and it was crumpled and ruined) and tried to make me take it off so that she could iron it, but I was out of the door quickly. From that day on I lived as if I were walking across the surface of a frozen lake, terrified that the fragile, apparent surface might at any moment give way, plunging me into the roiling darkness I had glimpsed beneath. Of course, no one else knew about our strange and strained relationship: who was there to tell, and what was there to say? Abandoned by one parent, afraid of another sudden glimpse of the terrifying void inside the other, I realized I was on my own; and so as the years rolled on I devoted myself to being self-sufficient, not just in terms of financial means but in all the ways that matter, sealing myself off from need and desire and pain, making a bubble around myself that no one could penetrate.

But that evening at my kitchen table when I reread the letter I knew that bubble was about to be shattered.

Forget this letter. Do not open the box. Sell the house and everything in it. Let sleeping beasts lie . . .

Was there ever a farewell letter so guaranteed to torment? Whatever did he mean by 'sleeping beasts'? The phrase plagued me. It also filled me with a mysterious, deep-seated excitement. My life had been so settled, so dull, for so long: but I sensed that something was about to change.

*   *   *

At the gym the next morning I determinedly ran and stepped and skied and pulled weights for an hour. I showered, dressed in Chanel and arrived at my office at precisely ten minutes before nine, as I did every working day. There, I switched on the computer, examined my calendar and made a list of the day's tasks, allotting times and precedence to each of them.

I had sought security in all aspects of my life, and as Benjamin Franklin's old saw goes, there is nothing sure in life but death and taxes. Not much fancying the trade of an undertaker, I had opted for the latter. As a corporate tax accountant my working life ran in a smooth routine from day to day. Most nights I'd leave the office at half past six, catch the tube and train home, put together a simple meal and read a book, watch the news on television and go to bed, alone, before eleven. Occasionally, I'd go into town and meet a friend; or a stranger. Sometimes I went to the indoor wall at the Westway or the Castle and climbed like a demon: my one concession to the lost Izzy trapped within. And that was my life.

I kept no ties to the girl I had been. Except for Eve.

I had known Eve since I was thirteen and she had moved into the area with her father. Eve was everything I was not: pretty, funny and more sophisticated than the rest of us, who were busy with trying to stick safety pins in our ears and join, rather belatedly, the punk revolution. Eve wore authentic Westwood bondage trousers and ripped T-shirts tied artfully at the waist; with all this and her dandelion-blonde hair she looked like Debbie Harry. Everyone loved Eve, but for some reason it was me she chose as her friend, and it was Eve I turned to that first Saturday morning after taking receipt of my father's bombshell of a letter.

'Come over,' I said. 'I need some moral support.'

At the other end of the phone, her laugh rang out. 'You hardly need me for that! Give me half an hour, I'll be over for some immoral support. Much more fun.'

She'd come to the funeral with me, and cried till her eyes were red, while I remained stone-faced throughout. Everyone who didn't know me had thought she was Anthony's daughter. 'He was nice, your dad,' she said now, turning her coffee cup around in her hands. 'Remember when Tim Fleming broke my heart?'

Tim Fleming had been seventeen to our

9

thirteen, louche, long-haired and leather-jacketed. Going out with him was just asking for trouble, which was exactly what Eve wanted, and got. I grinned. 'Who could forget?'

'Your father gave me that look of his—you know'—she put her head on one side and fixed me with a beady eye; it was an absurd exaggeration of his most quizzical expression but strangely accurate—'and said: "Pretty girl like you, you're wasted on a git like that." It was so funny, a word like that being said in that incredibly posh accent of his: I just burst out laughing. And that's what I told him myself when I saw him next, remember? "I'm wasted on a git like you!"'

I remembered Eve striding up to Tim Fleming outside the kebab shop, where he was mooching around that Saturday lunchtime with the rest of his friends, and shouting the words out, her blonde hair flying like a banner. She'd seemed so bright and defiant, and I was so proud of her. Hers was not the image of my father I most often remembered, though.

She read my father's letter, frowning in concentration, then read it again. 'Weird,' she said at last and handed it back to me. 'A box in an attic, eh? Do you think your mother's corpse is in it, mouldering away? Perhaps she never died in France at all.' She made a Gothic face at me. The eyeliner beneath her left eye had smudged. I itched to reach over and wipe it away, not out of any lesbian urge but purely for the sake of tidiness.

'Oh, she went back to France, all right.'

As soon as I left to go to university, as if abnegated of all responsibility for me, my mother had sold her share of the house back to my father

10

for some astronomical sum (I had not realized they were even in contact) and gone back to France. I visited her there twice before she died; and each time she was as distant and polite as a passing acquaintance. Each time I sensed dark shadows gliding beneath the composed exterior, and knew that if those shadows were to surface they would emerge with monstrous teeth and the power to destroy. It was probably a relief to both of us that I decided not to visit again.

Eve put a consoling hand on my arm. 'How are you feeling about it all?'

'I don't know.' It was true.

'Oh, come on, Iz. It's me: emotional trainwreck Eve. You don't have to stay buttoned-up with me.'

'To be honest, it was a bit of a shock to hear he was dead. The last time I saw him on TV he looked fine. But the money from selling the house will come in handy.'

For a moment she looked appalled. Then she gave me the bright, forced smile you might give a three-year-old that's just inadvertently (or not) stamped on a frog. 'You're probably still feeling a bit numb, from the shock of it all. Some people grasp the enormity of a death at once; it just takes longer with others. The grief will kick in later.'

'Honestly, Eve, I don't think so. He walked out of my life when I was fourteen. This wretched letter is the first time he's been in contact since. How are you supposed to feel about a father who did that to you? No matter how rich he is.'

My father might have ended up as a rich man, but he hadn't started out that way. Archaeology isn't an occupation known for making fortunes. He had a genuine passion for the ancient past, having

11

spurned the modern world as a thoroughly bad lot, which was not an entirely surprising attitude for a young man coming of age immediately after the Second World War, with all the horrors and inhumanities that liberation had revealed. When he met my mother on a dig in Egypt in the fifties he barely had the price of a meal. She, however, came of aristocratic French stock, with a smart house in the first Paris *arrondissement* and a small chateau in the Lot. They travelled together all over the world, from one ancient site to another. They visited the excavated ziggurat at Dur Untash and joined for a while Kelso's dig at Bethel. They saw the Neolithic plastered skulls unearthed at Jericho and marvelled over the rose-red city at Petra. They saw Imhotep's stepped pyramid and the city of the dead at Saqqara, spent time walking amid the Roman ruins of Volubilis and visiting the ancient capital of the Hoggar at Abalessa. They were, as they loved to tell me, academic nomads, always on the trail of knowledge. And then I came along and put a stop to their joyous quests.

My father got work as a researcher just as the new medium of television was taking off; soon every family in Britain was basing its evening life around its television set. Not long after, he got a lucky break and ended up presenting an hour-long segment when the regular presenter fell ill. He was good at it; he was an immediate hit with the public, with his slightly old-fashioned academic air. He was handsome without being overly distracting, a man whom women enjoyed watching and men would listen to, and infectiously enthusiastic about his favourite subjects. He was the David Attenborough of archaeology: he made history

12

entertaining, and the British have always loved history—they lay claim to so much of it. On the screen he radiated bonhomie and a generous delight in sharing his passion. I remember him on one programme horrifying a British Museum curator by trying on the Sutton Hoo helmet and getting it stuck on the crown of his head. Ancient peoples were smaller than we are today, he spluttered, struggling to wrestle it off, leaving his dark hair standing up in tufts. People loved him for gaffes like this: they made him human and accessible, and by association brought the subjects of his programmes closer to them. It was exceedingly odd to see him still walking and talking on television even after he'd left us, as if nothing had happened. The worst of it was that you never knew where he'd pop up next: he was a public institution, a national treasure. It was easy enough to avoid programmes about history and archaeology, but turn over to watch a charity appeal for some godforsaken corner of Africa and you'd suddenly be caught out as he appeared, running a hand through his increasingly mad hair and making an impassioned plea for funds.

'Come on,' Eve said, leaping to her feet and grabbing up her handbag. 'We're going to the house.' She saw my face and added quickly, 'We can make an assessment in preparation for the sale. Instructions for the agents, stuff to be cleared, that sort of thing. You're going to have to do it some time or another, so why not now, while I'm here? Bit of moral support, remember?'

I stared past her shoulder into the rain-sodden courtyard, where a pair of cats were squaring up to one another, one on the wall, the other on top of the shed. The one on the shed roof had its ears laid flat to its skull; the tabby on the wall looked ready to spring. I walked quickly to the window and tapped on the glass. Both cats turned to stare at me, their yellow gazes inimical. The cat on the shed stood up and stretched its back legs, then its front legs, and leapt neatly down on to the patio. The tabby started unconcernedly to lick its paws. Humans: what did they know?

Abruptly, I remembered the cat we had owned in my youth—Max, short for Doctor Maximus ibn Arabi, a lithe beast with huge ears and a sleek, sandy-brown coat like a fennec fox—and how he would lie stretched out in my sandpit at the bottom of the garden, blinking at the sun as if he had located himself in a tiny yet infinite desert. At the age of eight I asked my father why our cat had such a strange name. My friends' cats were called simple descriptive things such as Blackie or Spot or Socks. 'That's not even his real name,' he told me solemnly, as if imparting one of the world's long-hidden secrets. 'Nor is he even just a cat. He's the reincarnation of an ancient scholar and his real name is Abu abd-Allah Muhammad ibn-Ali ibn Muhammad ibn al-Arabi al-Hatimi al-TTaa'i. And that's why we call him Max.' Which left me none the wiser. But every time that cat looked at me I sensed it regarded me through the veil of hundreds of years of acquired wisdom. Other children might have been unnerved by such a concept, but I was fascinated. I would lie nose to nose with Max out in the garden to see if that wisdom would leap the gap between us, inter-species. I had completely forgotten not just that cat, but the entire sensation of magic and promise and possibility it had represented to the child I had been.

Remembering now, I felt like an entirely different person to that naive and trusting eight-year-old; but perhaps her shade was waiting to be reunited with me under the eaves of my childhood home. 'All right,' I said, making what felt like a momentous decision. 'Let's go.'

CHAPTER TWO

We took my car. On those rare occasions when other people drove me, my right foot hovered constantly over a phantom brake pedal; I had to grit my teeth to prevent myself from yelling 'Watch out!' or 'The light's changing!' I watched other road-users in the rear-view mirror, and out of the corner of my eye, anticipating their every move. My fingers itched to change the gears or take hold of the wheel. I was not what you would call a relaxed passenger.

We crossed the river at Hammersmith, manoeuvred around its clogged-up roundabout and took the A40 into the West End, overtaking the slow weekenders in their family saloons. As we were cutting up through the backstreets around Regent's Park we came upon two men loading a camel into what looked like a glorified horsebox. Or were they taking it out, delivering it to the zoo? It was hard to tell. The camel was single-humped and looked as if it had reached the end of its patience. It had planted its wide, padded front feet sturdily on the wooden ramp and wasn't budging an inch one way or another. Just before we turned the corner into Gloucester Gate, I looked in the rear-view mirror and it was still there, as immobile as a statue.

We reached the house twenty minutes later, having toiled through the clogged traffic of Hampstead Village. I hadn't been back since I'd walked out of it at the age of eighteen, with any illusions I'd had about the benevolence of the world lying in tatters around me and with only the hundred quid I'd raided from my mother's study to sustain me until my university grant came through. 'Give me a couple of minutes, will you?' I asked Eve, and left her sitting in the car on the driveway.

The house regarded me furtively through its shuttered windows. If it recognized me it gave no sign. But I remembered everything about it: the pattern of the creeper as it wound up around the eaves and how it turned to crimson in the autumn, then became plague-spotted and finally a sickly yellow before littering the garden with its annual death. I remembered the rhododendrons whose contorted branches hid the dens of my youth, and the smooth patches on the slate path up to the front door that had been worn by the passage of thousands of feet. It was a Georgian house and its proportions pleased the eye of the adult who regarded it now. As a child, it had seemed vast to me; now it seemed substantial but hardly enormous, impressive but not ostentatious, as if it had somehow shrunk over the course of the intervening years. I looked at it steadily, and knew that I would sell it. I did not even want to go inside. Too many memories waited for me, and not just in the box in the attic.

Instead, I took the path that led around the side

16

of the house to the back garden and gazed at its familiar landscape, hardly breathing, as if to move or make a sound might frighten away the delicate shades that lived there still. I felt that if I were to slip past the screening cover of the dense yew hedge I would surprise my six-year-old self, barefoot and sun-browned, my hair braided in untidy squaw-plaits, victoriously flourishing my latest find: a slow-worm or a toad unceremoniously disinterred from the rockery. Or that if I closed my eyes I would hear the whoops and howls of our little band as we chased one another between the flowerbeds with spud-guns. But the only sound I heard was the alarm cry of a blackbird high up in the cedar tree, liquid and shrill.

I walked on, into my past.

The pond where I had lain on my belly for hours on end, spying on the lazy meanderings of the ornamental carp through the murky depths, was now matted with weed and overgrown with convolvulus and meadow grass. There was the rockery, now little more than a random pile of stones overrun with ground ivy, nettles and dandelions. My father had been no gardener even in his youth; it was my mother who had set about keeping nature at bay. Armed with long-handled loppers, her gardening gauntlets and a pair of secateurs, she seemed like a medieval knight going out to do battle with a small but annoying dragon. Clearly no one had done anything to the garden in years. Wandering through the long grass, I half expected to find the remains of my old wigwam: tatters of faded yellow cloth flapping from skeletal poles like a becalmed *Marie Celeste*, my old rag-rug and toys still scattered where they had been

17

suddenly and mysteriously abandoned. I walked over to the spot where it had stood all those years ago, but there was not even the tell-tale crispy brown circle it left on the lawn when dismantled and packed away for the winter. It might never have existed; and neither might that laughing, bright-eyed child.

Dark clouds had gathered overhead and as I stood there, remembering, it began to rain. Sticking my hands deep into my coat pockets, I trudged back to Eve.

'Come on, then,' I said. 'Let's go inside.'

*　　　*　　　*

I avoided the subject of the attic for as long as I could, though I kept catching Eve casting her eyes towards it every time we passed through the hall, with its winding baronial banister. By the end of three hours we had made a rough inventory of the contents of the house, concentrating on the furniture, the paintings and the more valuable artefacts my parents had collected from around the world. I could not bring myself to enter what had been my parents' bedroom. My own room was along the corridor. Gingerly, I pushed open the door.

Everything was just as I had left it all those years ago, except that it was now rather dusty and faded. On the walls were posters for The Slits and Crass and The Rezillos, angry music for an angry girl; inside the wardrobe, a jumble of clothes that were probably back in fashion in the seedier streets around Camden. I closed the door. That was an era of my life I never wanted to return to, a chapter of a book I wished to leave closed for ever.

Back out in the corridor, I found that Eve had pulled the attic ladder down.

'You know you've got to,' she said gently.

I knew she was right. There was no avoiding it. Up I went.

*   *   *

I have heard of people with a morbid fear of attics. There are countless tales of ghosts and mad folk lurking in the hidden, dark spaces of our houses: all good psychological symbols for the Self and the Other, for the dark side of our personalities that we fear, for the irrational part of the world that we cannot understand and so feel threatened by. It was not the attic that made my hands shake on the ladder. I had no fear of ghosts, as such. I'd scared the kids at school half to death with stories of vengeful spirits and the walking dead. I had no idea where I got such stories from, except that as a child I seemed to be possessed of a ghoulish imagination and a strong stomach. When next door's terrier was run over in the road and I saw its guts spilling out on to the tarmac like great fat white worms, I didn't run away and cry but stood there, gripped by my own fascination. Who knew a dog's body contained such things? I elaborated my next ghost story with these gruesome details and Katie Knox was sick in a rosebush. But since then I'd spent a very long time suppressing my overactive imagination, straitjacketing it into the world that accountants and other such grown-ups inhabit. My fear as I went up into that dark, cobwebby space was of giving the dead power over

19

me in the form of things that would prey on my mind rather than on my body.

At the top of the ladder I reached for the flashlight that my father stowed to the right of the hatch; and there it was, in the same place it had always been. The memory of the last time I had been up here jangled at the edge of my consciousness and I pushed it away into the dark place it had come up from. I clicked the switch and a beam of light swept over the attic space. Boxes. Boxes everywhere.

What had I expected? A solitary box sitting in the middle of a great void, waiting just for me?

I climbed up over the edge and walked the boarded floor in search of the one with my name on it. I'll say this for my father: he was organized. I supposed I had inherited that trait from him. I wondered, scanning the neat labelling and the clarity of his archiving, whether he had known he was going to die, and, if so, for how long? There were boxes of books, by subject; boxes of shoes; boxes of archaeological records; boxes of old papers.

At last I found it. I had probably passed it two or three times, as it was a lot smaller than I'd been expecting; perhaps I'd been influenced by Eve's ghoulish suggestion about it containing the remains of my mother. I crouched down. *Isabelle*, it said on the top in my father's striking italic scrawl. The paper on which this had been written was yellow with age, and the ink was faded. I wondered just how long the box had been sitting there. It had been carefully closed with packing tape so that I could not simply rip into it then and there, tip whatever it contained over the floor and walk away. I picked it up. It was light, but as it tilted something inside shifted position and fell to the other side of the box with a dull thud.

What on earth could have made a noise like that? I stared at the box as if it might contain a skull, or a withered hand. Oh, stop it, Iz, I told myself firmly, and tucked the thing under my arm. It was hard descending the ladder with one hand, but I managed it without mishap. Eve eyed the box greedily. 'Go on, then, open it.'

I shook my head. 'Not now. Not here.'

CHAPTER THREE

London encompasses a vast space, covering well over fifteen hundred square kilometres. Into that space the best part of eight million people are jammed: in Victorian and Edwardian terraces, in seventies council blocks, in modern steel-and-glass towers, sprawling out into endless suburbs. In the past twenty years I had bought and sold flats all over London, forever on the move, forever moving west. I never stayed in one place for long, loving each new property for a year or two, then feeling restless, unsettled. Once I had finished renovating and redecorating and moved my focus outward to the world again, I felt uncomfortable. No matter where I was, no matter how attractive the area or how pleasant the neighbours, I never felt as if I fitted in. Each time I had itchy feet, I would find myself looking in estate agent windows and know that the time had come again to up sticks and move on. I was lucky: the property market moved with me, onward and upward. In the process I managed to trade up from a bedsitter in Nunhead with mushrooms growing between its bathroom tiles, to a one-bedroomed apartment in Brockley, to smarter two- and three-bedroomed Victorian conversion flats in Battersea and Wandsworth, to a mews house tucked away in the backstreets of Chelsea; and had finally ended up in a substantial property in the far south-west of the city, about as far away from my parents' house as you could be while still remaining in London.

Less than forty minutes after we had speeded away from Hampstead we were back in Barnes, having gone from one overpriced middle-class village to another. Both areas reeked of money, old money and new; and for a few sickening seconds, as I drew the Mercedes into the drive, I hated my own version of my parents' house almost as much as I had the original.

I said nothing of this to Eve: she wouldn't have understood even if I could have put it into words. Eve loved things, loved them in a visceral, sensual way, as if they filled the void in her life that should have been filled by a husband and kids. She'd had two husbands, but had never been able to have children. I wondered sometimes if I filled part of that void as well, for she could be bossy with me when I was being slower off the mark than she liked, as if she was playing the mother she had never been and I her child.

I cleared the table and set the box on top of it. It looked ridiculously out of place amongst the shining stainless steel and polished granite of the kitchen: a piece of old rubbish salvaged from the street. I ran a sharp knife down the top seam and

22

watched the paper and packing tape part. *Isa,* it said on one side of the cut, and *belle* on the other.

Eve and I craned our necks over it. Inside, at first glance there appeared to be just a load of dusty old papers. I took them out carefully: they looked fragile enough to disintegrate in my hands. The first sheet was small and a pale green in colour—my mother would have called it 'eau de nil'. It had been folded and refolded many times. On one side there were odd-looking squiggles, impossible to make out since the ink was so old. I turned it over and found an indistinct heading. Something *Maroc . . .* Whatever came next was lost in the fold. It looked as if it might once have been an official document of some kind, for I found a couple of words that appeared to have been printed. I picked out *provi . . .* and a word that began *hegir . . .* But whatever else had been written or printed on it had vanished over time, evaporating inside the box. For a moment it occurred to me that by opening it I had allowed this information to escape, that somehow it was in the air around us, invisible but full of meaning. Fanciful nonsense! I passed the thin green note to Eve. 'Not much help.'

She turned it over; held it up to the light, squinting hard. '*Maroc:* that's Morocco in French, isn't it?' she said after a while. 'And is that a stamp?'

In the bottom corner there was a small, embossed-looking rectangle. It bore a faint image, but even under the brightest of the halogen bulbs we couldn't tell what it was. I put it aside. Next was a sheaf of typed papers, brown at the edges, the printing obviously that of a manual typewriter, since missing serifs and filled spaces appeared in the same letters each time, and occasionally a full stop had punched a hole right through the paper. My father had always had a heavy hand when typing.

Notes regarding the gravesite near Abalessa, read the heading across the top of the page. I scanned it, frowning, taking in the phrases *confused jumble of stones, otherwise known as a redjem* and *commonly found in the Sahara*. At the bottom of the first page the word *skeleton* leapt out at me. Gingerly, I picked up the article, turned the page and quoted aloud to Eve: *According to witnesses, the skeleton of the desert queen had been wrapped in red leather embellished with gold leaf. She lay with her knees bent towards her chest upon the decayed fragments of a wooden bier secured with braided cords of coloured leather and cloth. Her head had been covered by a white veil and three ostrich feathers; two emeralds hung from her earlobes, nine gold bracelets were upon one arm and eight silver bracelets on the other. Around her ankles, neck and waist were scattered beads of carnelian, agate and amazonite . . .* I skipped a bit and then continued: *Professors Maurice Reygasse and Gautiers of the Ethnographical Museum believe this site to have contained the remains of the legendary queen Tin Hinan.*

'Wow,' said Eve. 'What fabulous stuff.' She closed her eyes. 'You can almost smell the desert, can't you? Treasure and a legendary Saharan queen. It's like something out of *Indiana Jones and the Temple of Doom*! But what's it got to do with you?'

I shrugged, feeling a bit sick. 'I haven't the least

idea. From the tone of the notes it doesn't even sound as if Dad was the one who excavated the site.' I put the papers aside: it was like going back in time, seeing their punched-out o's and feeling the impression made by the typewriter keys on the reverse side. It was some sort of message to me, a message from beyond the grave—both the Saharan queen's and my father's. The skin on the back of my neck tingled as if hairs were rising one by one.

The last item in the box was obviously the thing that had shifted when I picked it up in the attic. It was a cotton pouch with a cord wrapped many times around it. It weighed heavily in my hand, more heavily than I'd expected. A sudden electrical current ran up my arm, as if it had given me some sort of shock.

'Do you think it's something from the gravesite?' Eve asked eagerly.

I was shaking now; but whether from excitement or from terror, I did not know. 'I don't think this is a good idea,' I said, dropping the pouch back into the box, then shovelling the papers in after it. I closed the ruptured flap and put the knife down on top to hold it down. 'This is all too weird and cryptic. And so typical of my father. I remember something he once said on TV: "Curiosity in children is to be encouraged. Give a child knowledge on a plate and it will leave it there to dry up, craving something more forbidden. Let it ferret out a treat for itself with the aid of a judicious clue or two and it will learn something for life." Well, I hate being fed sodding clues like this. It's designed to draw me in and prey on me, and I just don't intend to let it. "Let sleeping beasts lie," he said in his letter; perhaps that's what

25

I should do.'

'It'll only prey on you more if you don't open it.'

I knew she was right. I wrestled with my irrational fears, then took a deep breath, removed the knife from the top of the box, delved inside and drew out the pouch. Swiftly, before I could change my mind, I unwound the drawstring and shook the contents into my palm, and we both stared at the thing that lay in my hand.

It was a solid chunk of silver, around five millimetres thick at its top edge, flaring to almost a centimetre or more at its base, the whole being the best part of four centimetres square. Circles of red glass or some semi-transparent stone embellished the central boss, and diagonal bands of complex, arcane patterns were engraved across the corners. A twisted leather thong was attached to the top. I picked it up by this and it swung from my fingers, twirling this way and that like a divining pendant, the red discs capturing the light like rubies. Against the backdrop of my modern kitchen it looked impossibly foreign and out of place.

'Oh, Izzy,' Eve breathed, her eyes round with wonder. 'It's . . . unreal.'

Its weight and massiveness made it feel very real to me; but what on earth was it?

Eve took it from my fingers and examined it closely. For some reason without it in my hand I felt strangely insubstantial.

'I think it's a necklace,' she said after a while. 'But what a barbaric-looking thing!' She wrinkled her nose. 'Not my style; not yours, either, my love.'

It was true: you couldn't get any further from what she called 'my style' than this curious object. I picked up the pouch. A slip of paper protruded from the bag. I eased it out and read there in my father's neat print: 'Amulet, date and provenance unknown, possibly Tuareg; silver, carnelian, leather.' A chill ran down my spine. Was this thing part of the grave-goods of the skeletal queen mentioned in my father's archaeological paper? I pushed it back into the pouch and stared at the lump it made under the cotton. Convulsively, I shovelled it back into the box, feeling quite illogically as if it might bite me. What had I brought into my home? I felt like running outside, digging a hole beneath the patio and reinterring it, along with the papers my father had left me.

*   *   *

That night, for the first time in years, I dreamt.

Through the narrow eye-slit in my veil I see palm trees and my heart rises. I have crossed the desert and survived. *Alhamdulillah*.

Before me, the other caravanners lope easily, their blue robes dun with sand and dust, their veils wound tight against winds that have stripped the fine patina of colour from my grandfather's saddle and torn the bundles from our animals' backs.

I blink and a herd of gazelles flashes past, their brilliant white scuts dancing in and out of the red granite boulders. I blink again and we are in a wide valley at the foot of a deep gorge and there is something watching me. A lion, vaster than any lion can be, gazing down from the cliff! I cry out in alarm.

When I look again I realize it is a natural feature, many camels in height, incised into the rose-red rock by God's own hand, and given

27

perspective by the scatter of adobe houses on the slopes below it and the tiny figures of black-robed women tending to the cultivated terraces. One bold soul accosts Soleymane, asks what we have brought. When he tells her salt and millet, her face falls. She is as old as my grandmother, her eyes outlined with kohl. 'No jewellery?' she asks. 'No gold?'

The days of gold and slaves are past. Times are harder now.

As we enter the oasis town, the muezzin calls out the adhan. We lead the camels to the caravanserai and some of the men go to the mosque, but I want to see the market.

In the souq, artisans are working iron over open fires. I give them a wide berth: the *inadan* channel spirits. Old men sit on blankets selling pyramids of spices, vegetables and, wonder of wonders, leather babouches, bright yellow, as yellow as the sun. Suddenly I imagine them on my feet, resplendent. Such slippers are sure to impress pretty Manta. The next thing I know my hand is reaching for my silver amulet to make a bargain.

Azelouane appears, as if by magic. 'What are you thinking of? That amulet is worth a hundred pairs of babouches; a thousand! What else will protect you from the evil influences of the Kel Asuf?'

But when I look down there are yellow babouches on my feet. They pinch: too new, too tight, but in them I look like an emperor.

Now it is night and we are sitting around our fire wrapped in our blankets and Ibrahim is telling me, 'God created the desert so that there might be a place where he could take his ease. But he soon changed his mind. So he summoned the South Wind, the North Wind and all the other winds and ordered them to become as one and they obeyed. He took a handful of the airy mixture and there came into being—to the glory of Allah, to the confounding of his enemies, and to the benefit of man—the camel. To its legs he bound compassion, on its back he laid saddles, and to its flanks he tied riches, and finally he fastened good fortune to its tail. The desert and the camel are God's gifts to the People.'

'*Allahu akbar*,' I say, because I know it will please him.

'God is great.' He pauses, then leans in. 'Those who are born to the Great Desert can never be free: no matter how far they travel, no matter where they go. The spirits are always with them, those beings that have inhabited this world before there was time, or rock, or sand. Beware the Kel Asuf: wear your veil high; keep your nose and mouth covered. They love the body's orifices, the spirits: they are always looking for a way in. When you make water, use your robe like a tent. When you shit, make sure you do it where the sand is undisturbed.

'You will see their marks if you look closely. Amongst the dunes you will sometimes see a spiral of sand rise in the air for no reason. Where the *sif* dunes ripple like serpents, you may see where their claws have raked the ground. Watch for the changing angles of sun-shadows and moon-shadows, for eddies and ripples, for the perfect tiny circles formed in the surface by blades of grass bent flat by the wind: they leave their traces everywhere. Keep your amulet close at all times: it

29

will keep you safe from harm, and remember, always, that the desert is your home.'

*　　*　　*

I woke before dawn and my mouth felt strangely dry and gritty and there was a strong, musky scent in my nostrils. I lay there for a while, luxuriating in the smooth coolness of my London bed; but it was hard to shift the sensation that instead of a quilted silk comforter and luxury Egyptian cotton sheets upon me, there lurked a smelly camelhair blanket somewhere in the room.

CHAPTER FOUR

I must have gone back to sleep, because the next time I looked at my watch it was well past ten: an event unheard of in my regulated world. I gulped down two glasses of water, put the coffee on, then ran down the road to fetch a copy of the *Sunday Times*, but when I got back found I couldn't sit still for long enough to get halfway down the front page. I felt filled with some kind of hungry energy that made me want to run and leap, to stretch and climb.

I called Eve. 'Let's go climbing.'

Had there been the geographical possibility of such a thing, I'd have selected a sea-cliff or a moorland tor, somewhere elemental and unfrequented where I could hang off my hands from a rock ledge, or pad up a sunlit slab, laughing with glee at the yawning spaces beneath my feet;

but the closest possibility of wild climbing lay several hours' drive away, so half an hour to the Westway climbing wall would have to suffice.

While I was waiting for her to arrive I looked up the word 'amulet' on the internet. The *Online Etymology Dictionary* offered me this:

> **amulet**
> 1447, *amalettys*, from L. *amuletum* (*Pliny*) necklace or brooch worn as a charm against spells, disease, etc. Of uncertain origin, perhaps related to *amoliri*, to avert, to carry away, remove. Not recorded again in English until 1601; the 15th century use may be via Medieval French.

I frowned at the entry, feeling none the wiser. Perhaps the necklace wasn't an archaeological find after all. Perhaps it had been something passed down through my late mother's family, though I couldn't imagine my petite, chic French mother ever wearing any piece of jewellery like it; nor, with her chilly pragmatism, ever resorting to superstition.

I had meant to look up 'Tin Hinan' and 'Abalessa' too; but I simply couldn't sit still for long enough: I had to move, to find an outlet for the monstrous energies that filled me. In the end I leapt in the car and picked up Eve at the corner of the road.

*   *   *

The climbing wall was packed: there were people hanging from ropes all over the place like stranded spiders, kids treated to a birthday celebration being tutored up the practice wall, shrieking their heads off with excitement and terror; serious soloers and boulderers applying themselves fiercely to the problems at the back of the hall. A miasma of loose chalk hung in the air, invading the lungs within minutes. I remembered the place when it had just been a scruffy outdoor facility: a basic traverse wall and a couple of large slabs of concrete bristling with holds from which you could see the traffic speeding past on the A40 flyover; at the top you could surprise drivers by being at eye-level with them. Now it was a state-of-the-art modern climbing gymnasium, its fifty-foot white translucent polyurethane walls anchored to the underside of the underlit flyover like a circus arena, lending real height and a sense of exposure to the routes inside.

At university I'd joined the climbing club but I never enjoyed being under someone else's control, especially that of the lads of the club, who liked to lord it around on the crag, showing off their superior strength and shoulder construction, barking instructions at us feeble women as we failed to reach the holds they pointed out to us, or swinging monkey-fashion in their flashy, slap-dash style. Having honed our rope technique, a couple of us girls sneaked off to try our better balance and more delicate footwork on some hard slabs. Ross Myhill, the worst chauvinist in the group, went straight up an easy crack system in the same rock face and deliberately pissed down the slab ahead of us, like a dog asserting its territory rights. We never climbed with the men again.

I watched Eve now make her way along the

traverse wall. She had good technique and dancer's feet, and she moved neatly, avoiding the bulges and overhangs with an undercut here, an interim toe-dab there. I followed, faster and stronger from pulling weights and circuit training at the gym, and soon caught her up. By the time I had covered the traverse wall three times my forearms felt as hard as wood.

Eve raised an eyebrow. 'Got energy to burn off or something?'

'You could say that.' I felt full of vigour and ready to take on anything. Warmed up now, we put on our harnesses, fetched the rope and worked our way up half a dozen routes of varying degrees of difficulty, clipping the *in situ* bolts and lowering off from the top with pumped muscles and a sense of easy achievement.

I enjoyed working out on climbing walls. I liked the sheer artificiality of them, the reduction of an outdoor adventure sport to a games board of coloured holds, delineated by French technical grades, by rules and protocols, and all in a controlled environment. Climbing in the outside world demanded a lot of you: expertise, risk and judgement, and a total trust in your climbing partner. It was the latter that had always been my sticking point: placing your life in the hands of another human being. At a climbing wall, you trusted your partner to hold the rope and not to let go if you fell: but even if they suffered a lapse in attention you'd still be hard pressed to kill yourself, with all the supervisors and crash mats around.

When we took a break I went off to buy some cold drinks and fortifying flapjacks; when I returned it was to see Eve's blonde head bent over a magazine someone had left on the café table. She looked up and beckoned me over. 'Look at this article about this place they're calling the new climbers' paradise: it's very laid back and easy-going, the weather's brilliant, and the climbing looks amazing. See this crag here: there's a fantastic 5a line going right up the front of it. It's called the Lion's Face or something.'

My gaze locked on to the photo in the double-page spread. The rock was the precise rose-red of the landscape I had seen in my dreams, and there was the very cliff that had towered above the caravan traders, its rugged features carved as distinctly as those of any Disney lion. For a moment it felt as if the world spun. My nostrils were filled with the scent of saffron; my skin felt hot and dusty. I became aware of a strange rhythm in my head, like a slow drumbeat, and for a moment the blood was so loud in my ears that it was like a sea, or like the wind over sand dunes, a susurrus turning to a roar, and I heard a nonsense word again, over and over and over: *Lallawa, Lallawa, Lallawa . . .*

I blinked and shook my head. Eve was staring at me. 'Are you OK?'

'What? I . . .' I frowned. I focused on the picture again. It was just a place, I told myself, a place in the world, a place someone had taken a photo of for a climbing article. What was so unnerving about that?

'It's in Africa,' Eve said. 'In the south-west of Morocco, to be exact, a day away from the Sahara.'

I stared at her, then back at the photo. A crawling sensation started halfway down my spine and worked its way up to the nape of my neck until my whole head was buzzing. 'Morocco?' I echoed, and it felt as if my voice were coming from a different continent. Morocco, land of gold and spices; and maybe the starting point for the 'story' mentioned in my father's letter. The idea was intriguing, intoxicating, and suddenly I was engulfed by a wave of positivity, sweeping away all doubts.

'Let's go,' I said, taking us both by surprise. 'Let's go there, Eve. Take a holiday, go climbing, maybe even drive into the desert. I can take the amulet with me; we can do a bit of detective work, find out something about it . . .'

'What's got into you?' Eve was round-eyed.

'I don't know.' My grin started to fade. I felt confused, hijacked by the force of an idea that did not even feel like my own. 'I don't even know if I want to find out more about the amulet. And I've never had the slightest interest in going to Africa.' A headache was starting to insinuate itself into the bones in my head: I felt as if opposing forces were trying to pull my skull apart.

*   *   *

On the way back I suffered a full-blown migraine attack, complete with little sunbursts and flashes of internal neon lightning. I managed to get home, somehow, as if the car were on auto-pilot. In the kitchen I grabbed a glass of water and turned to walk with it to the bathroom, where I would find the Migraleve. But there, in the middle of the table, was the box, just as I had left it. For some reason I found myself putting down the glass and picking up the pouch. The amulet within slid out on to my hand and nestled there comfortably. There was something reassuring about the solidity of it, the way it weighed in my hand, as if it had been made to fit there.

Suddenly, I had put it on. It lay heavy against my ribs, but not unpleasantly so. When I blinked, it was as if the neon sunbursts had become bright silver gazelles flickering past my eyelids. I went to find the Migraleve.

In the bathroom, instead of hitting the main light-switch, I activated the one that controlled the lights around the mirror. The brightness of the bulbs illumined my face and cast the background into shadow. I had never really appreciated the odd effect of this until now. I looked as if I had been cut out and pasted in somewhere else, on to a different background. My face and eyes glowed above the navy T-shirt I had on; and so did the amulet. Together, we were super-real, and the rest of the world was dark and indistinct.

The jewellery I usually wore was barely noticeable, never showy. I had never owned anything that made such an emphatic statement as the amulet. But it suited me. I could see that now. There was something powerful about its solid lines, something uncompromising and individual about its unashamed ethnicity. For the first time in as long as I could remember, I was rather pleased with my reflection. I looked like a different me: striking and confident.

I had inherited a darker than usual colouring from my French mother. Amongst the pale, golden-rose girls at the private school to which I was subjected between the ages of eleven and sixteen, those most sensitive of formative years, I had always felt myself to be the odd one out. They teased me for my differences, made fun of the shading of soft, dark down on my arms, the wiry blackness of my hair. I hated them for it; and soon began to hate myself. My breasts grew in more quickly than those of my peers, as did the dark triangle of hair that began to sprout between my legs. I took to undressing in the corner of the changing rooms, facing away from everyone else. I was the last out on the hockey pitch, the last to take a shower. I began to starve myself, taking pleasure in seeing my curves diminish. No one noticed, not for a long time; no one but Eve, and she thought thinness was a fashion statement rather than a problem. Then one day in the kitchen I turned around, aware of scrutiny, to find my father watching me.

'You've lost weight.'

I nodded, non-committal. I was thirteen and awkward: it wasn't something I wanted to discuss.

'You shouldn't, you know. Skinny women—' He made a face. 'Not attractive. And you're a beautiful young girl. Young *woman*. You shouldn't be ashamed of the body God gave you.'

I was startled by this. No one had ever called me 'beautiful', and it was certainly not how I thought of myself. But it was a word you couldn't trust, coming from your own father. Don't all parents think their children beautiful?

I put my hand to my face now and watched as my reflection mirrored the action. *Beautiful.* I hadn't thought of myself as even attractive, not for a long time, and yet the reflection told another story. In the mirror I glowed. It was the amulet that did it: it lit me with its own light.

I don't remember what I did with the rest of my day. Perhaps I watched TV; perhaps the migraine returned with a vengeance. I do remember that when I closed my eyes, flashes of another landscape flickered past my inner vision. At one point, with the clarity of hallucination, I saw the face of a girl with bold black eyes, who touched me on my arm as if she had something to tell me and I was not paying proper attention. She said my name, over and over and over.

Except that it wasn't my name she was saying. The word was foreign, unfamiliar; a syllable repeated into absurdity. I strained to hear better, and it was as if someone were speaking to me, telling me a story I couldn't quite hear . . .

CHAPTER FIVE

High above a mountain valley a girl sat sitting beneath a tree, gazing out over the landscape. She had a striking face, strong and distinctive, with a long, straight nose, bold black eyes and an uncompromising chin. No one ever called her pretty or likened her to delicate things—to moonlight or gossamer or the tiny, elegant songbirds that soared in the twilight air. The men who had attempted (unsuccessfully) to woo her spoke in their clumsy verses of wild camels and the great winds of the desert: elemental things over which they could hope to have little control. They strove, and failed, to find rhymes for her name (Mariata); and she repaid their attention with verses as abrasive as a sandstorm and they soon went away.

She had been sitting very still for some time, staring into space as if concentrating hard on something just out of reach. The tree was on the crest of a rocky peak: on the horizon Mount Bazgan loomed as a shadowy presence, and it was from this mountain that the tribe amongst whom she now lived took its name. At this altitude the air was cool and scented with wild thyme and lavender, but even so you could sense the presence of the desert that lay beyond the hills.

A long moment passed in concentration and then she bent to make a mark in the sandy soil at her feet. As she did so a fly settled on her cheek, and then suddenly there were hundreds, an iridescent cloud of them. She swatted them away.

'God curse all flies!' What use were the vile things, with their pointless meandering and their stupid noise? And so many of them, thousands, all over the food, the animals, the babies. Surely if God were a woman, there would be no flies in the world. She could almost hear her mother's voice scolding her for that: *Mariata, you cannot say such things: have some respect!*

But her mother was dead, and she was an outsider in the home of her father's sister. She sighed, and dragged her mind back to the poem she was attempting to compose. An image hovered: she was just beginning to frame it in words when she heard someone approaching. *Bones and dust!* She shrank into the shadows. If she were disturbed, the poem would evaporate like spit on a hot stone. Sarid would pay her if it was good, and when the travelling smith came back she

39

would be able to buy the earrings she had set her heart on. It was her first commission; if she did well, others would follow. It was demeaning to work for pay, but much to her disgust she depended on the charity of others now. Her Aunt Dassine and the other women of the Kel Bazgan treated her with no respect, and certainly not the respect someone of her lineage deserved. They even expected her to milk goats with her own hands—to bind them head to head and pull on their teats! It was disgusting. Everyone knew that such a task was designed only for the hands of the *iklan*. But, despite the lack of deference they accorded her, Mariata was beginning to wish she hadn't moved so far away from the rest of the tribe.

She stilled her breathing. It was probably just a goatherd, but there were bandits in the region, who came by night to steal camels or goats, and recently stories had reached them of peasants murdered as they worked in the garden-farms, of brutal attacks on villages; and here she was, alone and a long way from the camp.

A twig cracked under someone's foot and a moment later a figure moved into her line of sight: a man, his veil lying loose upon his chest. By this detail she knew he was alone and that he did not expect to meet any other man. By the lazy position of the veil and the carriage of the man's head, Mariata knew that this was no bandit but Rhossi, the nephew of the chieftain. Only Rhossi was so arrogant as to think himself immune from the spirits.

The thought of him made her skin prickle. Rhossi had been watching her since her father left her with the Bazgan tribe: she had felt his gaze crawling over her whenever she crossed the encampment, when she danced with the other girls, practising steps for the wedding dances, when she sat beside the fire at night.

He wasn't looking at her now; he was looking at the ground, touching something with the toe of his sandal. Perhaps he would pass by. She watched him kneel and touch the dry grass she had crushed underfoot. Then he raised his head, turned towards her and smiled.

'Are you well there in the shadows, Mariata ult Yemma?'

She saw his eyes fix on her, gleaming. 'Thanks be to God, I am well, Rhossi ag Bahedi,' she said, bringing the edge of her headscarf across the lower part of her face. Over the top of it she glared at him, furious at being discovered.

He grinned. His teeth were sharp, each set slightly apart from the next. The other girls said he was handsome and flashed their eyes at him; but Mariata thought he had a face like a jackal's, narrow and sly, and a regard that was calculating and without warmth even when his mouth was smiling.

'And is it peace with you, Mariata?'

'It is peace with me. Is it peace with you?'

'With God's blessing, it is peace, *insh'allah*.' He kissed the palms of his hands, brought them down his face and touched his chest, just above the heart, all the while maintaining eye contact. It was politeness and piety personified, but somehow he managed to make the gesture obscene.

Mariata glared at him. 'Are you a man, Rhossi ag Bahedi?'

41

He bridled. 'Of course.'

'I was always taught that only little boys and rogues go unveiled. Which are you?'

Rhossi grinned all the more widely. 'I veil only in the presence of my betters, Tukalinden.'

Tukalinden. 'Little Princess'. It was what some of the people of the tribe—those who honoured her lineage—had taken to calling her, for her mother's bloodline could be traced directly back to Tin Hinan, through her daughter Tamerwelt, known as The Hare; but in Rhossi's jackal-mouth the words were heavy with sarcasm.

Mariata got to her feet. Even grinding millet was preferable to passing time with the high chieftain's nephew; even milking goats or collecting dung for the fire. She made to pass him, but he caught her by the shoulder. His fingers dug into her muscle, and it hurt.

'And what is this in the sand, Mariata?' He touched with a toe the symbols she had drawn there while trying to compose the poem; a word here and there to fix the images in her memory, amongst them *yar*, the circle crossed by a line, *yagh*, the closed cross, and *yaz*, the symbol for freedom, and for a man. He squinted at them, suspicious. 'Have you been making sorcery?' His grip tightened. 'Are you casting spells?'

Idiot. He could not read. And he all of twenty-six or seven summers! Almost an old man. If he were able to read, he would have seen Kiiar's name and Sarid's too—the couple to be married next month; he would have seen the ideograms for palm trees and wheat, for a bird and for water. Her wedding poem so far regaled Kiiar thus:

Her skin resembles palm trees,
A garden of wheat, a flowering acacia.
Her braids are like the wings of a bird
Her glistening hair gleams with butter:
It mirrors the sun and the moon.
Her eyes are as round as a ring in the water
When it has been riven by a stone.

But this was lost on Rhossi. He had spent all his time learning swordplay and how to make his camel prance to show off to the girls, and none at all with reading; to him the symbols were nothing more than arcane marks; he could not perceive them as language, he could not understand them at all, and that which he did not understand made him afraid. He would know that women used symbols like these for making charms, harmless things for the most part; but not always, so she would let him think that, and serve him right for his ignorance. Besides, if he thought she made magic, he might just leave her alone.

'Perhaps I am.'

She was gratified to see how Rhossi touched his amulet to ward away the evil eye, but then with a sudden flurry he stamped compulsively on the symbols.

Mariata cried out and made a grab for him, but he pushed her away and she fell back against the tree. 'I'll have no sorcerers in my tribe!' he cried, kicking sand over the symbols, obliterating each one.

The poem was gone. Mariata knew well enough that she would never remember it perfectly. If she could use magic, she would do so now: she would send Rhossi to the demons, summon the Kel Asuf to consume his mind. She wanted to spit at him; she wanted to wound him, but she had seen how ferociously he beat his slaves. She got to her feet and furiously brushed the dust off her robe. '*Your* tribe?'

'It will be soon enough.' His uncle, Moussa ag Iba, had a painful growth in his gut and it was continuing to grow no matter what medicines he took for it. In the tradition of their people, the leadership would pass to the son of his sister.

'Is that what you came all this way to tell me?'

'No, of course not. How would I have known you were out here making spells?'

'But you followed me, didn't you?'

Rhossi's gaze narrowed, but he did not say anything. Instead, he caught one of her hands, gave it a twist and pressed it high between her shoulder-blades, lifting her close to him. His face was so close to hers it was a blur and his breath was hot on her face. She could almost feel the spirits flowing out of him, the fire and madness of them. Then his mouth was upon hers. She clamped her lips closed and began to fight in earnest to escape him, but all he did was laugh.

'If I want to kiss you, I will kiss you. When I am *amenokal* all the people of the Aïr will answer to me. Women will beg me to take them as my third or fourth wife, even my slave! Do you think you are better than them?' He held her at arm's length, watching her. Then he leant in close, his face darkening. 'Or perhaps you think you are better than *me*?' He could read the answer to that in her eyes. They were fearless eyes, dark and bold. And in that moment she could see that he hated her as much as he desired her. 'You need to learn that you are not!' He caught her by the hair, winding a hand in its black, silky length. 'You give yourself such airs, filling the children's heads with your stupid tales, boasting about your family, holding the Kel Taitok above us as if we are just some filthy vassal tribe. It's time you were taught a lesson—' He thrust his free hand hard between her legs and began to drag her robe up.

Mariata, crushed against him, was outraged. To touch a woman without her permission was taboo: forbidden, punishable by exile, or even death.

Down in the valley a wild dog's howl shivered in the air, followed by another and another and another. Something had disturbed them: normally they lay like dry, yellow carcases in untidy heaps in the shadows cast by the drystone terrace walls, while the *harratin* dug and weeded and watered on the other side. The howl hung in the valley like a vulture, buoyed up by the hot air currents; then faded away.

But the disturbance had broken the moment for Rhossi: his head came up; then he pushed Mariata away from him and walked fast to the crest of the hill, shading his eyes to see what had caught the dogs' attention. Keeping a good distance between them, Mariata moved to where she could also stare down into the valley, but all there was to see was a figure making its way up the mountain path, a figure that eventually resolved itself into a woman in a black headscarf and a long, patched blue robe, her head bowed, her shoulders bent as if she bore a burden on her back. Mariata did not recognize her, but since she had only been with the Bazgan tribe for a few weeks, that was no surprise.

But Rhossi was staring at the woman as if he

45

had seen a ghost. Mariata watched as he adjusted his veil, wrapping it swiftly around his face until just a slit remained. His eyes glimmered through the slit. He looked scared.

As if attracted by the movement, the woman looked up briefly and Mariata was surprised to see that she was old, her face a bag of wrinkles, her skin dark as acacia wood. She looked sad and exhausted; she looked as if she must have been driven by powerful forces to make this hard journey, up this steep, rocky path into another tribe's territory. Was it hunger that drove her, Mariata wondered? Or did she bring news? Strangers usually had a tale to tell.

As if it was the most natural reaction in the world, Rhossi picked up a rock and hurled it at the old woman, hurled it with real venom. It struck the stranger hard and she cried out, spun and lost her footing, slipping on the loose scree of the path and falling with some force. At once, Rhossi was off and running, leaving Mariata fixed in place, staring down at the injured woman, complicit in the attack by the mere fact of her presence.

When the woman did not get up, Mariata shook off her torpor and climbed down through the scrub and thorn and rock. By the time she reached the stranger's side, the old woman was groaning and trying to sit up. 'Salaam aleikum,' Mariata greeted her. Peace be upon you.

'Aleikum as salaam,' the old woman responded. On you be peace. Her voice was as harsh as a crow's.

A claw-like hand clutched at Mariata's robe, found her shoulder and began to haul. Mariata helped the old woman to sit upright. Her head-

46

covering had fallen off, revealing a twist of dark braids that had been intricately plaited and knotted with scraps of coloured leather, beads and shells. Here and there were bright threads of silver: these were no ornament but hairs coloured by age. The eyes that searched Mariata's face were a bright, deep brown, without the cloud of cataract: and though they were buried in a wealth of deep sun-lines, it seemed the visitor was not such a crone after all.

'Are you all right?' Mariata asked her.

'Thanks be, I am well.' But the woman winced as she moved her arm, and blood was beginning to soak through her robe where the rock had struck her.

'You are bleeding. Let me look.'

But as Mariata reached to examine the wound, the woman caught her by the chin and stared intently into her face. 'You aren't a local girl.' It was a statement, not a question.

'I come from the Hoggar.'

The woman nodded to herself and made a gesture of respect: it was an old-fashioned gesture, not one often made nowadays, when people were beginning to forget the old ways, the old hierarchies. 'My name is Rahma ult Jouma, and you must be the daughter of Yemma ult Tofenat.' Her eyes gleamed. 'I have walked for eight days to find you.'

Mariata was appalled. 'Why would you do such a thing?'

'I had the honour to know your grandmother. She was a woman with extraordinary powers.'

Her grandmother had died years ago. Flashes of memory offered a tall figure, very grand, decked

47

with silver and rather frightening, with fierce eyes and a nose as curved and sharp as an eagle's beak.

'What powers?'

'Your grandmother communed with the spirits.'

Mariata's eyes became round. 'She did?'

'She had great skill with words and she drove out demons; and I need someone who can do that. My son is dying. Someone has placed the evil eye upon him: he has been possessed by spirits. Every medicine woman and herbalist in the Adagh has visited him, every *marabout* and expert in Qur'anic texts, every *bokaye*; even a travelling magician from Tin Buktu. But no one has been able to help him. The Kel Asuf have him in their grip, and they care nothing for the Qur'an or for plants. It requires a specialist, and that is why I have walked so far to find you.'

'I'm afraid I don't have any magic in me,' Mariata said. Secretly she was flattered. She liked to be considered different from the women of the Bazgan. 'I can't help you—I'm not a healer. I'm a poet.'

Rahma ult Jouma made a face. 'Well, I can't help that. All I know is that when I cast the bones they gave me your grandmother's name.'

'I am not my grandmother.'

'You are the last of her line. The power of the Founder has been passed down through the women of your family.'

Mariata was beginning to think the stranger was herself mad, a poor, sun-touched vagrant, a *baggara*. The desert took its toll on many who lived within and around its fiery borders. She stood up and took a step away. 'Look, I'm sorry, I can't help you. I don't have any magical powers.'

48

Rahma caught her by the arm. 'I have come a long way to find you.'

'I'm sorry.' She pulled away, but the older woman was not letting go. 'I can't imagine how you knew I was here, anyway.'

'A travelling smith passed through our village and he told us a woman of the Iboglan was living amongst the Bazgan, a very imperious girl; fine-boned and *asfar*; and that she had asked that a pair of earrings bearing the symbol of the hare be made especially for her. Only a woman of Tamerwelt's line would ask for such an icon.'

The smiths carried news and gossip far and wide. So that explained it. Mariata's hand went to her face. It was true that her skin tone was lighter than that of women from the more southerly tribes; and the hare was the animal with which she and the women of her family had a special bond.

'The smith said she had been left with the Bazgan by her father, that her mother was dead. He also said the nephew of the chieftain was paying her a lot of attention, but that she didn't encourage his advances.' And here, the old woman spat into the dirt. Her spittle was red with blood: in the fall she must have bitten her tongue.

Mariata looked away, uncomfortable. 'And how did you know I was up here, so far from the camp?'

'I passed a tall girl herding goats down in the valley. She told me where you were.'

That would be Naïma. Mariata had shared her bread with her on her way up the mountain, and the goatherd had given her some wild figs. Fate seemed to be conspiring against her. 'She was the only one who knew I was here.'

'Apart from the man who threw the rock at me.'

Mariata nodded, embarrassed.

'Perhaps the son of Bahedi, the brother of Moussa.'

'Rhossi, yes. How could you know that?' You could tell a man of one tribe from the man of another by the way he wore his veil—an extra twist, a higher peak, a longer tail—but to be able to distinguish an individual from another tribe at such a distance? Surely that was impossible.

'His actions marked him out to me. He is a coward. In that respect he resembles the other men of his family.'

Any man speaking of the amenokal's kin like that would be forced to defend his words with his sword. It was as well they were alone, although Mariata had heard that sometimes the wind carried insults to the insulted, and so it was that feuds were continued.

'You know his family, then?'

Rahma's expression became guarded. 'You could say that. Come, there isn't any time to waste. It's a long walk back to my village.'

Mariata laughed. 'I'm not going with you! Besides, you're in no fit state to make such a journey. You don't look as if you've eaten or drunk in days. And now you're hurt too; and look, your feet are bleeding.'

Rahma looked down. It was true: there was blood oozing between her toes, staining the worn and dusty leather of her sandals.

'Come with me to the encampment. I'll make sure you're given food and water and a bed for the night, and maybe one of the men will take you back to your village tomorrow.'

The woman spat on the ground. 'I shall never

50

set foot amongst the Kel Bazgan ever again; it was with great misgiving that I have come this far.'

Mariata sighed. What a dilemma. She could hardly abandon a woman who had come so far to find her, and who had been injured in the process. 'Come with me to the harratin: they will take care of you.'

Rahma ult Jouma smiled. 'Such diplomacy. How like your grandmother you are.' She patted Mariata's hand.

Down in the valley the harratin, who worked the garden-farms for the tribal chieftains, had erected a village of little round huts made from river-reeds, mud and stones. They lived here all year, while the tribespeople led their traditionally nomadic life, travelling out along the ancient Saharan routes from one oasis to another, returning in the harvest season to take the crops they had financed, leaving the harratin the fifth they were due for their labour. Although they were used to Moussa ag Iba's overseers visiting to check on the progress of the winter foodstuffs, the sight of two desert tribeswomen walking unaccompanied into their midst made even the children stop playing and stare. A group of old harratin women stood around in a circle, pounding grain in a mortar, their black skin greyed by the flying powder, the slack flesh on their arms shuddering with every impact. They stopped in mid-strike at the sight of Mariata and Rahma. Two younger women, weaving a rug on a tall upright loom, gazed through the grille of threads at the newcomers, their solemn, dark faces sliced by the bright wool. Even the old men paused in their basket-weaving. No one said anything.

At last one of the men got slowly to his feet and

came forward, head high, eyes wary. He wore a patched and tattered robe; he did not look much like a headman, despite his air of authority. He made the customary greeting, then stared at the visitors, waiting.

Mariata explained that Rahma needed attention from a healer, and something to eat and drink. 'I have nothing to give you in return now, but I'll come back later with something for you, some silver—'

The elder laughed. 'What use is silver to us? Plead for some respite for my people with the amenokal: that would be the best reward you could give us.'

'I don't think the amenokal knows the meaning of the word "respite",' Rahma said.

The elder looked surprised but said no more.

'I'm not in a position to intervene with the amenokal for you,' Mariata said gently. 'But I will bring you tea and rice.'

The man put his hand to his chest and bowed. 'Thank you, that would be most acceptable.'

Mariata turned to Rahma. 'I'll come back to see you tomorrow.'

'Make sure you do: we must make haste.'

'I won't be going with you.'

'Oh, I think you will. Look around. Can you condone what is happening here?'

Mariata was bemused. 'What do you mean?' It was just a normal harratin village, shabby and poorly put together.

'Look: really look. Can't you see they are starving?'

Mariata looked around, focusing on the details of the harratin life for the first time. The children were huge-eyed, their bellies bulging, their arms and legs like sticks. The adults looked exhausted, as if they had worked themselves half to death, the bright patterns of their robes mocking the dullness of their eyes, sunken cheeks and desperate expressions.

Rahma gestured to the rug the women were weaving. 'Even that will be taken by Moussa's people. They will have been given the wool and the design: the Kel Bazgan will sell it for profit and the harratin will get practically nothing for it.' She walked over to the old women and said something to them in their own language, and they jabbered back. She gestured for Mariata to join her. 'You see that? They have only the spoiled grain from which to make their flour, the ears they have garnered from amongst the chaff—not even the fifth part of the crop their contract stipulates. And see the children playing over there—'

Between the huts two lighter-skinned toddlers squatted in the mud, while a pair of older children, leaning against the wall of a hut, watched them wearily.

Mariata nodded. Rahma clicked her tongue. 'Do the little ones look like true harratin children? I think not, with skin so fair. I think young Rhossi has been sowing his seed far and wide. The first child was made by force, they tell me; the second girl learnt enough from the first to make a bargain.'

*   *   *

On the way back to the encampment, Mariata once more passed Naïma with the tribe's goats and for the first time noticed how very many of them there were—black and brown, piebald and skewbald, white and gingery orange—all milling around amongst the valley trees, stripping whatever foliage they could find. On the outskirts of the camp she passed the flock of sheep, the ewes hobbled, the youngsters left to run free, since they never wandered far from their dams. They looked plump and lively, and there were so many that she could not count them. Now the tents came into view, and beside them were the precious camels—the sturdy Maghrabis and the long-haired Berabish camels, the short grey Adrars and the mehari, the prized white camels from the Tibesti uplands of Chad. The mehari were a great luxury, expensive playthings for rich young men, who rarely used them for what they had been bred for: to travel at speed through the deep desert to raid other tribes or caravans. Instead they just raced them, placing wagers on the outcome. She knew that two of the great white camels, with their haughty heads and skittish ways, belonged to Rhossi.

The Kel Bazgan's low-lying hide tents looked to be plain and simple dwellings from the outside, but inside the women kept their treasures: bright rugs, soft sheepskins, carved chairs and beds, boxes of silver jewellery, woollen robes, slippers and sandals decorated with studs of brass, gorgeously coloured and fringed leather bags. On the east side of the women's tents their husbands stored their most precious belongings: swords that had been forged from Toledo steel three centuries before and passed down the generations; *tcherots* and *gris-gris*; thick silver armlets and richly adorned saddles. There were boxes of rice, sacks of millet, bags of

54

flour; jars of oil and olives, pots of spices brought from northern markets. The women were plump; the children fat. Even the dogs were well fed. Only the poor were thin. The Bazgan tribe might not enjoy the legendary standing of the Kel Taitok, but it was a wealthy clan nevertheless. As Mariata looked around, it was as if she were seeing it all for the first time; and for the first time she felt ashamed. She had never once given a thought to the polarity between the lives of her people and those of the harratin on whom they depended, having always considered their relative estates the natural order of things. They were the aristocrats and the harratin were their retainers, paid to provide their services. That they were not paid well, or possibly even fairly, had never occurred to her before.

As she sat around the campfire that night with the other women eating spicy mutton with the fragrant flatbread the slaves had made that afternoon, the thought suddenly occurred to her that she had seen no livestock at all in the harratin village. She was quite certain none of them would be eating meat that night, or indeed that month, and the realization made the lamb stick in her throat until she coughed and coughed.

'Are you unwell, Mariata?' her Aunt Dassine asked. She was a sharp-eyed woman, sharp-tongued too.

'I have lost my appetite,' Mariata replied a little stiffly.

Seated at Dassine's side, Yallawa stared coldly at Mariata, then turned to her neighbour. 'The Kel Taitok eat only the most tender of gazelles: clearly our poor sheep are not sufficiently palatable for

55

our regal kinswoman.'

Mariata pushed the rest of her meal away from her. 'I am not hungry, though I passed many today who were.'

Curious eyes turned to her. 'Beggars, maybe?' Dassine asked.

'Your own harratin,' Mariata replied shortly. 'Their children's bellies are swollen with hunger. Even the adults are thin as sticks.'

People began to murmur. Mariata could catch only a word here or there, but the glances the women gave her were hostile. At last Yallawa said, 'This is not a subject suitable for discussion by ignorant young women.' She fixed Mariata with her cold regard. 'And it is especially unsuitable for a young woman who is dependent on the charity of others for her well-being to voice such foolish and unwanted opinions.'

'It is not my fault that my mother is dead and that my father treads the salt road. I would hardly have chosen to come here, but I wasn't given the choice.'

Dassine thrust her face at Mariata. 'When my brother took your mother to wife, the Kel Taitok treated those of us who travelled all the way to the wedding as if we were vassals bringing them tribute. The women laughed behind their hands at our darker skin and made fun of our best clothes, our jewellery and the way our men wear their veils. You may give yourself airs and boast of your elevated ancestry; but your bloodline does not impress me. You are lucky to be pretty enough to have attracted the eye of Awa's fine son: at least such a match will temper your arrogance.'

Mariata pushed herself to her feet and without a

word walked away, not trusting herself to respond in a civil manner.

She gave the men's campfire as wide a berth as possible as she made her way to the tents; but even so she saw out of the corner of her eye how Rhossi ag Bahedi detached himself from the group. She increased her pace, but he soon caught her up and stood in front of her, his dark eyes blazing.

'Walk with me.'

'I will go nowhere willingly with you.'

'You should do what I say, if you know what's good for you.'

'Since when did any man have the right to tell a woman what to do?'

'You will regret it if you don't.'

'I am sure I would regret it if I did.'

He caught her by the arm. 'I hope you haven't said anything to anyone you should not have said.'

'I can't imagine what you mean.'

He gave her a little shake. 'You know perfectly well what I mean.'

'Oh, like telling everyone how you so bravely threw rocks at a defenceless old woman?'

'Is she dead?' he asked, a little too avidly.

Mariata regarded him curiously. 'Why should the high chieftain's heir care so much about the fate of a poor wandering baggara?'

Rhossi glared at her. 'A baggara, yes, that's all she is. But did she live? Tell me at once.'

'I am happy to report that her death does not lie on your conscience.'

Rhossi let her go and drew back. 'I'm glad to hear it.' He did not sound sincere. 'Where is she now?'

Mariata hesitated. 'She went on her way,' she

said at last, and watched as relief flooded his face. 'And now I shall be on mine.' She yawned hugely. 'Today events have tired me out.'

'I will see you to your aunt's tent.'

Mariata laughed. 'I hardly need a companion to see me safely home over such a short distance.'

'Even so.' He took her elbow and walked her away from the campfires. 'Do not ever mention that woman to anyone, do you hear me?'

'Who is she, that you're so concerned that no one knows who she is?'

His jaw tightened. 'No one special.'

At the entrance to Dassine's tent, Mariata stopped. 'Good night, Rhossi.' Detaching herself from his grasp, she ducked inside. She bent, lit the candle-lantern and knelt to arrange her bed. She had brought the embroidered bedcovering that lay on top of the frame with her: it had come from the south of Morocco and she loved it. Rows of embroidered red camels, unrecognizable to any who did not understand the geometric abstraction, marched across a background of gold; around the edges stylized flowers made star-shapes like the mosaic tilework she had once seen in Tamanrassett. This item, more than any other, reminded her of home. They had left in such haste. 'Bring only those things you can carry,' her father had told her brusquely. 'Your Aunt Dassine will have everything you need and I don't want the caravan to be held up by having to cart your possessions all over the desert.'

She had left a dozen fine robes, boots for the winter, jewelled sandals and belts, many coloured headscarves and shawls, her sheepskins and the fine goat-leather her mother had been keeping for

58

her so that she could make her own tent when she married. All she had brought with her was contained in the wooden box beside her bed: her jewellery, cosmetics, a little knife and a spare robe. The clothes on her back and this bedcovering represented all she had left in the world—or at least in this place. She ran her hands over the embroidery, feeling homesick and lonely.

'Very pretty.'

She turned but before she could cry out there was a hand over her mouth. She could smell the stink of mutton-fat on it, and the char of the fire.

'Who are you going to call for? Your father and brothers are halfway across the Sahara, loading up their camels with cones of salt like the common traders they are. Your aunt? She can't stand the sight of you. Your cousins, Ana and Nofa? They've both been chasing after me for years: not that I've any interest in them—the hulking great oxen. All the men live in fear of my uncle, and I am his chosen successor. You're an outsider in this tribe, Mariata, while I am the heir of its high chief. No one is going to lift a hand to stop me. And afterwards, whose word are people going to believe?'

Rhossi pushed her face down on the bed and held her there, straddling her body, his weight suffocating her. She couldn't call out, could hardly breathe. The next thing she knew there was cold air on the back of her bare thighs and a hand trying to prise her legs apart, fingernails digging into her delicate flesh. 'Don't struggle,' he told her. 'You'll enjoy it: girls always do when they get used to the idea. Just stay still, damn you.'

Her cries of outrage were swallowed by the

bedding.

'You don't need to worry about the baby: you won't need to kill it—you'll be my wife. There'll be no shame.'

There came a moment when his hold on her lessened and in that moment Mariata felt herself filled by a spirit, a vengeful, ravening thing possessed of supernatural strength. An animal noise came out of her, rough and guttural as she bucked and twisted. Her right arm came free and she shot out a wild elbow that caught Rhossi full in the mouth. Everything stopped.

Mariata fought herself upright, dragging her robe back around her ankles. From her treasure chest beside the bed she took the little dagger and held it out in front of her breathing hard, ready to use it.

Rhossi's eyes were huge. He touched his face. The hand came away from his mouth covered in blood and he stared at it as if both hand and blood belonged to someone else. When he spat, a tooth fell out on to the beautiful bedcover, spotting it with a different shade of red. He looked at it in disbelief, then transferred his gaze to Mariata. A little whimper escaped him, and then he started to cry. He hurled himself to his feet and ran from the tent.

Mariata stared after him. Then she moved methodically around the tent, collecting the things she would need.

*   *   *

She arrived at the harratin village an hour later.

'Tell no one that you have seen either Rahma or

myself,' she instructed the headman carefully. 'And make sure everyone in the village—even the children—say the same thing. They will punish you if they know you have helped us.'

She gave him the rice and flour and tea she had stolen from Dassine's tent. Then she took Rahma by the arm and led her out to where two of the fine white, fully laden mehari camels that had once belonged to Rhossi ag Bahedi stood waiting complaisantly for them under the light of the three-quarters moon.

CHAPTER SIX

Had I forgotten to take off the amulet when I went to bed that night? You'd think it'd be a hard thing to forget, as massive as it was. But I was wearing it when I woke up the next morning.

As I swung my legs out of bed, I had the sense that I was in two places at once, but never fully present in either. And when I threw back the curtains it seemed to me that the London sun that shone in on me was dull, as if someone had changed a hundred-watt lightbulb for a low-energy equivalent.

On the tube as I travelled in to work I was aware for the first time in years that millions of tons of stone and earth and sewers and buildings were pressing down upon the tunnel through which we passed at unnatural speed. Trying to divert my attention from this uncomfortable thought, I cast my gaze around the carriage. An advert for holidays in Egypt, a line of camels silhouetted against dunes and pyramids; cheap flights to Marrakech . . . A knot of foreign women got on at Knightsbridge and stood swaying with the movement of the train, only their heavily kohled eyes visible in the slit black fabric of their niqabs. One of them looked right at me, said something to her companions and they all stared at me.

Disconcerted, I picked up a discarded *Guardian* and opened it at random. Under world news a paragraph leapt out at me: 'Four hostages, employees of the French nuclear company Areva, have been kidnapped by a splinter group from the Niger Movement for Justice, a group of so-called Tuareg freedom-fighters.' *Tuareg*: the word snagged my eye. It was foreign, unknown, yet somehow familiar. I had the sense I had come across it recently, and that it held some weighty significance, but I was unable to dredge up the relevant connection from my fuzzy memory. 'A spokesman for the group said the four captured hostages were "in good health" and being held in the Aïr, the conflict zone in Niger.' With sudden vivid force I remembered my mother talking about the huge reserves of uranium that had been discovered in what was then the French colony of Niger, a discovery that had enabled France to become a nuclear power. Ah yes, Niger. In my mind I heard her languorous accent playing over the two long, foreign syllables: *Neee-jhair*. My maternal grandfather had made much of his sizeable fortune there and elsewhere in the French colonies, mining. Or, as I had once put it to him in the midst of a furious teenage argument, 'raping African resources'. My youthful political fervour had soon given way to more inward, personal angst, and then to the cowed and cautious conservatism that had taken me through my accountancy training and into my comfortable career. Feeling a brief shudder of shame, I read on.

'Where once our families drove their livestock and pastured their camels, there is now nothing but a vast industrial waste land. No one asked our permission, no one paid us compensation. They stole our lands; they stole our livelihoods and our children's inheritance. Our people are left destitute. These hostages will not be harmed; we want only to make our point and have the world listen to us. We do not want your nuclear bombs, we do not want your mines. All we want is to live free in our ancestral lands.'

The article concluded by reminding readers how British prime minister Tony Blair had claimed in what later became known as 'the dodgy dossier' in 2002 that Saddam Hussein had sought to purchase from Niger huge quantities of uranium to create the 'weapons of mass destruction' that formed a major part of the justification for the 'pre-emptive' attack on Iraq, and showed a small and rather indistinct map of the region. I frowned and examined the map, feeling a gnawing uneasiness in the back of my head. At last, unable to focus on the tiny print of the place names, I shook out the paper and riffled through to the arts pages. There, as if planted by a mischievous force determined to torment me, I found a photograph of a group of veiled men, their turbans wound as intricately and comprehensively as those of the men who populated my dreams. 'Desert Blues Strike Gold', the headline read, followed by an appreciative review for a new CD by a band of Tuareg

63

musicians performing under the name of Tinariwen.

Tuareg. I remembered where I had come across that word now. In my father's description of the possible provenance for the amulet.

My skin prickled all over.

*   *   *

All day I had the sense of a low murmur in my head, as if someone was having a long conversation with a part of me I could not access, in another room, behind my back, just out of earshot, in a foreign language. Sometimes I found myself poring over a column of figures as if they had been inscribed in hieroglyphics or the Punic alphabet, unable to make head or tail of them.

Back at the house, I fired up the laptop and searched out flights to Morocco. It was years since I'd been abroad. Fear of flying was just one part of the reason; there had been no one to go with, for Eve was only recently divorced. And Africa, that'd take ages, wouldn't it?

It's closer than you think.

It was as if the voice were exterior to me now, somewhere in the room. I shook my head and devoted myself to tracking down the best flights. Then, task accomplished, I opened the box and took out my father's typed papers.

Notes regarding the gravesite near Abalessa
Abalessa (latitude 22°43'60N, longitude 6°1'0E,
at an altitude of 3,000 ft) lies almost at the
heart of the great desert. Terrain is rugged and
rocky. When the site was first discovered by

64

Byron Khun de Prorok in 1925, it would have been easily overlooked at first, appearing to be just one more confused jumble of stones, otherwise known as a redjem, such as are commonly found in the Sahara. The initial excavation revealed a large monument over 80 ft on its longer axis and 75 ft on the shorter, constructed using ancient techniques for drystone walling, the stones carefully selected and placed. The irregularity of the structure and the roughness of the style and masonry suggest Berber origins, not Roman, as has been suggested (see later notes).

Inside the exterior walls is an antechamber and various chambers, in the largest of which the sepulchre was found.

According to witnesses, the skeleton of the desert queen had been wrapped in red leather embellished with gold leaf. She lay with her knees bent towards her chest upon the decayed fragments of a wooden bier secured with braided cords of coloured leather and cloth. Her head had been covered by a white veil and three ostrich feathers; two emeralds hung from her earlobes, nine gold bracelets were upon one arm and eight silver bracelets on the other. Around her ankles, neck and waist were scattered beads of carnelian, agate and amazonite.

From such details it was ascertained that the body was that of a woman of high birth. Professors Maurice Reygasse and Gautiers of the Ethnographical Museum believe this site to have contained the remains of the legendary queen Tin Hinan.

Tin Hinan (lit. 'She of the Tents') is the founding mother and spiritual leader of the desert nomad people known to themselves as the Kel Tagelmust ('People of the Veil') or the Kel Tamacheq ('Those Who Speak Tamacheq'). To the Arabs they are known as the Tuareg. Tuareg is an Arab term and according to some means 'cast out by God', since these nomad people fiercely resisted the Islamic invasion in the 8th century. According to their mythology, Tin Hinan came from the Berber region of the Tafilalt in the south of Morocco and walked alone, or with a single maidservant according to another version of the legend, a thousand miles across the desert to the Hoggar and there established her tribe. She was given the title Tamenokalt (m. Amenokal, f. takes the Berber 't' beginning and end) and is known even to modern tribespeople as the Mother of Us All. Aristocratic Tuaregs claim to be able to trace their ancestry directly back to her.

Found by de Prorok amongst the funerary items in the monument was a wooden bowl commonly used for camel's milk. On its base was the impression of a gold coin bearing the head of the Emperor Constantine II (AD 337–340). The nature of the burial is incompatible with Muslim burial rites (Islam was introduced to the region by Arabs from the East c. the 8th century). There was also found a perfectly preserved clay lamp of common Roman design, well used and smoke-blackened. Experts have dated this style of lamp to between the 3rd and 4th centuries. Thus from these details we can with some confidence state that

66

*the gravesite is likely to date from the 4th
century AD and is certainly contemporary with
the later Roman Empire.*

*The amulet we found at the site is similar to
those tcherots worn as talismans by the men
and women of the Tuareg to ward off various
evils, but why it was overlooked by the 1925
excavators and then by those who followed in
the 1930s or 1950s, I cannot imagine. We
discovered it just inside the antechamber, lying
on the surface and showing no trace of having
been interred. Moreover, it bears inscriptions
from the Adagh region, and the red carnelian
discs are more recent than the carnelian beads
found in the grave-site. On the rock wall above
it we found an inscription, which I have copied
below; but no one has been able to decipher
it and the provenance of the object remains
a mystery.*

Beneath this was a series of odd-looking
symbols inscribed in blue ink.

I took off the amulet and regarded it solemnly.
Did I hold in my hand one of the grave-goods of a
legendary queen; or was the mystery deeper still?

CHAPTER SEVEN

In her haste to escape the encampment and the
wrath of Rhossi ag Bahedi, Mariata had been able
to carry only one saddle with her to the camel
enclosure: the one she had brought from her home
in the Alhaggar. It was a beautiful thing passed

down from her great-grandmother, made from leather and carved wood decorated with brass appliqué and copper nails. Sitting in it made her feel like the princess she considered herself to be. She didn't want to offer it to the older woman, but forced herself, out of politeness.

Rahma took one look at it and laughed. 'You think I need that unwieldy old thing?' She clicked her tongue till the mehari folded its legs, attached her sandals to its hobble rope, caught hold of the creature by its lower lip, threw a leg over its neck and settled herself in front of its hump, over the withers. She kept one leg folded under her as if in place of a saddle. She looked down to catch Mariata's fleeting gaze of admiration. 'My father only had girls; when times were hard, I went with the caravan.'

Mariata looked at her own mehari dubiously. She had travelled all the way from the Alhaggar to the Aïr, but most of the time she had been sitting in a palanquin, as befitted a woman of her status.

'Pull its head down,' Rahma instructed her. Mariata did so and the well-trained beast sank to its knees. 'Take your shoes off and keep them in your lap. Tap the right side of his neck to turn left and the left to turn right. Rest the soles of your feet against the curve of his neck so you can feel his movement. You can guide him like that as much as by using the reins. To make him trot, hit him on the rump—not too hard or he'll bolt; or dig your heels into his neck; or both. If you want to stop, pull on his head rope. And if you want to make him sit down, just tap him smartly on the back of his head and hiss loudly. Ready?'

Mariata twitched her camel's head rope, but all

it did was give a low bellow. 'How do you make it start?'

* * *

They rode all that night, down through steep river-cut gullies and rocky defiles, heading north and west. The moon shone out of a cloudless sky, outlining everything in silver. A jackal called and its mate responded, their cries shivering over the hills and down Mariata's spine.

At every night sound she turned her head, seeking for pursuers, but there were none. The Bazgan range rose up at their back, rugged and imposing; down below they could see where watercourses—some iridescent, others apparently dry—snaked across the grasslands to the south.

'Down there,' said Rahma, waving her left hand vaguely, 'half a day's ride away, lies Agadez, the gateway to the Ténéré.'

The Ténéré: 'the Emptiness' in their tongue, or simply 'the Desert'—over a thousand miles of barren rock and sand. Even now Mariata's father and brothers were tracking across it, moving along part of the ancient trade route between Fezzan and Egypt and the ancient Songhai Empire. For centuries caravans had ferried gold, ivory, cotton, leather and slaves through the Ténéré to the great civilizations at either end of the route, but the halcyon days were long gone: now the caravanners were reduced to trading dried vegetables and bags of millet for cones of salt and whatever meagre profit they could make once they had bargained hard with the Kanuri who ran the mines, and paid their fees to the men whose territory they crossed

69

and from whose wells they drew water. Sometimes raiders attacked the traders; sometimes dust storms or treacherous quicksands—*fesh-fesh*—swallowed entire caravans, leaving only their bones to be found years later. Sometimes no trace was ever found of them at all.

'Are we going into the Ténéré?' Mariata asked. The idea filled her with a mixture of anticipation and disquiet. She realized for the first time now, out in the quiet night air, her body swaying to the rhythm of the camel's strange gait, that she didn't have the least idea where they were going. All she knew was what Rahma had told her: that she had walked for eight days to find her.

Rahma laughed softly. 'Good heavens, no!'

She offered no more and they rode on in silence. Down out of the Aïr Plateau they came, into the wide *oueds* that gave out on to the floor of the valley below—shale-filled dried riverbeds in which the camels walked easily, their great pads crunching the loose stones underfoot. As the sun came up over the hills behind them, it cast long red rays across the landscape, filling the acacia trees with fire. But still there was no sign of Rhossi.

As the land flattened out into a broad plain, Rahma smacked her camel and immediately it picked up its pace. She looked back over her shoulder. 'Come on!' she urged Mariata. 'They are sure to be following us, given the value of the camels you stole; we must put as much distance between us and them as we can.'

Mariata nervously tapped her camel on the rump, but all it did was to swing its great white head around and gaze at her with its huge, languid eyes, managing to look both bored and infinitely superior. 'Please,' she begged, digging her heels into it, 'go faster.'

For a day and more the world was green and grey, an endless succession of vegetation and stones; but gradually the green gave way to brown, and soon the vegetation was no more than scrub-brush and yellowed grasses. They crossed open ground consisting of nothing more than bare rock and expanses of pitch-black gravel, punctuated by thorn and tiger-bush, with a scatter of tamarisk where the water-table was high. The next day came the sands, wave upon wave of them, tawny and wind-sculpted.

Mariata gazed out to where sand and sky merged in a shimmering haze and felt her mind drift wide as if it too were flowing into the vanishing point. A delicious peace spread through her, softening her muscles, soothing her bones. 'Beautiful,' she whispered. 'It's so beautiful.'

Rahma smiled. 'And, like all beautiful things, quite deadly if you do not treat it with the respect it deserves.'

'You came all this way on foot?'

'I did.'

Mariata shook her head, astounded. 'You must truly love your son.'

'I do.'

'Tell me about him. Is he handsome? Is he noble and a poet? Does he wear the blue? Is his skin stained with indigo from his veil? Does he travel the desert routes? Or perhaps he is a warrior, with a famous sword whose name he cries as he flourishes it in battle?'

The older woman clicked her tongue. 'You young girls are all the same: silly romantic

71

dreamers. And the boys are as bad: no, worse, with their dreams of war and foolishness. All I will say now is that he lies close to death. If he dies, you will need to know no more; if he lives, you can ask the rest yourself.'

Mariata was disappointed. 'Will you not even tell me his name?'

'His name is Amastan.'

'But what is his full name?'

Rahma sighed. 'So many questions.'

'If I am to cross a desert, I should know something about the one I am making the journey for.'

For a long while the old woman was silent, gazing out into the wilderness, her eyes narrowed against the brilliance of the air. At last she said, 'His name is Amastan ag Moussa.'

'Like Moussa ag Iba, the amenokal, high chief of the Aïr drum-groups?'

'Thanks be he does not take after his father.'

'He is the son of the amenokal?'

The older woman tapped her camel smartly on the poll of its head and hissed loudly. Obediently, it came to a halt and sank to its knees and she slipped easily to the ground.

'And therefore Rhossi's cousin?' Mariata pressed.

'Do not think to judge my Amastan by what you know of that one. Until my boy was born, Rhossi had been Moussa's chief delight. Rhossi had only to mention a thing and it was his—a pretty trinket, the best cut of meat, a play-sword fashioned from wood. But Amastan was Moussa's firstborn, and his heir; from the moment he set eyes upon him he adored him, and that made Rhossi insanely jealous. As my lad grew up, all the time I found bruises and cuts upon him he could not have come by from simple play, and once he came to me with clear fingermarks upon his throat as if someone had tried to strangle him. He never said a word against Rhossi; but a mother knows.'

'Was that why you left?'

Rahma pressed her lips together tightly. 'Now we walk,' she told Mariata.

'We walk?' Mariata was horrified.

'We must rest the camels.' She took a long drink from the waterskin, then passed it to Mariata, after which she wound her headscarf up around her face in a semblance of a man's tagelmust. Then, leading her beast by its head rope, she strode out briskly, her back arrow-straight.

Mariata half dismounted, half fell, from her own mount and followed suit, twisting the dark cotton of her headscarf around her face until only her eyes were visible. Unused to wearing a veil, she found it uncomfortable and stifling, but as soon as the first breath of wind came up off the dunes she understood why it was necessary. Particles of sand scoured her skin, stinging her eyes. Hot sand burned her feet through her thin sandals; her body moved stiffly and awkwardly after the hours on the camel's back.

Despite her age and the attack Rhossi had made upon her, Rahma moved easily, as if she made such journeys every day of her life. She walked, Mariata thought, like a man, like a caravanner or a hunter, and she could not help a welling admiration for the older woman, who was so hardy and so determined. As the wind whipped up, Rahma moved to the lee side of her camel so that

73

it sheltered her as she walked; Mariata did the same. They walked in this way till the sun was high in the sky, and still there was no sign of pursuit.

Mariata walked until she thought she could walk no more; then she walked some more. She walked as if in a trance, or a dream, her legs moving automatically, her arm attached to the camel by its braided head rope; she walked until she was no longer aware of the discomforts that had infuriated her at the beginning of the day. Freed by the demands of her body, Mariata's mind ranged far and wide. Why was she making this mad journey with a woman she had just met, and in such bizarre circumstances? Was staying with the tribe really so terrible? If she had called out, surely someone would have come to her aid, whatever Rhossi had said. The protection of women was sacred to her people; women were respected above all things. Her fear of Moussa's nephew had twisted her logic out of shape, driven her to make mad decisions. But then she remembered the starving harratin, and the furious temper of the high chief whom everyone said was dying. And when he died, Rhossi would be chief and then no one could protect her from him. He had even tried to strangle the son of the amenokal!

She mused about that. Whatever had happened between Rahma and Moussa must have been serious: for an amenokal to divorce his wife, or worse, for her to divorce him, was uncommon. She sensed a scandal.

All these thoughts moved through her head like moths around a fire, sometimes vanishing into the darkness, sometimes catching light and zigzagging crazily about.

At last Rahma turned to her and said something inaudible.

Mariata's head came up. In front of them were palm trees, shivering in the heat haze. Was it a mirage, she wondered. She had heard that the desert played tricks on the mind, and especially on novice travellers.

'Oasis,' Rahma said again, more distinctly. 'The oasis of Doum. We are more than halfway there now.'

They watered the camels, and let them graze. They refilled the waterskins, and while Rahma lay down in the shadows to sleep Mariata sat with her feet in the cool water of the *guelta* and gazed at the reflections of the date palms and the dazzling sky beyond. Such peace! She had never felt such peace. Before, there had always been the coming and going of family and neighbours, the noise of children, goats and dogs, the endless procession of the chores of daily life. She had been Mariata ult Yemma, daughter of Tofenat, daughter of Ousman, sister and cousin and tribe member. After that, she had been the niece of Dassine, outsider from the Taitok tribe suddenly displaced amongst the people of the Bazgan; taken from her homeland and set down amongst strangers, and somehow because the Kel Bazgan were strangers there seemed to be so many more of them, with names and patrimonies and stories she did not yet know, all milling about the camping ground, talking, shouting, going about business she knew nothing about. But now, in this moment, there was just herself—Mariata—and Rahma, fast asleep, a woman she had met only a day ago and to whom she was bound by neither tribal loyalty nor family ties; and the desert, beautiful, serene and eternal.

This moment of freedom, of perfect being, swelled inside her until she felt light-headed, as if she might float off into the gilded air like a gossamer seedhead . . .

How much time passed like this she had no idea, but she was shocked out of the moment by a sudden sharp report, like two rocks struck together close by the ear.

At once, like a cat that appears asleep but is napping with one eye open, Rahma was on her feet. 'Mariata, get your camel. Now, hurry!'

'Why?'

'No time for questions. Quickly!'

Mariata ran and took the hobble off her mehari, then stood there with the head rope in her hand, indecisive, not knowing what to do.

'Get on, get on! Head for the high dunes there and wait for me: they will not go there, the sand is too deep. Go!'

'But what about you?'

'Just do what I say, girl, or we're both dead.'

At last Mariata managed to get her camel to its knees and, as soon as she was on it, took off as if it had intuited the required action. She slapped its rump and it increased its pace, the sand flying up from the great pads of its feet. The dunes reared up, great sweeping hills of sand. She headed the animal towards the intersection of two of the biggest ones and by sheer will urged the camel up and over the other side. Then she hurled herself down from its back without waiting for it to couch, and crawled forward to look over the crest. The oasis seemed miles away, much further than the distance she had just covered in that short time, and for a moment she could not see Rahma and her camel at all. Panic rising, she scanned the landscape desperately: if she lost Rahma she was surely doomed. Then suddenly she caught a movement out of the corner of her eye—

Rahma, far to her right, her camel at a gallop, its ungainly limbs flying out at all angles. Mariata watched as their course veered towards the eastern edge of the long bank of dunes on which she lay, then disappeared from view.

Now there came another noise entirely, a rough growl of a sound, low and rumbling. Travelling towards the oasis at speed was a dusty vehicle: a truck with several dark-clad men sitting in the back, their rifles pointing towards the sky. Mariata froze. Had Rhossi brought in government authorities to ensure the return of the camels? To bring her back to the tribe? A chill shivered her stomach.

Surely not even Rhossi would involve the police? Their people lived beyond national boundaries and jurisdictions, and had done so for a thousand years. Mariata lay there, suspended in time, waiting for something to happen, for something to determine her fate. Don't let them see me, she mouthed silently, then swiftly amended her prayer to: don't let them see *us*. Let them leave and not see us . . .

Several heartbeats passed and all was silent, except for the rush of blood in her ears. Even her camel seemed to sense the need for quiet: it had knelt down on the cool lee side of the dune, where the sun had not yet reached, with its head up and its long-lashed gaze fixed on nothing in particular, the strange, clear membrane of its third eyelid flicking back and forth to dislodge grains of sand.

Then the jeep reappeared, accelerating out of the oasis along the well-beaten track to the east, which it followed for several hundred yards. Then suddenly it veered off, where Rahma and her camel had veered off just minutes before. Mariata stopped breathing; then her heart began to thump as if it wanted to escape her ribcage. She watched as the jeep began to climb the dune, then became bogged down in the softer, deeper sand of the flank. Two of the men vaulted out, guns slung across their backs, and began to search the ground. She saw them touch the surface, talk animatedly, then move upwards, leaving the rest to push the vehicle out of the sand. The two men wore trousers, not robes—a Western style of dress; and caps instead of a veil or turban. They looked like spiders, Mariata thought, thin and dark and fast and dangerous, as they picked their way up the dune. Soon the swell of the sand obscured their progress.

What should she do? Should she leap on her camel and flee before they saw her, or wait and hope they passed by? She had just about made up her mind to remount the camel and make a run for it when something hissed. Mariata scrambled to her feet intuitively, for the bite of a horned viper could kill—

'Get down!'

It was Rahma, leading her camel by a length of cloth she had tied around the creature's jaw.

Obediently, Mariata flattened herself against the hot sand. 'Who are they?' she whispered.

'Soldiers.'

'Soldiers? What soldiers?'

'There are soldiers everywhere now. On that side'—she gestured to her left—'the newly independent country of Mali; to the other'—waving to the right—'Niger. To the north, Algeria. They all have soldiers swarming around this quarter. They have found precious ores beneath these sands: all their governments will be wanting to get their hands on it. Ripping out the guts of the earth, destroying our ancestral lands; shooting us if we get in their way.' She took another length of fabric and briskly bound the second camel's jaw shut. It wouldn't render the beast silent, but it would stifle a bellow that might betray their presence. 'Now, if you don't want to die, follow me quickly.'

She led Mariata down the side of the dune, keeping the curving crest between them and any sight-line the two soldiers might have, and as they went Rahma used a palm frond to smooth over the marks of their passage. It wouldn't fool a nomad scout; but at a distance the dune would look relatively untouched.

Down through the soft sand they ran into a deep valley between sandhills, then Rahma led them into another intersection where the dunes towered up on either side.

Rahma shoved the head rope into Mariata's hand. 'Wait here.'

And with that she was gone, scuttling sideways up a tall dune to look for their pursuers. Mariata hugged her knees to her chest. Soldiers. Men armed with guns. Enemies. She had never even considered the possibility of having an enemy before, someone who might actually want to kill her. There were tribal rivalries, of course, duels

79

and raids; but these were things between men. No one ever threatened a woman with violence—except for Rhossi. But even Rhossi did not scare her as much as these anonymous, uniform-clad men. For the first time since they had entered the desert, she felt truly afraid.

CHAPTER EIGHT

The shadows were slanting deep into the valley before Rahma reappeared, striding out with her elbows jutting angrily and her feet kicking up puffs of sand. She looked like one of the spirits of the wilderness herself, her robe all dusty and her eyes shining with anger. Mariata hugged her knees tight to her chest. 'Did they attack you?' she asked timidly. 'Are you hurt?'

The older woman barely looked at her as she said, 'Get on your camel.' She unhobbled her own and mounted up nimbly.

'Have they gone?' Mariata tried again once she had managed to catch up with her companion, but all Rahma did was to give her a curt 'Yes', then fold her lips tightly and stare straight ahead, lost in her thoughts, thoughts that knit her forehead into a kinked maze.

Mariata tried several times to draw her further on the subject of the soldiers as they rode through dune after dune and then over a wide sandy plain, but the older woman kept her counsel and barely spoke a word during either day. Towards the end of the third day after they had left the oasis, the sun veered westwards, dipped and fell, stealing all the red from the landscape and leaving it violet and chill.

The rising moon filled the sand with light and rendered the solitary thorn trees they passed a ghostly silver. Mariata had never seen country like this: it seemed unending, unrelenting, and still they rode on. As the land flattened it became more solid underfoot, little tufts of vegetation poking up through the ever-increasing scatters of stones. Finally, in an area in which huge detached blocks formed towering, solitary boulders, Rahma drew her camel to a halt.

'We'll stop here till dawn,' she decreed. 'We can't go up into the hills by night: the ancestor spirits become vengeful by moonlight.'

Even the most benevolent spirits changed their nature as night fell. Mariata muttered a charm that might ward off such dangerous influences and stared into the shadowed hills. It was hard to tell what was night and what was land, but she could see no sign in the darkness of any camp, no fires, no lanterns. All she could see were the boulders, dumped all over the place as if by a giant grown suddenly bored with a game.

'This is an ancient, magical place, full of *baraka*,' Rahma said softly. 'No spirits will harm us here.'

The boulders were vast, but to Mariata they looked neither magical nor full of blessings. She closed her eyes, exhausted. Every muscle ached, every hair on her head. She had been looking forward to lying down in the shelter of a tent; she wanted to rest her cheek on a cushion, to cover herself with a blanket and sleep and sleep and sleep. She was so tired she found herself swaying and had to reach out a hand to the closest stone for

81

balance. The heat of the day had gone right out of it: it felt cold and rough beneath her fingers; rough and cold, but somehow alive . . .

A succession of images flitted suddenly through her head: a woman whose tears darkened the indigo of her robe where they fell; a round-headed child grabbing its mother's skirts; the flash of a sword thrown in the air, silver gleaming in blue. A swaddled baby with great dark eyes, lying helpless in the sand. A man's naked body rising and falling, the curve of his buttocks lit by the jumping light of a candle. Her eyes snapped open, shocked.

'What is it?' Rahma said sharply, taking her by the arm. 'Did you see something?'

Obscurely ashamed, Mariata snatched her arm away. 'No, nothing. I'm just tired.'

She took the blanket from her camel and lay down on the ground, but sleep was hard to find. The world moved within her, as if she were walking still; her head swam. Images came rushing at her—armed men shouldering rifles, Rhossi's leering face too close, a skeleton they had passed in the desert, its bones picked at by vultures and bleached by the sun; starved children, a weeping woman—until she felt sick with anxiety. When she sat up to clear her head, the only thought that came to her was that she was alone in the world and at its mercy, with no protection except for a strange, mad woman. Up above, the stars shone down, unmoved by her circumstances. Tears of self-pity stung her eyes, and it was then she heard the voice.

Remember who you are, Mariata. Remember your heritage. You carry all of us within you: we are always with you, all the way back to the Mother of Us All. Remember who you are and do not despair . . .

*　　　*　　　*

That night Mariata dreamt. She was back in the Hoggar: its hills rose jagged against a brilliant blue sky, and she sat in the sun watching her mother braiding Azaz's hair. The last time she had seen her brother he had been tall and skinny, almost a man in his robes and blue veil, but in the dream he was still a boy, with round, laughing eyes and a wide gap between his front teeth, and she remembered how they had run rings around the old women and told stories to keep each other from punishment when one or the other had been caught misbehaving. Baye, the youngest, crawled naked in the sand. Her mother was so beautiful, Mariata thought, watching her quick, deft hands and the way the sunlight fell across the elegant bones of her face. How long she watched this tranquil scene she did not know: she was in dream-time. Behind Yemma's head high clouds streamed; the sun fell and rose, fell and rose again as she plaited Baye's first braids, reaching over the huge and growing swell of her belly. And then a shadow fell across her and she looked up and smiled and the world stood still. What a smile that was! Mariata could have looked at that smile all day, all night. Such love was in it, such pleasure. For a moment she wondered what it was that had made her mother smile in such a blissful way, and then she saw herself walking beside her tall father, carrying a basket of figs, the figs her mother craved in this, her last pregnancy. And she knew, as she had always known, that her mother loved her, that she had not willingly left her in this world; that she

83

watched her always.

*   *   *

It was the first rays of sun on her own face that woke Mariata, and for a moment she did not know where she was; all she knew was that she felt refreshed and at peace. When she stretched, her joints did not crack or protest; when she got to her feet she was steady, and her muscles did not complain. Perhaps, she thought, there was something in what Rahma had said about the stones: perhaps they did hold some form of power. She folded away her blanket and went to have a closer look at one of the boulders.

Three quarters of the huge rock was in shadow. She walked around it, marvelling at its immensity, at the chill of the shadow it threw. But as she rounded the final side, she found the eastern face was now brightly lit by the rising sun. In the middle of the face, snaking from the ground almost to the summit fifteen feet above, were carved letters and symbols in the ancient language of her people. She craned her neck.

'Today we buried Majid, a brave man, husband to Tata and father to Rhissa, Elaga and Houna,' read one inscription.

A second read simply, 'Sarid loves Dinbiden, who loves him not.'

A third was the beginning of a poem. '*Asshet nan-nana shin ded Moussa, tishenan n ejil-di du-nedwa,*' she read aloud. *Daughters of our tents, daughters of Moussa, think of the evening of our departure . . .*

Another, slanting up and away to the right, she

84

read at first as 'Love endures, though life does not.' Then she realized it could be read as 'Long love is rarer than life.' She frowned, unable to decide on the correct meaning. A third possible interpretation offered itself as, 'Where love is found, remain.'

'Poetic, no?'

Mariata turned to find Rahma at her side.

'Who carved these—people from your village?'

The older woman laughed. 'Some of these inscriptions were made by the Kel Nad, the People of the Past. No one knows how old they are; they have been here before the memory of even the very old, before the memory of their parents and grandparents.'

Mariata frowned. 'But they seem so . . . new.' It was an inadequate word, especially for one who fancied herself a poet. What she meant was the sentiments in these carvings were the same as those felt by her own people, every day.

'The past is always with us,' Rahma declared. 'And people are all the same, in their essentials, whether they are modern or ancient.' She seemed more cheerful this morning, perhaps at the prospect of returning home triumphantly with the descendant of the Founder.

Mariata began to feel nervous now about what was expected of her. Leaving the Kel Bazgan had not been a difficult decision at the time. She had done it without giving much thought to the future and since then crossing the desert had largely emptied her mind. She tried not to think about it. People are all the same, in their essentials, she told herself. There is nothing to be frightened of.

They entered the village and the older woman greeted everyone who came out to see her (of whom there were many) at length and with great politeness. 'I am well,' she answered to all inquiries. 'Thanks be, I am well.' She would then ask about their family and news and listen patiently to the answers, although these were always the same: I am well, my wife is well, my sons are well, my daughters are well, thanks be to God. At last, she would turn and indicate Mariata and introduce her as 'Mariata ult Yemma ult Tofenat, daughter of the Kel Taitok, who has come down out of the Aïr Mountains from the Kel Bazgan with whom she was staying, and has crossed the Tamesna with me in order to see my son and drive out the spirits that have possessed him.'

Initial respect for Mariata's noble descent-group and the journey she had taken swiftly gave way to shuttered expressions at the mention of Amastan, she noticed, but everyone was polite and wished her well and that blessings would protect her from any evil spirits that she might encounter.

Rahma spoke to a small dark-skinned woman wearing a bright red headscarf and the woman ran off and returned moments later with a bowl of rice mixed with milk. 'To cool his heat,' she said, and Rahma agreed, taking the bowl from her. Mariata gazed at it longingly and her stomach began to rumble, but, 'We must try to return him to some sort of equilibrium,' Rahma was saying to the other woman, and it seemed there was no likelihood of breakfast until they had seen the patient.

They passed an enclosure where chickens ran

and pecked, which surprised Mariata: nomadic peoples did not keep chickens, for the creatures could not walk through the desert or overfly the route, and the camels and donkeys were always fully enough laden without adding chicken coops to their burden. She had also noticed that there were a number of permanent-looking adobe huts dotted about the encampment, and that some boasted well-grown-in vegetation—a fig tree here, tomato plants there.

'Does your tribe no longer travel the salt road?' she asked curiously.

'Some do. We still have a few caravanners, but we lost an entire caravan to the desert two years back; and disease killed a number of our camels last season. Poverty and unrest have caused many of our harratin and slaves to run away into the towns, and the new government is encouraging them in this: life is hard and getting harder. Our people are going to need young men like Amastan more than we have ever needed our young men at any time in our history. Without him and others like him, we are doomed to scratch a living in the dust.'

Mariata was aghast. 'But we are the masters of the desert, not poor peasants!'

'Our proud heritage will stand for nothing if things continue as they are.'

The last villager they came upon was an odd-looking person with a loosely wound tagelmust that exposed, shockingly, the lower half of the face, skin the colour of charcoal and heavy silver earrings that dragged down both earlobes. This odd personage now caught hold of Mariata's hands and held them tight. Mariata put this lack of reticence down to the fact that this person was clearly not properly one of the People of the Veil, and forced herself not to pull away. Not that she could even if she had wanted to, for the stranger appeared to have her in a remarkably powerful grip. But when he spoke, it was the voice of a boy whose vocal cords have not yet acquired the deep timbre of a man; and the hand he had in his grip was pressed against what felt suspiciously like a soft female breast, so now Mariata was entirely confused. 'Ah, the far-travelled daughter of the Hoggar. Welcome, welcome to the Teggart.'

'Thank you,' said Mariata, dipping her head politely. She tried once more to take her hands away, unsuccessfully.

'Lovely girl, the spirits take many forms. Beware the melancholy beauty of the Kel Asuf lest you be seduced. I can see there is a wildness in you; and wildness calls to wildness. I hope you have a complete head.'

And with these enigmatic words, the strange person let go of Mariata's hand and went on his way.

Mariata stared after him. 'What does he mean? Indeed, is he a he?'

'Tana?' Rahma smiled. 'We have no word for what Tana is. I have heard strangers called her an *homme-femme*, but that does her no justice. God has blessed her twice over, shall we say. In her is to be found the perfect symmetry between the genders and she is a most remarkable person. Sometimes she knows more than normal people know. She was the daughter of our smith, when the village was wealthy enough to keep one of its own, and when he died she stayed and carries out some of an *enad*'s duties.'

The inadan were smiths and masters of mystic ritual: a resident smith would oversee ceremonies, kill the sacrificial goats, command the fires and work the things of iron that no Kel Tagelmust, and certainly no woman, could safely touch.

'Can she not heal Amastan?'

'She went to see him once after he returned; after that she would not go near him.'

Mariata digested this silently. After a while she asked, 'And what did she mean about a complete head?'

'It's what we say sometimes about an apprentice of medicine coming of age, when their knowledge is complete.'

Mariata felt the panic rising again. 'But I have no learning of medicine! I've never apprenticed at anything.'

'There are some things that cannot be learnt: gifts from on high; gifts that run in the blood.' Rahma took her by the arm as if she feared Mariata might run away; and suddenly Mariata was filled with fear: fear that Rahma's son might be mad and raving, frothing at the mouth like a rabid dog, prone to bouts of violence. She was afraid too that he might look quite normal, except for the dancing of the spirits in his eyes. She was afraid she would have no effect on him, that despite her grand ancestry she would be found to be quite an ordinary girl after all. And somehow that possibility was the worst fear of all.

*   *   *

Beyond the last of the tents, huts and animal

enclosures lay a grove of olive trees, and beyond that, across a stretch of rock-strewn ground, a makeshift shelter had been erected between a pair of tamarisk trees, little more than a simple frame of branches draped with blankets and old grain sacks. In the shade beneath this, Mariata could make out the figure of a man in a black robe and a tightly wound tagelmust that left only a sliver of his face visible, a sliver through which a pair of dark eyes glittered balefully.

The man sat cross-legged on the ground, unmoving, his hands clasped in his lap. He did not change his attitude as they approached, making no effort to greet them in any way. He did not even respond when Rahma crouched beside him and laid a hand against his cheek.

'Blessings on you, Amastan, my son. You look better than when I left you, I am sure of it. Just take a little rice and milk to cool the excess of heat that is in you.'

She laid the bowl down on the ground beside an untouched dish of bread and dates. He did not so much as glance at it.

'And see, I have brought you something else as well, a visitor from far away. Mariata ult Yemma ult Tofenat of the Kel Taitok, descended straight and true from Tin Hinan. She has crossed the Tamesna just to see you. Won't you rise and greet her and make her welcome as befits the master of the house?'

She was attempting to humour him, Mariata saw, for this was no house, and he was clearly master of nothing, including his own wits. She scanned what little she could see of his narrow brown face through the slit in his veil, seeing only that the bones lay close to the surface, that his eyebrows were well formed and that while he was expressionless the crow's feet at the outer corners of his eyes stood out pale against the dark tan of his skin. He did not, now they were close up, look frightening at all, she thought with some relief, and was just beginning to relax when his gaze flickered away from the ground at which he had been staring so fixedly and came to rest upon her face.

It is said that when a gazelle is cornered by hunters it will often become paralysed and stand stone-still even though if it chose to spring away it could easily outrun its pursuers. That was how Mariata felt when Amastan looked at her: transfixed, terrified to the core of her being and utterly unable to save herself.

She found herself looking into the most expressive eyes she had ever seen. They were long and almond-shaped, the eyes of a poet, not a warrior or a madman; but in the instant that he pinned her with his gaze she was unable to think of anything except that that gaze was as deep and dark as water glimpsed at the bottom of a well: the last water of the season, before the well runs dry and those who rely on it go thirsty and eventually die.

Mariata's heart began to beat fast. She felt the muscles in her legs twitch as if they would carry her away, very far, very fast, whether she consciously asked them to or not. But despite this she stayed where she stood, as if she had suddenly taken root.

Then the moment passed. Abruptly, Amastan's eyes filled with tears, tears that gathered and brimmed and then fell, unchecked. It was shocking to see a man cry. Men were reticent with their emotions: it was part of the code of *asshak*, the code of pride and proper behaviour. Mariata felt her heart go out to him.

There are some women who cannot resist trying to set to rights something that is broken, women who feel the weight of responsibility for restoring the order of the world—even if it is just in the little things such as washing the dirt out of clothes, the sweeping of a tent or the reweaving of an unravelling basket. Mariata had never considered herself to be one of these women. But before her she saw a man whom life had snapped in two and suddenly she yearned to put the two halves back together.

*   *   *

'How long has he been like this?' Mariata asked as she and Rahma walked back towards the village. As the distance increased between her and the possessed man, her heart resumed its normal rhythm; but even so she could feel his presence, as if a cord had been tied to each of them, which became tighter with every step she took.

Rahma said nothing for a time. At last she arrived at a boulder of rock. Here she stopped and sat down, turning her face up to the sun so that Mariata saw the faint trace of tear tracks that had dried on her cheeks. 'It was his camel brought him back, as if it knew its way home, even though he had not been here for a year or more. He was slumped over it, in a daze. He had no idea where he was: his eyes were open, but he did not even recognize his own mother. There was blood all over him. I thought . . .' Her voice faltered. 'I

92

thought he was dead . . . or at least mortally wounded. His sword was gone—the Reaper, which had belonged to my brother, his *anet ma*, and to his *anet ma* before him. He would never willingly be parted from that sword: it was his pride personified. He had nothing with him: neither food nor water. How he survived I can't imagine, except that the spirits must have kept him alive for their own purposes.

'But he did have one thing. It was clasped in his right hand. We tried to prise his fingers open, but he turned on us like a wild animal. He has it still. I am sure that if we can separate him from it we can save him. The Kel Asuf draw their power from it, I am sure of it. We've tried everything: medicine women have offered him sleeping herbs, but he would not take them. The enad sang the song of the winds and we played the drums to dance out the spirits, but all to no effect. The marabouts have prayed over him and pinned Qur'anic verses to his robes. I could have told them that wouldn't work: he tore them off in a rage and ran about naked! The magician from Tin Buktu surrounded his tent with charms and fetishes he had brought out of the south: Amastan ignored them all, and lay down to sleep with his right hand pinned firmly under his body. Anyone who tries to force his hand open is met by the fury of the wild spirits inside him. He has been this way for three months and more: he can't go on like this much longer.'

Mariata bit her lip. 'I want to help, but I don't know what I can do.'

Rahma turned to look at her. 'He wept when he saw you, Mariata: it is the first recognizably human emotion he has shown in all this time.' She sighed

93

and stood up, suddenly looking exhausted. 'As a boy, Amastan loved poetry,' she went on. 'He loved to make songs and verses; he dazzled the local girls with his skill with words. They all wanted to marry him, but he would not marry, he said, until he had walked to the Arbre de Ténéré, seen the sea and touched the snow that fell on the highest mountains.'

Mariata smiled. These were just the sort of romantic notions that appealed to her. 'And how many of these things did he accomplish?'

'All three. And, having reached these goals, he became at last betrothed. To a girl from the N'Fughas Mountains. He had gone there to fetch her back to meet me and his grandmother before they married. My mother was too old and ill to travel, you see. She died before he returned. That was probably a blessing.'

Mariata felt a sharp stab of discomfort at this news. He was betrothed? She reminded herself it was none of her business that a man she did not know should be handfasted, but something in her felt a sudden keen disappointment. 'Where is she, his beloved?'

Rahma looked away. 'I do not know. No one does: it seems she has disappeared. But do not listen to gossip, I beg you.' Before Mariata could make anything of this odd request, Rahma went on hurriedly, 'Words are the most powerful magic of all: your grandmother knew that. The power of words has run through your family since the time of the Mother of Us All: how else could she have persuaded others to come to her in the desert and establish our people? She was just an ordinary girl—no older than you—just a girl from a dusty little village in the south of Morocco. Yet she had such power in her that she left a safe and settled place to make a new life in the wilderness. To do that she must have communed with the Kel Asuf, become one of them, or bent them to her will, for they helped her shape our people. That power of hers will have passed down the female line as with all such things of value, so it must reside in you. I have to believe that, or Amastan is lost to us for ever. Will you help him? Sit with him and tell him stories, make poetry and charms for him; quiet the spirits, bend them to your will. Try to persuade him to give up the thing in his right hand. Will you do this?'

'I will try,' Mariata said, but dread gnawed at her. Amastan had come back to the village covered in blood and without his betrothed. She was not to listen to gossip. But abruptly she remembered a folk tale from the Aïr, told often around the fire at night: 'The Bloody Wedding of Iferouane'. It told how a handsome, richly arrayed stranger had ridden into a village to the great excitement of the local girls and over the subsequent weeks had chosen the prettiest of them and wooed her with fine words and then promptly married her with the blessing of her family; but on the first night of the wedding celebration a great commotion was heard coming from the tent of the newlyweds, and much piteous wailing from the girl. The elders had shaken their heads: it was rash of the groom to want to have his way with the bride on the very first night. A child conceived by moonlight was a child cursed for life. No good would come of it. And indeed when one of the old women came to bring the couple their breakfast the next morning she

95

was met by a grim sight: a tent full of blood and hair and bone, and no sign of either bride or groom. The bride's brothers, however, found the tracks of a great cat and they followed it to its mountain lair, and killed it after a great struggle. Inside its belly, they found the remains of their sister, but none at all of the groom; and from this they deduced that the handsome stranger had been a shape-changer, a spirit of the wilds, whose true form had been released on the wedding night.

She could not help but wonder: was Amastan another such monster? Had he, possessed by *djenoun*, killed his beloved? She did not want to find out; and yet she had to know.

*   *   *

Rahma took her to her tent. It was a fine affair, made from more than a hundred goatskins.

'I brought it with me when I divorced Moussa ag Iba,' she said, before Mariata could ask. 'That, twelve-year-old Amastan and one old donkey, long since dead. The damned marabout ruled that I must give my bride-wealth back, although it was my right to keep it. He told me it was God's burden to me to endure Moussa taking a second wife, that I was in the wrong to divorce him over such a small thing. I showed him the bruises on my arms and legs; he just smiled and said sometimes men have to beat their wives to teach them proper behaviour. Since that time I have returned to the old ways. The marabout is dead now; and Moussa's gut gives him great pain, I hear.'

Mariata stared at her. 'You cursed him?'

'I cursed them both. It's just that Moussa was

96

always such a strong man. He's held on a long time.'

Something inside Mariata shuddered. 'If you can manipulate the spirits, why can't you save Amastan?'

Rahma gave a bitter little smile. 'There is balance in the universe: I think this is the spirits' way of teaching me that.'

*   *   *

For a little time each day over the next few days Mariata put on a white robe and head cloth that Tana lent her—for luck and to balance out the blackness inside Amastan—and went to sit with him, making quiet poetry at first in her head, and then out loud. He did not seem to mind her presence; indeed, he did not seem to take any notice of her at all. There were no tears, no heart-stopping glances and no sign of the spirits that possessed him. If he heard her poems and stories, he did not betray any response to them; after a while she found his presence restful; inspirational, even. Soon she was making some of the best poems she had made in her life, manipulating the words, forming them into intricate acrostics with the power to trap magic between their lines. Some she scratched on the ground with a stick, but mainly she kept them in her head. None seemed to have any effect on the patient.

Each day, she took away untouched the food she had brought for him the day before. How could he live without eating? He must, she thought, be fuelled by other means, by something unnatural, maybe even unholy. Then one day she found the

97

bowl overturned, the milk soaking into the earth. This was taboo and surely evidence of the spirits' work. She scratched charms in a circle around the bowl to try to cancel out the malign influences.

A few days later her period started. A marabout would have banished her to her tent, but Rahma laughed. 'You're at your most powerful now: blood is stronger than the power of the spirits.' And indeed when she took Amastan that day's bowl of milk and rice he picked it up from the ground and ate it. But he did so with the fingers of his left hand, which was an abhorrence.

All the while he kept his right hand curled closed and she noticed that when she looked at it, the knuckles whitened, as if he clenched it harder.

One day, inspired by the ancient inscriptions on the rocks where she and Rahma had passed the last night of their journey before entering the village, Mariata made this poem, and started to recite it aloud:

Daughters of our tents, daughters of Moussa
Think of the evening of our departure
The saddles of the women lie ready on the camels
The women are coming now, stately in their robes
Amongst them is Amina, with her eyes shining
And Houna, a new scarf upon her head.
Beautiful Manta, as fresh as a seedling palm . . .

'No!'

His cry was ear-splitting, heart-rending. Mariata leapt to her feet, suddenly terrified to see Amastan's face contorted in some terrible excess

98

of emotion. She half expected to see fangs spring from his mouth, claws from his hands, fur to push through his skin, but once the cry had escaped him he seemed exhausted and sank in on himself. He opened his right hand and she saw a glimpse of the object inside it.

'Manta, oh, Manta,' he whispered, or at least that was what Mariata thought she heard. Eyes closed in anguish, he pressed the thing in his hand against his forehead.

It was an amulet, she saw, a solid square of metal with a raised central boss embellished by circles of carnelian and bands of etched patterns. Something had dried all over it, like rust.

CHAPTER NINE

I had a lot of vacation days to take: I'd not used up my holiday allowance in over three years. In some trepidation I went to the senior partner and asked if I might take a six-week sabbatical, three weeks unpaid. To my shame, I used the excuse of my father's death as my reason for wanting such a long break: there was so much to do to get the house ready for sale, and after that I would need a change of scene.

Richard agreed with an alacrity that was almost insulting.

I felt guilty; but then I would look at the box and feel the anticipation rising up inside me again. I was going to Africa, following what my father had called 'waymarkers' on the path of my life: I was going to take the amulet back to the continent from which it had come and stir up that sleeping beast. I had looked up Abalessa in an atlas and found it marked as a tiny place in the south of Algeria. Morocco–Algeria; Tafraout–Abalessa. On the grand scale of the dark continent the distance between these places didn't look too formidable. With three weeks at our disposal Eve and I could head south into the Sahara on the road trip to end all road trips.

I was impatient to get started; but impatient in the same way I had been when faced with exams. I wanted them to start, so that I could stop worrying about them, wanted to be in the midst of the experience instead of building it up into a worse nightmare than it needed to be. In truth, all I wanted was to stop thinking.

I threw my untapped energy at the problem of getting the house sold and devoted myself to the reams of red tape, the endless useless reports, guarantees and documents that new legislation had made necessary. I had the collectibles valued and taken to be auctioned, and a clearance firm came in and took the rest. I appointed an agent and listened to her tales of woe about the state of the housing market, about the need to 'dress' the house in a more modern style to attract the 'right sort' of buyer, to hire in furniture and pot plants and spray fake coffee and bread smells about the place before viewings. 'Is there a sun-warmed cut grass scent we can spray about the garden?' I asked sarcastically, as we stood in drizzle gazing out over the bramble-grown wilderness that had once been the site of the vegetable patch, and watched as she digested this suggestion. 'What a good idea,' she said thoughtfully, and got out her notebook and wrote it down, oblivious to my incredulous stare.

*   *   *

On the day we were due to fly I awoke at five in the morning, sweating and crying out because I had been left under the burning desert sun, too weak even to crawl towards the far-off gleam of water. I sat up in bed, my heart thudding. Now, where had that come from? Was it a displacement dream prompted by my fear of flying, or something even less explicable? I tried not to think about either possibility, and by the time I had packed the amulet and the other contents of the box carefully into my handbag alongside my passport the sensation had been replaced by a distinct sense of anticipation.

*   *   *

We were not the only climbers heading for Morocco, it seemed. In the check-in queue at Gatwick, punctuating the usual mixture of sun-seeking tourists and families with wailing children, there were four or five teams porting climbing sacks, rope-bags, even a bouldering mat or two. They were mostly in their twenties and looked painfully young to me, in their frayed Fat Face jeans and colourful fleeces, the girls with pale, dreadlocked hair, the boys with leather bracelets. We manoeuvred our trolley into line and Eve's sack promptly tumbled off with a rich clank on to the concrete floor. All the gear was in it, packed down tight: it weighed a ton. She hauled it upright and was trying to muscle it back on to the cart when a young man swooped in and effortlessly swung it up into place, then turned and smiled at us. He had a broad, pleasant face, sandy hair and a lazy eye, yet the combination was somehow piratical. 'Hiya, I'm Jez,' he said in a broad Sheffield accent. 'We saw you arrive and said: climbers! Just like that. Could tell from the way you moved. Didn't we, Miles?'

His companion was a year or two older and more smartly turned out. He nodded, a little shy, not much wanting to engage. 'The rucksacks were a bit of a giveaway.'

Jez had obviously taken a bit of a shine to Eve. 'Going to Tafraout?'

Eve grinned, and you could see he was dazzled, and why. 'Sure. Are you?'

'Of course. Best place in the world to climb at this time of year, and a lot less of a hassle than the rest of Morocco.'

'Well, there were those carpet touts,' Miles reminded him. 'Desperate to get us in their shop, they were. Chased us up the street!'

Jez laughed. 'Yeah, dressed as Tuaregs. They were no more Tuareg than you or me. Still, it was a nice carpet. Put it in my room: reminds me of Morocco every day.'

They were easy company; we sat and had a coffee in one of the cafés in Departures and swapped tales of climbs we'd enjoyed, crags we liked, epics we'd had and avoided, falls taken and held. In no time we were on the plane and I'd had no opportunity to obsess over my horror of flying.

A short-haul flight may pass in the blink of an eye to the seasoned traveller who isn't terrified of falling out of the sky in a blaze of aviation fuel; but for those of us who play this image on an unending loop, time becomes torturously subjective, minutes stretching out into infinite panic with every lurch and bump; and, whatever airlines may believe, the truly flight-phobic remain undistracted by the relentless round of drinks and duty-free trolleys. 'Honestly,' Eve said, watching my knuckles whitening as I alternately flexed and balled my hands, 'how you can nervelessly tackle an unprotected 5c slab and get so terrified just sitting on a plane is quite beyond me. Here, read the guidebook: it'll take your mind off things.'

As Jez and Miles had said, there were acres of rock to be climbed around Tafraout, thousands of routes and thousands more waiting to be charted. I distracted myself by working through the guidebook, selecting likely targets, but time after time I came back to the photograph of the crag known as 'Assgaour; or, the Lion's Head' with its strange, iconic face. The route up the nose of the Lion would have to be done: I could feel it in my bones. It kept staring back at me, a challenge, a rite of passage into the heart of Africa. I touched the amulet in my pocket and the fears receded. Even when I heard the crunch and grind of the landing gear as we began our descent into Agadir, I did not immediately think of freefall and fireballs, but tucked the climbing guide calmly into my bag and did not tense at all when the wheels hit the tarmac.

At the airport everyone else's hire cars appeared to have turned up except for mine and Eve's. Disorientated after the long immigration check, we stood outside the terminal building in the baking sun while Eve called the number she had scribbled in the back of her diary, got a series of loud beeps and no dial tone, and had to experiment several times with codes until eventually she managed to get a response and explained in her mangled French that our car had not turned up. The woman on the other end of the line said something back to her and her face contorted with horror. *'Plus lentement!'* she wailed, and thrust the phone at me. In the course of a long and convoluted conversation it transpired that somehow when making the booking, by phone, long distance, Eve had managed to order the car for midnight, rather than midday. *Midi, minuit.* I sighed. Eve thought it was hilarious; except that it turned out they had no cars available until the evening. Eve looked at me, stricken and remorseful, as I relayed this piece of unwelcome information.

'Hey, girls!'

A silver-blue Peugeot 206 had pulled up below us. Miles was driving it; Jez had wound down the window and was grinning at us.

'Come with us!'

I waved them away. 'No, honestly, it's fine. We've got a car, it's just going to be a bit late arriving.' A bit late . . . as in eight hours away.

But Jez was already out of the Peugeot, stowing Eve's rucksack with some difficulty in the already laden boot, and Eve was climbing into the back seat.

'Hey!' I called to her. 'We're going to need our own vehicle, you know, for the Sahara.'

She looked back over her shoulder. 'We can always pick one up later in Tafraout.'

I shrugged, apologized to the woman at the hire car company and followed Eve into the crush of rucksacks in the back of the tiny car.

'It might be a bit cosy,' Miles said reluctantly, sounding as if he wasn't entirely thrilled at the prospect of being lumbered with us, but he soon warmed up as we drove through a small town thronged with every imaginable sort of traffic: buses, cars, scooters, bicycles, donkey carts, all travelling at variable speeds and unpredictable trajectories, with hundreds of pedestrians thrown into the mix, all trying to cross the road at unsuitable points, even stopping and chatting with drivers and donkey carters en route. There were men in long robes with characterful faces of walnut-coloured skin and a mass of wrinkles; veiled women; children in pastel-coloured playsuits; girls in white school overalls or jeans and colourful headscarves. Horns sounded constantly; people shouted, laughed, whistled; donkeys brayed. Arabic music blared out of a rusty Mercedes that veered perilously close when it overtook us on the inside, the high-pitched voice of a female singer threading reedily through a thump of drums.

We passed rows of lock-up shops: grocers and paint shops, mechanics, hardware stores, bakeries, carpet shops; shops with mattresses, rolled mats, white plastic garden furniture or tyres piled up outside on the pavement; and one shop that apparently sold only painted blue metal wheelbarrows. I turned to point this oddity out to my companions, only to spot on the opposite side of the road a mule drawing a long cart bearing the eviscerated, cut-down carcase of an old Dacia car. A man sat on the bonnet, on some sort of makeshift seat, twitching the reins; behind him, sitting in state within the body of the car, were three black-robed, veiled women. I half expected them to wave formally to the crowds, revealing long white gloves, like the Queen.

'Look!' I cried, but Miles had his eyes fixed on the road ahead, trying to avoid hitting the myriad obstacles in our path, and Jez and Eve were engrossed in a heated debate about a band I'd never heard of. By the time they looked away from one another the hybrid carriage and its occupants were far behind us, replaced by a parade of municipal buildings, a sentry point manned by armed, uniformed men and the long ochre walls of a fort that managed to look both ancient and modern at the same time.

After this, the countryside began to roll past: acres of agricultural land devoted to crops grown beneath polytunnels and bird-netting; fields of chilli plants and banana palms, olive groves, orange and lemon trees, palms bearing heavy clusters of dates. The landscape opened out, became drier and redder. A group of women in robes of purple, yellow and black stood out vividly against the dusty orange of the soil they worked. Prickly pears, cactus and thorn bushes formed natural hedges between fields where shepherds sat in the shade beneath solitary trees, watching as flocks of skinny sheep and black-haired goats foraged for whatever they could find. A ghostly interzone, where everything—trees, rocks, road and fields—was covered in white dust, marked the transition between the seaboard and the uplands. Just after a sign for the Atlas Quarry, where a huge hill of white stone had been eaten away on two sides as if by two rival giants trying to scoff the lot,

106

we took a turning off the main road and started the long climb towards the haze of blue mountains on the horizon.

In first and second gear the Peugeot ground its way through a series of narrow and vertiginous switchbacks. The views were so stunning and the potential for disaster so great that at last everyone stopped talking except to remark on the dizzying drop falling away to our right. 'How on earth do cars pass each other on a road like this?' Eve asked, appalled, and at that moment a tall, unsteadily laden truck garlanded with good luck charms and painted with garish scenes of palm trees and camels came careening around the corner towards us and we quickly found out: you veered off the road into whatever nook in the cliff face you could find in order to avoid oncoming traffic, or you were likely to find yourselves in a head-on collision with someone who believed more in fate than in careful driving. In the back of the car, my foot stamped down hard on a phantom brake pedal.

'Eh, that were fucking close!' Jez turned to survey us.

I tried to divert myself from doubts about my life being in Miles's hands by devoting myself to correlating the landscape with the map of the area I had bought from Stanfords in Covent Garden. It had been printed in Morocco and looked nothing like the Ordnance Survey maps I was used to. The scale was off, the colours different, the roads hard to make out against the contouring of the terrain, and some of the Berber place names were so exotic that I could not even begin to form the sound of them in my head: Imi Mqourn, Ida Ougnidif and

107

Tizg Zaouine. After a while the sheer bleak romance of the landscape and the luxury of being able to pay attention to its jagged skyline, eroded massifs, stone-walled terraces and dry watercourses lined with almond trees, instead of having to concentrate on the road, began to seduce and calm me. I had not expected Morocco to be so beautiful—although its beauty belonged not to the lexicon of soft green curves and planes of the English countryside but to a harsh, wild, rugged idiom. The people who lived here would be harsh and wild and rugged too, I thought then; they would have to be in order to survive in such a place.

We crossed the Tizi-n-Tarakatine Pass as the sun was beginning its lazy descent towards the horizon; but the air was clear and the shadows were indigo-sharp as we negotiated the winding road that passed through the col, and as we rounded the corner into the valley I gasped. Before us lay the magnificent Ameln Valley, snaking away to the horizon with the vast wall of the Jebel el-Kest's mountain range looming over its right flank.

'See the crag up there?' Miles called back over his shoulder and pointed up at the rock wall. I followed the line of his finger towards the crag. Even at first glance it was massive.

'There's a classic Joe Brown 5b goes right up through the middle of it; Middle Ground, it's called. Brilliant: steep and sustained, incredible exposure.'

I grinned. His enthusiasm was infectious, and it was typical that that down-to-earth Yorkshire climber, no doubt one of Jez's heroes, should have given a route such a prosaic name amongst all the tongue-twisting Berber exoticism. As we made our way down the valley even Miles seemed to cheer up and started pointing out other routes they had climbed, or wanted to: Great Flake, Old Friends, the White Tower, Black Groove, Black Streak, Great Slab and Agony Arete. All the way down the red walls reared over us. The idea of climbing them made my palms itch, and then sweat, as I felt by turns fascinated and unnerved by the sheer size of the routes: some looked to be three hundred metres tall, or more. I'd never tackled anything so large; any expertise I owned had been won on British crags, and those mostly single pitch. Multi-pitch climbing meant at most a hundred metres of Cornish granite in gentle sunshine with the sea lapping the feet of the cliffs and an ice cream to be bought from the van at the car park when you finished the route. Here, you'd be climbing from dawn to dusk in African heat, on unfamiliar rock, in a country that had neither rescue services nor easy ways down; and certainly no ice cream van waiting at the top. I glanced at Eve to see her reaction to these monster rock faces, but she was a less experienced climber than I was and didn't seem to have clocked the level of difficulty we faced. Given her lack of big climb experience, I'd be making all the decisions, and probably doing most of the leading too. Abruptly, I felt terrified at the idea of climbing alone with her in such a place. While I might crave control, the weight of responsibility seemed suddenly overwhelming. Perhaps it wasn't such a bad thing to be with the guys after all: they knew the rock and the area. Perhaps we could climb in a four until I had my eye in.

My nerves were still jangling as we reached the base of the valley and Jez turned around to grin at both of us. 'See that up there?' he said, gesturing out of the window at the tallest crag in the range. 'We'll take you up there tomorrow. You'll love it, won't they, Miles?'

Miles cast a sardonic glance back over his shoulder. 'Consider it a freebie: guided climb from the experts. You can buy us dinner in return.'

'Aye, all week.' Jez winked, or was it just a droop of his lazy eye? 'It's a great walk in, fabulous views. You park at Assgaour and walk up through the ruins of the ancient village, then take one of the goat-tracks up to the crag. Takes a good couple of hours, unless you run it like we did last year. Pull up, Miles: let the ferret see the rabbit, eh?'

Miles pulled the car in to an unpaved turn-off and we all got out, glad to stretch our legs after the three-hour drive. After the air conditioning of the car, the air felt hot and dry and carried with it a sort of musty scent, at once earthy and spicy. I closed my eyes, savouring the odour, for it smelt nothing like anything I had ever smelt in Britain. Yet somehow it was familiar.

'It's not that scary, is it?' There was a hand on my shoulder and I jumped. Miles was peering at me intensely. He had very blue eyes and for some reason this seemed weird to me; for two or three seconds I stared at him as if he were an alien until he looked away awkwardly to where Jez was pointing out the various pitches to Eve.

'Sorry, no, it wasn't that,' I said. 'I was miles away.'

'It's a big route, most of them are. Three hundred metres. It says 5a in the guide but there's not too much of it at that grade. Bit of loose stuff to get through: you know, pick a hold; if you don't like it, put it back.'

We both grinned and the awkward moment passed. 'Look,' he said, 'it's amazing, isn't it? Like a cartoon. Some people just can't see it, and I have to say it's easier when it's in full sun. Once you've spotted it you can't *not* see it whenever you look at the mountain—it's like Magic Eye.'

I looked. The wall of the dark red gorge loomed above a village of scattered mud-brick houses in shades of pink and terracotta, dwarfing the little white mosque, the tiny trees. Vast pyramidal rock formations appeared to have been piled one on top of another, their jagged edges delineated by indigo shadows. The scale was impossible to judge: the whole thing was immense. Under Miles's instruction, I followed the line of an enormous ridge flanking the right-hand edge of the tallest peak and moved upward. It took a moment to see what he was trying to show me, but when I did I could not look away. There! Two deeply shadowed eyes, a long nose and curving muzzle: a lion's head: *the* Lion's Head. It was bizarre; unmistakable. My heart began to hammer. I closed my eyes, but when I did I found superimposed upon the image of the lion the proud face of a young man, black-eyed and intense . . .

CHAPTER TEN

Tafraout was full of black-eyed men; but none was the man I had 'seen' in my reveries. It had to be said, though, that the local Berbers were a handsome people, with strong facial bones, arresting faces and lithe frames. I watched them strolling around the town in their dusty robes, talking and smoking, laughing at each other's jokes, sometimes holding hands.

'They do that a lot round here,' Miles said, nodding in the direction of a pair of elderly gentlemen in hooded robes and the region's distinctive yellow leather slippers walking by hand in hand.

'Aye, we were a bit worried when we first come here,' Jez added. 'Thought they were all arse bandits or something.'

Eve burst out laughing. 'Very enlightened of you. Anyway, I think it's rather sweet. It's good that men show their feelings, that they can be affectionate towards their friends and family in public. I think the world would be a much nicer place if everyone could walk around holding hands.'

Jez looked towards Miles and raised an eyebrow. 'Fancy a stroll?'

'Don't mind if I do.'

Off they went down the road, hand in hand, hamming it up for their audience. The locals looked on, puzzled at first; then they began to grin broadly. A couple of boys in Manchester United shirts who had been kicking a ball around in the road outside the café where we were drinking coffee and reading our guidebooks pointed and laughed, then followed them down the street, aping their gait with uncanny accuracy.

'Not sure who's won the mickey-taking contest,' I said to Eve, but I was glad no one had taken offence at Jez and Miles's horsing around.

My first impressions of the town were those of pleasant surprise. I didn't know what I had been expecting of the place in which we would be staying, for all the photos I had seen had been of the outlying area and of the climbs. Maybe a crumbling adobe village like those we had seen beneath the Lion's Head, quaint and otherworldly. Most of what we had seen of Tafraout was modern: a sprawl of low-rise buildings lined the main street in from the valley with ground floors given up to little businesses—lock-up shops and cafés, three mosques and a kasbah-style hotel on a hill. We arrived just as the sun was going down and there were not many women around. 'They're probably all inside cooking for their menfolk like good little housewives,' Eve said, but I wasn't so sure. The few I had seen so far had been working in the fields, or coming home from them, wrapped head to toe in the traditional black robes of the area, the fabric draped to display as much of the intricately embroidered hems as possible. They wore red leather slippers on their feet and shuffled along under back-breaking loads of greenery that must surely be fodder for their animals. Husbanding livestock in such a region would be demanding and difficult. The only vegetation I'd seen on the way up from the valley had been cacti, palm trees in a dried-up riverbed and some gnarled-looking trees I didn't recognize but that were dotted about the orangey-red landscape at such regular and widely spaced intervals that I could imagine the complex root systems marking each tree's territory beneath the surface, snaking out in all directions in a desperate search for water. For all the modern trappings of the place—the pharmacies, cars and satellite dishes—this was clearly a region bordering on desert, rocky, dry and dusty; it would be hard to make a living here. I'd read in the guidebook that most of the men of the area worked away from home for much of the year in cities across Morocco, bringing their Berber values of shrewdness, determination and a strong work-ethic to bear on thriving little businesses in Casablanca and Marrakech, and sending money home to sustain their families. The lion we had seen presiding over the valley was said to watch over their women, children and old folk while they were away, and indeed I'd noticed that the majority of the men we had seen here had been elderly, or young lads. Women in such a community would have to be pretty tough and self-reliant.

I watched a pair of them now coming up the road carrying a huge basket of vegetables from the market by one handle each. They stopped to exchange greetings with some men standing outside the bakery; one of the young men took the hand of the older woman and kissed it, then returned it to her and touched his hand to his heart. It was a gesture out of the fourteenth century, a touch of ancient chivalry. I found myself smiling broadly and was still doing so as the two women came towards us, chattering to one another. As they drew near, the older of the two paused in her conversation as if feeling my eyes upon her, then quickly drew her veil across her face with her free hand, covering her mouth and nose, and her friend immediately followed her example. They quickened their pace and walked past us, heads averted. I felt obscurely disappointed by this, marked out as a tourist, an intruder in their world. Which, of course, I was.

The men seemed to be doing a better job of cross-cultural bonding. Down the street, Jez and Miles had joined their mockers in a kick-around, and some of the older men had joined in too, shouting and laughing, running and tackling with a joyous enthusiasm rarely seen except in children.

'Ah,' said Eve. 'Football: the universal language.'

We sat there companionably sipping our coffees and watching the world go by. Across the road a pair of cats—striped, tigery beasts with sharp yellow eyes and long limbs—lay in the shade of a barber's shop awning and did the same. A metre away a large feral dog lay on her side with three puppies sucking at her teats. People coming out of the shop stepped carefully over them, even though I was sure I had read somewhere that Muslims disliked dogs, considering them unclean. It was all very laissez-faire: I could feel myself relaxing moment by moment, the little tightly wound Isabelle inside me uncoiling by fractions.

*   *   *

That night we ate at a restaurant Miles had discovered on his first visit, and found we were sharing the place with at least three other climbing teams. Some of us had already hit the hotel bar, since it was the only place in town with a licence to sell alcohol, and several were a bit the worse for wear. There was a lot of giggling and shouting as we stumbled in the darkness down a narrow alleyway bordered by old adobe houses. The doorway to the restaurant was lit by an ornate lantern and framed by hibiscus and bougainvillea. A huge, grinning sun had been painted in bright primary colours on the wall outside: a fitting symbol for the town and its attitude to life. Miles knocked on the door and moments later it was opened by a tall man in blue Berber robes and a red turban. His dark eyes glittered as he surveyed us—a dozen Western climbers in scruffy jeans and fleeces, breathing beer fumes out into the night air, the women with their hair unabashedly uncovered—and I wondered what he made of us, loud and dirty and irreverent: infidels all; but then he caught Jez and Miles in a huge embrace that somehow managed to encompass the whole group and swept us all inside.

'My home, your home!' he declared in heavily accented English, and we all trooped in, dutifully removed our boots and approach shoes, and sat where we were told, on tabourets and cushioned benches around a series of low circular tables. With candlelight flickering on the carved stucco-work and bright brocades, we feasted on spiced lentils and flatbreads, spectacular tajines of lamb and prunes with almonds, and a fragrant chicken couscous jewelled with bright vegetables and garnished with a scarlet sauce that made all of us gasp in awe and beg for the recipe.

The restaurateur tapped the side of his nose. 'Is family secret,' he told us. 'It contains mixture of over twenty different spices. If I tell you how is made, you have no reason to come back here. The magic is lost. Mystery is very important in life, no?'

And with that, he swept our empty dishes away and strode back into the kitchen with a swirl of his blue robe.

Eve and I raised eyebrows at one another. 'He's quite something, isn't he?'

'Very striking,' I agreed, thoughtful. There was something self-contained, confident and easy about the manner of the people we'd encountered in the few short hours we'd been here, which was attractive to someone who was used to the cocky one-upmanship of London men, a competitiveness that masked a deep insecurity and distrust of others. 'Don't get too interested,' Jez said, eyeing us with amusement as we craned our necks to get a glimpse into the kitchen. 'Someone got there first. We met his wife last year.'

Talk turned inevitably to climbing and plans for the next day. It was a mixed group—in age, ability and ambition. Three other women, one of them grey-haired and in her fifties, the other two (Jess and Helen) younger and flaunting rather more flesh than was wise, and five men other than Jez and Miles: two middle-aged guys and three young hotshots who boasted about the new routes they were here to bag. 'Acres of unclimbed rock,' the blond one was saying, 'dozens of routes just waiting to be taken.' He spoke as if he were in the vanguard of a conquering army about to ravish the virgins of the city.

Helen now leant across and batted her eyelashes at Jez. 'It all sounds a bit hard round here. The climbing, I mean. Jess and I were wondering if you and Miles'd be up for taking us out with you tomorrow, since you've been here before, as guides, like. Give us a bit of an introduction to the rock?' She admitted they'd never climbed outdoors before.

Miles's face was the very picture of horror, but Jez was kinder. 'Sorry, girls, love to, but we're taking Eve and Iz out with us tomorrow. You should try bouldering on the granite; there're even a couple of bolted routes you could have a go at— technically difficult but not dangerous.'

Helen shot me a look of pure female jealousy, hard and witchy. I gave a little shrug—not my battle, honey—but Eve was loving every moment of it. 'Yes, we're going to do the Lion's Face,' she said, putting her hand territorially on Jez's thigh, and I watched his face go very still as he tried not to betray a reaction.

Someone took pity on the girls: an older man with a pale, lugubrious face and glasses who was here with his wife—the woman with short grey hair—and brother-in-law. 'We're climbing just above Oumsnat tomorrow,' he said to Helen. 'There's a single pitch wall there with lots of good introductory routes on it—you can come with us.'

I could see that Helen was not going to give up without a fight, but luckily our conversation was interrupted by the restaurant manager coming back with a large tray bearing a silver teapot and a dozen glasses. He was followed by a blonde woman in a Moroccan tunic and jeans who surveyed us all and grinned, enjoying our surprise at seeing a European emerge from a Berber kitchen rather than one of the ubiquitous black-robed ladies. He poured out the mint tea from a ridiculous height with great élan so that it formed a frothing foam in the little decorated glasses that she passed amongst us along with some exquisite little almond biscuits. When she got to me, she stopped in her tracks and bent forward.

118

'How lovely. Did you buy it here?'

I had forgotten I was wearing the amulet: the climbers were all far too interested in their sport to comment on it. I ran my fingers over it and it suddenly felt warm to the touch, as if it had taken in the warmth of the candles and the food and stored it in the red glass discs.

'Ah, no. It was . . . a gift.'

'Do you know anything about it?'

'A little,' I said cautiously.

'I reckon it looks like a Moack,' Jez grinned. 'Don't you, Miles?'

Miles made a face, uninterested. 'Who climbs with Moacks nowadays? Bloody antiques.'

'My dad gave me his: best runner I ever had,' Jez said cheerfully.

The restaurateur's wife grinned. 'I doubt it was made in Sheffield,' she said, astutely guessing his accent. 'It looks as if it's from the desert, or at least inspired by work from the desert tribes. Tafraout's on the ancient trading route out of the Sahara towards Taroudant and the coast. There are a lot of southern influences in the jewellery made here.'

'From the desert? Are you sure?'

She laughed. 'Sorry, no, not really: I'm no expert. But you should ask around. Mhamid has similar necklaces at his stall in the souq. Houcine too. You could ask them if you want to find out more about it.'

Her husband appeared at her shoulder and fixed me with his glittering black eyes. 'It is to Taïb you should talk. My cousin. He is expert in antiquities, he has business in Paris'—*Paree*—'but he is in Tafraout now, for *vacances*. I arrange meeting for you if you wish.'

119

'No, no, thank you; it's very kind, but no,' I said, flustered, and he shrugged and continued pouring out the teas. I could feel people looking at me, could feel the *weight* of their gazes on me, weighing me down; weighing upon the necklace. I swallowed fast, closed my eyes. Panic rose up like a black wave, worse than anything I'd felt on any climb I'd ever attempted; worse than the time I'd been halfway up Bubble Memory, stranded amid decayed limestone and flaky holds, and my only apparently good runner had popped out. I felt hot, then cold, and my heart hammered and hammered. Bile rose in my throat. I swallowed it down and forced myself to breathe steadily. *Get back in the box*, I told the panic fiercely. Back into the place in the back of my head where I stashed the things that mustn't get out. I enfolded the amulet in my hand and felt it beat with my own pulse, slower and slower. When I opened my eyes, I found that actually no one was looking at me at all, not even Eve. Especially not Eve: she was hanging on Jez's every word, her whole body angled towards him, mouth open and her eyes shining with such fervour that I had to look away. It was as if I'd walked in on them naked and sweating. I felt obscurely ashamed and appalled, as if I were in some way responsible for her. I tucked the amulet away beneath my jumper and tried hard to concentrate on getting back into the flow of the conversation.

*   *   *

That night I slept badly, woken at various times by the mournful cries of the feral dogs and the pre-

120

dawn call to prayer. I lay there in my narrow single bed and listened to Eve's steady breathing on the other side of the room. The tatters of a dream flickered and tantalized on the edge of consciousness, but no matter how hard I tried to go back to it somehow it evaded me, leaving me with a sense of unfocused dread, as if something awful had happened just out of my sight, something that had a bearing on my fate: a warning or a premonition.

CHAPTER ELEVEN

Mariata sat on her heels in the palm-branch shelter a little distance away from the camp and watched the enad's deft hands working the piece of iron over a flame so hot that it seemed to burn white at its heart. The hammer rose and fell with a rhythm that almost lulled her to sleep. There was something primal about the process that fascinated her; fascinated and repelled her in equal measure, if truth be told, which was largely how she felt about the enad too. Although many weeks had passed in her new home, and despite the fact that she went to the smithy almost every day to watch the enad work, Mariata still did not know what to make of Tana, with her big hands and her small, but undeniably womanly, breasts, her loose veil and men's clothing. It was taboo for a woman to work metal over fire like this; taboo too for a woman to come here to watch; but Tana was not an ordinary woman, and neither was Mariata, and something about the enad and her craftsmanship

121

called to something inside her. Did she find a parallel for the working of her poetry in the way Tana shaped iron and silver, hammering away incessantly and with a critical eye, exclaiming at imperfections and assailing the metal with angry little dinks and beats until it had succumbed to her will? Or was it that she identified with this strange person who stood with one foot inside the tribe and one foot without? Or possibly it was that after her long hours at Amastan's side she felt the need to seek out someone else who communed with the spirits and might understand the exhausting demands that such work made upon her. Or maybe it was because she felt she could release the pent-up spirits into the enad's fire. Certainly, the piece Tana was working now was proving to be more recalcitrant than usual. The smith grasped it in her delicate tongs and squinted at it critically, the firelight adding a fearsome red lustre to the planes of that uncompromising face. It was a key, a hand's span in size, notched and incised along its length: it would when finished fit the intricately crafted lock that Tana had made the day before, the lock that would be fixed to a great wooden chest to contain a chieftain's treasures. The smith now held it in front of her face and peered at Mariata through the open-worked circle at its tip, the circle that represented the world. At the other end, the key ended in a crescent, representing the endless sky. 'Has he said anything to you yet?'

Mariata felt herself flush. She dropped her eyes to the coin she had been fiddling with, one from a pile of assorted silver pieces the enad would melt down for the next jewellery commission she received. 'This morning, when I brought him his porridge, he spoke.' What she did not tell Tana was that he had accompanied these first words he had addressed directly to her (for you could not count those inadvertent explosions of anger or fear that seemed to come shooting up out of some dark place in his memories, sparked by something in her poetry or some movement she made, eruptions that often terrified her and made her run away) with a slight touch upon the back of her hand, a touch she had felt like a lightning bolt through the very core of her.

Tana's still face registered not a flicker of reaction. 'Are you sure it was Amastan who spoke, and not the spirits inside him?'

Mariata turned the coin over and furiously applied her concentration to it. Only when she had stared at it for several moments did she realize that what she was looking at was not a random arrangement of lines and engravings but a design, a representation of things that belonged in the living world, and not on dead metal. Images made on carpets and shawls were a different matter: textiles came from living things, from the wool of sheep and camels, or from the cotton plants that grew by rivers. But images made on metal, there was something wrong about that. She turned it back, realigned it, turned it around again. On one side there appeared to be a fierce bird with two heads and wings spread so that the primary feathers fanned out like fingers; on the other was the profile of a rather fat person of indeterminate gender whose head grazed a series of strange-looking symbols ringing the edge of the coin. 'Who is this?' she asked, holding the coin up. 'Is it a man or a woman?'

Tana frowned. 'Is it so important to know?'

Mariata had never seen a visual representation of a person before, nor one of any living thing that looked as it did in life. Those who followed the new religion said that it was blasphemous, disrespectful, to imitate Allah's work: even the symbols they worked in their woven rugs were heavily stylized, triangles for camels, diamonds for cattle, dotted circles for the frogs that stood for fertility. She had certainly never seen anything rendered so minutely that you could make out curls in the hair or the drapery of a robe falling off a shoulder. She peered at the silver disc more closely. The marks around its edge looked nothing like the Tifinagh, but somehow she felt sure they constituted some sort of language. How she knew this she was not sure; it was no more than a twinge of recognition. 'Perhaps. I was curious. I just wanted to know.'

The enad's smiled widened, though her eyes remained cool. 'They all want to know. "Is it a man or a woman?" That is the question I always feel on their lips, hovering behind their tongues like a bee vibrating with its own importance. How can we know? Shall we crawl into her tent at night and watch to see when she disrobes which organs she owns? Shall we jostle her in a crowd, feel through her clothes and pretend we were just brushing past?'

Mariata was dismayed. 'I'm sorry, that's not what I meant at all. I just wanted to know why there is a person on this coin and who it might be.'

'The coin is a thaler, and the woman on it was called Maria Theresa. She was a great queen. The coin was made during her reign in the eighteenth

124

century as the Christians reckon their years.'

'I have never heard of her.'

Tana laughed and her heavy silver earrings spun and caught the firelight. 'Ah, so the child of Tin Hinan's line believes there is only one great queen, does she? It will be news to you, Mariata of the Hoggar, that there are many queens in the world, and many lands beyond those you know. This was a queen—more than a queen, an empress. The Holy Roman Empress, Queen of Hungary, Bohemia, Croatia and Slavonia, Archduchess of Austria, Duchess of Parma and Piacenza, Grand Duchess of Tuscany, mother of Marie Antoinette, queen consort of France and wife to Louis XVI, whose head was cut off by her people.'

Mariata had heard of none of these places other than France; their unfamiliar names washed over her and left her untouched; but the last detail caused her to stare at Tana in horror. 'Her head was cut off?'

'With a guillotine: a great sharp knife lowered, very fast, by ropes.' Tana chopped her hand down so hard that Mariata jumped.

'But if the head and the body are separated in death, the soul will roam for ever. The Kel Asuf will capture it and it will become one of them, one of the People of the Wilderness.' There was no worse fate in the world. She shuddered at the very thought of it; and that such a horrible thing should happen to a woman who was the daughter of a great queen too. Almost, she could feel the cold blade on her own neck . . .

'They were cruel people.' Tana cocked her head on one side, considering this. 'The world is full of cruel people, which keeps the Kel Asuf thoroughly

125

satisfied.'

'How do you know these things?'

'Do you think I have lived here all my life? I have travelled, more widely than you would imagine.'

'I thought this was your home.'

'The inadan have always travelled. We are the news-carriers and the messengers of the Kel Tamacheq, as well as the smiths and the makers. We keep the knowledge of the tribes, and we know the things they do not wish to know for themselves.'

Mariata was not sure what to make of this last pronouncement, so instead she asked, 'Have you taken the salt road, then?'

Tana took up her file and ran it along a rough edge on the key. 'Both literally and symbolically.' Her smile was wry, lopsided. 'My father was a travelling smith who often accompanied the caravans; my mother a slave from this tribe. In the beginning they treated me as a boy. Maybe they did not even know my secret: my mother kept me covered, and called me son. Who was to question a mother's word? I learnt my trade from my father and I travelled with him too. With the *azalay* I have crossed the Djouf, taken salt from Tawdenni to the Adagh and the Aïr, even to your homeland in the Hoggar. Then my courses came and my breasts began to grow.'

Mariata leant forward, fascinated now. 'Then what did you do?'

'To start with I bound rags between my legs and pissed in private. I let no one see my body. It was not difficult: no one washes in the desert, or ever disrobes. But then I fell in love with another

126

caravanner.'

'Did you tell him?'

The file rasped and rasped. 'What, that I loved him? Or that I was "not as other men"?' She paused. 'Nor women either, for that matter. No, I did not tell him either thing, though I made such sheep's eyes at him that he avoided me at night. All through that long journey, though the sun burned down on me like a fire and there was not enough water to go around, it was not the heat or the thirst I thought I would die of, but love. Every time I looked at him and he looked away it was like a dagger to my heart. When he laughed with the other men and fell quiet when I passed, I wept inside. When we reached his village he announced he was to be married to his cousin, and I went out into the desert and lay down and begged Allah to send me my death. *Baghi n'mout*, I told him. I am ready: it is my hour. But he did not take me and so here I am, and I am happy enough in my own way. I have accepted my place in the world, and that I will never be either a husband or a wife. But even so, you should know that I understand what it is to love a man.'

Mariata felt like one of the pieces of the coloured glass the smith worked into her creations: transparent to her eagle eye. Her heart began to beat very fast; she could feel her pulse throbbing around the coin she held tightly in her fist.

Tana put down the key and the file. 'Such a fiery love is never a good thing, child. The desert lies outside you: why bring it within?'

'He needs someone to love him,' Mariata said, not looking at her.

'His mother loves him enough for everyone,'

Tana said drily.

'She crossed the Tamesna to find me because she believed I could help him. I must make him better: I must! And he will get better, I know it.'

'You are very young and the young never listen to the old, especially in matters of the heart.' Tana shook her head. 'You will have heard the rumours, I am sure. Well, I am no great advocate of rumours: heaven knows I've been subjected to enough of those in my long life; but what I will say, child, is that you must beware of Amastan. He carries the scent of death with him. He does not smell like a lucky man, or one who brings luck to those close to him.'

The hairs on the back of Mariata's neck rose.

'You must ask yourself why the spirits follow him,' the enad went on. 'Do they haunt him for the lives he may have taken, or for those he has yet to take?'

Mariata stared at her, dismayed. She could not believe him a murderer—she could not. 'He is beset by spirits, that is true: they invade his dreams. But it is not his fault,' she said steadfastly. 'They gather around the thing he has clutched in his right hand.'

'Have you seen what it is?'

'It is an amulet. And there is dried blood upon it.'

The enad gave a little hiss, or maybe it was just a sudden spurt of flame in the fire. Then she said, 'When he first came here there was much of his father in him: his tongue was as sharp as a viper's, and there was a lot of anger in him. It can be hard to shake one's first impressions of a person.' She pushed herself to her feet and walked across the smithy. 'But I should have helped him when he came to me with that amulet. All actions have consequences; things come back to haunt you later in life.'

From a plain leather box Tana took a small pouch on a black string, and this she hung around Mariata's neck. It smelt musty and unpleasant, and when Mariata craned her neck to look at it she was sure she could see something that resembled a chicken's foot inside, as well as other, less identifiable things.

'The gris-gris will protect you from what we are about to attempt,' Tana pronounced. 'But I am trusting you never to mention what you will see me do here today. It is hard enough to be an enad who is not precisely a man, without adding the accusation of sorcerer to my reputation.'

Mariata's eyes became round. 'You are a sorcerer?'

'Not really, child, no. I make divinations; I speak with the spirits from time to time. But there are some in this tribe who might look for a reason to chase me away, even though I am just one weak creature.'

The tall smith did not seem weak to Mariata—not in the least, with her well-muscled arms, her big hands and her considerable height, as well as her fierce golden-brown eyes that seemed so bright in comparison with her charcoal skin.

'Come, let us visit your Amastan and I will see what I can do.'

*   *   *

When he saw them coming, Amastan adjusted his

veil and set his back against the wall of his shelter, looking, Mariata thought, like a dog that fears a beating. As they approached, his eyes never left Tana's face.

'Amastan ag Moussa. It is time to give up the amulet.' And the smith walked right up to him and held out her hand, palm up.

Amastan's eyes went so wide you could see the white above and below the dark pupils. Then he clutched his right hand to his chest, while holding his veil close against his face with his left, as if he were using it as a shield against the enad. They remained like this, unmoving, for long moments. Then Tana began to chant in a language Mariata did not understand, although she heard Amastan's name repeated over and over amongst the unfamiliar sing-song words. Taking a piece of silver on a long string from beneath her robe, she started to swing it back and forth in front of him. Mariata watched his eyes flicking from side to side, captured by the movement of the pendant.

This went on for so long that Mariata began to feel light-headed. Then she heard Tana stop her melodic chanting and say, quite distinctly, 'It is the amulet that is holding you prisoner like this, Amastan ag Moussa. All you have to do is to give it up. The spirits inside it must be released: it is as cruel to them as it is to you to keep them trapped in this way. I will not ask you to relinquish the amulet to me; I know you fear me, as do the spirits you guard. But perhaps you will give it to one whose heart is open to you.' And she beckoned for Mariata to come forward. 'Give up the amulet, Amastan ag Moussa. Let Mariata ult Yemma, daughter of the line of Tin Hinan, take it from you.

Place the amulet in her hand. Do it now.'

For several heartbeats the air hung still and heavy between them. Then, like a man in a dream, Amastan uncurled the fingers of his right hand and held out the talisman.

Without pausing the pendant in its action or taking her eyes from him, Tana said quietly, 'Take it, Mariata. Take it from him, quickly now. You are protected against the spirits, I promise you; but only you can do this. There is a bond of trust between you.'

Mariata hesitated. What if the spirits were to swirl out of the amulet and engulf her? Would she be haunted by them all her life? Would she become mad, an outcast, condemned to live outside society, exiled to a mean shelter like this one, like a diseased dog? She shook the thoughts away: it was in her power to save Amastan. Tana said it was so, and, for all her oddness, she believed the smith when she said this was true. She dropped to one knee before him and quickly took the amulet, strung on a long cord threaded with bright black beads, into her own hand. For a moment she felt it throb in her palm, as if transferring the power it contained from Amastan to her; then the connection was broken.

Amastan's entranced gaze slid from the smith's pendant to Mariata. She watched him frown and look down at his empty hand, where the impression of the amulet was still deeply imprinted. The frown deepened. Then his head came up and he looked away from Tana and fixed his eyes upon Mariata. Dipping his head so that Mariata blocked Tana's view, he dropped his other hand from his face, letting his veil fall. Mariata found herself staring. It was only the second time in her life that she had seen the naked face of a grown man, but Amastan's gesture was one of vulnerability, and a gift to her, unlike Rhossi's arrogant disregard for propriety. Neither did he resemble his cousin greatly: his bone structure was finer, and the cheeks that showed above his ragged beard were stained a dull blue. Here was a man who had travelled the world, buffeted by the desert winds, protected by a tagelmust whose powdery indigo dye had transferred itself to the skin. Then he bowed his head, ran a hand across his face to feel the rough and unaccustomed hair growing there, and slowly and very deliberately rewound his veil tightly about his face. 'Would you ask my mother to let me have my shaving things, and bring me a bowl of water so that I can see who I am now?' he asked after a while. 'You can assure her I will not use the knife to slit my own throat.'

*　　　*　　　*

From that day Amastan returned to the tribe, though he largely kept to himself and exchanged few words with the other men. To begin with people tended to avoid him, casting askance glances at him when they thought he was not watching. His mother treated him like a recovering invalid, bringing him special foods and saving her meat for him. She was very pleased with Mariata, to whom she ascribed Amastan's miraculous return to his true self. At first Mariata did not know how to respond; she could not tell Rahma what the enad had done, for she did not really understand what that was. Tana had employed some sort of strange magic; the spirits had left of their own accord; removing the amulet had indeed enabled Amastan to regain his sanity; or he had simply decided for some reason known only to himself to give up his long and perturbing period of desolation—any of these could have been true. And so she decided to smile and say how glad she was that Amastan was well again and that she had been able to help.

'You must stay with us as long as you would like,' Rahma told her, as if she had other choices. 'I regard you as I would a daughter.'

'That is very kind of you,' Mariata returned, acknowledging the formal invitation, but she could not look the older woman in the eye: for she knew she had no wish to be seen as a sister to Amastan. She wore his amulet, washed clean of blood, beneath her robe, against her heart.

CHAPTER TWELVE

The nightmarish images that had plagued my sleep that first night in Tafraout remained with me in uncomfortable flickers as we made the hard two-hour walk-in up through spectacular rocky terrain to reach the foot of the Lion's Head. For the next four hours, as we made our way by increments in two teams of two—Miles and me, followed by Jez and Eve—up the three hundred metres of the route, I moved from pitch to pitch with greater caution than was my usual style, feeling those unsettling dreams nagging at me. I placed my feet with exaggerated precision, consciously checked

133

each hold before putting my weight on it, backed up every belay in textbook fashion, and checked knots and harness buckles with such neurotic care that I knew I was driving Miles mad with impatience. As it was, it was clear he would rather have been climbing with Jez alone, swift and Alpine-style. He was lucky: at least I pulled my weight, alternating leads with him and carrying out my duties with some degree of efficiency. Eve, being the slowest and least experienced climber of the four of us, led no part of the route, meaning that Jez had to lead each pitch, which necessitated a slow and tedious pulling-through of ropes at every belay, and inevitable tangles and further delays.

Miles had been tutting and swearing under his breath for the past two pitches, even though the sun was glorious, and the climbing sound, for the most part, and elegant. But when we reached the crux traverse beneath a vast, unclimbable roof, a long sideways expanse of unstable rock whose upper layers were exfoliating in thin skins due to their long exposure to heat and cold, he skittered sideways across it impatiently, not stopping to place any gear to protect me when I seconded the pitch. I paid the ropes out angrily. Long traverses like this were as dangerous for the second as for the leader. Take a fall on a vertical pitch and the rope is always above you, so that you fall only a metre or two at worst; but take a fall seconding a traverse and you'll swing all the way from the point of the fall to beneath the point where the leader has taken his belay; and from where I stood that was a good twenty metres away. Unable to stop myself, I looked down, something I could usually do without feeling any great terror, and realized that the traverse was deeply undercut and that when I started out over it there would be a yawning void below me, a sheer drop of more than fifty metres. Or so I reckoned: the scale was simply impossible to calculate. All I could see down there were the tiny dots of trees green against the ambient orangey-pink of the rocky ground, and below those some tiny black dots like ants but which were probably goats.

I looked back, but Miles was out of sight now, having climbed over the lip above, and the rope had gone still. I looked to my left. Far below I could see Jez's blue bandana bobbing as he made his way up the pitch. Of Eve there was no sign because of the curvature of the cliff. I was on my own. The temptation to wait until Jez made it to the belay ledge became immense; I found it cold and dark and lonely in the shadow of the overhanging roof, a nerve-racking place at the best of times, and all the more so when faced with the prospect ahead. But after a couple more minutes the ropes jerked three times: the signal that Miles had reached a safe place and made his anchor point. I detached the lead ropes from the belay device and watched them snake away across the rock till they went tight on my harness. *Jerk, jerk, jerk.* The next signal: that he had me on belay, and pretty much what I thought of him too. With shaking hands I removed the gear with which I had protected our belay and tugged the rope in turn. *Ready to climb.* I touched my amulet, which I had hung for luck on the back of my harness, out of harm's way, and started the traverse. I teetered across the first two moves feeling acutely exposed.

I was at the furthest extent of the rope now: one false move and I'd pendulum across the rock face, taking a leader fall that at best would rip the skin from my hands and face, at worst would put such force on the belay that it would see us both plunge down the mountain. The tremor in my hands transferred itself into the muscles of my forearms, then into my thighs and knees. I was balanced on five centimetres of flaky rock, without a handhold, both palms pressed against the quartzite: precarious, to say the least. *Get a grip, Izzy,* I told myself fiercely. *Just bloody well get a grip. You're on a rope and you're not going to die.*

But I might . . .

I made another sideways move, leaning into the rock. Still no decent holds. Another move; toe in a crack. A tiny piece of rubble detached itself at the pressure of my foot and went bouncing away down the rock. I heard it go, *click, click, click*; then there was no sound at all as it peeled off into the void. The tremor became a shake.

Get a fucking grip, Izzy: it's only 5a.

I looked down, seated my left foot as well as I could in order to move on again with my right, and reached across. Nothing, well nothing much. Nothing much would have to do. My whole body made a tremor of intent as I prepared to transfer my weight; then I saw the ropes. A great loop of them now hung between me and my invisible belayer: Miles, bored and annoyed, was not taking in as quickly as he should have been. I shouted up to him—'Tight!'– but the word fell like the stone into the empty air. A tight rope would pull me off-balance anyway, I reminded myself. Hell. I took a deep breath to steady myself and transferred my weight to the right . . .

A chunk of quartzite the size of a house brick came away beneath my leading foot and down I went, tumbling over and over against the rock, too fast even to yelp or fully register the pain as I knocked, hard, an ankle here, my cheek there, nose, hip, knee, forehead . . . There was a disembodied cry, sharp and hallucinatory: from far below me, or was it inside my head? I had no way of telling. I waited for the plunge into space as the rock ran out beneath me, but then, with a jolt that nearly dislocated my hip, the fall was halted. I was hanging sideways, looking down the mountain. How bizarre. Surely if the ropes had caught me, I'd be facing in, or out, not sideways at this odd angle. I looked up. The ropes, two garish pink and blue snaking things, lay flaccidly along the rock high up against the deep red of the quartzite, unconcerned by my fate. I hung where I was, afraid to move, hardly daring to breathe. So it wasn't the rope that had held me but my harness. Probably one of the gear loops had snagged a spike of rock. Panic flared up again: gear loops weren't made to resist a shockload; any moment now whatever held me would snap and I'd be hurled down off the cliff, and that would be that.

Slowly, I moved my head to examine what had stopped me. My vision was blurred; my head rang from the knocks it had taken. For several woozy moments I couldn't trust my eyes. Impossibly, it looked as if the amulet had wedged itself inside a crack and that I was hanging from its narrow leather thong, clipped with a mini-karabiner on to a gear loop. I stared at this unlikely combination of cause, effect and sheer uncanny luck, unbelieving.

137

Then, compulsively, I twisted to get my feet and hands back on to the rock and take my weight off that fragile point of contact. A decent foot-ledge; a handhold. Thank God. And just as I breathed out, the leather thong holding the amulet snapped. I pressed my face against the rock, my heart beating so hard it felt as though its hammering might propel me off my precarious hold on the mountain.

Danger soon steadied my swimming head. Swiftly, I fiddled a piece of gear into a crack, ran a sling through my harness loop and back again and clipped it; did up the karabiner's gate. That gave me the courage to stare at the amulet again. There it was, wedged across its broadest point, the sun winking off the silver. It looked positively smug, as if it had been designed for this very moment in time. But the force of the fall had deformed it: I could see how it was bent and awkward-looking. It was probably never going to be shifted. I would have to leave it behind as a sacrifice, a thank you to the Lion's Head, which had once again extended its legendary protection to a woman. I reached out to it, brushed my fingers over its outside edge as if in farewell; and it fell into my hand.

Shaking, I slipped it into a pocket in my climbing pants and zipped the pocket closed over it. Then, fiercely pushing away my fear, I removed the gear and climbed towards Miles with my heart thudding like a trapped bird's. Going up was a whole lot easier than going sideways. When I appeared over the lip of rock where he had made the belay he was still taking in rope at speed. 'Slow down,' he said. 'I can hardly keep up with you.' He huffed and puffed as he clipped me into the belay, then looked at me properly for the first time.

'Christ, look at you, what happened?'

I put my hand to my face and it came away covered in blood. I realized suddenly that various bits of me were hurting, quite badly.

'Ah . . .' The words would not come. I looked down, my head throbbing with the effort. Blood was seeping through the knee of my climbing pants, but, though the kneecap smarted, I knew instinctively that I had a worse injury. Now that the adrenalin of the fall and the desperate need to reach the safety of the belay had worn off, I could feel a dull, foreboding pain in my left ankle. Gingerly, I pulled up my trouser leg to examine the damage. The ankle was swollen, flesh spilling grotesquely over the top of my climbing shoe. Abruptly, I found it would not take my weight. I thought I might vomit.

Now Miles looked horrified. 'Jesus, what have you done? How the hell did you climb that pitch like that? Can you move it?' He stared at the ruined joint but made no attempt to examine it more closely. Instead, I saw his gaze slide away down the rock towards the long, rugged expanse of mountain beneath us, and I knew he was already anticipating the difficulties of the descent while hampered by an injured woman. He ran a hand over his face, a gesture that said quite articulately, *This was not what I signed up for.*

'I'll strap it up,' I said briskly, angry at myself for allowing this ridiculous situation to have occurred at all, angry to have put myself at the mercy of a stranger. 'I'll bind it and put my walking boot on to support it.'

Miles pulled at his lip. 'I'm not sure about that.' He looked at a complete loss. Then he readjusted

139

his belay and picked his way across the shield of rock to where he would have a view of the progress of the other team. Where he should have taken the belay in the first place, I thought savagely, so that he could keep a proper eye on his second. But there was no point in apportioning blame: it was my own fault for falling. I hadn't checked the crucial foothold before trusting my weight to it, despite all the caution I'd employed right up to that fateful moment. In climbing you soon learn to take responsibility for your own mistakes and live with the consequences. It was one of the things I most liked about the sport: cause and effect was clear-cut, the way life should be but rarely was.

Miles returned to the belay looking relieved. 'Jez'll be up in a few minutes.' Then he sat down and mutely fiddled with his gear, rearranging it on his rack, head bent to avoid eye contact, and not another word passed between us.

Time ticked leadenly by. About fifteen minutes later Jez's blue-bandanaed head appeared over the lip of the ridge. He was grinning from ear to ear, clearly loving the sensation of the Moroccan sun on his back, the warm rock under his fingers, the gulf of air beneath his feet, the delicacy of the moves. When he saw the state of me, though, the grin faded. 'Fucking hell, Izzy, what have you done?'

I waited until he'd made himself safe on the belay and gave him a carefully edited version of events. No point in mentioning Miles's failure to protect his second; or his lack of patience or communication. Jez whipped off the bandana, wet it with some water from his pack and made to clean my face. I pushed his hand away, took the cloth from him and dabbed at my nose.

'Not broken?'

I shook my head.

'It's her ankle,' Miles said flatly, staring out across the landscape. If we were on Everest, I thought, he'd be consigning me to my fate, leaving me behind in the death zone, every man for himself. But Jez came from different stock. He ran a practised hand over the mass of bruised and fluid-filled flesh, and I tried unsuccessfully not to wince. 'Can you move it?' I couldn't, and the attempt elicited a moan. 'Bloody hell, Izzy, I think it's fucked.' Even as my mouth opened in shock, he took the edge off this by winking. 'That were a technical term. You just sit back and leave it to the doctor.' With a swift gesture he ripped the bandana in half, spliced the ends together and soon had the ankle expertly immobilized.

'I was going to put my walking boot back on to stabilize it a bit more.'

Jez looked dubious. 'I worry you won't be able to get it off again. Let's have a look.' A couple of minutes later he had removed my 5.10, clipped it to the back of my harness by its pull-on loop, modified the lacing on my Salomon mountain boot so that it would fit over the ruin of my ankle, then laced it up as hard as he could without my fainting. When he saw my colour, he patted me kindly on the shoulder. 'We'll get you off, don't mither yourself.'

'I'm really sorry,' I said, though the apology came hard. 'Not the best start to your climbing holiday. Hope you don't believe in omens.'

Miles said nothing. Jez shrugged. 'Accidents happen in climbing. That's why we love it, eh?' He

141

paid out a loop of rope, twisted a figure-eight knot into it and secured it to his harness, then downclimbed to where he could belay with Eve in sight. I watched him give her a thumbs-up and wondered how she would cope with the traverse, but when she eventually appeared over the top, her eyes huge with concentration and panic, I saw that her gear loops were festooned with runners: Jez had clearly protected the pitch all the way for her. The two of them shared a swift, quiet conversation that I couldn't quite catch and then Eve came padding up to the belay ledge and clipped herself in.

'God, Iz, I'm so sorry. Jez says he thinks it's broken.'

That was not what I'd wanted to hear. Shit. Now I was really in trouble. I forced a grin. 'Maybe. Ah, well, an excellent chance for us to practise our rescue techniques, huh?'

Miles put Jez on lead and off he went out towards the arête, armed with gear and slings and a ferociously purposeful expression. Some while later he headed back again, crabwise, across the slab. 'Right,' he said, 'we'll get you across this section and from the edge I reckon we've got enough rope to lower you into the upper reaches of the gully. Then Eve can abseil down to be with you while Miles and I clear the gear and finish the top pitch, and we'll make it down the col to you, OK?'

'I'll be fine,' I said firmly. 'If you can get me into the gully, I can get down to the car, even if it takes me a week on my bum. Finish the climb, Eve: get it ticked. Don't worry about me.'

She looked appalled. 'I can't do that. I won't

leave you.'

'Honestly, I'd rather deal with it on my own; no need to ruin everyone's day, eh?' I said, sounding a lot braver than I felt.

The setting up of the abseil ropes seemed to take an age. No one would let me do anything: at a stroke I'd gone from experienced climber to invalid, a burden to be lowered off over the edge of the route. I seethed inwardly and tried not to think about what lay ahead: the descent; the seeking of medical attention; and, if it really was broken, spending the rest of the holiday as useless, and deeply bored, baggage.

With a mixture of hops and slithers I made it to the stance and looked over the edge. It was a long way down. I hoped the sixty-metre ropes would reach the ground, but it would be impossible to see precisely where they landed from here, since the line of the cliff bowed out and away before cutting back in again. The only way to find out would be to make the ab. I leant against the hot rock, sweating as I watched Jez make knots in the ends (it seemed he was thinking the same thing), then coil them expertly and hurl them out into space. We both held our breath, listening for the sound as they hit the ground, but at the crucial moment all we heard was the cry of a goat. Jez grinned at me. 'Ey up, sounds like I just killed our supper!' He handed me the loops from the belay. 'One thing I don't understand,' he said, lowering his voice, 'is how come you didn't fall all the way. I saw Miles hadn't protected the traverse.'

I wouldn't tell him about the amulet. What had happened seemed unreal now, too strange to have actually occurred. 'My harness,' I said brightly at last. 'It caught on the rock, pulled me up short.'

He gave a low whistle. 'You're lucky to be alive.'

I really didn't want to discuss it any more. My head was swimming in waves of pain now, the specific agony of the ankle pulsing up my thigh and into the core of me. I felt alternately nauseous and faint, then horribly present, a boiling bag of nerves and blood beating against the rock. 'Right, then,' I said briskly. 'Better get going.'

'Just find some shade and wait for us. We won't be more than an hour or so.' He leant across and checked my harness buckles, the descender and screw-gates. 'I'll look after Eve,' he said suddenly.

'Eve can take care of herself.'

'Sure, I know. Independent modern woman and all that. Still, it's just, well, I really like her.' The lazy eye was suddenly wide and alert to my reaction, his whole being focused on my response. What was he waiting for: my blessing?

I mustered a grin. 'Good luck with that.'

I manoeuvred myself to the edge and let the ropes take my weight. Abseiling has always terrified me—that initial step into space, like the Fool in the Tarot pack, trusting everything to chance, and a decent anchor—but once I was started it wasn't so bad. I hopped the first twenty metres SAS-style while contact with the rock was still possible, then I was dangling in clear air like a spider on its line of silk.

Down I went by increments, trying not to overheat the descender, surveying the surroundings, looking for a likely landing spot. I couldn't quite make out the ends of the ropes against the bright colours of the ground; then with a jolt of realization I understood why. The ends were hanging free at a distance of five metres off the ground where the gully fell suddenly away into what looked like the dry course of a waterfall. My head started to throb and swim. Was I concussed? That was all I needed. Damn. There was no way I could jump that last section, not with a damaged ankle. I made a hitch in the ropes and clipped them back into the harness system so that I could stop and think. Jez wouldn't be able to see me now that I had vanished under the angle of the cliff. I looked down: could I swing myself further up the gully? I thought not: it would probably mean a punishing drag and fall back into the cliff . . .

'Hoi!'

It was a voice, somewhere below me. I spun round, stared down. Two figures in native robes, with dozens of little black goats and some scrawny-looking sheep milling around them, and a dark brown burro laden with panniers. The man who had shouted shaded his eyes and called something again in a language I couldn't understand. Then, quite clearly he shouted, *'Voulez-vouz de l'aide?'*

Well, yes: but what could he do? Here I was hanging on a rope! *'Oui, merci!'* I shouted back, largely because it seemed polite.

The man came clambering further up the gully and called in French, 'Can you see the ledge there?' He pointed to a place above him on the cliff, and when I looked down I could see that about ten metres or so below me was a wide ledge with a cave behind it. The rope might just get me there: but the cliff was undercut, and swinging into the ledge would be hard, but I called down, yes. The man ran back to the donkey, rummaged in its packs and returned a moment later with a short

145

rope weighted with a stone. Then he shrugged off his robe, revealing jeans and a T-shirt underneath, and monkeyed up the rock to the ledge with the rope slung over his shoulder. When he turned his face up to me, grinning, I could see that he was indeed one of the local Berbers, despite the polish of his French accent. Under the grubby white turban he wore he had the deep walnut-brown skin and sharp cheekbones of the region, the bright black eyes. 'Can you come down more?'

I released the hitch in the abseil ropes and lowered myself closer, then wrapped them around my leg as a brake that would leave at least one hand free. Adrenalin and the need to concentrate banished the pain and wooziness as he sent the weighted rope up towards me, and I caught it neatly. It was a hobble rope for the donkey, a worn length of old blue polypropylene, frayed and sun-bleached, its nylon fibres harsh and prickly against my palm.

'I'll swing you into the ledge.'

And he began to pull me towards him with the hobble rope, until the knotted ends of the abseil rope came within his reach. Anchored, I abseiled the final few feet of available rope until I was standing, one-footed, on the ledge. 'Broken ankle,' I said, indicating the left foot. *Cheville cassée*. 'I think.'

His face went very still and grave, then he called down something in his own language to the other figure, who I saw now was a woman, her head swathed in a blue scarf tied in a knot at the nape of her neck. 'My sister will bring the donkey up the old goat-track,' he told me, indicating where the ledge disappeared behind a huge tree that seemed to grow right out of the cliff.

The pain and relief were so intense I could only nod. With fumbling fingers I released myself from the abseil ropes, gave them a sharp tug to let Jez know I was down, and watched as they magically retracted and then vanished altogether.

Sometime after this I must have passed out, for I have no recollection of the woman appearing, of having my rucksack removed, or being laden on to the donkey, of the goat-track down the rock into the gully. All I recall of the later passage occurs in vivid blasts, like snapshots, or isolated frames of a movie: a cactus with brilliant white flowers; a lizard disappearing into the shade of a crack with a flick of its brindled tail; one of the little goats almost nose to nose with me, regarding me curiously with greedy yellow eyes. The rose-red rock in vast blocks and pillars, boulders and canyon walls, striated with grey and green, striped with light and shadow. Tiny white-shelled snails like little quartz pebbles; flat purple flowers like amethysts; the lyric hum of the couple's low conversation in counterpoint to the high cries of the goats. I sensed the brooding presence of the mountain that had broken me moving away, and then I passed out again.

CHAPTER THIRTEEN

Over the weeks that followed the tribe welcomed Amastan back little by little into their society in their courteous, reserved manner, accepting outwardly at least that he had recovered from a long and mysterious illness. By the end of this recuperative period no one mentioned the nature or cause of his erstwhile madness; no one gossiped any more about the fate of the sweetheart he had left in the mountains. He was his own self again: the spirits had left him, cast out by the girl from the Hoggar, and they were proud to count Mariata as one of their own. Mariata found herself accepted by the other women, encouraged to take her place amongst them. After the antagonism of the Kel Bazgan it was a relief to be treated with a measure of acceptance; more pleasant still to have her lineage acknowledged with a degree of respect. Here, no one poked fun at her or called her Tukalinden—Little Princess—with a curled lip or a sneer, and, while she knew that it was Tana who had proved to be the real catalyst in Amastan's return, Mariata found that she did not mind at all that they credited her with the cure. The older women brought her dates and listened to her poetry with real appreciation, bringing drums and setting her words to music with which they all joined in; the mothers urged her to teach their little ones to write the Tifinagh, and the unmarried girls came to her increasingly for slips of paper to put in their amulets—the more devout ones asking for verses from the Qur'an to carry around for good luck, the more superstitious amongst them seeking love charms and magic to ward off the *tehot*, the evil eye. In return, they offered advice of their own: 'You should marry and stay here with us,' said Khadija.

'Don't be silly,' Nofa chided. 'Mariata is Kel Taitok: why should she lower herself to marry a man of the Kel Teggart?'

There was a certain amount of head-nodding at this, but Yehali said fiercely, 'Our men are as good as those of the Hoggar! They are tall and handsome and toughened by much hardship. It has made them sinewy of limb and serious of spirit.'

'Too serious, where Ibrahim is concerned!' someone said, and they all laughed. 'But his brother Abdallah is a good man, and Akli is good company. She need not marry if she does not wish to spoil her descent-line.'

'She must want to dance!'

'Ah, well if you want to dance, then Kheddou is the one.'

'He likes to dance too much,' said Nofa, and they all brought their headscarves across their mouths and laughed uproariously, and Mariata suddenly realized that here they used the word for dance to mean other things entirely, and found herself blushing.

'Ah, we have all danced with Kheddou in our time,' agreed Tadla. 'He is an excellent dancer. But you'll have to be quick if you wish to take your pleasure with him, for he marries Leïla next moon.'

'Poor Leïla: she will have her hands full with that one,' Nofa said with mock seriousness, and they all took the double meaning and fell about laughing at her wit.

Mariata shook her head, grinning. They were a scurrilous lot, these women of the Kel Teggart; they worked hard, for without many slaves or harratin to do the daily manual work there was not much time for leisure, but when they did enjoy themselves it was clearly with a whole heart.

Tadla sighed. 'It is not easy to find a good

husband here, it is true. We have lost men on the salt road, and others have gone into the mountains. There are not enough good men to go around.'

'There is Bazu.'

'Too fat.'

'Makhammad?'

'Too religious.'

'Azelouane?

'Too old.'

'There is Amastan ag Moussa,' someone said. 'He is the son of an amenokal after all. He would not sully Mariata's bloodline.'

There was a pause as if people were weighing their words before letting them free. After a time Yehali said, 'He is very handsome, the son of Rahma. He has the most beautiful hands,' and after that they all joined in with good things to say about him.

'He is the best poet in the region. He beat all comers at the *ahal* in the year before the locusts came.'

'And he can dance too—no, really dance; don't be so rude, Nofa, you will shock Mariata. He has the most nimble feet and he can leap as high as a gazelle.'

'He is most expert when it comes to racing camels.'

'He can wield a sword.'

'He is a good shot too!'

'He has travelled far.'

From all this Mariata learnt that before he had 'gone away', as the girls put it, Amastan had been a celebrated visitor to the settlement, passing through infrequently en route from his annual

150

trading trips to visit his family and bring treats for the girls. He had been popular and admired, a proper figure of a man, and one they all would have wished to marry. They were sad when they learnt he had found a bride elsewhere. But then . . . Tadla changed the subject. 'Well, maybe not Amastan. He is not a lucky man, and in these days we all need lucky men, eh, Nofa?'

'Lucky and rich,' Nofa agreed. 'Five camels at least.'

'Ten!'

Mariata let their joking float like a cloud around her. She had not needed their praise of Amastan to rekindle her interest in him, for in truth she thought of little else. But it was curious to note that the other girls had not noticed his attention towards her over these past weeks, and for that she was grateful. Every evening as the sun set, he would seek her out and they would walk together and talk a little; once he had taken her hand and brushed it with his lips. When he looked at her she felt as if his eyes were burning her; it was not a comfortable sensation, but even so she longed for it and a day was not a good day unless it ended with him gazing from his place at the men's fire to where she sat amongst the other women at their own fire.

And because she was a part of his community she found herself embracing a way of life she once would have thought beneath her. She immersed herself in the quiet daily rhythms, every morning rising at dawn to help to milk the goats, and on those days when she did not accompany the animals while they foraged she was content to stay behind at the village, pounding the grain to make the day's *tagella* with the other women, listening to their chatter and gossip, entertaining them with her poetry as they prepared and drank endless pots of green tea. It was perhaps the very simplicity and absorbing practicality of this new routine that brought her this unaccustomed sense of peace.

Even so, every morning before setting out with the goats or going about her other chores she would walk out to the highest vantage point beyond the village and gaze eastward for any sign that Rhossi ag Bahedi had come to take her and his camels back with him to the Aïr. But one day she realized that five full moons had come and gone since she had fled the Kel Bazgan, and that if he had still not managed to link her disappearance to his hated aunt, or persuaded the harratin to give him the information they held, that it was unlikely he was going to suddenly turn up in the Teggart. For her part, Rahma had arranged that the two distinctive white mehari be taken to the camel market far to the north, at Goulemime, and there their Bazgan brands were subtly changed and they were sold for an excellent price, for it was unusual that two white Tibestis of such quality should make it to market in that area. She had given into Mariata's hands all the money the animals fetched, which was a not inconsiderable sum, even after the traders had taken their cut, and refused a small commission for her part in arranging the sale. 'You are a woman alone now, and as I know to my cost it is hard to be a woman of no family and no wealth. You might think to invest some of it in a caravan when the *azalay* sets out again, maybe entrust it to Amastan when he takes up the trade once more.'

Mariata did not think this was likely, for in the conversations she had shared with Rahma's son in these past weeks he had professed little interest in returning to the salt road; not that she had managed to persuade him to talk of many serious things, for every time she moved towards dangerous ground, he would become silent and withdrawn. But she raised the subject again when they walked together down by the river that night.

'I have seen enough of the old trade routes in my time,' he said, his low voice a contrast to the singing of the frogs, which was shrill with challenge and desire. 'I shall never travel them again.'

'Tell me what you have seen,' Mariata begged, her eyes shining. 'Your mother told me that you once swore to walk to the Arbre de Ténéré, to see the sea and to touch the snows on the highest mountains; she also told me you achieved all of these things.'

Amastan's eyes glittered with the red light of the sunset, but since the rest of his face was hidden behind the very proper arrangement of his veil Mariata could not read his expression. Then he sat down on a rock and spoke as if addressing an audience, all the while turning over a dried twig of oleander in his hands as if the repetitive movement enabled him to channel his memories, and all at once she remembered the storyteller who had once visited her home in the Hoggar, who came with a bag of pebbles, each pebble relating to one of the great tales, and how he had offered the bag so that the women might choose the story they wished to hear. Amastan spoke with just the same authority.

'I have crossed the desert of stone and the desert of rock and the desert of sand; on foot and

153

on camel I have traversed the old roads. I have seen the sun come up like a fire over the dune-sea; I have seen night steal every colour from the world, leaving everything a ghostly grey, while above the stars shone like a houri's jewels. I have carried indigo from the dyeworks at Kano, millet and dates to and from Ingal and Ghat. I have seen the gold markets of the Tafilalt and crossed the great Atlas; it was there I saw the pure white substance they call snow, which though cold burns the skin like flame. In the famed city of Marrakech I walked the central square and was assailed by the clamour of dancing boys and snake charmers and speaking birds, magicians, soothsayers and charlatans by the hundred. I have seen the wide blue ocean at Agadir, which like the endless dunes shimmers and shifts beneath the caresses of the wind just as our own sands do; I have followed the foot-worn market-routes through the Anti-Atlas Mountains from the fortified walls of Taroudant over the mighty Jebel el-Kest and down into the lovely oasis town of Tafraout . . .

'It was while we crossed the Great Emptiness on our way to the saltworks at Bilma and Kauar in the Sudan that I saw the famed Arbre de Ténéré: a solitary acacia standing like an ancient sentinel in the middle of the cruellest waste land in the world. Our *azalay* ringed it and paid our respects as caravanners have for centuries; it endures, blind and thorny, alone and hardy, in the blasting heat of the desert as a talisman for the survival of our people. It is said that if the Arbre fails, so will the People of the Veil. I wanted to see it, just once, to ensure it lived still. But that was five long years ago, and, given what I have seen since, I fear it is dying, or may even be dead.'

The twig snapped loudly between his hands, and even the frogs fell silent at the sharp report. Amastan sat staring into space as if seeing the bleakest of futures playing itself out on the vast, reddening sky.

Mariata sighed, entranced. 'If I were a man I would surely spend my life on a camel's back travelling from wonder to wonder.'

Amastan snorted, brought back to himself. 'Ah, little wanderer: what a romantic view of the world you have! I have learnt to spin words like dervishes, to bewitch and blur reality. You don't often hear the poets telling of the difficulties of digging out a drifted-in well, of the stench of decayed bodies and shit found rotting in the base; of the disgusting taste of brackish water that you have to drink to stay alive, of the foul gripes that rack you; of how your skin feels like old leather tanned by the flying sand and your arse is so pained by the wood of the saddle that it is easier to walk than to ride, even though the hot ground burns through the soles of your sandals. They never make songs about how even in the deepest wilderness weevils get into the bread and the dried strips of goat meat you eat become so hard you can break your teeth on them because there is no water in which to soak it and all your saliva has dried up; nor do they make verses that tell how the tongue swells till it feels as if your mouth is full of wadded cotton; how fear and thirst lead you to hatred and distrust of every stranger. And no one says a word about the scorpions, the horned vipers, the jackals or the bandits. I do not think the *azalay* is a place for a girl.'

Mariata bridled. 'You underestimate me.'

'Do I? Haven't you heard the saying that neither women nor goats have the hardiness to cross the desert?'

'Well, how do you think I got here, then?' Mariata demanded, rising to his bait. 'Do not forget that I was born in the Hoggar and had already travelled far to reach the Aïr before I crossed the Tamesna to order to persuade the djenoun to leave you in peace! And never forget that I am descended in direct line from the Mother of Us All, who walked a thousand miles into the desert to establish our people!' By the end of this tirade, her cheeks were flushed and her fists balled.

Amastan was delighted; she could see it in the crinkling of the skin about his eyes. Then he reached up and picked a bright pink oleander blossom from the tall shrub behind them and, leaning forward, tucked it behind her ear, a gesture so uncharacteristically intimate that Mariata's colour deepened to a shade even darker than that of the flower. When he spoke again his voice was gentle. 'When Tin Hinan made her epic journey it was through a landscape that rippled with wind-blown grass where acacia trees spread their shady limbs and herds of antelope and gazelle grazed. It was no desert then but a very paradise.'

Mariata stared at him. 'How could that be? The desert is eternal. The desert is the fiery heart of the world, the cauldron in which life began. Everyone knows that. Even the djenoun originated here, and they are creatures of heat and flame, fiery spirits; how could they have come out of a grassland?'

'I could take you to caves in the Tassili and show

you rock engravings by the Kel Nad, the People of the Past, by hunters who made pictures of the animals they hunted—antelopes and gazelles, striped horses and giraffes; creatures of the savannah and the plain—and it is believed by the elders that these pictures were made even before the time of the Mother of Us All.'

Mariata turned her head away. This was not what she wished to hear. 'They dreamt those scenes,' she said contemptuously. 'I have seen such depictions myself in the caves of my own homeland. I have seen the White Lady of Inawanghat carrying the horned Moon on her head, with a river of stars stretched beneath the horns and seeds shining in her belly and falling from her hands. Is this some picture they made from the life too?'

'Ah, you have me there, with your woman's logic. Perhaps you do not have the heart of a poet after all.'

'At least I have a heart,' she returned, suddenly reckless.

Amastan stood up all in a rush and strode away from her with jagged strides; then, as if changing his mind, turned on his heel and stalked back to tower over her. 'Never say such a thing!' he demanded angrily. 'Never.' He took the blossom from her hair and threw it down in the dust, ground it underfoot with a sudden furious gesture and stalked away into the falling darkness.

*   *   *

The next evening he did not come to her; nor the next, and she wept herself to sleep. On the third

157

morning she rose before the sun, milked the goats, reunited them with their kids, and led the troop down to the river to forage and feed. There, she laid cold river stones against her hot and swollen eyelids until the redness receded and she did not look like a frog any more.

'I am sorry.'

She whirled around. Amastan detached himself from the bole of a tree, one shadow emerging from another. His veil was wound high; he looked as tall as the tree; taller. He looked as tall as the sky. Kohl made his eyes brilliant.

'You have not slept?'

Mariata shook her head, not trusting herself to answer.

'Nor I. Sleep doesn't offer me the refuge that others find in it.' He fell silent, brooding. After a long pause he said, 'I am no good for you. No good for any woman. But I will not trouble you any longer.'

She stared at him dismayed. 'Why would you say such a thing? I enjoy the time we spend together. I had . . . hoped . . .' She did not dare say what was in her heart.

'Do not hope, Mariata. It is too dangerous.'

'Dangerous?'

He turned away from her. When he looked back at her she thought she saw madness in his eyes once more. When he opened his mouth, she thought he might howl, but all he said, so quietly that she could hardly catch the words, was, 'I have a heart; but it is torn in two.'

He still thinks of his dead sweetheart, Mariata thought, and pain lanced through her. 'What do you mean by that?' she asked in dread.

Amastan lowered his long frame to the rock beside her. 'I wish that the world was a different place, Mariata. I wish I could erase the past.' He paused, glanced at her, then away again. 'I wish I could make a fresh start. Take a wife, have children; be happy.' It was almost a whisper. 'But I cannot.'

'You cannot?' she echoed.

'The world is not the place I thought it was a year ago; and I am not the same man.'

Silence settled heavily between them, and in that moment the sun rose over the horizon and poured its red light all around them. The river at their feet ran like blood. Mariata said gently, 'The world is never the same. Everything moves, and we must move too. There is a stream that runs through the rocks close to our winter camp where I lived as a child. When I was small I placed a line of stones by the side of its flow; and when we returned to our camp the next year I searched for them, but they were gone. So I placed some more; and the next year those pebbles were gone too. I searched for them, thinking someone was playing games with me, but there was no sign of the stones. At last I realized that the stream's course was moving sideways across the ground, just a hand's width with each passing year. But I knew that by the time I was an old woman it would be a different stream to the one I looked at then. Nothing in this world stands still, Amastan, and because the world changes around us, we change with it. We are never the same person from one day to the next, because our experiences change us. I am not the naive child who left the Hoggar.' The look she gave him was eloquent, but he turned away.

'What you say may be true,' he said, 'but I am too much changed by the things I have seen. The things I have done.' He paused for a long moment. 'What I am going to tell you now I never intended to tell anyone. It is hardly the stuff of poetry or songs. But I have carried it inside me for long enough, and I owe you the truth.' He took a deep breath; exhaled it slowly. 'The last woman I loved died, and in the most horrible fashion.'

This is it, Mariata thought. He is going to tell me how he killed her now, and then I will know him for the monster he is. She wanted to run; but she had to know, and so she stayed.

'Her death lies heavy on my conscience,' he started, confirming her worst fears; but the story he dragged out of himself, word by agonized word, was not at all what she had expected.

He had met Manta when he was little more than a boy and had passed through her village with a caravan. She had made a great impression on him, for she was not shy like the other girls; she had kissed him before he left and the touch of her lips had lived with him through the long winter months as he travelled through the desert. He bought her gifts with the money he earned; at last, on his third season's visit, she had promised to marry him. He had given her an amulet to seal their betrothal.

'It should have kept her safe.'

Mariata felt the heavy piece of silver pressing against her skin. Her hand rose to touch it through the thin cotton of her robe.

'You have it with you.'

She started guiltily and found his eyes upon her.

'I don't want it back; it carries bad luck. You

160

should not wear it either; it brought no luck to the last one who wore it.'

Mariata took out the amulet from under her robe and pulled it over her head. It sat there in her hand, the light glinting on the black beads of its string, and they both stared at it. 'But I love it,' she said softly. 'How could it be unlucky? See how it has the symbols for *tefok*, the sun, here and here.' She ran her fingers over the carnelian discs. 'Red is a lucky colour.'

Amastan's expression was grim. 'Open it,' he said.

Mariata examined the talisman, turning it over and over. She slid a nail into the seam at top and bottom, but the amulet was solid and nothing moved. She spun the carnelian discs and pressed the raised central boss: nothing. She turned the amulet over and searched for an opening on the back but found no solution. 'How?'

Amastan reached across and gripped the central boss, moving it sideways.

Mariata watched as the amulet offered up its secret: a hidden compartment containing . . . nothing. She looked up and found Amastan had not moved, that his face was very close to hers: she could feel the warmth of his breath as he exhaled. 'There is nothing in here,' she said, stating the obvious.

'I went to the enad—to Tana—to ask for a protective charm to put inside it. But she . . . she saw something when she touched it. She knew . . . something. She tried to take the amulet from me, said it was touched by the evil eye. I was angry. I took it back, forcibly, and left her with insults. I meant to visit a marabout to buy a Qur'anic verse

161

instead, but I never got around to it. I don't know what stopped me: superstition, maybe. Or pride. I thought the gift itself would be enough, that my love was so strong it would protect her.' He shook his head. 'I don't know what I thought. She was so happy to be given it. It's very old, and of the finest silver. She wore it all the time, until . . .'

'Until?' Whatever was coming, she had to hear it.

Amastan took his time. She heard his breathing, ragged, slowing as he composed himself. 'This new government, which calls itself independent, is filled with men from the south, those who hate us most. They accuse us of enslaving their ancestors, of abusing their people: they have decided to use this as their excuse to persecute us. Elements in the government have been using its power against us, enforcing arbitrary boundaries, stopping our people from crossing them without the papers they have decreed necessary; but what do the Tuareg have to do with borders and papers? We have always traded far and wide, from the Sahel to the sea. Who are they, with their Russian guns and their Western uniforms, to call us "uncivilized" and "barbaric", to try to force their way of life upon us? They have always hated our people because we are free and they are poor, because we refuse to live in the squalor of their cities, to subject ourselves to their rules, to be imprisoned by their boundaries. They call what they do "law": but it is no more than murder and oppression. They are cowards!' He thumped a fist down on to the rock. 'They use any resistance as an excuse to attack old men, unarmed women and children.'

His voice caught in his throat; with a sideways

glance, Mariata saw his eyes glitter with unshed tears.

Manta lived, he told her, in a northern village. She told him there had been trouble; petty stuff mainly. Made bold by the change of government, by the French withdrawal, Songhai villagers had been raiding whatever property they could lay hands on, be it ever so meagre: livestock, foodstuffs, blankets, even cooking implements. Complaints were made but never addressed. Rumours abounded of injustices and attacks. The young men who were either out on the salt road or on hunting trips would come home to find their camp desecrated, their mothers and sweethearts insulted or robbed, but there were no official reprimands. Worse was happening elsewhere. People were disappearing, taken away for 'questioning'. Ancient grudges resurfaced; wells were poisoned, crops destroyed.

The young men of the tribes tried to make some resistance; but there was no coherent strategy, no coordination of forces, just a number of small-scale reprisals against the brutalities visited on their people, and all this seemed to do was to make matters worse. But it was better than doing nothing at all. Amastan joined a resistance group in the N'Fughas Mountains. 'We followed the example of Kaocen, the hero of the first uprising: we fought like jackals, not lions. We attacked and ran, doing what damage we could.' He paused and took a long breath. He ran a hand over his face. One day word had reached them of incursions by soldiers into the remote regions to the south, where Manta lived. The rumours were unsettling: women were being raped to pollute the vaunted

163

bloodlines of the Tuareg; Tuareg children were being forcibly removed to the cities. He tried to persuade other fighters to come with him, but they were engaged in their own struggles and so he took off alone.

'I was going to bring her here out of harm's way.' He closed his eyes. The sky that hung over them was a pale and pitiless blue. Mariata felt that it might fall upon her if she uttered a sound.

At last, Amastan continued, his voice flat with suppressed emotion, his gaze fixed on a still point in the river. 'I rode all night up through the foothills, starting at every sound. For some reason, I had never been so afraid in my life. When my camel flushed a bird from the bushes, it scared me to the edge of death. Every shadow seemed filled with menace. The landscape with which I had become so familiar over my years of journeying through it by day in the dark seemed a different world, filled with *afrits* and *ghûls*, and the vengeful spirits of the dead. I smelt the village before I saw it. I cannot describe to you the peculiar quality of that smell: you could never imagine it. All I can say is that if like me you had smelt it, it would remain with you for life. I will never be clean of it. It made my camel skittish: it did not want to go further. It dragged its feet, became obstinate. Its bellow split the night. I had to exert my will over it to make it move at all. Even in the darkness I could tell that a pall hung in the air: a thick, black smoke with a filthy taste to it, a taste that coated my tongue as if with fat. Not a sound came from the encampment—no dogs barked, no goats bleated, no one sat round a fire. I thought perhaps people had evacuated the place, moved further up into the mountains . . .

'As I got closer, I smelt petrol in the air. That was not a good smell. What use do the Tuareg have for petrol? It was a foreign odour. My senses were spiky with presentiment. I wanted to turn back. But I knew I could not.

'I saw that a cairn had been piled up by the entrance to the village. I almost passed it without a thought; but the moonlight was suddenly too bright. It was heads that were piled there, not rocks. The shock knocked me from my camel: I hit the ground and lay there insensible till the sun rose the next day.

'There were thirty-four heads, to be precise. I counted each one of them. Thirty-four people whose spirits would wander for eternity. I could feel them in the air around me, swirling angrily. Manta's was the thirty-first I found. I sat with it cradled in my lap. She who had been so beautiful, so charged with life, reduced to hard, cold flesh, all blood-clotted and split apart. Her shining eyes dull and glassy . . .'

The words ground to a halt, but it was as if he reached down inside himself and forced himself to go on.

'I begged her spirit to speak to me, but it was silent with reproof. I had not been there to save her, and the amulet I had given her for protection had done nothing to ward away the evil that had come to her village.

'I found the amulet, still on her body: they had not burned her as they had so many others, and the goats and cattle too, split apart by machetes, their limbs scattered, stinking. I will say no more about how Manta was arrayed when I found her. I tried

165

as hard as I could to reunite her head with what was left of her body, but the pieces would not knit, though I raged and wailed at them. It must have been then that my wits finally left me and the Kel Asuf came for me, for I remember nothing more. I have no idea of how I returned to the Teggart; I do not know how I survived, whether I ate or drank or slept. I was human no longer. I was not human till you came to me and looked into my eyes. I thought you were her, that she had come back to me. And then I knew that you were not.'

'And that was why you wept.' Mariata took his hand into her lap; but as soon as she did so she was assailed by the horrible image of Amastan sitting there on the ground of the murdered village with his beloved's severed head in his lap, talking to it like a madman, stroking the dead skin.

The next thing she knew, she was running, running as if a thousand djenoun were after her. She did not stop until she reached the camp; and when she found herself in Rahma's tent she stared around, bewildered, not knowing how she had got there.

CHAPTER FOURTEEN

Where was I? I blinked and tried to focus, but my head was muzzy and the ground was moving past my face, and before I could do anything about it I was throwing up uncontrollably, heaving and retching, till it felt as if my stomach was going to flip right out of my mouth.

'*Comment allez-vous?*'

The voice was kind, but the question seemed absurd. I swallowed the last of the bile and tried to reorient myself. It dawned on me gradually that I was travelling face-down over the back of a donkey.

'Can we stop, please?' I croaked. *'Pouvons-nous arrêter?'* Given current circumstances, some small distant part of me congratulated myself for possessing such wherewithal as to be able to attempt to communicate in two languages.

Miraculously, the world stopped moving around me and the nausea began to subside. Firm hands helped me reposition myself on the beast, and then an unfamiliar, dark face hove into view.

'Ça va? Vous allez bien?' he asked, and I remembered the young man in native clothing who had helped me off the mountain.

'Where are you taking me?' I demanded ungraciously, feeling panic at being at someone else's mercy.

'To Nana's house,' he told me.

'Nana?'

'Our grandmother, Lalla Fatma. She is a renowned healer and herbalist. There are plants growing here that grow nowhere else in the world, and Nana is expert in their use.'

The panic took a grip. 'No, no, that won't do at all,' I said, trying to muster the firm voice I used on the ditzy temps they sent me when my own assistant was away, enunciating slowly and with exaggerated clarity. 'It's very kind of you, but no. You need to take me to a *hospital*. For *X-rays*.'

The man laughed; but what was amusing about wanting to go to hospital with a suspected broken ankle? I forced myself to try again. 'Look, it needs to be X-rayed and set in a cast so that it can mend properly. I really don't think a few plants are going to do the trick.'

But my rescuer turned away without a word and it struck me suddenly that maybe his French was not as fluent as I had thought. I sighed. Over his shoulder I could see the beginnings of a medieval-looking peasant village—a jumble of adobe buildings in the same rose-red hue as the surrounding rocks, as if they too were excrescences of the natural landscape. They had flat roofs and tiny, iron-fretted windows, and some were so ancient they appeared to be crumbling back into boulder and crag. Not much chance of a hospital here. Black-robed women stopped chopping vegetation or digging in the ground and silently watched us go by with their wary, sloe-black eyes. By contrast, the children ran about shouting and laughing at the sight of a European on a donkey. Goats and sheep jostled around us, baaing in confusion; this was not the time they usually came down from grazing on the mountain. What was going on? An enormous white cockerel standing on a wall flared its carnal red coxcomb at us; its harem of chickens clucked and scratched in the dust below.

'There is no hospital here,' the man said conversationally, confirming my worst fears, 'not in the sense that you mean. There is no X-ray machine; and the doctor . . . well,' he paused, 'my grandmother is more skilled than any doctor. People come to consult her from Taroudant and Tiznit; even from Marrakech.'

My thoughts raced ahead to a time when I would walk with a stick because of a joint that had healed badly; no, my frantic brain amended, with a prosthetic leg to replace the one lost to blood poisoning and gangrene brought on by the use of weird herbs . . .

'For God's sake!' I cried out, on the edge of hysteria, feeling all control slip away, now and in my future. 'I need a *doctor*!'

No one paid me the least attention, except the ragged children with their dark, laughing eyes. They thought I was hilarious.

The girl leading the donkey handed its rope to the man and ran ahead calling, 'Lalla Fatma! Lalla Fatma!'

Women of all ages and descriptions emerged from the mudbrick houses to see what the commotion was all about; seeing me, a European woman, they pulled their veils up to hide their hair and faces as if I might suddenly assault them with a camera, like any other ignorant tourist. A few moments later the donkey came to a halt outside a wall washed in the same pinky-ochre as the rest of the village. My rescuer pulled me down off the animal and into his arms, revealing surprising strength in his wiry frame, and carried me through a garden fragrant with orange and lemon trees, olives and roses. Up the beaten-earth path he went, then over the threshold, ducking almost double to take me through the low door.

The contrast between the virulent sunlight and the cave-like interior was so intense that for a moment I thought I had gone blind. When my eyes adjusted I realized that the large chamber we had entered was full of women in the midst of domestic tasks, or sitting with their backs against the walls chattering like birds, their henna-patterned hands

169

gesturing busily. One woman ground something in a large stone mortar; a second attended to the coals in a brazier in the centre of the room over which a big, tarnished copper kettle sat steaming; another sorted through a dish of lentils, discarding small stones from amongst the pulses; a fourth carded wool. The fifth—vastly fat—assembled a number of clay pots on a low circular table, helped by the girl who had led the donkey down the mountain. If this was not enough for me to take in, four goats now came bursting through the open door after us, bleating wildly. One of the women lumbered to her feet, grabbed the broom and, addressing each one by name—*Teaza! Imshi! Tufila! Azri!*—shooed them all out again. Already my head was spinning.

The big woman got to her feet and said something to the others. One by one they all got up, kissed her hands respectfully and departed, leaving only four of us in the room. Where there had been bustle and noise there was an abrupt and pregnant quiet. The Berber man set me down gently on a mat on the floor, but the old woman scolded him furiously until he made me a bed of cushions. I lay there, looking up at her, not knowing what to do or say. She was extraordinary-looking, dark-skinned and imposing; unlike the other women in their plain black robes she wore a long blue chemise and over that a vibrantly striped swathe of silk in orange and black knotted over her ample chest, and draped up over her head. Around her neck was a necklace of amber beads, each bead as large as an egg; heavy silver earrings weighed down her pendulous earlobes. The sleeves of the under-dress were pinned back to reveal muscled forearms glittering with silver bracelets that rattled and clacked as she gestured at me.

'*Marhaban, marhaban!*' she exclaimed, and then began chattering loudly at the pair who had brought me to this place. While the three were engaged in what seemed to be a heated discussion, I looked around. Great oil jars, of such a size that they might easily have hidden Ali Baba's band of thieves, lined two walls; a series of sacks of what I thought would be grain or flour or rice sat next to them; and all around the uneven adobe walls were jars and boxes and tins—vintage caddies of Tetley and Lyons and Chinese gunpowder tea—that, from the look of their brands and packaging, must have originated in the pre-war period, although their gilt and glitter were as bright as new. And now a new sensation assailed me: a dozen different odours, some rank, some pungent. Amongst them I clearly identified animal shit, lanolin, cooking oil, spices and sweat; and over all something entirely unidentifiable and foreign. My head reeled from the pain, the noise and the smells, and the sheer strangeness of it all, waves of nausea washing over me, accompanied by the dancing black stars that presaged loss of consciousness.

The young man knelt beside me and gently raised my head. 'Nana says I am very impolite and must apologize to you.' He placed his hand on his heart. 'I am Taïb' –*Tie-yeeb*—'and this is my sister Hasna.' He nodded to the slim, solemn girl who stood behind him. 'This is the house of my grandmother, Lalla Fatma.'

Recognizing her own name amidst the foreign words, the old woman inclined her head and patted her capacious bosom. 'Fatma, *eyay*, Fatma,'

171

she repeated. They all looked expectantly at me.

For a moment I couldn't remember my own name. Then, with a Herculean effort, I wrestled the information out of my head. 'Isabelle Treslove-Fawcett,' I said, and watched their faces go blank. 'Isabelle,' I amended, and finally, giving up, 'Izzy.'

At that, they all burst out laughing. Grandmother Fatma made a low, buzzing noise, and they laughed even more. My disorientation was complete.

'I'm sorry,' Taïb said at last. '*Izi* is the Berber word for housefly: cursed and wretched things.'

Cursed and wretched: lucky me.

Now, Taïb turned to his grandmother and off they went again, chattering away in their guttural language. He gestured out of the door and up at the mountain, then back at me, still in my climbing harness, and the old woman looked with amazement at me. She said something loud and emphatic, hit a palm with a fist, shook her head. The subtext was clear: these modern European women who think they can do what the men do! Climbing a mountain, whatever next? Is it any wonder she has come to grief?

She waved her hands in resignation, then bustled off to supervise whatever Hasna was preparing over the brazier, and a moment later the scent of rose of attar mixed with something strange and bitter added itself to the layers of odour in the room. Having thus cleansed the atmosphere, she placed a thick sheepskin on the floor and lowered herself cross-legged on to it with the neat, controlled power of one who has trained her thigh muscles over long decades, and without further ceremony laid hands on my injured ankle. My cry ricocheted off the walls, but no one took any notice. Instead, they stared at my Salomon mountain boot as if it were a truly foreign object. It was, indeed, an old model, a dear favourite of mine, the intricate eyelet-lacings concealed beneath a flap of zipped Goretex. To the untutored eye it must have looked impenetrable, impossible to open: a magic boot. Taïb flourished a knife and made to start cutting it open. 'No!' I leant forward, despite the nausea, and showed him where the zip was that would unlock the secret. *Mais doucement, s'il vous plaît. Très doucement.*

True to my request, he worked the zip down, opened the lacing as wide as it would go and eased the boot off my foot with infinite care—which still managed to bring acrid tears to my eyes. Then for some reason he passed me the boot. I clasped it to my chest like a talisman.

Lalla Fatma folded her hands around the injured ankle, then with what seemed extra-ordinary expertise immobilized the joint while interrogating the swelling all around it, her fingers busy and probing. It all hurt, but nowhere near as much as I feared. *'La bes, la bes, la bes,'* she murmured over and over, as if to reassure me.

Soon I found myself relaxing: which was a mistake. The next thing I knew she had clamped the ankle down with one hand and twisted and pulled the foot hard with the other and there was the most tremendous popping sound, as if someone had discharged a gun. A scarlet sea engulfed me, not pain exactly but something deep-seated and primal as if a flood of adrenalin had been released by the sound, a wild red inundation. And then it was replaced by a wash of white light

173

and someone applauded; people chattered.

When I opened my eyes again I found that the old woman was looking remarkably pleased with herself, as if she had achieved something that added to her great renown. The other women, as if on cue, had come back in and she immediately began to boss them around, clapping her hands to chivvy them along, and the room after its moments of suspended quiet abruptly became noisy and bustling once more. Hasna passed her grandmother a dish containing a muddy green paste and the old woman promptly broke an egg, drank the white and added the yolk to the mixture. She set the dish down beside the brazier to warm and went to the shelves, returning with a clay jar whose lid was stoppered with wax. This she opened, after applying some force to the lid, and at once a powerfully revolting smell exploded into the air: rancid, decayed, indescribably rank. She sniffed it appreciatively, then dug her hand into the jar and came away with a handful of the dark goo within. Then she grinned at me, revealing a serious lack of teeth, and held out her hand. There was no way she was coming anywhere near me with whatever witches' brew she had there. I jacked myself up against the wall. 'No,' I said, shaking my head. 'No, no. Water, please; just water.'

Taïb translated, but his grandmother was having none of it. '*Oho, oho,*' she said over and over. '*Aman, oho.*' She waved a finger at me. Then, with her surprising, brutish strength, she seized my ankle and set about slathering the foul substance into it with long, firm strokes. After my horror of the smell wore off, I realized this was in fact quite a pleasurable sensation, a deep tissue massage that

174

radiated heat out of the injury and up into my leg, where it proceeded to disperse. Perhaps she really did know what she was doing.

My ankle gave an involuntary galvanic jerk. It moved! Not broken then, after all, I thought with a sudden surge of hope, though it hurt like hell. Now she slathered on a thick layer of the warm green paste, set into this a handful of reeds for splints and bound it with strips torn from Taïb's proffered white turban. 'Two weeks,' he translated for me. 'You must stay off it for two weeks. You have damaged the ligaments and perhaps the tendon, but the bones are intact.'

This was good news compared to the lost-leg scenario; but not so great for a climbing holiday. I hadn't even completed one route, I thought bleakly. I grimaced, then remembered the manners my French mother had beaten into me, and thanked her. '*Tanmirt*, Lalla Fatma.' It was as much of the language as I'd picked up so far but the old woman seemed delighted. She beetled off to the sacks by the wall and came back with something of a deep, maroon red. Taïb suppressed a smile, like a magician allowing his audience a glimpse of the rabbit before making it vanish, poker-faced. I stared at him, but now the old woman was saying something to me and uncurling her fingers to make her offering. My hand reached out from a long habit of politeness, then retracted in horror.

'Locusts,' Taïb translated, trying to keep a straight face. 'Locusts eat only the finest plants and they have great strength in their jumping limbs. If you eat them, their strength will pass into your ankle and it will heal quickly.'

'I am *not* going to eat locusts,' I said, pushing

175

Lalla Fatma's hand away gently but firmly.

'But they've been dry-fried and coated in sugar. Delicious,' Taïb went on. 'We eat them like bonbons. See.' He popped one into his mouth and crunched down on it and I watched him, aghast, then laughed aloud as he made an appalled face and palmed the pulpy remnants into his hand. 'OK. They are quite revolting. Nana will be very disappointed in both of us.'

His grandmother looked from him to me, clucked her tongue and left the room. Had I mortally offended her? I had little way of knowing. But a couple of minutes later she was back with something shiny that she began to fasten around my ankle. 'Baraka,' she said, as if I should know what this meant. 'Baraka.'

'For good luck,' Taïb translated. 'To keep the evil eye at bay, and help you heal. Since you won't eat the locusts, that will make you well.'

I bent forward. There, bound to the bandages with thin leather bindings, was a small square of silver. My heart jumped. Then I unzipped my pocket, took out my amulet and held it out on the palm of my hand for her to see. 'Look.'

Taïb and his grandmother stared at the giant version of the thing that had been pinned to my ankle and started talking very fast, their heads bowed close together, hers swathed in the bright black and orange silk, his close-cropped black peppered with solitary grey hairs. He was older than I had at first thought.

'It's very similar, isn't it?' I asked conversationally.

Taïb looked up. 'They're from different regions. The small one belongs to our Mauretanian ancestors; this other is from further south, I think. They are both clearly Tuareg in origin. Where did you get it from?'

'It was a . . . gift.'

'An expensive gift. This is a very good piece. Do you know where it came from?'

'I believe it was found near some grave in the desert,' I said vaguely, unable now to remember the name of the woman mentioned in the archaeological paper. 'Someone whose name meant "She of the Tents" or something similar.'

He started. 'You don't mean Tin Hinan?'

The name sent a little shock of recognition through me. 'Yes. That was the name. But it may not have anything to do with her at all.'

Taïb was regarding the amulet very intently. Then he shook his head. 'It cannot be that ancient: it must be a coincidence,' he muttered, almost to himself. 'Would you let me buy it from you?'

Was this some sort of polite code for making a gift of the amulet to the family for their rescue of me? I felt a sudden irrational fury: all they had done was brought me to this old witch with her smelly goo and peasant medicine. The amulet was mine and I would not part with it. I closed my fingers tight around it. 'It's not for sale.'

He shrugged. 'Even if we cannot prove the provenance it would fetch a good price, you know. In Paris. There are a lot of collectors for this sort of artefact: an original *inadan* piece, not a modern nickel copy.'

I looked at him askance. 'You seem to know a lot about it.'

'You mean for a poor backward Berber?' He gave a short, sharp laugh. 'The truth is I am only

back in the region to visit my sister Hasna here'—
he nodded to the girl, who smiled back—'and
Nana and the family. The rest of the time I deal in
North African antiquities, in Paris, for the most
part.'

And suddenly I knew who he was, and felt a
fool. The cousin the restaurateur had mentioned.
'Ah,' I said. 'You're *that* Taïb.'

When it became clear I was not going to explain
this odd remark any further he said, 'Could I take a
closer look? It really is a fine example.'

Reluctantly, I made to hand my amulet over to
him, but, as I did so, something inside it seemed to
shift. I turned it over and stared at it. 'Oh! I think
it's broken. It must have happened when I fell.'
Abruptly, I felt nauseous. The amulet had saved
my life; and now it was broken.

Taïb craned his neck. 'It's not broken: look.'

The central boss was out of place, pushed
sideways by the impact of the fall. Behind it lay a
second level, a hidden compartment. I had
forgotten all about my injury now, for inside the
hidden compartment nestled a tiny roll of what
looked like paper, or was it parchment; or even
papyrus, or whatever the ancient peoples wrote
upon? With trembling fingers, I tried to winkle it
out, but it had been in there a long time: it was
recalcitrant.

'You try.' I held it out to Taïb, but his
grandmother laid a hand on his shoulder and said
something very loud and very fast that drew from
him a look of consternation.

'Nana is superstitious. She says it's best to let the
dead rest.'

'The dead?'

'It's just a saying. Not to disturb the past. She's worried it may contain bad magic, a curse, and she doesn't want it to pass to her family.'

Let sleeping beasts lie. All of a sudden I remembered the words of my father's letter. No chance of that! I fiddled determinedly with the narrow opening until the curl of paper fell out into my hand and waited for the weird tingling sensation I had had when I first touched the amulet, but there was nothing. The paper just felt very fragile, very brittle: I was afraid it might disintegrate as soon as I tried to open it, but I had to know what it contained. Carefully, I smoothed it out. What had I been expecting to find inside? Something like a message in a bottle spelling out 'Help me!'? I stared uncomprehendingly at the arcane glyphs: amongst them a circle with a horizontal line across it, like a no-entry sign; a triangle with a line sticking out of it like a dropped umbrella; a stick-figure man, arms upraised; an X with the top and bottom closed; a symbol like an overturned picnic table; two tiny circles, one on top of the other. The writing seemed to go from side to side and from top to bottom, intricately inter-woven as if to ward off interference from an interloper like myself. I looked to Taïb. 'Do you know what it is: can you read it?'

He shook his head. 'It's Tifinagh, the written form of the language of the desert tribes, kept alive by the women of the Tuareg, the Kel Tamacheq. But can I read it?' He shook his head. 'My family has Tuareg roots, but those who could read the Tifinagh are long since buried.'

'Not even your grandmother?' I saw the old woman craning her neck to see what we had found;

her eyes were wide, as if she knew something but was keeping it to herself. Then she put up her hands as if to ward off evil influences, turned and walked away. We both watched her duck under the low doorway into the courtyard outside and disappear from view.

CHAPTER FIFTEEN

Mariata avoided Amastan's company after his hard confession. She could think of nothing to say to him. Why could she not find the right words? Why could she not respond to the huge sacrifice he had made in opening up to her? What sort of poet was she; more, what sort of woman? Her failure to speak was causing him a new order of pain: she could see it in the way he gazed at her, then glanced quickly away; always the shade of Manta shimmered between them. Mariata imagined her as she must have been, vital and full of confidence; prettier than most, a bit of a rebel, not afraid to kiss a young man she liked, willing to trust her heart to him even though she hardly knew him. In other words, a girl rather like herself. And making this connection made it even more difficult to go to Amastan: in some strange way to do so seemed a betrayal of the dead woman and the tragic love she and he had shared.

About a week later Amastan left with a group of hunters heading north to look for game for the wedding feast for Leïla and Kheddou. For the first few days she was relieved not to bear the constant reminder of his presence, but soon after that she began to miss him so badly she felt as if her heart would calcify if she did not set eyes on him again soon. As if by way of revenge for this yearning, Manta insinuated herself into Mariata's dreams night by night, waking her in a sweat. She heard a disembodied voice; saw the decapitated body moving of its own accord; the head rolling to her feet, opening its mouth to reveal within the bloodied amulet Mariata now wore around her neck . . .

One morning Rahma came to sit beside her as she pummelled the dough for the day's tagella.

'You look tired, daughter.'

Mariata had to admit she was not sleeping well.

'It has been hotter than usual,' Rahma conceded with a half-smile that told Mariata she knew very well there was more to it than that. When once more she raised the matter of her son taking the salt road, Mariata smacked the dough down hard. 'I do not think your son is ever going back to the caravans.'

Rahma stopped brushing the dust and sand from the proving stone and looked intently at Mariata. 'What has he said to you? Has he told you what happened to Manta yet?'

Even the name was like a knife to her, but she said nothing. It was not her tale to tell, even if she could bear to tell it.

Rahma pressed on. 'I think we must find out; but it is you who will need to ask him; he has always kept secrets from me, even as a child. When his uncle gave him a knife when he was five, he concealed it in the sand behind the tent, lest I found it and took it from him. When he hurt his knee playing with the older boys he was too proud

181

to tell me about it in case I stopped him from playing with them any more: the congealed blood stuck to his breeches and he hid it from me for a week, until the cotton had grown into the wound. He bears the scar still.' She looked sad. 'Promise me, Mariata, that you will find out. Promise me, for both our sakes.'

Mariata regarded her curiously. 'Why do you ask this of me?'

'I have seen the way you look at him—' She waved a hand to flick away the girl's denial. 'We both love him. When he returns to us, I will do what I can to help you in this, and you will do what you can to help me, and between us Amastan shall have what he needs.'

'And that is what?'

Rahma watched her with hooded eyes. 'He will stay here with us both and raise the family that will be the making of him and give him the hope he needs to remake his world.'

'I do not think he is ready to do this,' Mariata said warily. 'In fact, I am quite sure he is not, with me or anyone else.'

'Then we shall have to make sure that events overtake him,' Rahma said, and folded her lips.

*   *   *

Guests began to arrive for the marriage from the surrounding area, from as far away as Tafadek and Iferouane: aunts and cousins, brothers and uncles and old friends. Resources were stretched to feed and accommodate them: some of the precious goats were slaughtered, chickens too, though the older people would not eat them, regarding them

182

as taboo. As sweetmeats, a dish of locusts cooked and coated in sugar was prepared—a special treat.

Some days later the hunters returned with a number of rabbits, many of the pretty speckled fowl that ran wild in the hills and two gazelles they had chased down on the plateau above the village. The elderly ram that had that day been earmarked for slaughter if the hunters returned empty-handed was reprieved. The men of the village joked about this and one of them hung a leather amulet around its neck to ensure it was blessed with baraka, and everyone was in fine spirits. Everyone, that is, except for Rahma and Mariata, for Amastan had not returned with the group. He had, the hunters said, gone his own way, but they did not know where.

Mariata tried to throw herself into the preparations for the marriage celebration, but her heart was not in it. She spent the morning baking loaf after loaf of bread: pummelling the dough, proving it on the sun-warmed bread-stones, keeping fire after fire alight till the embers were glowing, laying the embers of each fire aside and placing the dough into the hot sand beneath the fires to cook with the glowing charcoal replaced on top; then turning the loaves halfway through the cooking time. It was a process that required concentration, and, even though Amastan's absence had left an unfillable hollow within her, she was meticulous in the bread-making and won praise even from the wizened old women who had been preparing bridal loaves for half a century.

In the afternoon, when it was too hot to prepare food or move around in the burning sun, the women took to the tents, to sleep and gossip and

183

select their clothing and jewellery for the night ahead, and to apply their kohl and henna; while the men took themselves off to the shade of the trees on the other side of the encampment.

While Nofa painted the bride's hands and feet with flames and flowers of henna paste, Leïla begged Mariata to braid her hair in the Hoggar style, which seemed glamorous and outlandish to the women of the Kel Teggart. Hours passed in a comfortable haze of plaiting and chatter, and once they had seen the results all the other single girls clamoured for similar treatment, but Mariata waved them away. 'This is only for the bride: how will she feel herself to be special if you all look the same?' They looked so disappointed that in the end she relented and rebraided some of the youngest girls' hair in a different fashion. Her fingers were sore before she got to the end of the jostling queue and found there Idrissa, four years old and determined not to miss out on whatever excitement his older sister was a part of. 'Me,' he demanded. 'I want my hair done too.'

Tired and heartsore though she was, Mariata had to hide a smile. Like all the other infants in the tribe, he had a single braid that sprouted from the top of his shaved head, and she took hold of it. 'But, Idrissa, if I braid your hair flat against your head like your sister's, how will the angels catch you if you fall?'

He looked thoughtful; then sly. 'Do my hair like Tarichat's and I promise I'll be careful not to fall. Then you can redo it for me tomorrow.'

All the girls laughed. 'He'll be a trader, this one.'

'Already he strikes a hard bargain,' Mariata

184

agreed. 'But you know, Idrissa, that if I do your hair like Tarichat's you'll look like a girl and all the other boys will laugh at you.'

Idrissa considered this solemnly, then declared, 'I don't want to look like a girl.' And with that he was off, laughing and shouting, to hurl himself into a noisy game the other boys were playing with dogs and sticks on the far side of the goat-pens.

Mariata was still smiling as she walked out into the enclosure, until she became aware that someone was watching her. She turned. Behind her were the women's tents, loud with laughter; but everyone was engaged in their happy tasks and paid her no attention. To her right were the animal pens and the playing children; to her left, the deserted olive grove; in front of her, the area where the men of the tribe were drinking tea, smoking and talking. No one looked her way. The prickling sensation came over her again, and she turned back to the olive grove. Very slowly, as if interpreting some lost language, her eyes made out the still form of a tall figure, his dark robes a pool of shadow against the silver-green foliage. Her pulse raced suddenly: even at such a distance it was impossible not to recognize Amastan. Why was he just standing there, watching her? All around there was the buzz and hubbub of the wedding preparations: people laughing and singing, carrying pots and cooking implements, food and rugs and drums towards the feast-ground. He was an outsider looking in, an isolated still point amidst the bustle. Mariata felt her heart drawn to him as if on a wire. I must go to him, she thought. I must talk to him, heal the rift between us, on this day of all days. She trembled on the edge of her decision;

185

and someone stepped in front of her. It was Tana, her hands still bloody from dressing the meat.

'Don't,' she said, staring intently down at Mariata.

'Don't what?'

'Don't go to him. Leave him be.'

'I was doing nothing,' Mariata said, unnerved. How could the enad know her mind? Her hand went to the amulet under her robe.

Nothing escaped Tana's sharp eyes. 'I see it is already too late. Well, that talisman won't help you, and it's hardly me you need to be warding away. I'll say again: don't go to him. No good will come of it.'

'I don't know what you mean. I was just going to help Leïla with her jewellery.'

'She has her sisters to help her with that.'

'Why are you speaking to me like this, as if I were an intruder, one who has no place here?'

Tana's gaze was black and opaque, her secrets shuttered behind it. 'I saw death in the entrails and came to warn you straight away. You should leave. You can take my mule.'

Mariata stared at her. 'What? Whose death did you see?'

But the enad was already walking away.

'Where would I go?' Mariata called after her, but the enad did not reply.

She felt hot, then cold. She had thought of Tana as a friend, another outsider who had been embraced by the tribe. But the smith's gaze had been no more friendly than her unsettling words, despite the offer of the mule. Did she so badly want Mariata to leave the tribe? Had she really seen death in the entrails, and was that death

Mariata's own? Another thought struck her, somehow worse than the first: perhaps it was Amastan's death that Tana had seen, and somehow she, Mariata, was the cause of it and that was why she had to leave. All through the long hours of the feasting, through the joyful music and the dancing, through the ritual abduction of the bride and the shutting of the bridal pair into Leïla's new tent, Mariata felt the enad's words looping back and forth in her head, making a spider's web of thoughts in which she felt trapped like a fly. When the sun went down, she could not get warm. She found herself shivering even when she sat next to the fire, and her heart was not in the singing, which she usually loved. When she danced it was as if to a different rhythm to the other girls, to a drumbeat heard at a great distance, one that beat out a slower, more insistent tattoo. The poetry did not fall from her lips as easily as it normally did during the song-challenge: she lost her way, forgot the link-words she was supposed to follow, became tongue-tied. At one point she intercepted a glance between Yehali and Nofa that was eloquent in its exasperation. What is the matter with Mariata tonight? She can do nothing right: she is making us all look stupid! She even caught Amastan watching her quizzically, the ridge of a frown visible through the opening of his veil. At last she could bear it no longer and slipped away from the gathering. From the tent she took the few belongings with which she had come here, a goatskin for water that she was sure no one would begrudge her, and some of the bread she had made that day. Then, as if in a trance, she walked out of the encampment towards the enad's forge and the little enclosure where she kept her mule, and at last found herself at the post to which the beast was tethered. She stared at the mule, and it stared back at her incuriously, its eyes glinting in the darkness. 'Well, there you are, and here I am,' Mariata whispered to it. 'Though where we shall go who can say?'

The mule, of course, had no reply to this, but the air behind Mariata seemed to stir and then a low voice said, 'Wherever you want to go, I will take you there,' and when she turned around, there was Amastan, his indigo robes all of a piece with the night.

'Do you want me to leave too?'

'I? No.'

'Even though I have been cruel to you?'

He said nothing to this but she thought she saw the small flame of a smile light his eyes. Night insects chirred; from the distant river the mating cries of the frogs were carried on the breeze. At last he said, 'Cruelty and kindness; kindness and cruelty. Who can tell which is which? Toss them in the air, they are but two sides of the same coin.'

Mariata frowned. 'Surely you have seen tonight that I am not in the right frame of mind for a game of words, or to be teased like a child.' She took the mule's panniers from the ground where they lay, placed them across the beast's back and arranged her few things in them. Then, sighing, she turned back to Amastan. 'Since I am about to leave I had better speak plainly. When I first came here, it was to help a man everyone believed was mad, a murderer possessed by the djenoun, who had in all likelihood killed his sweetheart while in the grip of evil spirits. Your mother crossed the Tamesna to

188

find me, convinced that because of my lineage I could help; but it was soon clear there was no magic in me at all, for I couldn't do anything for you. It was Tana who released you from the spirits, not I; and she did it for my sake, not yours. Because, you see . . . ah, this is so hard . . .' She ran a hand over her face, and continued quickly in an almost-whisper, 'Because, you see, it was not you she took pity on but me.' She darted a fearful look at him to see how he would respond to this, but he gave no sign of understanding her at all. 'And then you told me the true story of what happened . . . to Manta. You opened your heart to me and instead of showing you the sympathy I should have shown to one who had experienced such horrors, I ran away, like a child running from a tale of monsters! You had held those terrible memories inside you for so long, and I . . . ran away. I am ashamed of myself for it. Perhaps I am not as grown up as I thought, but, even so, you should not tease me like a child.'

'The effect you have on me is not that of a child, I can assure you,' Amastan said gravely. 'Indeed, you disturb me.'

'*I* disturb *you*?'

'I was safe in my darkness, hidden from all. No one could touch me there; and my demons were my shield from the world. And then you came and struck through that shield with the light in your eyes and the sharp words of your poetry. Tana may have released the demons, Mariata, but it was you who opened the door through which they fled. Your grace pierced me; but your silence terrified me. When you would not speak with me or even look at me, it was as if the night had come to

189

swallow me once more. I felt there was no hope left. So when the hunters set out, I went with them. Away from you; away from the tribe, away from everything. Then I left the hunters and walked alone. I walked far, without food, without water, and waited for death to come to me. But while I sat there, waiting, I saw that the world went on around me as if I were insignificant in it; no more important than a stick or a stone. Rock-squirrels ran around me, burying the nuts they had gathered and watering them to mark their cache; but while I sat still they thought of me as no more than an inanimate obstacle they had to run around. A lizard skittered past on feet that moved so fast they barely touched the hot ground, and I saw before it did the viper that darted out from between the boulders and caught it in its jaws. When night fell, I lay on my back and watched the stars wheel overhead, watched the Guide with his three-starred stick shepherding the constellations across the heavens, and felt both as great and as small as one of those specks of life. And I realized there was probably nothing I could have done to save Manta; no magic that would have kept her death from her, that the plan of the universe is too great for one man to rearrange, that maybe there is no such thing as the world of the spirits, of magic or curses, and that these are things that men speak of in fear because they cannot accept the harsh truth: that death and danger are around us all the time, and there is nothing we can do to ward them off. That life is hard and short and vicious, but the stars—those tiny jewels of light up there amongst the darkness—they go on for ever. And perhaps it is where we go too, when all is done. Do you believe that, Mariata? Do we become stars when we die, little specks of brilliance in a relentless field of black? Or do we just go into the ground and rot?'

Mariata stared at him unhappily, not sure what to say. For a moment it seemed as though his mind had been turning towards her, towards matters of the heart and things that might be understood and discussed between a man and a woman. But then he had veered away into a dangerous quicksand. She had been raised to believe in the spirits—the djenoun in all their varied forms. To discuss them so was surely tantamount to inviting them to appear in numbers, and at this time of the night, it would not be the good djenoun who would be visiting but the Kel Asuf, the People of the Wilderness, those who seduced the minds of the living away from their families and the safety of the campfires to become as jackals, feral scavengers of the wilds; the afrits and demons, spirits of the night; the ghûls, those vengeful spirits of the wronged and the damned, which haunted the sites of their untimely deaths, hungry for others' pain to assuage their own; the *qareen*, the personal demons ever ready to whisper wicked desires into the fertile mind and lead the good soul astray.

And all this talk of stars and death: where had that come from? Her grandmother had taught her the cosmology of their world, framing each element of it in stories and poetry from her own grandmother's time, which in turn had been passed down by elder generations. She knew that the unquiet dead walked the earth; that you had to inter a body immediately upon its death, intact and

191

with its face turned to the east, and top the grave with seven flat stones to keep the soul in its right place, thorny branches to stop wild animals tearing the flesh. The physical body would surely rot away down in the ground: surrounded by death all the time—of goats and dogs, of camels and babies—it was impossible to deny such a fact; but the life of the spirit was another matter. Those who followed the new religion spoke of some nebulous heaven for the souls of the elect, but people like her grandmother, and those like Rahma who rejected the call of Islam, held a darker, more elemental view of the world. But none of them had ever spoken of spirits in the stars. The wild concept of the dead hanging over her head in the endless sky seemed at once oppressive and revolutionary; she could feel her mind rebelling even as it entertained the possibility. She shook her head. 'No one should speak of such things by night. It attracts the wrong sort of attention.' And she touched the amulet she wore about her neck.

Amastan smiled. 'You are still wearing my amulet.'

'I have worn it ever since we took it from you.'

'I once believed that all the ills of the world resided in it.' He took a step towards her, took hold of the bright string of beads on which it was suspended and lifted it out on to her robe. 'But when I see it on you, I know that cannot be true. It lifts my heart to see you wear it, Mariata.' He gave her a steady look. 'Before Manta, there was no one who stirred my heart. I thought there never again would be.'

'And now?' she asked unsteadily, the longing plain in her eyes.

He was silent for such a long time that she thought she had pressed him too hard, overstepped the bounds of respect. Then he took her hand in his, turned it over and gazed at it intently. 'Such a little hand,' he said, and pressed her palm to his lips.

Through the soft cloth of his veil she felt the warmth of his mouth against her skin and thought her knees might fail her.

'Come with me,' he said at last, and led her down to the river.

CHAPTER SIXTEEN

The sound of a child's agonized screaming jarred me out of a pleasantly sensuous doze. I turned around to see a blond toddler lying on the path where it had fallen, beating the ground with its fists, its face scarlet with fury. Its harassed-looking mother, equally blonde, marched across the hotel's plant-festooned terrace, and scooped it up.

Behind them, the peaks of the Ameln Valley glowed in the sun; the Lion looked as if it were dozing in the heat.

'He's bored to death! I can't imagine why you thought it was such a good idea to come here: there's bugger all for him to do!' she shouted back over her shoulder to her husband, a balding man poring over a set of maps spread out on the table a few metres to my right. And with that, she stalked back and deposited the shrieking child unceremoniously on his lap. The man looked at it with a puzzled expression as if he had no idea what it was. Then he reached across, picked up an almond biscuit from the tea tray and stuffed it in the child's mouth; taken by surprise, it abruptly ceased its wailing.

I felt a reluctant sympathy with the toddler. If I could have got away with throwing a similar tantrum, I'd have done so in a heartbeat. But there was no one in the vicinity who was likely to pick me up and dust me off and give me an almond biscuit to shut me up. Well, at least I could do the almond biscuit thing for myself: I'd ordered mint tea with its delicious accompaniments and had forgotten all about it, instead dropping off to sleep. The boy who was waiting tables had obviously been too polite to wake me. I poured myself a glass of tea; but it had gone tepid and orange from over-brewing, and was as bitter as poison when I tasted it.

I'd spent three days of my precious holiday cooped up in the Tafraout hotel, or on its terrace, resting my wretched ankle while everyone else was off having adventures. On the first day after Taïb had rescued me from the crag and brought me back here, Eve had stayed with me, but bearing the burden of guilt for the boredom she tried so hard to veil from me was worse than being on my own and at last I couldn't take it and sent her off with Miles and Jez.

The second day I'd almost enjoyed having time on my hands with nothing to do and nowhere to go. I'd sat out on the terrace, with my face turned up to the sun like some heat-seeking flower, and felt my kinks and nerves slowly unwind themselves from the tight coils in which they'd been knotted. I'd gazed out over the impressive scenery and

194

marvelled at being for the first time on the continent where all human life began. Surveying the vast, unchanging quartzite cliffs, the piled-up tors of red-orange granite and the bright splash of green in the oasis in the valley floor, I could easily imagine life going on here since the earliest times: the endless procession of people and animals travelling to trade their wares and barter their crops and artefacts for those goods they could not make or grow themselves. Seeing the local people go slowly about their daily routines in the long robes and head-gear—scarves for women; turbans for men—that people in this region must have been wearing for centuries, I could almost imagine myself a time-traveller as well as a tourist, one who had crossed not only a thousand air-miles but also millennia.

But the novelty had soon begun to pall and I'd long since started to regret being abrupt with Taïb when he'd dropped me at the hotel after his grandmother had worked her odd magic upon me. Well, not dropped exactly; he'd insisted on carrying me from the donkey and into the lobby, like a groom carrying his bride over the threshold. This over-familiarity had so unnerved me that I'd leapt out of his arms and been positively rude to him, not wanting the stern-looking man behind the reception counter to read anything illicit into the scene.

'I'll come and fetch you tomorrow or the day after, give you a tour of the area in my car if you'd like,' he'd offered generously. I'd demurred, and was now regretting it.

I looked at my watch. Just gone three o'clock. It was incredible how time dragged when you had no

195

useful way of passing it. I applied myself to the much thumbed guidebook, hoping in vain to find a secret chapter I'd yet to read, but of course there wasn't a page left unturned. I'd also already read the only other book I'd brought with me—a biography of Gertrude Bell—and in desperation had raided Eve's luggage, only to find a girlie novel that utterly failed to hold my attention after two pages of inconsequential chatter about shoes and boyfriends. Work and its constrictions usually confined me like the boning of a corset; climbing took its place on holidays such as this, bringing its own structure and routine to bear. Without either, I was at a loose end: a formless, shapeless jellyfish of a creature. I hated to feel so helpless, so empty of inner resources. Was I really such a robot, so programmed by the dull, repetitive exigencies of modern Western work-life that I couldn't find any other way to amuse myself when hampered only by a twisted ankle? How did other people manage, with far worse handicaps to contend with in their lives?

Angry with myself now, I made my mind up to get down into the town, whatever it took. Perhaps visit some of the jewellery stores the woman at the restaurant had mentioned, ask more about the amulet. Given my reasonable French, I might also be able to have a conversation about the local area, its culture and customs. Or perhaps I'd just mooch around the stalls in the little souq I'd glimpsed when we'd bought provisions for our day's climbing on the Lion's Head. Who knew what other bizarre things I might find in a place where they ate locusts for fun?

Having fuelled myself with these tentative plans,

I was ready for action. Before I could change my mind I put twenty dirham on the tray for the tea, shovelled my guidebook into my shoulder bag and stood up carefully, balancing on my good leg. Then, gingerly, I put my injured foot to the ground and experimentally placed some weight on it. Jesus! Hot aches rushed up my leg, making me suck in my breath. I clutched the table and waited for the pain to pass and a moment later it eased. But when I flexed my toes to make a step another lesser surge ran up into my calf. Ow. If I had to spend one more day at this blasted hotel, one more hour . . . I took one step, then another.

'*Mademoiselle?*'

The voice came from behind me. I spun, taken off guard, lost my balance and fell in a crumpled heap, knocking my ankle on the metal chair leg as I went down and grazing my face on the patio stones. Pain regressed me from civilized human being to foul-mouthed child. 'Shit! What the fuck do you think you're doing sneaking up on me and taking me by surprise like that? Jesus, my bloody ankle. Christ almighty!' I raged and swore and then swore some more for good measure in my best climber's English until the fury and hurt had poured out of me. And all the time I did so a small part of me, like a little demon sitting on my shoulder and whispering in my ear, reminded me how down in the town I had seen a man with no legs knuckling himself along on a little cart, joking with the local children who ran alongside; an old woman bent almost double by some severe scoliosis turning her face up at an extraordinary angle and smiling at everyone she passed, wishing them good day and baraka; a painfully thin boy

197

falling off his donkey and on to his head in the middle of the street, bouncing straight back up again as if on a spring, dusting off his robe and laughing to ward off the fact that everyone else was laughing at him and it had hurt so badly. And here I was with only a twisted ankle, making a ridiculous scene, as my mother would have put it. *Izzy, don't make a scene.* As if to do so was the worst sin in the world. I looked up and found that even the blond toddler was watching me open-mouthed. 'That's right,' I thought savagely from my undignified and uncomfortable position on the uneven ground. 'Take a long hard look: this is how to throw a proper grown-up tantrum, sonny. Why don't you learn some good Anglo-Saxon vocabulary and then you can really shock your smug middle-class parents?'

Someone took hold of me under the armpits and hauled me upright and into the chair, and then there was a flurry of activity and a barrage of unintelligible Berber and moments later an attendant came running out with a jug of water and a small white hand towel, and the next thing I knew someone was dabbing at my face and murmuring in soothing French, 'It's only a graze, no real harm done.'

I thrust the towel away from my face, feeling suddenly ferocious at having my personal space invaded. 'Leave me alone!'

'Forgive me, I was just trying to help.' It was, of course, Taïb, his strong-boned face grim with concentration beneath the folds of his turban.

'Sorry,' I said, embarrassed by my overreaction. 'I'm just fed up with needing everyone's help.'

'I thought you might like to come with me to a

village up in the hills to meet a very old woman who might just be able to tell you what the inscription in your amulet means.'

I stared at him. 'Really?' Curiosity warred with wariness. Could I trust this man I had only just met? *Can you trust any man?* a voice in my head goaded. I took a deep metaphorical breath and pushed that unworthy thought away. 'OK . . .'

'Had enough of lazing in the sun, have you?'

I grinned at him, won over. 'Afraid so.'

He took a seat and gazed at me intently. 'Europeans simply aren't used to sitting around doing nothing.' He laughed. 'We Moroccans can do nothing for days on end. In Paris I work, work, work: all day, sometimes all night. Here'—he spread his hands, taking in the town and the magnificent hills—'I become myself again. I slow down, sometimes come to a complete stop. I get up late, I take a long, slow breakfast, then sit in a café and talk with my friends. I visit all the neighbours and relatives I missed when I was in the city, catch up on their news, pass the time of day with them. I watch the sun changing the colour on the rocks. I sleep a lot, or sit and watch the world go by. But I can see you're finding it hard to do that.'

I shook my head. 'I can't bear doing nothing. It drives me mad.'

'Too bad. It might do you good.'

I shot him a look, but decided to bite my tongue. 'So . . . this old lady. Where is she and how did you find her?'

'She lives in a village a couple hours' drive south of here, a place called Tiouada. Nana knew her when she was a child: she's a . . . a distant cousin.'

'And she can read Tifinagh?'

He shrugged. 'That's what Nana said. But what have you got to lose? At the very least you'll spend time with one of Tafraout's most charming sons, and get to see some spectacular countryside into the bargain. I'd say that was a good deal.'

'Is that so?'

He gave me a sly look under his lashes, which were, I noted with some annoyance, longer than my own. 'It's what I'm often told.'

'And do I have to pay for the privilege?' I was getting used to the expectations of the local populace, who seemed only too keen to fleece tourists under the smiling pretence of doing them a favour.

Taïb looked offended but quickly masked it. 'If you wish to, you can offer something for the petrol,' he said shortly and got up to leave. 'You might want a coat. When the sun goes down it gets very chilly in the uplands.'

I watched him walk briskly down the steps towards the hotel's car park and felt a brief frisson of irritation. Then I hopped and hobbled my way to my room to fetch my mountain jacket.

*   *   *

Back down in the car park I looked around and saw no sign of Taïb. A couple of ordinary saloon hire cars had been left to bake in the full sun by their unsavvy drivers; the hotel manager's antique Renault sat smugly in the shade beneath the fig tree. Other than that, there was an empty Dacia pickup and a gleaming black SUV. Even in the short time I had been in Morocco I could tell a local's car from a foreigner's at a hundred paces:

200

Taïb must have gone off to fuel up his vehicle in preparation for the drive, I decided. So when the SUV turned in a purring circle and drew up beside me, I was surprised.

'VW Touareg,' I said, falling into the waiting passenger seat. 'Did you choose it for the name?'

'Absolutely not,' he replied straight-faced, and off we went in leather-seated, air-conditioned luxury.

Down the long hill from the hotel we rolled: past terracotta-painted modern houses; an internet café with handwritten signs in the window; a shop selling local antiques; an elderly man sitting side-saddle on an emaciated mule; and a truck disgorging hundreds of crates of soft drinks into a warehouse that already seemed stacked high. I craned my neck.

'Full-fat Coke,' I observed. 'Horrible.'

'Ah, yes,' Taïb said. 'No one likes the diet version: people here were brought up to regard sugar as currency. If you drink Coca Light, you must be poor. Even though it costs the same. We traded in it, you know: Moroccan sugar was used all over the world. People still give sugar cones to couples getting married, and for special occasions. My mother has the cones she was given for her wedding, and the one to mark my birth.'

'Really?' I was intrigued. 'Sugar cones? I don't think I've ever seen such a thing.'

'You will.'

In the centre of the town there seemed to be schoolchildren everywhere, chattering excitedly or drifting along in pods of three or four, the boys in market-stall rip-off jeans and T-shirts and mock-Nike trainers, the girls all thin and dark in trousers and white coats, as if it was kicking-out time for a convention of trainee dispensing chemists. Hardly any of them covered their hair, though the few women I saw—their mothers and aunts and older sisters—all wore the regulation black *haik*, covering everything except their faces, their lively brown hands and brightly shod feet. The men sat at roadside café tables, smoking and drinking tea and talking, though their eyes lazily took in every detail. The atmosphere was relaxed: no one was doing much work, except perhaps the café staff. In the central square, Taïb drew up and got out, leaving me alone in the car. I looked around. A row of dusty shops lined one side of the square. Carpets whose bright dyes had daily been leached by the sun to the shades of an old colour photograph were displayed; striped woollen cloaks and hooded robes that looked far too substantial to be worn anywhere except the South Pole; ornamental swords and daggers, silver jewellery and chunky bead necklaces against a faded felt board; copper kettles gone green with verdigris, lots of big old clay jars like the ones I had seen in Lalla Fatma's house—all tourist goods but shabby enough to be authentic.

It was getting stuffy in the car: I turned the ignition key and buttoned down the window. Just as I did so two teenage boys on a beaten-up bicycle rode idly past, and one looked back over his shoulder at me. He said something to the friend who sat in front with his feet up on the frame, a bundle of knees and elbows, and then turned the bike and wobbled past me in the opposite direction.

'Gazelle!' they declared loudly in unison, and

rode off, giggling.

Gazelle? Was this an obscure form of insult, or a compliment? I had no way of knowing. I supposed it was better than having someone shout 'Hippopotamus!' at me or 'Elephant!', but even so . . . I looked around and found that this had set some of the men in the nearest café to laughing. Others watched me out of their lazy black eyes, their expressions unreadable. I was relieved to see Taïb returning, even if he did appear to be in a heated discussion with someone in a royal blue robe with smart gold-embroidered facings and a vast black turban. Furious, guttural words shot out of the two of them like gunfire; hands waved wildly. Then Taïb grabbed his companion by the shoulder and I thought they were about to fight; but a moment later they embraced heartily and burst into uproarious laughter. Clearly, I understood neither the verbal language nor the body-language involved in this culture.

Reaching the car, Taïb opened the door and drew his companion into view. 'This is my cousin, Azaz.'

They bore very little resemblance to one another, for members of the same family. Where Taïb was fine-boned and long-jawed, Azaz had fat, merry cheeks and a large Saddam Hussein moustache. 'Welcome, welcome,' he said, shaking my hand vigorously. 'I speak English very good, French and German too; all tourists come to me for advice. I am very sorry to hear about your accident on the Lion's Head.'

I was taken aback by this. 'Does everyone in Tafraout know?' I asked rather crossly.

'Oh, yes,' he assured me. 'Everyone! Everyone

knows about the young English woman on the mountain. But we are very glad our Lion took care of you and sent Taïb to help.'

'Half English, actually: English father, French mother.'

'I think your friends were worried they did not find you when they came down from the Lion!'

'You know them too?'

'Of course! I know all climbers who come here. Lots of English! I have met Joe Brown and Chris Bonington and the journalists who write guidebooks and magazine articles: they all come to me and I tell them about the mountains and routes here. So, yes, I know your friends Miles and Eve and her nice husband, Jez.'

'He's not her husband,' I said.

Azaz didn't appear to be shocked by this at all; quite the opposite—he laughed hugely and clasped his hands together. They were very plump and soft-looking, I noticed, and covered in extraordinary silver rings. *Not* the hands of a rock-climber. 'Ah, we are very wide-minded here; very relaxed. We shall call him her *copain*, her very good friend.'

Azaz stepped back. In my peripheral vision, I saw how he and Taïb exchanged a glance and then they both got into the car, with Azaz in the back; though he leant so far forward between the seats he might as well have been sitting in the front with us. He and Taïb kept up a barrage of Berber chatter, not bothering to translate for me as we roared out of the town and up the long hill towards the plateau. A mild sense of panic began to wash over me: where were we going again? I could not even remember the name of the village we were heading for: how could I take the basic precaution of texting Eve my whereabouts? It occurred to me again that I really didn't know anything about Taïb, much less his cousin. Might they drive me somewhere remote and subject me to some appalling ordeal? Would my body be left out in the wilderness to be picked over by jackals and vultures? Did they even have vultures here? I thought of the men in the roadside cafés in their smiling male complicity with the teasing boys on the bicycle: if I disappeared would the entire community turn its face inward and present an incommunicative blankness to the world, in the same way their architecture hid its secrets behind tall walls and shuttered windows?

'I must let my friend Eve know where I've gone, or she'll be worried,' I said loudly, breaking into their conversation.

'There's no need,' Taïb assured me. 'Everyone knows you've come with us to Tiouada—there's a *fichta* there tonight.'

'A what?' But they were chattering again. *Tee-wada. Teeooada*. How would you spell that? I dug in my bag for my mobile phone, turned it on and was about to start texting when a loud beep sounded and an envelope icon appeared. I had a message, it seemed. I opened it up.

SOME GUYS HV INVITD US 2 DINNER IN THR VILLG. HOPE U DNT MIND! C U L8R, EVE X

Great. I was about to respond when the signal flickered and then vanished. Even better.

'What's a *fichta*?' I asked into a momentary lull in the conversation.

'*Une fête*, a celebration: a party!'

'Beeeg party,' Azaz beamed. 'Many musicians,

205

everyone will be verrry happy. And Taïb and I will play.'

'Play?'

'The drums! *Agwal* and *tamtam*; and Mohammed will bring the *ganga* . . .'

Ganga? Did he mean *ganja*? What sort of party was this going to be? My panic levels notched up again. 'Where are they, then, these drums?' I demanded.

'In the back, behind Azaz.'

I turned. Beyond the back seat was a pile of jumble: blankets and boxes, a crate; and indeed, two large unidentifiable objects obscured by an old multicoloured rug. 'I thought we were just popping in to see an old lady to ask her about the amulet and then coming right back.'

Taïb turned an impassive face to me. 'No one ever just "pops in" to see anyone in Morocco,' he said smoothly. 'We have a great tradition of hospitality. There will be food and tea and music—'

'And just how long will all this take? I have to get back to the hotel.'

'You have so much else to do.'

I glared at him, flushing hotly. I knew I was being ungracious, overreacting to a kind invitation and the chance to see something of the real life of the country; but I was unprepared for it and feeling all semblance of control slipping away from me. For a moment I contemplated demanding that he turn the car around and take me back to Tafraout: but, indeed, what did I have waiting for me there? More dull hours to spin out on the hotel terrace as the sun dipped and went down into shadow; a solo dinner in the not-very-good hotel dining room . . . *For God's sake, Izzy,* I chided myself: *live a little.*

206

Take a chance. I forced a smile. 'OK, sounds great.'

'You'll love it,' he promised, and then he and Azaz were chattering again in their harsh, unintelligible tongue. Berber was an emphatic language, full of glottal stops and hawking noises made deep in the back of the throat, and it sounded, as all foreign languages do when you don't speak them, both fast and aggressive. With all the insistent hand gestures that accompanied even a simple conversation between friends, or cousins, it seemed confrontational, but after a while I began to find it calming, a sea of meaningless noise I could just tune out as I watched the landscape rolling past the window.

And what a landscape it was. Vast and rugged, cinematically widescreen, it stretched out ahead like a promise, or a threat. There was simply nothing this big, or this empty, in Britain. Even the plain we drove through was spectacular, dotted as it was with enormous boulders carved by the elements into fantastical shapes: five-metre mushrooms, their once-sturdy pillars weathered to apple-core stalks by blasts of windborne sand; great tors like a mass of fat pancakes piled one on another; huge peaks with jutting outcrops like eagles' beaks; rounded forms like crouching hares and sleeping women; and dozens of thrusting towers.

Taïb touched me on the arm and pointed to one of these, an isolated and striking example. 'See that? We call that the Aglaïn.'

In the back of the car, Azaz snorted with sudden laughter.

'And what does that mean?' I asked; and then stupidly wished I could call the question back,

207

since the answer was grotesquely obvious.

'The Cock and Balls,' he said, his eyes shining with mischief.

'Women who want babies walk all the way out here to touch it,' Azaz added helpfully. 'And it works! My cousins have many babies after visiting the Aglaïn.'

'Would you like to drive over to there so that you can touch it?' Taïb asked innocently. 'This car will tackle any terrain.'

'No!' I exploded. 'I would not. What primitive nonsense!'

'You already have children?' Azaz did not seem to be playing the same game as his cousin, but I was still unnerved.

'No.'

'But you are very old not to have children,' he continued, quite oblivious to the usual social mores, and to my growing alarm.

'In my culture women have careers,' I told him, tight-lipped. 'And we think that's just as important as having children.'

'Nothing is as important as having children,' he said solemnly, as I turned my head away from their prying eyes.

A little while later we took a left and soon the road began to climb, zigzagging up through a series of switchbacks, bounded on all sides by dizzying tumbles of red rock. Turning near the summit so that I could survey the landscape we had passed through, I gasped, astounded by the immensity of it: a huge, almost barren vista of raw rock, scattered boulders and scant vegetation, not a soul or a house to be seen. Far, far away I could see the dark, forbidding wall of the Jebel el-Kest louring over the Ameln Valley and was amazed to see how the incised features of the Lion's face were clear even at such a distance. No wonder it was enshrined in the local mythology: no one could get lost even in this wilderness with such a landmark to aim for. I imagined bygone traders making their weary way north out of the desert with their camels laden with gold and ivory and ostrich feathers, topping out on this mountain the Touareg was grinding up and setting a course directly for the Lion's Head with relief in their hearts, beckoned by the promise of a lush oasis after weeks, maybe even months, of their harsh journey.

On the other side of the mountain pass the landscape changed again, opening into a magnificent winding valley cut through by some vast and vanished river whose course had left behind it precipitous red cliffs resembling a not-so-miniature Grand Canyon, their layered strata laid bare for all to see, like a diagram in a geology textbook. But there was no great Colorado River here, in fact nothing at all to indicate the power of the torrent that had created such an impressive gorge, for way down in the riverbed there were nothing but dry boulders, worn smooth and white by the ancient passage of the water. Down we went, sheer drops on one side, masses of towering, unstable rock dotted with little orange starburst flowers and spiky Barbary figs on the other. Goats watched our passage with their slotted eyes as the road forded the ghost-river. We sped along a bumpy causeway, our tyres raising clouds of detritus that masked the way we had come. For one brief, surreal moment I felt as if all my future stretched before me like the narrow ribbon of tarmac ahead of us, leading into the unknown, and that everything in my past was slowly but surely being erased, turning to ashes and dust in our wake.

CHAPTER SEVENTEEN

Tiouada, when we finally reached it, was an unprepossessing sprawl of crumbling old adobe and modern breeze-block buildings. Compared to Tafraout it looked poverty-stricken and scruffy, a village balancing on a knife-edge of existence. Everywhere it was dry, dry, dry. We passed an enclosure in which a donkey stood tied to a post by a frayed piece of old rope. It lifted its head and eyed us dully, expecting nothing from life and in that expectation not being disappointed. I could see nothing green in its enclosure, not a leaf, not a plant; the rope that hobbled it looked the most edible thing it could reach.

The village was deserted, shutters closed, doors shut, even the iron grille of the obligatory grocer's shop drawn down; nothing stirred. Rusting cars stood baking in the afternoon sun, no children played in the street; not a feral cat or even a dog lazed in the shade beneath the papery leaves of the eucalyptus tree in the square. It certainly was not a place that gave the impression of somewhere a mystery might be resolved, a place in which the sole guardian of a lost ancient language might reside: it did not look as if anyone lived here at all. You sensed the entire population might have gathered during the day and after much debate had taken the long-put-off decision finally to abandon the village to drought and desertification, packed up their bags and belongings, and tramped off to find a better life elsewhere: somewhere with a higher water-table and some vegetation.

'Where is everyone?' I asked at last.

'You will see,' Taïb replied shortly.

We drove past a row of administrative buildings outside which the red-and-green national flag hung limp. Someone had daubed in large graffiti VIVE LE TIFINAGH! Long live the Tifinagh! And beside it what looked like a dancing stick-figure, legs akimbo and arms upraised, in black paint on the farthest wall, a figure that seemed at once defiant and delirious. For some reason it looked vaguely familiar to me. I asked Taïb what it meant.

'Berber pride,' Taïb said cryptically. 'That's called *Aza*: it's the symbol of the Amazigh'—*Amazir*—'the Free People.'

'Really?' I was curious. 'Who are the Free People?'

Taïb smiled darkly. 'We are. The Berbers were the original people of North Africa. Before the Romans came, long before the Arabs, we were here, with our own language and culture; our own religion and beliefs. The Arabs came from the eastern deserts in the seventh century, bringing Islam with them like a flaming sword. The invading Arabs made speaking the Berber language and writing in the Tifinagh alphabet illegal—even speaking Berber in our own homes became an act of subversion. But the Berbers are a proud people, and because they've always lived on the edge of hardship, they know how to persist against the odds. They resisted, and were brutally suppressed.

211

But still they fought, on and on through the centuries, stubbornly resisting integration with the Arabs, then with the French. A Berber separatist movement was formed. In the time of the last king, Hassan II, anyone supporting the Berber cause risked a beating, or worse. But the harder you tread on a snake, the more it'll want to bite you.'

'Yes,' said Azaz, his usually merry face solemn. 'It was a bad time. Many people simply disappeared.'

'Azaz's father was a member of the separatist movement, but he didn't take up arms: all he did was to campaign for free elections. He died in prison,' Taïb said grimly. 'No one speaks of such things now. The new king is different. He is more progressive than his grand-father, Mohammed V, or his father, Hassan II. He knows that if he is to succeed in making Morocco a successful modern country he's got to avoid disharmony and political unrest.'

We turned another corner and found a flock of skinny sheep blocking the road. I couldn't quite believe my eyes: where was their pasture? There was no shade of green to be spotted anywhere. Truly, the animals here must be as hardy as the people. It seemed a shame to eat them.

'Why hasn't there been more support for the movement?' I asked.

Taïb considered this, drumming his fingers on the steering wheel in a complex foreign rhythm as we waited for the sheep to move away. 'Most Moroccans have Berber roots, but not that many regard themselves as Berbers first and foremost any more. They can't afford to. The last century has been particularly hard. The French colonized

Morocco and siphoned off its resources. Wars came and went: widespread poverty was the inevitable result. If you want to get on in life, you have to speak good Arabic, and good French. If you speak Berber, people think you're an ignorant peasant and treat you accordingly. The younger generation have given up trying to scrape a living in the countryside: they've moved into the cities and adopted a Western way of life. Become a part of the system rather than fighting against it.' He sighed. 'My family is a good example, though Lalla Fatma remains the anchor to our heritage. We've lost our connection with the old language and the old ways. Even in the remotest places our people do not read or write the Tifinagh any more. We've managed to keep the language alive orally, but we've long since lost the use of our alphabet. At least there is support now to begin to teach it in the schools: the king has called the Amazigh culture "a national treasure". But the damage has long been done: I feel it as a great shame that you cannot simply walk up to someone in Tafraout and ask them to read the inscription in your amulet; that no one can do so, even though it is the written form of our own language, a dialect of the one we speak every day.'

Until that moment, I had not realized that the language I heard being spoken around me and the weird symbols in the amulet bore any connection to one another at all. And suddenly it came to me why the sigil on the wall seemed so familiar: it was one of the symbols in the inscription. How extraordinary: I felt at once uplifted and confused by this unexpected connection.·

The last sheep bounded up the stony bank, and

we turned left and rolled up an unpaved track, the wheels crunching loudly over rubble. 'And where do the Tuaregs fit in to all this?' I asked.

Taïb negotiated the potholes expertly, flicking the wheel to the left and right. 'A good question. We were all the same people once: Berbers spread right across North Africa, from Morocco in the west as far as Egypt in the east. But when the Romans conquered the Maghreb some of the local population capitulated, some resisted and some fled into the desert. The Tuareg were those who went into the desert. There, living outside all political boundaries and control, they managed to evade even the Bedouin raiders; and they took the roots of our culture with them, including our ancient alphabet. Now, they're the sole guardians of the Tifinagh, particularly when it comes to the ancient uses, like the inscription in your amulet.'

'Do you really think it's ancient?'

'The style of the amulet itself is certainly traditional. The thing you have to remember about the Tuareg is that until very recently their way of life has remained largely unchanged for a thousand years. But in the last generation they've suffered droughts, famine and persecution; their numbers have dwindled radically. And of course the modern world has impinged to some extent. When I say your amulet looks ancient, I mean its design is ancient, passed through generations of smiths from father to son down the centuries. So your necklace could be anything from a thousand years old to a hundred, or less: it's hard to say. I recognize the motifs, but I'd need to know more about its provenance to know for sure how old it is. The inscription inside it should give us a better idea, though. And that's where Lallawa comes in.'

'Ah,' said Azaz, cheered up by this mention no end, 'Lallawa: she makes the best *m'smen* in the world!'

Lallawa. It was the name I had heard over and over in my dreams. Something cold brushed against my heart.

*   *   *

But Lallawa did not answer when we knocked at her door. Taïb peered through her window, calling her name loudly. 'She's getting very deaf,' he confided to me, 'and she sleeps a lot now.' But there was still no response.

We walked around the back of her little mudbrick house, washed with the same terracotta shade as its neighbours, and found there an empty enclosure. There were chicken feathers and dried goat shit in the dust; but no sign of either creature apart from the musty smell that hung in the heavy afternoon air.

Azaz frowned and said something to Taïb, who shook his head. 'Her animals are gone; and she was so proud of them. Something must be very wrong. I'll go and find Habiba. She'll know.'

'And who is Habiba?'

Did I imagine it, or did he look uncomfortable?

'She is a . . . cousin,' he said at last. 'A cousin to me, and to Azaz. Lallawa used to live with Habiba's family.'

Back down the track we drove, back into the deserted town, past the civic buildings bearing their subversive graffiti. Just off the square we drew up in the shade of a wall painted with a bright mural mixing Disney cartoon characters, famous footballers and elegant swirls of Arabic writing.

'Habiba teaches here,' Taïb explained as we all got out of the car again. The late afternoon sun was like a hammer on the back of my head, and it occurred to me belatedly that I'd eaten and more importantly drunk nothing for hours. He came to my side and without a word or permission put an arm around my waist to help me walk. I opened my mouth to protest, thought better of it and shut it again. He was only trying to help, and the shade beckoned across the school-yard; but even so I felt uncomfortably aware of his proximity, of the bump of his hip against mine, of the sinewy muscles I could feel moving in his shoulders; the heat of him through his cotton robe.

At the doorway to the school—a small prefabricated building, its entrance reached by a set of rickety wooden steps—Azaz went ahead of us. He disappeared into the darkness inside and a moment later I heard the usual staccato burst of Berber, followed by a lot of high-pitched shouting and laughter. Taïb helped me up the steps and into the welcome shadow within.

Despite the late hour, thirty or forty children of all possible ages were crammed inside the single room. They grinned away like mad at the sight of a hopping tourist, their teeth startlingly white in the gloom. Some of the younger ones plastered their fingers over their mouths and gazed at me over the top in sheer delight; others shouted out words I had no way of understanding, and laughed and laughed. At last their teacher, a thin man with large, earnest eyes and a dusty brown robe like a mendicant priest, motioned for them to calm down and be quiet, and they subsided into some kind of order. Then he turned to Taïb and Azaz, and the three of them entered into an intense and lively discussion.

I looked around. As my eyes got used to the light it occurred to me how different all the children were from one another. In Tafraout, only a couple of hours' drive away, the children all looked much the same: with skin of a milky coffee colour and shining black hair. Here, every shade under the sun was represented, except for the palest European white. One girl, sloe-eyed and as pretty as an Arab princess in her pastel headscarf and bead earrings, had skin as pale as mine in winter; her neighbour was a deep, rich ebony, with a round ball of a head, her hair braided into intricate cornrows. Next to her was a little boy of maybe six, almost half her size and age, with the sharp cheekbones and fine features of the local Berbers; next to him an elfin creature of indeterminate gender sporting a head entirely shaved except for a single long braid sprouting from the crown of its head. A couple wore T-shirts that looked as if they belonged to someone else, or several someone elses, but most wore traditional robes in pale blue and mustard-yellow.

The classroom was spotless, which was just as well, since everyone was sitting on the floor. All around the walls were examples of the children's handiwork: the same sketchy houses and smiling suns and stick figures you'd find in any school anywhere in the world, displayed between swatches of embroidery and little hand-woven rugs bearing the same simple geometric patterns as those I'd seen fading their lives away in the Tafraout market.

Someone tugged at my sleeve. I looked down to find a little girl with missing front teeth grinning up at me. *'Asseyez-vous, madame!'* she insisted, pulling me towards a cushion placed ceremonially on the floor at the front of the class.

I arranged myself awkwardly, and as soon as I was settled the children were upon me like locusts, giggling and babbling and demanding my attention, as if being down on their level gave them licence to treat me as one of their own. One of them plonked herself squarely in my lap.

'Bonjour!' she trilled, gazing up at me with huge black eyes.

'Bonjour,' I returned uncertainly. I could not remember the last time I had touched a child, let alone had one fall in my lap with such happy confidence. 'What's your name?' I couldn't think of anything else to say.

'Voyez!' she demanded, thrusting her notebook under my nose. Written across the page in great wobbly biro lines were five simple icons: small circle, vertical line, large circle with a dot in the middle, small circle, large circle bisected by a vertical line. *'Mon nom!'* she declared in triumph. 'Hasna.'

I looked at Taïb, startled. 'She's written her name? In Tifinagh?'

He grinned proudly. 'Yes, Habiba is not here and in her place Abdelkader has been teaching them, just for today. It is the greatest good luck: he is a pioneer of Berber studies. Why don't you show him your amulet?'

Now that it came to it, I found that I really wasn't sure I wanted the mystery my amulet

218

contained to be revealed. What if the inscription was as simple as a name, written by some long-dead man or woman, a name with no relevance to any living person any more, and certainly with no relevance to me? What if it contained the ancient curse Taïb's grandmother believed it might hold? My heart began to beat faster, then faster still. But with all eyes expectantly on me and having come all this way for this express purpose, it seemed ridiculously contrary to refuse. I took the amulet out of my handbag and handed it to Taïb, who thumbed the central boss carefully to one side and shook the roll of paper out into his hand. Abdelkader took it and smoothed it out, the vertical line between his eyebrows becoming increasingly deeply furrowed as he stared at the complex inscription.

An unaccustomed silence engulfed the schoolroom as if somehow even the children realized an event of some significance was taking place, that a little bit of magic was about to reveal itself in front of their eyes, if they were quiet, very quiet. No one moved; it almost seemed that no one breathed.

After a while, the teacher turned the little square of paper around and scrutinized it that way. He took it to the window and held it up to the light; returned to the front of the classroom and paced up and down. The children watched him, wide-eyed and expectant. My palms began to itch and sweat the same way they did when I contemplated a hard route. At last he gave a long and heartfelt sigh. 'This is well beyond my limited abilities with the Tifinagh,' he told me in his precise French. 'I can make out a number of the characters, of course; but the letter forms do vary significantly across the wide region where Tifinagh has been used, which is after all half a continent! Also, I have to say that I cannot work out which way around it should be read—no, no, don't laugh: it is not such a simple matter. The writing in it is crosshatched and I'm not sure which way to start to read it. Right to left is more common; but the older inscriptions may use a bottom to top orientation. The language, after all, originated as a way of writing upon rock, so to start from the ground upward makes a lot of sense. And of course the Tuareg use the most ancient version of the language of all, and the purest: it leaves the vowels inferred. Since then the forms have deviated both geographically and linguistically. And I'm afraid, as such, this is rather beyond my understanding.' He spread his hands apologetically.

Taïb said something to him in their own language, and Abdelkader scratched his ear and nodded, then gestured again at the paper, pointing something out; and then they both looked at the amulet. And then Azaz asked something and they all spoke loudly together at the same time. How they could understand one another I couldn't imagine, but they seemed to be communicating together just fine.

By now the children were getting restless, and so was I. 'What?' I asked peremptorily. 'What are you talking about?' It was *my* amulet, after all.

Taïb turned to me. 'Sorry. Abdelkader is of the opinion that this is old, and most certainly Tuareg: he says there are none of the modern additions to the alphabet, the modifiers that have come into use to make up for those sounds and characters that the original alphabet does not allow for. Vowels, for example: older forms of Tifinagh rarely mark the vowels that we are used to including nowadays. It's all quite complicated . . .' He tailed off as if the subject was simply too difficult for a mere woman to get her head around. I felt myself bristle, and almost as if he intuited this he raised his hands defensively and added, 'He also says that Habiba is with Lallawa, who is very ill. All the women in the village are taking turns to look after her. We should at least pay our respects since we are here.'

*   *   *

Habiba's family home was bland and modest, two storeys of rendered breeze-block with small windows covered by dusty iron grilles and a doorway surrounded by garish factory-made tiles. The door was open: Taïb walked right in, calling out as he entered.

A woman came running out of a room, drawing a veil over her head. As she saw who her first visitor was, her anxious expression changed to one of utmost delight. Taïb strode forward and kissed her four times on the cheek, an effusive greeting, intimate and warm, containing little of the usual reserve I had thought characterized relations between men and women in this country. I watched as she held his hands still between her own as they talked, their heads close together, and felt like a voyeur.

Then she looked past his shoulder and saw me and for a moment her eyes narrowed.

When Taïb turned back to us, his face was grave.

221

'Lallawa is very sick, but Habiba says that we must come in and see her.' His tone implied that it might be the last chance to do so.

'Perhaps I'll wait outside,' I said. Habiba's glance had made me feel like an outsider intruding into a private world of sickness and pain. But Taïb was having none of it. As Azaz also greeted his cousin, rather less intimately, it seemed to me, Taïb ushered me into the living room. In there, sitting on the low couches that lined three walls of the gloomy little room, were half a dozen women in black robes and head-coverings, and between them an unmoving figure lay on a pallet on the floor. They looked like crows gathered around a corpse, but as soon as they saw Taïb and Azaz the sombre mood changed and suddenly they were all on their feet, chattering. Kisses all round and the pressing of hands; then Taïb knelt by the prone figure. I craned my neck. For a moment, I thought she was dead, then a hand rose slowly and patted his face. Azaz knelt too and the old woman turned her face first to one, then the other, and smiled gummily at them. Her skin was the colour of spent charcoal, as if most of the life had already gone out of it. The sclera of her eyes was a bright, unhealthy yellow, and the pupils were milky with cataracts. At last Azaz gestured for me to come forward and I heard my name as Taïb explained to her who I was. I knelt awkwardly. '*Salaam*,' I said, putting to use what I had absorbed from the glossary in the back of the guidebook, and extended my hand. Her fingers grazed my palm as lightly as a butterfly's wings, the touch frail and papery. '*Salaam aleikum*, Lallawa.'

The filmy eyes fixed on me with fierce attention

and her fingers closed around mine like claws. I tried to pull away, but she held on, her grip surprisingly strong for one so ill. Her lips formed a shape, but the sound that came out seemed more like a gurgle than a word.

'Show her the amulet,' Taïb urged.

'Are you sure? She seems very ill and I don't feel right bothering her with it.'

'No, please.' Habiba appeared beside Taïb, resting a hand on his shoulder in a gesture that seemed at once relaxed and proprietary. 'It will remind her of the good life she has lived. It will delight her, really.'

I took out the amulet, and the claw-like hand fumbled for mine and brought the amulet so close to her face that her breath misted the silver. Then she pressed it to her lips with a sigh. When she laid her head back down on the pillow, one corner of her mouth turned up while the other lay lax, and I realized belatedly that she must have suffered a stroke. She made an indistinct sound; frowned and tried again. 'A . . . daa.'

'Adagh?' Taïb asked and she nodded. He opened the compartment and took out the piece of paper, then handed the amulet back to me, carefully unfurled the paper and held it out.

Habiba shook her head. 'She won't be able to make it out: she's almost blind now.'

But the old woman seemed determined. We watched as she narrowed her eyes and strained, her head coming up off the pillow as if the effort of trying to engage with the inscription was a physical fight. She touched the marks and mumbled. Taïb leant closer so that the paper was barely an inch away from her face. I could see the frustration in

223

her eyes as she tried and failed to focus; and at last a fat tear squeezed out of one eye and ran in a deep runnel down the side of her nose.

'Stop,' I said softly. 'You're upsetting her.'

Taïb patted the old woman gently on the cheek and sat back on his heels. '*Tanmirt*, Lallawa. *Tanmirt.*'

He rolled the parchment up and replaced it as the amulet sat in the palm of my hand. His fingers brushed my own and I felt a sudden charge of electricity run up my arm. Bemused by this sensation, I was slow to respond to Habiba as she touched my shoulder. 'Come,' she said. 'Come with me.'

I followed her out of the room, past the black-clad women who watched me curiously with their bright black eyes, down a long corridor where doorways gave off into other small, dark rooms, and at last we emerged into a small square courtyard roofed unevenly with reeds through which the sun slatted down in sharp white contrast to the dark shadows. In the middle of the courtyard sat a dry fountain. Habiba gestured me towards this, then flicked a switch on the wall and with a rumble a pump started up and a trickle of water began to fill the conduit that ran to the fountain.

'I'm sorry you've travelled so far for no good reason. Her sight's been failing for a couple of months now and her latest attack seems to have made it worse. Wash your hands and your amulet in there,' she said. 'The running water will appease the spirits.'

Spirits? Such superstition. But I hobbled over and did as she suggested, washing my hands, then rubbing my wet fingers across the etched silver and glass, making sure no water got into the hidden compartment. Something about the ritual of this act was obscurely comforting; although maybe it was just the silky-cold feeling of the water on my hands on such a hot day after the gloomy confines of the sickroom. Habiba passed me a towel and I dried my hands and the amulet carefully.

'It is a beautiful thing,' she said. 'Lallawa has pieces like this. I remember when she lived with us when I was a very small child, and I found her jewellery hidden beneath her sleeping mat and took it all out and put it on and looked at myself in the mirror. I thought I looked like a Tuareg princess, but she caught me and smacked me.' She gave me a smile that transformed her face. 'I screamed and ran to Mother to complain; but she said Lallawa was right to smack me because every woman's property is her own, no matter how low her estate. She is very old, Lallawa; no one knows how old, least of all Lallawa herself. She has had a very long life, and a good life, too, considering what happened to her. She really loved the desert. Before her latest stroke I promised her she would see it one more time—' Her voice hitched and I realized that she was fighting tears, and abruptly found my own eyes pricking. 'I promised she would take the salt road one more time before she died. But, as you see, she is too ill now.'

'The salt road?'

'The desert tracks to the salt mines in the depths of the Sahara, the routes the traders took with their caravans of camels. The roads to and from the markets at which slaves were bought and sold, exchanged for salt and other goods. The Tuareg

225

often use the term to mean "the road of life", or even "the road of death". And sometimes it is used to mean all those things at once. I feel bad that I cannot do this one last thing for her; it will be harder for her to die in peace. But your amulet has brought a little of the desert to her.'

I felt something wet upon my face and a moment later realized the tears I had felt pricking my eyes were running down my cheeks. I could not remember the last time I had cried: I had come to despise such sentimentality. Part of me felt infuriated by myself; but another part—some new aspect I had developed, or perhaps one that had been long-since buried—was unashamed.

Habiba, though, turned away from me to gather mint from an overflowing tub outside the kitchen door. Then she beckoned me inside and I watched as she set about making tea, boiling water over a single butane ring, warming the silver pot, adding a handful of gunpowder tea, a generous handful of the fresh mint and three huge bars of sugar. 'My God, is that the amount of sugar that goes into every pot of mint tea?' I thought of all the glasses of this stuff I had drunk since arriving in Morocco, and shuddered.

She laughed. 'I was going easy on you: you Europeans don't like too much sugar—I have noticed how even Taïb's tastes have changed since he went away to Paris.'

There was a certain sharpness to her tone as she said this, and I found myself wondering what it meant, or whether I had imagined it. 'Do all the young men go away? To work, I mean.'

'It's hard to make a living in the area. You've seen it: it's poor and dry, and getting poorer and drier by the day. There's no work here, no money, no luxuries. So, yes, the young men—and often the young women nowadays—go away to get an education and a job and send money home to the ones left at home. It's how we do things in Morocco.'

'It's hard on those left behind,' I said, watching as she tipped the first glass she had poured back into the pot and swirled the ingredients around. 'Especially the women.'

'It's hard on everyone. Sometimes they don't come back.'

'Like Taïb?'

She shot me a hard look. 'Taïb and I were promised to each other when we were children.'

'That's a very long engagement.'

'We put off the wedding until we had the means to set up house. I went to Agadir to continue my education and to train as a teacher; Taïb went to France. And, well, he stayed there. He likes the . . . lifestyle, I think.'

The way she said the word 'lifestyle' carried such a weight of disapproval that I could hear all the contempt of the Islamic world for the wayward, selfish, loose-moralled ways of the West in it. Needled, I asked, 'So, you're a qualified teacher now, and he's made enough money to be driving around in a brand-new car, so when are you getting married, then?'

She pressed her lips together, as if holding back a retort, and with a furious flourish poured out a stream of bubbling golden liquid into the first of the decorated glasses on the tray. 'Who *do* you think you are to judge us? It's not always about money,' she said scathingly. 'I lay no claim to Taïb

227

now beyond the bounds of kinship. You're perfectly free to sleep with him if you want to.'

Actually, 'sleep with' is my euphemism. Her use of the French verb *baiser* struck me as hard as a slap in the face. I saw the flash of triumph in her eye as I registered the word; then she turned, swept up the tea tray and marched off to the salon, where the crow-like women awaited their refreshments, leaving me to stumble along behind her, bemused, astounded and not a little outraged.

I wanted to grab her by the shoulder and spin her around so that that lethally sweet tea flew everywhere and demand what she meant by that remark. Of course, I did nothing of the sort, but sat meekly on the edge of one of the couches and sipped the horrible tea and did not meet her eye or say a word to her, or to anyone. I did not need to: they jabbered away in their hellish language without a thought for my presence; but every so often I found the unseeing gaze of the dying woman upon me, peculiarly intent, unblinking and unsettling. I was relieved when, long hours later, we left.

CHAPTER EIGHTEEN

'You looked uncomfortable in there,' Taïb said to me in the car.

I shrugged. 'Things to think about.'

He nodded slowly. 'Yes, I know what that is like. I too have much to think about.' But he did not say what.

Habiba's attack had shaken me, though my

initial anger at the insult had long since subsided. She was, I had decided, a jealous woman who saw me as a threat and I wondered whether she and Taïb were still formally linked, whatever she had said. Their warmth towards one another had seemed genuine, but it was difficult for me to judge how much emotion their kissed greeting masked, or contained. And had she read into his gestures towards me something that simply did not exist? Or did her hostility spring from feeling that she had lost him to France and its women? Given her straitened circumstances, buried away in that dusty little village, in that gloomy house with its contingent of beady-eyed old women and its dying guest, I could understand her frustration. How easy it would be to envy a modern European woman who waltzed (well, hobbled) in on the arm of the man you had expected to marry, her hair immodestly uncovered, a Longines watch on her tanned wrist and a Prada handbag over her shoulder, a woman who could (if she chose) take her pleasures where she would, with no social censure or other unwanted consequences, and move on. But a thought nagged at me: that it had not been jealousy, or not only jealousy, that I sensed in the tenor of her attack but a deep-seated and haughty contempt. What was it that Habiba had seen in me that had triggered such disgust? I had, I thought, been polite and respectful, for all my Western trappings and bare head. True, I did not speak her language, and it is common to regard foreigners who cannot understand or communicate with you as ignorant. But there was more to it than that: her attitude had not been merely dismissive but pointed. It had involved a judgement, as if she perceived in me someone who had made the wrong choice in life, someone who had stepped from the true path into a moral morass.

I was used to being treated with a certain level of respect, I realized. I moved in a world in which I was viewed within a social spectrum, a professional hierarchy. At work, I was defined by my role within the company, by the authority I carried, by the important clients I dealt with and the superior salary I earned. Even outside work, on the streets of the capital, I was used to people reading the signifiers of my appearance—my well-groomed hair, my manicured hands, my expensive clothes, my discreet but high-quality accessories, my manner and my confidence—and deducing from those my social standing. Even I derived my sense of self-worth, I realized, from these shallow trappings. But just who was Isabelle Treslove-Fawcett? Who was I really? When examined closely the successful edifice seemed fragile and behind it I felt insubstantial, like a dream of myself. The money was all very well, but money in itself means nothing: it represents only a covenant with the future, and what was my future? I had no family, few friends and no faith, in any god, or in anything much beyond my own experience. I had, I realized, closed myself off from the world all my life, had kept its difficult and random elements at bay so that it could not damage me, had walled around myself with financial independence and a job that involved no emotional input. There were good reasons behind the defensive position I had so painstakingly erected to protect myself, I knew, and the strategy I had chosen had got me thus far in life apparently unscathed; but Habiba had rocked its foundations.

And then there was the old woman expiring slowly on the living-room floor. The way Lallawa accepted her lot with such good grace moved me greatly, the way she warmly grasped the hands of her visitors, all the while smiling lopsidedly out of that gentle, careworn face. I thought of how her face had turned itself unerringly towards me on and off for those many uncomfortable hours in that little room, as if she too questioned my identity, and maybe even my worth. How must she feel, uprooted from her desert home and set down in a place like Tiouada? To lie there, yearning to see the bleak beauty of the desert dunes once more before she died, to ease her soul in a wide open space like the ones she remembered in her prime, but instead having her senses robbed from her one by one, and being imprisoned within four gloomy walls and a low ceiling, peered at by the crow-women, tended by the sharp-tongued Habiba?

Taïb and Azaz were uncharacteristically silent as we made our way along dusty roads rendered violet by the sinking sun, lost in their own thoughts. In the stillness, above the low rumble of the tyres on the uneven ground, I heard our destination before I saw it: a deep thrum of drumbeats pulsing through the twilit air, accompanied by some high-pitched stringed instrument, or a woman's voice strained to breaking point. We pulled to a halt outside a tall adobe wall; when Azaz opened the door for me, the noise was deafening.

Taïb put his mouth close to my ear; I felt his breath hot against my neck as he said, 'Welcome to

231

a proper Berber *fichta*!' And a moment later he had swept me up into his arms and into an extraordinary scene. Dozens of lanterns hung from trees already decked with pomegranates and oranges, their candle flames flickering with the movement of the dancing figures below them: men in turbans and whirling robes; women with kohl-rimmed eyes and glittering silver earrings, their henna-patterned hands waving rhythmically above their heads. Children ran amongst the throng in their best clothes: boys in white tunics and bright yellow slippers; girls in coloured kaftans, toddlers with huge black eyes and gap teeth, their fists twisted in their mothers' black robes and embroidered veils. A group of stripe-robed men wearing white turbans and ceremonial daggers beat a variety of drums, sending a powerful, complex rhythm out into the night, one that threatened to swallow every trace of individuality in the vicinity, and to swallow it whole. Feeling overwhelmed, I stared around for some comforting point of reference, but I was not to be reassured.

Around the edges of the garden, arranged along low couches and perched on little wooden stools, were the same crow-like old women as those who had been gathered in the salon at Habiba's house, waiting for death to claim the old woman—black-clad from top to toe, their faces as brown and wrinkled as walnut shells, their hands clasped like claws around little glasses of tea.

Taïb swung me down on to a vacant cushion beside a group of laughing girls tending to their younger siblings and abandoned me there. 'Stay here,' he told me, as if I had any choice. 'I'll be back in a moment.'

When I looked up to watch him pass through the crowd, I felt the bright black eyes of the old women upon me, piercing and inquisitive. They caught me watching them and held my gaze implacably; then they began chattering again like magpies, shooting sharp looks at me, waggling their fingers. I knew what they were thinking: I had had a privileged insight into the minds of the women of the region now. Feeling acutely uncomfortable under their damning scrutiny, I dug in my handbag for my mobile phone in order to try to text Eve again—anything for a bit of friendly contact in my own language—but it was the amulet that fell into my hand.

I felt its square edges, and then it was in my palm, resting there, sturdy and familiar and comforting. A sudden small wave of warmth washed up my arm, suffusing my skin, and abruptly I felt that maybe things were not so bad after all, that I was not an enemy intruding into this private celebration, a stranger in a foreign land, surrounded by the inimical Other, but a welcome guest here. No, more: that I was somehow a part of it, one amongst many; that the drums that beat so loudly that they reverberated in the marrow of my breastbone were a part of me and the beat of my heart was a counterpart to that rhythm. By the time Taïb finally made his way back to me I was sitting there cheerfully with one little girl in my lap and another happily braiding my hair, clapping my hands and nodding away to the music as if I had been doing this all my life.

He grinned at me and subsided gracefully to the floor beside me bearing a heaped plateful of food. Behind him came Azaz with a silver jug and ewer and a white towel draped over his arm. He knelt at my side and poured water for me to wash my hands in. How courtly! I smiled at him as I washed and dried my hands and he smiled back, restored to his merry self, then whisked the ewer away. The children disappeared, but not before Taïb had pulled handfuls of almonds out of his ears for them, making them giggle delightedly.

'Clever trick,' I observed into a lull in the music.

'Many nieces and nephews. A lot of practice.'

'You've never wanted children of your own?'

He passed me a plate of steaming lamb and vegetables with a large piece of baked flatbread balancing precariously beside it. The fragrance of spices and fruit rose from the dish, and my nose practically twitched like a dog's. He watched me eat without answering, and I was so absorbed by the delicious food, so rich and well balanced—the juicy meatiness of the lamb complemented by the soft, sweet prunes, the chilli and garlic mixing with flavours I couldn't quite place, flavours that hinted somehow of rose petals and sandalwood, or spices that had no name except for those given them by the Berber people who used them—that I failed to remember that he hadn't answered my question until I was halfway through demolishing the meal. I looked up guiltily and found him watching me with a mixture of amusement and intensity.

I swallowed the mouthful I held. 'No children?' I repeated.

'That's quite a personal question.'

'Is it? I've had a personal sort of day. Your cousin Habiba was quite rude to me.'

His eyebrows shot up. 'She was?'

I wasn't going to divulge exactly what she had

234

said: it was too crude, too uncomfortable, as if I were somehow trying to shock him, making some sort of advance upon him by a rather contrary route. 'And she told me you and she were engaged.'

His face went very still, close and remote, as if a set of shutters had come down. 'We were,' he said after a long pause. 'A long time ago.'

'So what happened?'

'That is a matter between her and me and our family, not a subject for discussion with strangers.'

Well, that told me. I sat back, affronted, while Taïb applied himself to finishing the plate of food. After a while, he got to his feet, took the empty plate and without a word disappeared into the crowd. A few minutes later he was back with a drum like a huge tambourine under his arm and another, consisting of two clay pots covered with skins, in his hands. He passed the larger one to Azaz, and then sat down cross-legged on the matting in the middle of the party and started tapping out a lively syncopated beat. Soon a dozen or more men had made a wide circle around them, augmenting and elaborating on the rhythm with instruments of their own, or by simply clapping their hands. A tall young man with what looked a lot like a banjo came and sat with them, adding his jazzy strings to the melody that now threaded its way through the gathering.

I watched as Taïb sang and played, his eyes shut, lost in the music. He had a pleasant light tenor voice, soulful and haunting, and he sang with a passion and lack of inhibition that made the tendons stand out on his neck. For some reason I was surprised by this: he had not to this point struck me as a passionate man, nor as one

235

charismatic enough to lead a room in song. People were dancing now, the men shuffling sideways a pace or two, clapping their hands together, stepping back again. The younger women shimmied in a sort of chaste and fully clothed belly dance, their hands flicking here and there, while the older women swayed and bobbed and laughed and looked a lot less crow-like than they had before. The song went on and on, merged into another, and another. Someone brought around glasses of mint tea, little almond-flavoured cakes, dates and something that I thought looked like fudge and to which I helped myself enthusiastically. Unfortunately, it turned out to resemble nothing so much as balsa wood, instantly removing every drop of saliva in my mouth, shocking me out of my pleasant reverie.

I glanced at my watch. Good grief! It was almost midnight. During a lull in the music I caught Taïb's eye and he came over. 'When were you thinking of heading back?' I asked. 'I should let Eve know.'

He looked distant, preoccupied. 'Of course.' He rubbed a hand across his face. 'Look, I need to go and see someone. Give me a few minutes. Call your friend and let her know you're OK and will be back soon. There should be a good signal here.'

There should? In the middle of nowhere it seemed unlikely, but when I took out my phone the reception bars were almost full. I retrieved Eve's number from the contacts list and waited as it rang. And rang. *Oh, Eve,* I sighed to myself. *Where the hell are you*? A moment later, as if she heard my chiding, she picked up.

'Hello?'
'Eve? It's me?'

Some sort of rustling as if she were shifting the mobile from one ear to the other. 'Oh, hi, Iz.'

She sounded a bit out of it: vague and displaced, as if she'd been asleep. 'Sorry, didn't mean to wake you up. Just to say don't lock the door, I'll be back, though it'll be really late.'

In the background I heard her say something but it was muffled, as if she had put her hand over the phone. I tried to focus, but there was too much chatter and laughter around me. 'Is that OK, Eve? Are you OK? Did you have a good day?'

'What? Er, oh, yes. Great, thanks, really good actually.' And then, as if ambushed, she gave out a shriek that turned into a loud and unmistakable giggle. There was another failed attempt to muffle the phone and then I heard her say, quite distinctly, 'Get off, Jez. No, get *off*! Ssh, quiet, it's Izzy.'

I gazed bleakly at the phone as if I could see projected on to its opaque little screen our unimpressive hotel room with its dull brown tiles and dun curtains. Had they lit one of the scented candles Eve had brought with her, rather than given themselves up as hostages to the unforgiving sixty-watt bulb that swung unshaded from the centre of the ceiling? Had they pushed the two single beds together, I wondered, or were they jammed on to Eve's narrow mattress, bare limbs entwined, the sweat sheening their well-exercised skin?

'Oh, Eve.' Suddenly I felt exhausted, emptied out.

'What? Are you OK? Where are you?'

'Look, it's nothing: I'm fine. I'm with Taïb, at a sort of party-thing, in a village to the south. Not

237

sure how long it'll take us to get back from here, but don't worry about me, OK?'

I cut the connection, feeling suddenly very alone, and looked around at the sea of humanity in which I was a still, small island. Some of the drummers were warming the skins of their drums over the fires and a group of women were now playing stringed instruments like small, oddly shaped violas; the children at their feet were sucking on dates. Taïb returned hand in hand with an older man with greying hair and a heavy moustache.

'Mustapha will drive you back to Tafraout,' he said without preamble. He looked weary, as if he'd had a hard job of persuading Mustapha of the efficacy of this arrangement.

I stared at him, feeling ever more isolated. 'You must be joking! I don't know him. I don't know anything about him.'

'He's my uncle. You'll be perfectly safe with him. Besides, there'll be my aunt and her three daughters travelling with you.'

'And you're just going to hang around here, party till dawn?'

He took a deep breath. 'I'm going to drive Lallawa to the desert. It's her last wish, and I have both the time and the vehicle to do this thing for her.'

My jaw must have dropped. 'Oh.'

He squatted down beside me. 'You know, I was going to ask you if you'd like to see the Sahara since we're only a few hours away from it here; but then I thought that would be a crazy thing to do. You hardly know me; and Lallawa, for all her stoicism and courage, will require some looking

238

after, and that's not really something your culture prepares you for, so then I thought I'd better ask Mustapha to take you back to your hotel. But if you won't go with him . . .' He sighed, spread his hands helplessly. 'I'm sorry. I promised to get you back to Tafraout, and I gave you my word on that. We'll leave now and I'll come back for Lallawa tomorrow—'

'No.' It was as if someone else was acting through me; someone reckless. I saw, as if from another place, how my hand reached out and touched his mouth to stop his words. 'No, I want to go with you. I want to see the desert too. With you and Lallawa. Take me with you, into the Sahara.'

It was just like starting out on a lead, or making the first step out into the void on an abseil. Just like that, it was done, and my life would never be the same.

CHAPTER NINETEEN

Over the days and weeks that followed, Mariata's thoughts spun constantly around her awakening into the new sensual world Amastan had introduced her to. She thought about it so often that sometimes she wondered whether her personal demon had access to these thoughts and was using them to haunt her in a new and inventive way. She remembered every detail of their time together in an hallucinatory fashion, as if she were reliving it again from within and without. She could recall how as they lay beneath the oleanders, with their heavy perfume filling the air above

239

them, Amastan unwound his tagelmust with slow and deliberate calm; how hungrily she had gazed at the planes of his face, revealed to her for only the second time and in such different circumstances to the first. How he had laid his naked cheek against hers and she had held her breath until it seemed she might pass out. How his breath had been hot on her neck, then her breast. The memory of it still made her shiver with rapture and anticipation for the next time he touched her.

She found herself looking differently at everyone in the tribe. Had they too experienced such wonder? The harder she stared at them going about their daily business the more unlikely it seemed. Old Taïb there, sitting on the rock working a piece of coloured cloth with needle and twine: had his heart ever beat so fast at the sight of someone that he thought it would break his ribs? Or Nadia, her brown face seamed with lines made by sun and laughter, whose husband was away trading: did she lie in her tent at night and think of him, with her hand between her legs? Or bad-tempered Noura: with six children she must surely have felt something for Abdelrahman, though you'd hardly think it to see the two of them now, chiding one another over the moths having got into the wool, or a lack of sugar in their stores. She could not imagine they had once eaten one another with their eyes the way that she and Amastan did. And when the subject in the women's camp turned to Kheddou and Leïla, the newly-wed couple, the tone of the girls was not one of envy or of wistfulness but of ribaldry and coarseness. Yet Leïla's eyes were sparkling and her cheeks reddened when at last she emerged from the bridal tent; and Mariata saw in the days that followed how she would sometimes stare off into the distance, or into the heart of the fire at night, and smile secretly to herself, and then she knew she was not the only one in the world to feel the way she did. The world was bathed in a glorious haze: she could hardly distinguish one day from the rest. Her mind wandered during her tasks. She burned the bread, overfed the chickens, overslept when it was her turn to milk the goats. She wished the daylight hours away: all she wanted to do was to lie down in the dark with Amastan and feel their blood beat together. Sometimes, she was aware of Tana watching her narrow-eyed, but the enad said no more to her about leaving the tribe and it seemed to Mariata that nothing could dent the perfect sphere of happiness in which she spent her days, shielded as she was by the power of her own sensuality. Even the sight of Amastan and the other men talking with two dark-robed figures who rode in to the edge of the camp one night as the sun was going down did not alarm her as it might have done, despite the glimpse of the bandoliers of ammunition they wore criss-crossing their chests, or the rifles slung across their backs. When he came to her that night, later than usual, all thought of asking who these men were fled her head, washed away by her desire. But as he started to rewind his veil before stealing back to the men's camp, she put her hand on his arm.

'Who were they, the men you spoke with?'

Amastan's regard became shuttered. 'Some friends. Just some friends. Nothing for you to concern yourself with.'

Mariata bridled. 'Because I am a woman?'

241

'Because it does not concern you.'

'Do not say that! Everything that concerns you concerns me!'

'There are some things we can never share.'

Jealousy flared through her. 'You mean like Manta?'

'I will always honour her memory.'

'I will make you forget her!' She pulled his face down to hers and kissed him ferociously.

After a while, Amastan handed her away gently. He cupped her face in his palm. 'I will never forget Manta, even though you own my heart now.'

'Then shall we be married?' She stared at him, her eyes sparking a challenge. The word reverberated in the air between them. Amastan's expression was unreadable.

After several long beats he asked softly, 'Would you really take me as your own, a woman of your lineage? You know I have neither fortune nor an honourable bloodline to offer you.'

'We will make our own fortune and a new bloodline: together.'

He nodded slowly. Then he drew free of her and got to his feet. 'I need to think about this.' He would not meet her eye, and bundled the cloth of his veil clumsily around his head as if he could not wait to be away from her.

Mariata shot to her feet, her fists balled as if they would strike him; instead, she beat violently at her robes, dislodging the dust, the dried leaves and crushed petals that clung to it. She felt the hot liquid he had left inside her run slowly down the inside of her thigh. 'There is nothing to think about,' she said through her teeth. 'Have we been playing like children, lying together these past weeks? Did you think I did so lightly, taking my pleasures where I would? Or perhaps I had decided to perfect the skills—learning to dance, as the women of your tribe so delicately put it—I would need before choosing a proper husband elsewhere?' She glared at him. 'Whatever *were* you thinking?'

Amastan raised a hand, palm up, placatory. 'Please, Mariata, don't. I have not been thinking at all, if truth be told. The time we have spent together has been a blessed balm poured on old wounds; but I should have thought about more than my own selfish needs. There is too much at stake for us to marry now. For you; for all of us.'

Mariata eyed him haughtily, feeling herself invested with the power of her ancestor; the power of all women over men. 'Please do not try to tell me what is best for me. Other men have tried to do so in my life, quite wrongly. When I was young my brothers told me that the best thing for a scorpion sting was to rub hot sand on it, which is the worst thing you can do: my finger swelled up like an egg. When my mother died, my father took me away from my tribe and left me to the mercies of the Kel Bazgan, and that was a worse mistake. It was I who made the decision to cross the Tamesna with your mother; I who chose to lie with you and no other, because I knew we should be wed. Only I know what is best for me; and since you love me, as I love you, I do not see what obstacle there is.' She took hold of the amulet she wore about her neck, and declared, 'I take you Amastan ag Moussa to be my husband for all time, and I wear your talisman as a sign of our union.' Then she reached down and picked up her scarf, shook it out vigorously and covered her head with it like one of the married women. 'You see? It is easily done. Tomorrow we will go to your mother and make our declaration of betrothal and she will arrange our wedding and send word out to find my father and brothers to invite them to join us in our celebration. There is nothing more to think about.'

Amastan took her by the shoulders; but it was not a tender embrace. His fingers, tense with suppressed anger, dug into her. 'Mariata.' He had not finished rewinding his veil: the long tail of his tagelmust hung down his robe, leaving his lips, which minutes before had been kissing her greedily, naked to the night air. The corners of his mouth were downturned unhappily. 'Now is not the time for weddings and celebrations. There is a war coming, a war that must be fought if our people are to survive. If we run, if we fail, we shall be the Free People no longer, for no trace of us will remain. Those men who were here tonight belong to a group the government call rebels: they are part of a resistance movement dedicated to creating an independent Tuareg state—the Azaouad, which will stretch all the way from the Aïr and the Adagh, even as far as your Hoggar. They are seeking fighters from every drum-group in the region. We will all go: me and Kheddou, Ibrahim, Bazu, Amud, Azelouane, Illi, Makhammad, Gibril, Abdallah, Hamid and the rest; all of us who are fit and able. We must, because if we do not stand and fight, what happened to Manta's village will happen here and throughout the Adagh. What happened to Manta—rape, murder, desecration—will happen to my mother, my cousins, my friends. It will happen to you, Mariata; and that I could not bear. They hate us. They want to see us destroyed, obliterated from the very ground on which we walk. They begrudge us the air we breathe and the water we drink. Our very existence challenges them and all they believe in. So we must fight them as cruelly as they would fight us: for only fire can combat fire. Violent resistance is all that is left to us now, though we will have to call on all the strength and cunning and baraka of our ancestors if we are to withstand their guns and their gas and their wickedness. You have to let me go so that I can do this, Mariata; and when we have won the day and made our people safe, we can turn our thoughts to marriage. Only then can there be a chance of happiness and hope for our future, and a future for the children we will have together.' His eyes shone with anger and zeal, as if he could see this future stretching out before them.

'What about Kheddou and Leïla? Only weeks ago you danced at their wedding and spoke no word of war.'

'I cannot make others' decisions for them.'

'Then do not seek to make decisions for me! I am not some feeble creature that has to be protected from the wicked world. My mother always told me that everything important in life starts from the heart'—she made a circle on the ground with a dot in the middle—'and we move wider and wider still into the Circle of Life, just as the world's horizon circles around you and the herd of your tribe. We are part of everything and everything is a part of us. If there is to be war, there will be war,' she said fiercely, 'but we shall face it together, wed in the eyes of the world. And

245

if you fight, I will fight too. Put a spear in my hand and a sword in my belt and I will fight like any man. And if everything is to come to an end in a sea of blood, I too will be swept away by it; and if we win, I will share your triumph.'

In the darkness her eyes glinted with moonlight as if she were filled with cold fire, and to Amastan she seemed at that moment more like an elemental spirit than a flesh and blood woman. Many men would have quailed at the sight, but Amastan was suddenly filled with a brief chest-bursting pride in the force of her determination, the power of her love for him. His loins were immediately afire once more. What could stand in the way of such a force? If you did you would be immolated by it; and some essential part of him welcomed the immolation. He caught her to him and kissed her hard. 'You are a lioness.'

She shook her head, laughing. 'A lioness? Not I. My spirit-animal is just the humble hare.'

'Humble? I think not. The hare is the most noble of creatures; as is the woman who will be my wife.'

*   *   *

The next morning they went to Rahma and declared their intentions.

Rahma kissed her son's hand, pressed it to her heart. Then she took Mariata in her arms. 'Ah, daughter, you could never have brought more welcome news!'

Seeing the two of them facing one another, Amastan thought how similar they were, with their strong profiles and gleaming dark eyes: like a pair

246

of lionesses, afraid of nothing, ready to take on the world to defend their own. I am not worthy of them, he thought but did not say.

*   *   *

News of the betrothal spread around the area like locusts through a crop. Everyone was buzzing with it. Opinions were mixed: although Mariata had generally made a favourable impression on the tribe, there were some who saw her as too elevated to be marrying a man of the Kel Teggart, even if his father was an amenokal of the Aïr drum-groups. The older people remembered their misgivings over Rahma's marriage to Moussa ag Iba. They had nodded and sucked their teeth when she had come running back to the tribe with her tail between her legs and nothing more to show for her twelve years of trouble with a man known to be overweening and cruel than the tent with which she had left, a failing donkey and a sullen child, small for his age, prone to rages and sharp of tongue. Time had served to amend their opinion of Amastan somewhat, for he had grown tall and strong amongst them, had become a master of verse and dance, and was valued by them for his hunting skills; but they distrusted his temper and his judgement, and he was regarded as something of an unlucky man, one who too often attracted the evil eye. The idea of him settling here with his new bride made them nervous: how long would it be, they asked, before the good djenoun abandoned him once more and the Kel Asuf came for him, and for anyone else who stood too close? And so they greeted him as politely as ever and gave their

247

felicitations, wished him baraka, long life and many children, and prayed fervently that he would do the right thing and take Mariata ult Yemma back to her mother's encampment in the far-off mountains of the Hoggar. As was only fitting, they reminded one another, given her fine ancestry.

But the younger women had few of their parents' and grandparents' misgivings and treated Mariata as they would any of their number marrying a handsome young man. They painted the moons and flowers denoting betrothal on the palms of her hands with a dark henna paste. After a day the paste flaked and fell to reveal deep red-brown designs stained into the skin, to which Amastan pressed his lips during their nightly trysts. In the privacy of the tents, they taught her bawdy songs and verses that made her bellow with such loud laughter that old Nadia came in, thinking one of the heifers had strayed where it should not have. Leïla, playing the worldly new wife, took Mariata aside to impart to her the secrets of the marriage bed. 'On the first wedding night you must resist his advances: he should act towards you only as a brother. That is the correct way. On the second night he may kiss you as a friend and hold you as you sleep; no more. It is only on the third night that he may behave towards you as a husband to a wife.' And then she went on to explain, in much practical detail, exactly what this was likely to entail, and was surprised by the younger girl's unblinking equanimity in the face of such earthy descriptions. For her part, Mariata thanked Leïla solemnly and slipped one of her fine silver bangles on to her slim brown wrist as a symbol of their friendship. Leïla later reported to Nofa and Yehali that she thought Mariata as frightened as a young gazelle at the very idea of it all.

The only thing that marred Mariata's happiness was having no family around her to share it with. Messengers were sent out with anyone of the routes south and east towards Bilma in the hope of finding her father and brothers. Travellers were questioned as to whether they had encountered them on their journeys. Some traders passing through from Zinder to Tin Buktu reported that tales were circulating in the *funduqs*, where the traders spent their nights in town, of a caravan returning from the salt mines of Bilma that had come to grief out in the Ténéré, a caravan that had included a father and his two sons; but no one could recall their names and since such a description could be applied to the vast majority of trading expeditions, no one took the news too much to heart. Mariata, though, trying not to show her anxiety, at last worked up the courage to approach the smith to have her read the omens regarding this rumour.

She found Tana sewing leather in the shade of a huge tamarisk on the edge of the encampment. The colours of the thing she sewed gleamed as bright as fruit. Mariata wondered what it was, with its complex motifs and decorative fringes; but she had rarely seen anything so lovely and could hardly take her eyes from it.

Tana regarded her gravely. They had not exchanged a word since the night of Kheddou and Leïla's wedding. 'It is a travelling bag,' the enad said without preamble, holding it aloft so that its fringes swayed and jounced. 'You will need one.'

'I will?'

'You are going on a long journey.'

Mariata wondered about this. Was the smith trying to make her leave again? On the other hand, she herself had proposed to Amastan that after their marriage they should make the journey to the Hoggar to bring the news to her cousins, the last remnants of her revered mother's family, and stay with them in the rampart of the hills beyond Abalessa in safety for the winter. She dearly wanted to show her beloved the mountains where she had grown up, the jutting pinnacles that turned to scarlet as the sun went down; the cool, shady gueltas in which water stood all year round. Amastan had been polite but non-committal on the subject. He would not speak them aloud, but she knew his thoughts turned on the conflict that edged ever nearer. Even so, she was sure she could persuade him once they were wed, so she did not press Tana for her meaning but instead asked the question she had come here to ask.

'Will you make a divination for me and tell me if you see my father and brothers still amongst the living?'

Tana's sharp eyes fixed upon her, boring into her so hard that Mariata felt as though her gaze was piercing her through like a lance. At last the enad sighed and put aside the leatherwork.

'Come with me.'

In the gloom of the smithy, Tana brewed tea using *tehergelé* and *tinhert* and another herb Mariata did not recognize. She hammered fragments from a loaf of hard sugar and stirred them into the pot. Then she stood and poured it like a man, from a great height, so that the golden liquid fell foaming like a winter waterfall into the

250

glass. 'You must drink a glass from each of three pourings,' she told Mariata sternly. 'The first is as strong as life.' She sat down opposite the girl and pushed the glass across the tray towards her, and Mariata drank it down, savouring the complex taste of the aromatic herbs.

Tana refilled her glass. 'The second is as sweet as love,' and with these words she regarded Mariata almost as if she hated her. Mariata tipped the glass to her lips; and indeed this second pouring did seem to taste more sugared than the first.

'And one final glass—' Tana pushed it towards her and waited.

Mariata took the tea glass up and watched the specks of tea and herb swirl in the amber liquid. It seemed cooler and darker than the previous two glasses: she supposed the tea had brewed for longer in the pot, but when she sipped it she almost choked. She set it down. 'It tastes horrible.'

'You must finish it.' The enad sat back on her heels and regarded Mariata implacably until the girl had drained the glass. Then she smiled as though well satisfied and said, 'The third glass is as bitter as death.'

Mariata felt the aftertaste on her tongue, and wondered for a chilling moment whether the smith had poisoned her, and was not at all reassured to see Tana closing the doorway with a long curtain of leather, and setting a series of gris-gris in the sand at the threshold. Gloom fell throughout the smithy: Mariata sat still, not daring to move, hardly daring to breathe. The light of the fire flared, rendering her strong features suddenly grim and demonic. Then she marked out a space on the floor, smoothing down the sand into a rough square, at each corner of which she set an amulet. At last, the smith went to the pole that supported the roof and looked up. Pale daylight filtered down through the smoke-hole into the room, illuminating a plain leather pouch that hung from a hook overhead. The air around the bag shifted and shimmered; dust motes and ashes danced in the draughts that spiralled up past it and out into the world. They spun and writhed like dervishes so that, for a moment, Mariata thought she was seeing spirits that were trembling on the edge of incarnation, about to spring to life. Something in the tea had made her head swim. The enad reached up, took down the pouch and weighed it in her hands. Something inside chinked.

'What is in the bag?' Mariata asked, trying not to sound too frightened.

Tana tipped some of the contents into her large brown hand. Her thumb played over them, consideringly. Then she held out her hand so that Mariata could see. In her palm were pebbles, water-smoothed, such as you would find on the bed of a river. But out of the water they were dull and unimpressive: Mariata was disappointed, they seemed so ordinary.

The smith dropped them back into the pouch with a clatter. 'Each one contains a spirit,' she said, and watched with satisfaction as Mariata recoiled. 'That's how I chose them: the spirit in each one called to me as I searched along the oued in the dry season. It is too dangerous to select stones when the river is flowing: everyone knows that water is where the spirits meet. They are not so strong when they are dry, but when they are dry I

252

can control them. I will read for you the Roads of Life and the Roads of Death and we will see what we will see.'

She touched Mariata's amulet, tapping it three times, then touched her forehead, her shoulders, feet and hands. Apparently satisfied by whatever protection this afforded, she drew out a handful of the stones from the pouch, tossed them into the air with her left hand and caught some of them again in her right. Some she caught in pairs; others singly. She laid the caught stones out in a vertical line, like the engraved lines of Tifinagh on the boulders outside the encampment: one; a pair; another pair; one. Then she threw another set of pebbles up into the air, caught them and examined the contents, her lips moving as if she were counting. From time to time her eyebrows rose as if she were surprised; or she pursed her mouth, or frowned.

Two pairs and two singles followed in a different configuration. It looked almost random, but with the smith investing the divination with great concentration and attention, Mariata could tell there was a system involved in the selection and display that she simply did not understand.

More stones rose and fell, and the remaining pebbles were laid out alongside the first two lines: three pairs, a single solitary red stone. The smith hissed and made a face: she did not seem best pleased.

'What do you see?' Mariata asked, unable to bear the tension any longer, but Tana shook her head. 'Do not interrupt the spirits while they do their work,' she said sharply.

The final line took shape: two pairs; a single

stone, black this time; a final pair. The enad sat back and regarded her handiwork thoughtfully. She picked up the single red pebble, turned it over and replaced it. Now its upmost side was a dark brown: it seemed less ominous. Or was it more so?

'Your father and brothers walk the Road of Life still, but death trails in their wake,' she said at last. 'Blood will be spilt.'

Mariata did not know what to make of this cryptic pronouncement. 'They are alive?'

'They are.'

The enad ran her hand over the configuration of four lines, making marks with her fingertips in the sand, moving stones around at great speed as if playing some frantic game of strategy such as the old men played sometimes with stones, capturing an enemy line with just two jumps of a pebble. 'Journeys, journeys, journeys,' she said crossly. 'Well, we knew that.' She appeared to be talking to herself. 'From the unknown to the known; from the known to the unknown. A sacrifice; a betrayal; an ineluctable sequence of events.' She picked up a white pebble, examined it closely. 'What are you doing there, on the Road to Death, if you represent new life?' she interrogated it angrily, as if it might somehow find a mouth and respond. Of course, it said nothing. She put it back in its place in the sequence, picked up a black one, frowning. 'The spirit that inhabits this pebble is contrary,' she pronounced. 'It loves to try to lead my divinations astray.'

Mariata waited. Then she asked, 'What does the black one represent?'

Tana sighed. 'Chance. It throws off the entire reading.'

254

'Then they might be dead? My father and brothers?'

'No, no: I see no member of your family dead.' She folded her lips, and added under her breath, 'Just a lot of other people.'

'What?' Mariata leant closer. 'What did you say?'

The enad pushed herself to her feet, threw open the leather doorflap and let the sunlight come streaming in. 'It does not matter. It is already written, and there is nothing I can do to avert it: I cannot see the time or place, just the blood and the eyes. Death is the door through which we all must go; we just pray we do not reach it too soon, *insh'allah.*'

CHAPTER TWENTY

No one seemed to think it at all odd when we turned up at Habiba's house at three in the morning to collect Lallawa for her visit to the desert. Instead there was much smiling and agreement from the crow-women that an early start was a good idea. The old woman was beside herself with joy at the news. She caught Taïb's hands and kissed them over and over, mumbling all the while. I kept hearing the word baraka.

'It means "blessings",' Habiba told me. Our earlier falling-out appeared to have been put aside. She seemed pleased that we were taking Lallawa into the desert; but the uncharitable thought did cross my mind that she was relieved that Taïb and I would not be on our own, that the old lady would be acting as a sort of chaperone, a ghost at our feast. Or maybe she was just happy at the prospect of a break from nursing for a little while.

The crow-women took Taïb away with them to prepare some breakfast and essentials for the journey, but as I turned to follow Habiba caught me by the arm. 'Come help me with Lallawa.'

It took an age to get the old woman dressed, and not simply because of my unfamiliarity with such a process. Lallawa was determined that she be arrayed in her best finery for the journey, and it was this determination that caused the delay. I had thought she would wear the ubiquitous black robe worn by the crow-women: but oh, no. Habiba was dispatched to bring an endless list of items, the old woman clutching her forearm exigently, punctuating each demand with an emphatic finger. The idea of visiting her desert again seemed to have filled her with energy, like a magical fuel.

Left alone with Lallawa, I couldn't think of anything to say to her, since we shared barely a word of language. Instead, I found myself grinning inanely, because she unnerved me so. Suddenly animated, she patted me on the hand and gabbled at me and touched her neck, moving her hand to mime a square. The amulet. I fished it out of my bag, guided it into her fingers and watched as she held it close to her eyes and turned it over and over as if examining every aspect of it. What could she actually see, I wondered? Could she make out the shape of the necklace, or any of the etched markings? Or was she just feeling its dimensions, the glass discs and the raised boss? It did not seem to matter, for the smile she gave me was one of pure joy, and when she handed the amulet back to me, she unerringly cupped my cheek with a gesture of such unwarranted affection that I almost choked.

Habiba returned with an armful of fabric and a bag of other items, and Lallawa gave herself up to our attentions, as compliant as a child. We changed her out of the nightclothes she'd been wearing and Habiba took out a great bundle of dark blue cloth with a faint metallic sheen. 'It's a *tamelhaft*,' she said, folding the fabric lengthwise and draping it around the old woman as I held her up. 'Very traditional; old-fashioned nowadays.' Fastening the result with two big ornamental silver pins at the shoulders, she smoothed out the pleating and stood back. 'Beautiful.'

Lallawa smiled beatifically, then patted one of the silver pieces with pride. 'They're very old,' Habiba told me. 'It's hard to come by such good quality fibulae now.'

More jewellery went on: a pair of heavy silver earrings; dozens of bangles, some as thin as a sliver of light, others sturdy with chunky geometric designs; two heavy strings of cowrie shells; and three small amulets that Habiba pinned at various places on the dress. Last of all came an embroidered shawl, which she draped over the old woman's head.

I was curious about the motifs that were repeated in all of these items. 'So many triangles.'

Habiba laughed. 'The sharp point wards off the evil eye, maybe is even designed to puncture it.'

'How gruesome!'

She shrugged. 'The old folk swear by such things: they say there are evil influences everywhere. Not just the evil eye but also evil

257

spirits—the djenoun.' I must have looked clueless, for she leant towards me. 'You've not heard of the *djinn?*'

I shook my head. Then a thought struck me. 'Unless you mean "genie", like in Aladdin?' And I gave her a swift explanation of the story in the *Arabian Nights* that I'd last read as a child.

She frowned, then laughed. 'Ah, you mean Ala al-Din and the lamp the sorcerous Moor sent him to retrieve in *Alf Layla Wa-Layla*. Yes, your "genie" is a djinn, a great and powerful spirit, though he's rather more biddable than the wicked creatures the old people believe in, which lie constantly in wait to lead the weak and foolish astray, to confound plans and spoil food and addle people's wits. Almost everything Lallawa wears is designed to ward off such spirits: from the dye in her robe to the kohl around her eyes; even the henna on her fingers.' She said something to the old woman, who nodded vigorously and replied at length. 'She says she will need such protection for going into the desert, for the desert is not only her home, but is home also to a legion of evil spirits. She's very glad that you have your own amulet to protect you. But she insists that you wear it.'

'Really?' I took it out of my bag and weighed it in my hand.

'It would please her.'

Reluctantly, I put it around my neck.

Habiba regarded it gravely. 'Good.'

Her scrutiny made me uncomfortable. Swiftly, I changed the subject. 'Now, what about her medications?'

Habiba laughed. 'She won't take anything the doctor gives her, only the herbal remedies the old women make. But lately she's refused to take anything at all.'

'She'll be all right, won't she?' I asked nervously. It struck me suddenly and rather belatedly that taking such a sick old woman into the greatest wilderness on earth might not be such a good idea.

Habiba quickly read the look on my face. 'She'll be fine, *insh'allah*. And if she isn't . . .' She spread her hands. 'Taïb will deal with it: he's very capable. *You* needn't worry.'

I felt suitably chastened, sensing that she had caught me out yet again in my Western selfishness. I was, if I were being truthful, suddenly terrified at being in the proximity of death. But for these people death was ever-present, a part of life, in a way that it simply wasn't for us in the West, where it was hidden away, made distant and clinical and more taboo than it had ever been, as if the idea that we did not control everything in the world would somehow bring the whole shaky façade crashing down around us.

Taïb put his head around the door. He looked as if he had taken a shower: his head was wet and he wore his turban draped loose around his neck, over a T-shirt and jeans that I realized he must have been wearing under the robe that was now bundled under his arm. Seeing Lallawa in her regalia, he beamed. *'T'fulkit,'* he said; and whatever that meant wreathed her face in smiles. Then he looked right at me. His glance brushed the amulet, then returned to my face. 'Beautiful,' he said softly and held my gaze until I looked away. Then he bent and swept up the old woman, just as he had carried me into the hotel; but where I had been stiff and resisting, Lallawa grinned so widely that I could

259

see the back of her throat.

We got her safely stowed in the back seat of the car in a cocoon of blankets, held upright by the seat belt, and I came back for the bag of food and drink the crow-women had put together to sustain us on the journey. At the doorway Habiba gave me a short, fierce hug. 'Thank you for doing this,' she said, her dark eyes intent on mine. 'Thank you. I am sorry I was harsh with you yesterday. This is a good thing you are doing, you and Taïb.' Then she turned, waved and went back into the house.

'*Vous allez bien, madame?*' I asked the old lady, though I knew she couldn't understand me. Her little wrinkled face peered out at me from amidst her headscarf and jewellery: she looked like a gypsy fortune-teller abducted from an end-of-the-pier show. The blanket stirred and out came her hand, as brown as a monkey's paw, and a moment later her thumb came up in the universal gesture of all good things.

We left Tiouada just as the sun came up over the hills, flooding the car with its bright beams. Nothing stirred in the still dawn except for a group of sparrows taking a dust bath by the side of the road; they burst up into the air, their dun wings full of light, which suddenly rendered them golden and magical, little streaks of fire against the azure sky.

I turned to point them out to Lallawa, but her head was already nodding, her folded hands rising and falling rhythmically over the swell of her bosom. 'She's asleep,' I told Taïb softly, and he glanced in the rear-view mirror.

'No need to whisper: she's very deaf.'

'Poor thing. And her eyes too. She's got glaucoma, hasn't she?'

'Cataracts, certainly. A life in the desert sun is harsh on the eyes,' he agreed. 'But she can still see.'

'I thought she was almost blind. I hope this won't be a wasted trip for her.'

'She will see the desert, blind or not,' Taïb said cryptically. 'It's a gift she shares with the People of the Veil.'

'The People of the Veil?'

'The Kel Tagelmust: the people who wear the veil. It's what the desert people call themselves. The term "Tuareg" is not often used.'

'But it's what you said to me when you were talking about your family's roots. You said you were Tuareg.'

He gave an almost imperceptible shrug. 'It's an easy shorthand. Actually it's an Arab coinage. Some say it derives from the region known as the Targa in Libya, since the word for one Tuareg is "Targui"; others that it means "cast out by God" or "those whom God has cursed"; but that's probably because they resisted the Bedouin tribes who invaded from the east in the eighth century bringing Islam with them so fiercely.'

'And the Blue Men? I've heard them called that too.'

'They prized indigo robes and turbans over everything other than their camels: good indigo cloth is hard to come by and very expensive. It's been a form of currency throughout Africa for centuries and to achieve a really good-quality fabric takes a lot of work: the Hausa dye-masters dye the cloth ten times over and then beat it till it acquires a glittering sheen. And the better the quality, the more dye there is in the cloth, and the

261

more of it will come off on the skin, marking the wearer indelibly as Kel Tagelmust. The odd thing is that it does actually protect the skin: it keeps moisture from escaping the body, and the women swear by its cosmetic properties too. So that's what makes them Blue Men.'

'Or Blue Women.' I smiled. 'But Lallawa . . . forgive me . . . Lallawa is much darker of skin than any of the rest of your family. She doesn't bear much resemblance.'

Even in profile, he looked embarrassed. 'She's not exactly . . . of the family, not originally. She's *iklan*.'

'*Iklan?*'

'A slave.'

'A *slave*?' I heard my voice rise an octave.

Taïb sighed. 'Lallawa was bought by Habiba's great-grandfather for cones of salt from traders in the south of Algeria. No one knows exactly where she came from, least of all Lallawa herself: she was no more than a child when she was captured. She was probably a victim of a tribal war in Guinea or the Ivory Coast, taken prisoner along with other members of her tribe by the victors and sold to passing traders. That was during the time when all of our family still lived a desert life, of course, and while Lallawa was young and able. She's been with the family ever since: *iklan* are not treated like slaves in the way you think, but like regular members of the tribe. They shared the same encampment, travelled the same hard road, shared the same food; they chose their own husbands and wives and raised their own children; and when they became old and could no longer work, they were looked after just like the elderly of the tribe. And

262

so when Habiba's father made the decision in the sixties to give up the nomadic life and move to Tiouada, it was quite natural that Lallawa should come with the family. She said she had always wanted her own house, her own animals: it was Habiba's brothers who built her house for her and set up her smallholding, before they went to work in Casablanca. She was sad to leave it, but Habiba said she was just too ill to be left there alone.'

I stared at him, taking all this in. How unimaginable to have been a slave in this day and age, to have been forcibly uprooted from your home and family, to have been carried off and sold like merchandise. It was hard to believe that a woman who had suffered this fate should exist in this, the twenty-first, century; that she should be fast asleep in the back of the car in which I now sat. The concept was impossible to assimilate, let alone justify, no matter how easily Taïb spoke of it. 'And just when did this sort of thing, this slavery, come to an end?' I tried and failed to keep the outrage out of my voice.

After a long pause, Taïb said, 'Well, it varied. The Tuareg are a people without boundaries, so traditionally they have not been subject to any form of central government or law, only to their tribal chiefs and the leaders of a regional drum-group. And you have to remember that much of North and West Africa was until quite recently subject to colonial control, mainly by the French. The colonials largely turned a blind eye towards slavery, simply didn't address the issue. It wasn't until the individual countries won their independence from colonialism in the sixties that slavery was formally prohibited and the Tuareg way of life was dismantled, often violently.'

'And how do you feel about this part of your heritage?' I asked, curious.

He shot me a look. 'How do you feel about *your* heritage? With a French mother and a British father I would imagine you must have your own share of slave-owning forebears.'

This didn't seem entirely fair, but I couldn't think of a useful rebuttal, and so for a while we drove in silence through the dusty vistas, past towers of crumbling rock and dried-up riverbeds bordered by scrubby vegetation and the occasional shocking burst of green oleander or palm. The few scattered settlements we passed were half-hearted affairs: squat, single-storey adobe buildings of the same dull red-brown as the soil out of which they rose. The further south we went, the more rudimentary these hamlets became, the higher the incidence of bare breeze-block, as if no one could raise the optimism or the energy to complete the buildings with render and paint. Man was losing the battle with the natural environment here, his influence losing traction, slipping backwards; for several kilometres we did not even pass another vehicle.

Clouds of dust swirled in the air outside; even with the air conditioning on I could smell it, spicy and musty, clogging the hairs of my nostrils; feel it coating the inside of my mouth and settling heavily at the top of my lungs. Dusty flatlands gave way to a rugged lunar landscape of barren peaks and jagged outcrops of jutting slate, all stabbing at an angle into the hard ground like foundered ships in a sea of rock, bringing to mind, despite the different colour values and environment, the north

Devon coast at Hartland and Sharpnose where I'd climbed one summer and refused, superstitiously, to return to. The area had a grim, forbidding air to it, even on a sunny day. It was a coastline haunted by shipwrecks and drownings, a place that had long been seasoned by death and disaster. I'd had the same sensation there that I had here: that we were intruders in a place where the natural world didn't want us to be, and that it had made itself ugly and unwelcoming in a determined effort to keep us out. I was still turning over this Gothic notion in my mind when Taïb said suddenly, 'Look!'

He brought the car to a halt just in time for me to see an enormously bushy-tailed fox propelling itself in great galvanic bursts of adrenalin-fuelled energy up an almost-sheer rock face, terrified by the noisy thunder of our approach.

I watched it in amazement and admiration: admiration for its flamboyant brush and thick, glossy coat of rust and black; amazement that a thing so vital and beautiful could exist in this dusty cauldron of a place. It seemed a minor miracle of life in the midst of such deadness and I said so to Taïb.

He snorted. 'Of course there are animals here! Did you think that just because you did not see them they did not exist, or that because there are no people to be seen there's no living thing in this zone? This fox lives here because there are rabbits to hunt; the rabbits are here because there are tender plants and good burrows to be had amongst the boulders. Keep watching and you'll see hawks and owls too. And when the sun goes down you'll hear jackals and wild boar. Herds of gazelle pass through these valleys on their way to their grazing

265

grounds in the north. There is life everywhere, as you'll see, even in the depths of the desert.'

'And what sort of fox was that? I've never seen one with such a bushy tail, or with such a dark coat.'

He looked at me oddly. 'It was just a fox,' he said.

A few minutes later a white-tailed black bird jinked low across the ground in front of the car and vanished into the branches of a thorny tree. 'What was that?' I asked.

'The tree's an acacia. The bird? I have no idea.'

'I thought you knew everything about the wild world,' I teased, and watched him bridle.

'Our people don't share the European mania for naming and categorizing,' he chided me. 'You think that just because you can give something a name you know something about it; but if I told you its name, what more would you know about it? Nothing essential about its nature, nothing important at all: just an artificial word some man has randomly attached to the creature that won't make it fly any better or produce more young. It is another form of colonialism, this naming of our world.'

This stung me. 'Look, it wasn't *me* who colonized your wretched country! I didn't even like my French family.' I saw his lips twitch and realized I had just swallowed the bait.

'So, Isabelle, tell me about your family, your childhood.'

'I'd rather not,' I said primly.

'What, you will punish me now for being sharp with you?'

'It's not that. It's just . . . well, there's not much

to say.'

'That's the saddest thing in the world to say about your childhood. Can you really dismiss it so easily?'

'I was a different person then.'

'How can that be? When I look back at who I was at the age of four, then nine, or fifteen, I can see that I am still the same person now as I was then—whether I am walking the streets of Paris or in the Tafraout souq. Nothing has greatly changed who I am. I have just learnt more lessons about life, about other people, and myself. But I hope I haven't lost the essential innocence or joy of the boy I was back then.'

I sat quietly, thinking about this, envying him such simplicity, such clarity in his life. Could I remember my four-year-old self? I could, if I tried, quite clearly—little Izzy, always out in the garden, making things: castles and hides and daisy chains and wormeries and nests for birds who never used them. I smiled, but the memory was tinged with sadness, for I was not that Izzy any more. 'Tell me about your childhood,' I said instead, deflecting the awkward subject. And so we drove through endless wastes of fractured rock and low scarps and black pyramidal hills rising mistily through the dust-filled air, while Lallawa snored softly on the back seat and Taïb told me tales from his youth. How he had been the leader of a band of boys who ran riot through the town, stealing fruit from the orchards, playing war-games amongst the rocks, creeping into the donkey-park on market day and letting loose all the hobbled donkeys, driving them into the hills so that all the poor folk returning with their sacks of shopping from the souq found

267

their transport home to the outlying villages milling around in noisy confusion. How they would run off into the mountains with whatever food they could cadge or steal. It had one day been Taïb's task to bring a chicken as a dare, and so he had sneaked out to where the neighbours kept their livestock and made off with a struggling bird stuffed down inside his robe. How they had got up into the mountains and prepared to butcher the poor thing only to find their only penknife so blunt that even sawing at the chicken's neck caused no harm but a great deal of squawking, and how in the end the chicken had wrestled itself free and gone staggering off into the wilds with its neck at a peculiar angle and its wings shedding feathers as it ran, and they had all laughed so much no one had thought to go after it. 'I like to think it's still out there somewhere,' Taïb said, his black eyes gleaming, 'having founded a dynasty of wrench-necked, rugged mountain chickens.'

On the road signposted to Akka, Lallawa awoke suddenly. I watched her hunch closer to the window and peer out myopically, her hand cupped against the glass and her breath frosting the pane. She said something to Taïb and he pulled the car to a halt and handed me a box of paper tissues with the word 'Beauty' and a coy-looking Arab princess with a beaded headpiece, kohled eyes and a discernible moustache emblazoned across it. 'She needs to . . . you know.'

Lallawa and I managed this pit-stop with a remarkable degree of dignity, despite my injured ankle and her age and infirmity and apparent bulk. In fact, she was very frail beneath the acres of cloth: I could feel the knit and jut of her bones, the slack flesh and wasted muscles in my grasp as I helped her back to the car, and my misgivings began to surface again. I glanced across at Taïb as he made Lallawa comfortable, but he appeared to be sharing some private joke with her and was not looking at me. Seeing him with his eyes downcast and the smile-lines etching his cheeks, with all his attention focused on Lallawa, I realized with a sudden shock how attractive he was—not just physically, with his strong-boned face and tall, spare frame, but in the way he engaged with the old lady: with a genuine warmth and open-heartedness that made my concerns seem petty and selfish.

We drove for another half an hour before Taïb swung the vehicle off the road to a lookout spot, and we gazed out over the edge of a huge escarpment at the most amazing vista. Directly below, a series of oases burst out of the red and dusty ground in vibrant emerald-green; beyond these the landscape flattened out and stretched into infinity: a never-ending blanket of rock and sand spread across the world.

'South of here is the gold mine at Akka, and beyond that, the Sahara.' Taïb shaded his eyes, then added casually, 'The gold mine is one of the biggest in Africa.'

I watched as Lallawa made a face and touched one of her amulets.

'She heard the word "Akka",' Taïb said with a smile, seeing my expression. 'Not so deaf after all. And she knows the legend.'

'The legend?'

'When gold was first found in this part of Morocco, people went crazy. They gave up their

269

wives, their children, just to search for gold; they spent every day and night digging and digging. They were possessed by greed; or by the djenoun. Seeing this, God sent a great flood out across the land, followed by a drought and a plague of locusts, to teach them the value of the things on which life depends. Gold is unlucky, in our culture. Wealth brings nothing but unhappiness, exploitation and death.'

'I'd have thought poverty brings with it a good deal more death and unhappiness than a bit of gold,' I said acidly.

'Men never die for lack of gold,' he said softly. 'But many die in the pursuit of it; and many more are trampled underfoot. In my experience, the rich never become rich by honest means.'

'So what are you doing in Paris, then, rather than staying here and marrying Habiba?' I asked, stung. 'Trading your culture's artefacts, no doubt for hugely inflated prices, to rich clients?'

The look he gave me was so direct that it felt tangible. 'The money I make from trading Tuareg goods goes back into the Tuareg economy. With the proceeds we have established a travelling school so that nomad children can learn the skills they need to negotiate the modern world and pass their knowledge on to their children. They are learning the history of their culture, and passing on the stories they hear from their grandparents, and recording the oral tradition in written form, for posterity. We also fund a travelling doctor who visits the encampments.'

I flushed. 'I'm sorry.'

'And what do you do, Isabelle, when you're not on holiday, falling off mountains?'

270

As I started to explain the nature of being a corporate tax accountant, I found myself gradually overcome with an emotion I had never once associated with my work before: a profound and all- encompassing sense of shame. I had prided myself on my much envied portfolio of blue-chip clients, on my knowledge of tax loopholes and procedures, on my diligence and cunning. As I explained the job I had done for the best part of twenty years to Taïb, I felt progressively disgusted, with myself and with the system in which I had played a part. 'And so, you see, that's what I do,' I said at last, wearily. 'I help fat cats avoid paying the taxes to the government that would make life better for the rest of the population, the money that would pay for more benefits for the poor, and heating for the old, and better hospitals and schools . . .'

'Fat cats?' he interrupted. In the heat of my discourse I'd slipped into franglais, dropping an English phrase in where I didn't know the French equivalent.

'Les gros chats,' I translated, which made him even more confused. I tried to explain further until at last he said, *'Ah, les rats dans un fromage!* The greedy ones who leave nothing for the rest.'

Like rats in cheese. I nodded glumly. Yes, that described them well, those greedy, exploitative, immoral corporations with whom I dealt. I realized that for some time I must have been harbouring a deep-seated resentment of all those sly, complacent businessmen in their Savile Row suits and private-dentist smiles who were disgorged at our offices from sleek, chauffeured limousines; whose carbon footprints were the size of the

271

Arctic; whose faceless global companies were cheerfully mining, drilling up and shipping out Third World countries' mineral resources, and whose social consciences had been clinically excised in a private hospital at birth. All those captains of industry who employed me, for a handsome salary and bonuses that were several hundred times the average national wage, to find all those slippery loopholes in the tax law, of burying their profits in 'research' and other tax-saving devices. I'd only been away from it all for a few weeks, and suddenly I found myself wondering whether I could ever go back to it . . . The realization of this made me feel deeply uncomfortable.

*   *   *

We drove past dusty tarpaulin-covered trucks on and on through kilometres and kilometres of dry, unrelenting scenery, through the ugly modern town of Tata and the checkpoint at Tissint where Taïb spent several fraught minutes in a police hut proving his ownership of the vehicle, showing my passport and his and Lallawa's national identity cards, explaining our route and answering many apparently irrelevant questions. Just before Foum-Zguid, Taïb swung the Touareg off the road on to an unsignposted and unmetalled track. Soon the car was made to prove its mettle as he switched into four-wheel drive to negotiate the boulders and craters. Dust flew everywhere. On we went, juddering over the rutted ground until every tooth in my head was rattling and I was blessing the fact that I was small-breasted and supported by a good

272

underwired bra. I reached back and took Lallawa's hand. *'La bes?'* I asked her, being one of the few phrases I had managed to pick up, and *'La bes,'* she answered, grinning like a loon. *'La bes, la bes.'*

After one particularly violent passage of track I looked at Taïb with some concern. 'Does this go on for long, or is it a shortcut to a better road?'

He shot me a glance. 'Did you think there would be a motorway into the desert?'

'Well, no, but . . .' I felt rather stupid, and shut up.

'Don't worry, I know the piste well, but it's certainly not one for tourists.'

'Do people ever take it and get lost, or break down?'

'Oh, yes,' he said cheerfully. 'All the time. They think the Sahara's some sort of adventure playground. It's good for them to learn it's not.'

'What happens to them, then?'

He kept his eyes trained on the track ahead, but I saw his grin widen wolfishly. 'Have you not seen the bones scattered around?' He pointed out to the left, where a scrubby-looking tree had broken through the crust of rock and compacted sand. At its base lay a scatter of . . .

'Oh . . .' I stared in horror, then realized belatedly I was looking at a fall of sun-bleached sticks.

Taïb laughed silently to himself for several minutes. Chastened, I watched him expertly change through the gear modes, noting despite myself the flex of his muscled forearm, the sleek brown skin beneath the fine curling black hairs, and felt a thoroughly unexpected shiver of pleasure run through me. Normally I hated to be

273

driven, hated to be in someone else's control. What was happening to me? Was it Taïb who was effecting this change in me, with his effortless confidence and capability, a man unfazed, it seemed, by anything, least of all carting a dying woman and a lame foreign tourist into the Sahara; or was there something innate within me that was changing its nature?

I felt abruptly like the landscape through which we passed: in a state of transition, caught between control and powerlessness, civilization and the wilderness; the known and the unknown.

But a moment later my meditation was jolted as I noticed the fuel gauge arrow had slipped into the red. 'Taïb! We're nearly out of fuel!'

He flicked a glance towards me, unmoved by my panic. 'I know.'

'Well, hadn't we better turn around and head back to get some?'

'No need.'

No need? Were we going to run on air; or walk? I stared out into the horrible stony wilderness that now stretched all around us. It was all but featureless in every direction. Behind us the plateau from which we had come rose as a distant blue haze; to either side stone-strewn terrain broken by the odd outcrop of bare rock; ahead, flat, raw ground merging with the pale sky in a shimmer of heat-haze. I stared out across the dead and stony plain, searching for a point of interest, a speck of life, but nothing met my gaze except endless rock and dust. It looked as if a vast sea had millennia ago been rolled back, leaving its bed naked beneath the sun's burning eye. And all the time the needle on the fuel gauge fell lower and lower.

After a time, Taïb took his mobile out of the door's side pocket, pressed in a number and started talking into it. The modern world reached its fingers everywhere, making a mockery of the word 'wilderness'. As a product of such a world I should have found comfort in knowing that help was no more than a phone call away. I thought of stories about climbers in Everest's death zone calling the rescue services; and now it seemed even the Sahara was not impregnable. Something inside me felt hollow with disappointment, as if my one and only experience of the desert was being stolen from me.

At no apparent landmark, Taïb veered the Touareg off the track along which we had been crunching on to a barely discernible piste at right angles to it. Patches of sand started to appear between the endless scattered rocks and stones, and the vegetation became ever more sparse and spiky, trees giving way to tortured-looking shrubs and cacti. The land dipped down into a dry riverbed and then rose and the car spidered up the other side one tyre at a time. As we topped out on the rise I saw in the distance a tiny splash of green shimmering amidst the dun. The more I stared at it the more distant and indistinct it seemed to become, but Taïb aimed the car at it, and after what seemed an interminable time the spreading fronds of date palms showed themselves clearly against the merciless blue of the sky, the water below them a sheet of silver mirror reflecting back a perfect reversed image. In their miraculous shade, Taïb parked the Touareg and we helped Lallawa out. I watched as she steadied herself with one hand against the hot metal of the side panel and sniffed the air, her eyelids pressed tightly closed as if even the blurriest of images might spoil the acuity of her other senses. At last she turned to Taïb. 'Zair Foukani,' she said and his eyebrows shot up in surprise.

'She knows where we are,' he said to me. He looked shaken.

I smiled, nodding. No great mystery to realizing we were at an oasis: we were in the shade and even I could probably smell the water if I tried.

'No, she knows our exact position: she knows the name of the oasis and the direction we take from here to the old trade route, the salt road.'

I felt myself shiver, despite the heat of the day.

CHAPTER TWENTY-ONE

We ate a basic but delicious meal of goat's cheese and bread and almonds and dates, the sort of meal that thousands of travellers must have eaten here beneath the palms for centuries. Shading my eyes against the bright land beyond, I could easily imagine a caravan of camels silhouetted against the pale sky, wending their weary way out of the cauldron of the Sahara, relieved by the proximity of the end of the desert and the promise of shade and water. But it was not camels that appeared on the skyline as we were finishing our picnic, but what looked like an army jeep, the sort you see in black-and-white war movies, its khaki sides pitted and dented and covered in dust. It looked almost as if a part of the desert had grown wheels and was rolling towards us. Should we be concerned? I had read in the guidebook alarming stories about tourists attacked and robbed in the desert, their vehicles stolen, the passengers left for dead. I shot a look at Taïb, but he was on his feet, a little half-smile on his lips. Then he started to loop his turban cloth around his head.

The jeep pulled in beside our vehicle and three men got out. They wore the same odd combination of East and West as Taïb: jeans and shirts topped by turbans; but where Taïb wore his loose around his face, all I could see of these men were their eyes, dark and glittering, out of a narrow slit in the fabric. Were they hiding their identities? I felt myself tense and turned to say something to Taïb, only to find that he now wore his own head-covering in a similar fashion. Two of the men came forward and greetings were exchanged: head nods and a sort of tentative handshake that seemed a mere touching of fingers and palms, very different from the effusive greetings I'd seen in the Berber villages. The third man hung back, keeping his distance. His eyes slid to me, then to Lallawa. He waited for a pause in the conversation, then addressed Taïb loudly and abruptly. Taïb gestured towards me in a dismissive manner—just a tourist—and, as if mollified, the man nodded and turned to take something out of the back of the jeep. By craning my neck I could see that it contained stacks of large olive jerrycans. Three of these were hefted out, money exchanged hands, and the third man counted it carefully while the other two helped Taïb refuel our vehicle. Then polite farewells were made, and the men got back into the jeep and drove away.

'Well, that's the most unusual petrol station I've ever visited,' I said laughingly as we made our own way south from the oasis.

'That's how we do things here,' Taïb said quietly. He had pulled the turban loose so that his nose and chin were visible again. He was smiling.

I looked at him suspiciously. 'Who were those men?'

'It's probably better not to ask.'

I bridled. 'I'd like to know.' A thought occurred to me. 'Smugglers?'

His gaze slid from the road, rested briefly on me, then returned to the route ahead of us. 'If you like.'

'Where the hell do they get the fuel from?'

He shrugged minutely, as if it was a stupid question, hardly worthy of an answer. 'Algeria is one of the world's major producers of oil. There are pipelines everywhere, and huge refineries. A few barrels go missing here and there . . .'

Contraband fuel. Stealing it was probably a crime you'd get shot for in these parts. If they caught you. 'Are we close to Algeria here, then?' I asked after a while.

'We're *in* Algeria.'

'What?' I stared at him in amazement, remembering with a sudden frisson the mention of Abalessa in my father's paper. 'I didn't see any border, no checkpoint or anything.'

'You can't cross legally between Morocco and Algeria. It's been a closed border since '94. In fact, relations have been strained between us ever since the War of the Sands in 1963.'

'Sounds like something out of Tolkien!'

He smiled faintly. 'It probably had a lot more to

278

do with oil than sand. But isn't that always the way? There's no war now, but it's still a tense situation. Both sides try to police the border as best they can, but it's eighteen hundred kilometres long: impossible to patrol without phenomenal manpower and at terrific expense. Both countries try to keep some sort of eye out from their respective army posts with high-powered telescopes and the like, but people slip past them every day: Polisario, *trabandistes*, refugees, nomads.'

'What will they do to us if they find us?' I asked weakly, images of filthy, rat-infested Algerian prison cells forming themselves insidiously in my mind. We hit a bump harder than expected and I yelped.

'Sorry. But look around: this is the desert. It's ridiculous to think anyone can police something as notional as a political line between one country and another in such terrain. How can anyone "own" territory like this? It's a wild place: it belongs to all of us. Might as well put barbed-wire fences across the Atlantic and forbid the fish from crossing them.'

I watched the sand begin to pile up higher and higher around us and wondered just what it was I'd got myself into here. But things were soon to get worse, as the piste all but disappeared. Taïb nipped smartly out of the Touareg and let some air out of each of the tyres, but still we glissaded this way and that as if driving through snow. We passed through a region in which a brittle crust of clay lay upon the surface, poked through here and there by spiky grasses, and then suddenly we crested a rise and found ourselves in a great static sea of dunes, wave

279

upon tawny wave of them stretching away into infinity.

I gasped, it was so beautiful. That was the word that came into my mind. Not empty, or deadly, or terrifying, but beautiful. When you come from a city, emptiness is beautiful. And there was something elegant about the endless replication of all those sweeps and curves and folds. My eyes followed the graceful lines and for some reason I found the panic in my brain receding, soothed by the reiteration of similar forms, by the alternating bands of light and shadow, by the clean delineation between one sharply drawn dune and the next. The repeating patterns distracted me for a moment from the knowledge that amidst all that glorious space desolation and death lay in wait for the unwary and unprepared, and very possibly for us. It seemed quite extraordinary that in the space of barely six hours we should have passed from the relative civilization of the Berber villages, with their houses and shops, schools and tarmacked roads, to this, and I said as much to Taïb.

'Eight hours in a *quat' quat*', but over a week by camel or on foot.'

'No, really?' I whistled. And what a walk it would be, what a feat of endurance, knowledge and determination. And yet we were still only on the northern fringes of the world's greatest desert. It was impossible to imagine how the caravan traders who had crossed the whole desert, bringing gold and ivory, salt and ostrich feathers, had managed to survive in such a place. It was a mighty achievement, by heroically hardy men. Then I remembered that gold and ivory and salt and bird feathers were not their only trade goods, and that they had also brought with them from the sub-Saharan states thousands of slaves.

I turned to look at Lallawa and found her looking right back at me.

'*Bîdd!*' she said suddenly, and Taïb put his foot on the brake and pumped it gently till we slid to a halt. Concerned, he turned and asked Lallawa something and she answered him swiftly. He asked another question and this time the response came back fast and furious. It sounded as if she might be in need of an urgent toilet stop and inwardly I groaned, then chided myself for my selfishness, released my seat belt and opened my door. After the air conditioning the change in temperature was shocking, and within seconds it felt as if the hairs in my nostrils were crisping. The sun was a hammer on my head. I helped Lallawa out into the furnace and winced as I put my weight on my damaged ankle. She stood there, swaying slightly, her face turned up to the sky, her eyes closed and the sunlight glittering on her jewellery and bringing out the oily gleam of the indigo cloth. Then she started to move forward. Immediately, I put an arm around her waist for support, but she batted me away. '*Oho, oho!*'

One foot shuffling in front of the other, the sand riding up in ridges over her leather slippers, she started to walk: not like a blind woman, with her arms out for balance or to ward off obstacles, but like someone trudging through an Antarctic storm, with great difficulty and against all the odds.

I made to go after her, but Taïb caught me by the arm. 'Let her be. She is determined to do this. She will not fall, and even if she does the ground is not hard. Let her do this for herself: she wishes it.'

And so we watched her slow progress from a safe distance until suddenly she sank to her knees. I ran towards her, thinking she had collapsed, but at that moment she started to sing, an ethereal warble that rose into the air like birdsong, and out of nowhere the image of the sun-drenched sparrows came back to me, their dull feathers filled with golden light; the hairs rose on the back of my neck.

The inadan say that all things have their time
The beetles that creep, the bird that flies
The flowers that bloom when the rains come
The female camel whose calving days are done.
My days now are as dark as my nights
The tinad says we begin and end in darkness
In darkness I come to you now, spirits of the wild
You who have waited patiently for me
I have heard you calling me in the night and on
*   the wind.*
The time of butter and dates is now long gone
And my days have become as dark as my nights
The sun has gone down like a fire in the west
The time has come for me to take the azalay,
To follow the long, hard salt road to my rest.

Were these the words of the song, or were they just words I heard in my own head as she sang? To this day I don't know; all I do know is that as the last notes died away, I found that I was gripping my amulet so hard that its edges left red indentations in my palm.

When I looked towards Taïb, I saw there were tears rolling down his cheeks. He made no attempt to stop or hide them: they fell, making dark

282

patches on the folds of the turban beneath his chin, and when I turned back I saw that Lallawa had lain down in the sand.

'What's she doing?' I whispered, but he didn't answer.

Instead he walked over, knelt beside her and took her hand. I heard quiet words exchanged, and then he rose and went past me to the car. When he came back it was with a bundle of white cloth under his arm. He gestured for me to sit down on the sand and then sat down beside me with the white fabric draped over his knee and stared out into space as if waiting for something.

Overhead the sun beat down, the sky becoming almost white with its heat, the sea of sands beneath it a shifting palette of grey. The blood beating in my ears seemed to be the only sound in the world. I picked up a handful of sand, so hot that it burned the tender places where the amulet had left its mark, and let it run through my fingers. A million tiny grains, each one worn down from a boulder, deposited here by desert winds in a mysterious process that had taken millennia. As if time had slowed almost to a stop, I watched each grain fall and merge with the billions beneath it, picked up another handful, let it drain. The action became addictive, obsessive, the repetition somehow necessary to keep the panic I could feel rising inside me safely at bay.

After an unknowable time something snagged my peripheral vision. It was a long-legged black beetle, skittering across the ground like a waterboatman flicking its way across the surface tension of a pond. I watched as it set about climbing a ridge of soft sand, sand that fell away beneath even its balletic feet. Up it went; back down it came. Up, down. I found myself willing it on, as if the power of the thought I trained upon it might make a difference. Eventually, it tried another angle up the ridge, and persistence carried it over the edge and out of sight, leaving behind it only a series of hieroglyphic tracks in the sand.

How long we waited, or how Taïb knew when the waiting was over, I have no idea, but one moment he was sitting as still as a stone and the next he had uncoiled his long limbs, got to his feet and gone to the old woman. He stared down at her for a long moment, saying nothing, and I knew from his stillness that Lallawa was dead.

My heart began to beat hard, but what had I been expecting? Ever since we had left Tiouada this had been the sure and final outcome of our journey, had it not? The twenty-first-century part of me—the Isabelle who worked in the City of London and obeyed the rules imposed upon me there, who wore a professional uniform and turned away from the raw nature of the world—was appalled that I could have allowed such a thing to happen, that I had not demanded that Taïb simply bundle Lallawa back into the car, albeit against her will, and drive her to the nearest hospital. But the old, wild part of me rose up exultant at the old woman's courage and dignity and envied her the serenity of her passing. I walked over to Taïb and looked down at Lallawa's dead body. Her expression was beatific, her eyes closed, her mouth curved up in a smile. Her amulets, necklaces, bracelets and earrings all glinted in the sun.

'Here,' Taïb said. 'Help me undress her.'

I stared at him. 'What?'

284

'We must wash the body.'

I stared around us. Yes, just as I thought: we were in the Sahara. 'There's no water,' I said stupidly.

He sighed. 'Just help me undress her.'

I had never seen, let alone touched, a dead person before. Some squeamish, superstitious part of me was repelled by the very idea, but Taïb fixed me with a stern glare. 'I can't do it on my own, and in our tradition it should be a woman who does this for Lallawa. You're not in London now, you know: you have to stop thinking like a Londoner.'

I swallowed hard. 'OK.'

Together we carefully unwrapped Lallawa from her complex clothing and laid her pieces of jewellery aside. When she was nearly naked, Taïb stood up. 'It would be considered improper for me to continue now, so I will tell you what you must do. I know it is hard for you, but, Isabelle, remember you are doing this for Lallawa, you are honouring her memory and our traditions. First you must rinse the interior of her mouth. I will bring you some water from the car.'

He brought me the two-litre plastic bottle of mineral water he had given me in Tafraout, back there in relative civilization, where it was possible to buy things and no one talked about burying dead slaves in the desert. There was not a lot left; enough, I supposed, to rinse out a dead person's mouth. I took the bottle from him, steeled myself and put my hand gently on the old woman's face. Rigor had not yet set in, and she was still warm, though that might have been from the sun. Touching her did not immediately give me the shock of disgust I had been expecting, but it was not long in coming. I opened her mouth and found myself looking into a toothless cave, the tongue grey and fallen backwards. Trying to close off my imagination, I poured water into her mouth, then shut my eyes and ran my fingers around the inside. It felt alternatively slick and slightly sticky, and there were hard protuberances at intervals like rocks in a sea. At last I tilted her head, and the water ran out and dribbled away into the sand.

'Now wet your hand and wash her face three times.'

I did as I was told. By the third time it was easier. I washed the top of her head, feeling her braids coarse and dry and springy beneath my fingers.

'Now take clean sand and rub it gently over her hands and forearms, her elbows and feet and knees, working always from left to right.'

This took some time, and all the while a little voice in the back of my head kept reminding me that I had my hands on a dead woman's skin, skin of an unfamiliar colour and texture from any other I had touched. I sand-washed the old woman's legs, feeling the muscles move like dough beneath my palms. Her breasts lay deflated and slack against her ribs. I glanced at Taïb. He looked away. 'Yes, you must. And the rest of her too.'

I firmed my jaw and carried out my task without complaint, doing my damnedest to shut down the outraged voice of the woman who rarely touched anyone if she could avoid it, and simply could not understand what was going on. At some point Taïb turned her over and I 'washed' her back and buttocks, and at last he pronounced the job well-enough done and we dressed her again and adorned her with her jewels.

I stood looking down at her. Clothed once more and with her hands folded over her bosom, she looked serene and impressive, and I felt a sudden perverse surge of pride in her, and in myself. Taïb went to the car and came back with a length of white cloth. 'It's her shroud. She asked me to bring it with us.'

'You knew, all along, that she . . .'

He nodded. 'She knew, and so did I. But if I had told you this was the likely outcome it would, I think, have been a more difficult day than it has been, no?'

It was hard to disagree. I helped him wind Lallawa into her shroud until every part of her was covered. Then he turned and walked back to the car and a minute later returned with a spade.

'You're just going to bury her, here, all alone?' It was a stupid question: what else did I think was happening? Why else had I carried out the death rites; and why had we wrapped her in her shroud? Maybe some small part of me had thought that after all this we would carry her back to the Touareg and drive back to civilization.

'Of course. It's what she wanted.'

'But what about the authorities? Don't you have to report her death? Get a death certificate, all that sort of thing? Won't there be an inquiry if she just goes missing?'

He gave me a long and telling look. 'Isabelle, forget London and remember where you are. Lallawa is of the desert, and the desert has taken her back.'

'But she's not "of the desert". She's from another place entirely. She was stolen from there

287

and brought to the desert,' I said mulishly. 'Why would she want to die here? Why would she want to be buried, in the sand, away from everyone she knows? I don't understand. I don't understand anything at all . . .' I gulped, determined not to break down.

Hesitantly he touched my shoulder. 'She knew what she wanted, Isabelle. Why else do you think she decked herself out like a queen? If I have half so peaceful a death when my time comes I'll count myself a lucky man.'

Like a queen . . . The phrase echoed around my head. Like a queen, decked out in jewels and finery, buried in the desert sands. I pushed him away. 'Oh, God.'

'What? Isabelle, what is it?'

'Something . . . something weird. I, I don't know. Ignore me, I'm just a bit upset, that's all.'

He touched the back of his hand to my forehead. 'Touch of sunstroke. I should have thought. Go and sit down in the car, Isabelle, I'll do what's necessary.'

I watched from the front seat of the Touareg as he aligned and dug the grave. By now the sun was dipping. At last I steeled myself, got out of the car and went to help. Together we laid her in the ground and covered her white form with sand. I watched over her as Taïb went in search of stones to top the grave. He brought back seven flat pieces of rock one by one, and reverentially we laid them down on top of her.

'May the earth lie lightly over you, Lallawa,' he said softly.

Solemnly, I took off my amulet and weighed it in my hand, then bent to place it on the grave. 'To keep her safe,' I began to say, but the words were drowned out by the sound of vehicles rumbling across the desert towards us.

Taïb shaded his eyes against the falling sun. Then he caught me by the arm and hauled me upright so roughly that I yelped. 'Go back to the car,' he said. 'Now.'

'Why? Who are they?' The amulet hung from my hand, sunlight flooding the red glass discs.

'Just get back to the car,' he urged fiercely.

But before I could do as he said, two big SUVs pulled up in a cloud of dust, and men in dark clothing and tightly wound turbans clambered out, several of them carrying guns.

'*Merde*,' said Taïb. 'I think we're in trouble.'

CHAPTER TWENTY-TWO

Time passed. The girls practised their dances and their songs. The men went about their business, and no one talked of anything out of the ordinary. Mariata's courses came and went. Life went on as usual. Word was sent, despite her protests, to the Kel Bazgan of the forthcoming marriage, in case her father and brothers rode through after their journey to Bilma. But that was not the only reason. 'I, of all people, understand your reluctance,' Rahma said wearily, 'but, Mariata, you have aunts and cousins there. It is our duty to let them know of the wedding. If we do not, can you imagine how angry they will be, how they will rail against us and accuse us of scandal, even abduction?'

'What about Rhossi? He will still be furious

289

about the camels.'

Rahma firmed her jaw. 'What camels? I know nothing of any camels. Do you see two white meharis amongst the poor beasts of the Kel Teggart?' She shaded her eyes. 'I do not.' She turned to the girl. 'If you want to do this, Mariata, it must be done correctly. The evil eye will fall upon you otherwise, and Amastan has already suffered more than his fair share of bad luck. They will not come: it is too far, too uncomfortable, and they will know better than to expect rich feasting or fine accommodations here. Can you imagine your Aunt Dassine or Moussa's new wives putting up with such conditions?'

It was true: Mariata could not. Even so, she felt nervous about the prospect, and her level of anxiety was not helped when Amastan and a number of the other young men disappeared, ostensibly to the market three days away, to trade goat's milk and cheese, leatherwork and skins, for rice and spice and honey for the wedding. A week passed and still they had not returned; ten days. No one seemed to notice. They polished their silver with sand, shook out their best robes and mended the embroidery; braided one another's hair and rubbed butter into their skin. The betrothal henna on Mariata's hands faded to a pale tracery of brown, as fine as lace, barely visible against the tan of her skin.

Then some of the men came back with the foodstuffs, and with cones of sugar as gifts for the couple. But Amastan was not with them. Neither, she noticed, was Bazu or Azelouane. Bazu was unmarried and his father was away with the azalay; no one seemed concerned that he had not yet returned.

'He's probably courting a girl down in Kidal,' said Tadla, and they all laughed.

'Beggars can't be choosers!'

'But why hasn't Amastan or Azelouane come back?'

They fell quiet. Noura looked at Nofa, who gave an almost imperceptible shake of the head. She was Azelouane's niece. Mariata caught the interchange and felt her heart catch in her chest. 'What?' she said. 'What aren't you telling me?'

Nofa leant over, placed a hand on Mariata's arm. 'It's nothing. Don't concern yourself. Azelouane is not as young as he once was; they're probably taking it easy, taking an extra day or two over the journey.'

Mariata left it at that, but she wasn't convinced. Azelouane might be elderly now, but he was as tough as an acacia tree, weathered by time and wind and habit to withstand even the worst hardships. No: she suspected that Amastan's absence had nothing to do with Azelouane at all, but that he had changed his mind about marrying her, that, as her people said, his liver had lost its fire. That, or something terrible had happened to him. She imagined him thrown by his camel in some rocky defile, blood leaking from his ears and nose. Murdered by bandits; or, worse, in the arms of a woman in another encampment. She knew these were irrational thoughts, but she could not help herself. They stopped her sleeping, stopped her doing anything but the most simple tasks, and even these she spoilt. She invoked Amastan's name when peering into buckets of water drawn from the river, but the water did not give up its secrets. She sent her spirit-form out at night to quest for him on the dream-paths, but to no avail. When she could not sleep, she paced the encampment under the silent stars until the goats sensed her presence and bleated for attention in the hope of an early release or an unexpected feed. One night, when the moon hung as thin and curved in the sky as a dagger, she climbed the hills to the west of the camp right up to the Eagle and the Hare, the two oddly shaped peaks on the horizon, defying the djenoun who might be abroad, and looked out over the landscape for a sign of him. She had no real expectation of finding Amastan, but doing something felt better than doing nothing; there was something bold and invigorating about being outside when the rest of the world slept, no matter how many of the Kel Asuf might also be abroad. So when two mounted figures came into view approaching silently up the col, she was shocked almost to the point of panic.

The riders rode tall and straight, leading a further two camels laden with bundles. They were veiled to the eyes and carried rifles across their backs. She stared and stared. Did the first rider resemble Amastan? At this distance it was impossible to tell. Could one of the others be Bazu or Azelouane? Or were these bandits coming to rob the camp? Whoever they were, they would be upon her position in moments. She should retreat now, run back down the hillside and raise the alarm; but a terrible curiosity had come over her and she knew she could no more turn and leave than fly like an owl. Instead, she slipped into the cold, dark, narrow crevice between two tall boulders and stood there in the chilly darkness with her chest pressed so hard against the rock that she could feel her heart pulsing like a mouse she had trapped there.

As the riders topped out on to the summit, she recognized the leading camel as one of their own: an ugly, piebald Mauretanian that belonged to Bazu ag Akli. Behind it was a big pale animal she thought might be the camel they called Taorka, which Azelouane owned. Bazu and Azelouane. The disappointment made her eyes sting. Where was Amastan?

One of the men said something and she knew the voice as that of the wily old caravanner Azelouane. The riders halted, brought their camels to their knees and dismounted. Together, they brought the third and fourth camels down; and it was only then that she realized the dark shapes on the third animal were not bundles after all but a man: either dead or sorely wounded. A whimper escaped her, but the men were talking and did not hear her. The figure moved, raised its head. Even at this distance, even in these circumstances, Mariata knew Amastan. She was on the point of dashing out of her hiding place when she heard him say, quite distinctly, 'Well, I'm not dead yet,' and the other two men laughed. He looked around. 'It's a fair way from the camp. What if they come—'

'They won't come.'

'You sound sure.'

Azelouane shrugged. 'We can't keep these in the camp. You can't trust people. Their sympathies are suspect or divided. They don't know what they want. It's not like the old days.'

'No one can know,' said Bazu. He sounded

nervous.

'And what do we say about my arm?' Amastan just sounded impatient.

'Don't let anyone see the wound.'

'Even Mariata?'

'Especially Mariata. She is Kel Taitok: Kel Ahaggar. The Hoggar capitulates: it always capitulates. It was auxiliaries from the Hoggar fighting for the French who killed Firhoun when he escaped from the prison in Gao; my father told me this.'

'Azelouane's father fought alongside Kaocen in the great insurrection,' Bazu reminded Amastan.

Mariata shrank back into the shadows. She wanted to leap out and confront them, defend the name of her people against their slurs, but she could not declare herself now: it felt too dangerous. She had a very good idea of what must have happened to Amastan, and what must be in the two large bundles they were taking down from the fourth camel. Puffing with effort, Azelouane and Bazu took down the first bundle and set it on the ground, where it chinked dully. Azelouane straightened up and looked around. At last, he pointed to the crevice where Mariata hid. 'There,' he said. 'Between the Eagle and the Hare.'

Oh no. Mariata risked a last glance at Amastan, who was now at least standing on his own two feet, then pressed herself far into the back of the crack, where no moonlight penetrated to give her away. Bazu and Azelouane brought the first bundle into the mouth of the crevice and she heard it thud down into the sand. With a great heave, Bazu shoved it as far as it would go, until it was stopped by Mariata's shins. Whatever was in the bundle was heavy and hard; when he pushed again she almost lost her balance and fell forward across it, but he seemed satisfied that it was well-enough hidden, for he withdrew. Minutes later they were back with the second bundle, which they threw down on the first, pinning her up to her waist against the rock.

'That should do it,' Azelouane said. 'Let's get down to the encampment. With luck we can attend to the camels and sleep for a few hours before sun-up.'

Their footsteps shuffled in the sand as they retreated. A little while later she heard the camels gurgle with protest and the creak of the wooden saddles as they remounted, and then they were gone and she was alone in the darkness with the contraband.

She shouldn't look, she knew. She should just climb up over whatever was in the dark bundles and run back down to the encampment by another route to the one the riders had taken. She shouldn't look: but she had to. There were numerous tales amongst the People of the Veil about curious women who came to grief for opening up someone else's panniers, jars or boxes. Women who were swallowed by a djinn, changed into a crow; sucked into a no man's land in which there was only the endless howl of wind-borne sand. But, like those women, she couldn't help herself. Stealthily, she scrambled up over the bundles, feeling their hard contents shift under her weight, out into the opening of the crack. There, with the moon shining its thin light over her shoulder, she peeled back the blanket over the lower bundle. Beneath it she found a pile of heavy black canisters, and had no idea what they were.

When she picked one up it rattled, small, heavy objects shifting inside the casing. Frowning, she put it back, then replaced the blanket and investigated the second bundle. Inside was a heap of dense wood-and-metal objects that seemed to absorb the moonlight into their strange dark forms. Mariata picked one up, and recoiled. She knew immediately it was a gun, but it was like no gun she had ever seen. It did not resemble the rifles the men used for hunting, still less the elaborately decorated antique weapons used in the ritual *fantasie*. This was lighter, more complicated and altogether more dangerous-looking. It reminded her of a scorpion. There was writing on the stock, writing that looked a little like Tifinagh, but she could not read it, and that in itself frightened her into putting it down and drawing the blanket over it again.

Guns. Foreign guns. Stolen foreign guns. And a mountain of ammunition.

She sat back on her heels. Insurrection. The great insurrection. Her thoughts raced. Rebels; rebellion. The Free People—the Imazighen—free no longer. The words spun around her head, and she knew that the war Amastan had spoken of had begun, that he was no longer a bystander; and so, by association, neither was she.

CHAPTER TWENTY-THREE

'Where did you go?'

They were lying in their secret place, the hollow between the oleanders down by the river. The frogs were silent now; the water was all but gone, dried up by a sun that burned hotter every day as the earth turned slowly. In her homeland, they would have moved up into the hills by now, where water could still be found in the shady gueltas, or into the lowlands, where the pasturage was irrigated by the harratin who worked for them; but the Kel Teggart were too poor to keep harratin, too weak to stop them deserting to the towns.

Amastan reached up and brushed her hair from her face. Her skin was sticky with sweat as she sat astride him in the darkness, and the mystery of the joining of their two bodies was curtained by the rucked-up fabric of their robes. He ran a finger across her forehead, feeling the ridge of her frown, and considered how they tempted fate every time they did this, making themselves prey to so many evil influences by being out here in the night, without shelter or protection. 'To the market,' he said lightly, pressing the frown away. 'You saw the things we brought back. Think how pretty you will look in the headscarf I bought for you. The shells on it are called cowries: they come from the islands off the coast of the Indian continent, far away to the east. It is said that traders first brought them here in the time of the great pharaohs: imagine that, before the time of Tin Hinan! Who knows, some of these very shells may be even older than your ancestor, older than the Mother of Us All. They've been circulating as currency all these years, from the Maldives to Egypt and through the Great Desert into the hands of the most beautiful girl ever born. What a glorious sight they will be, adorning my bride on our wedding day! They are as white as your teeth, as white as the whites of the eyes that are glaring down at me like stars in the night. How they will gleam!'

Mariata bit her lip. She loved it when he spoke like this, spinning words about an exotic world she would never see, but she would not be distracted. She said again, 'Where did you go? Apart from the market?' And when he did not immediately answer, she squeezed her thighs so that he winced. 'Painful, is it, your arm? How did you do it again? Remind me.'

Amastan narrowed his eyes at her. 'You shouldn't question your husband so. It demeans my honour.'

'You are not my husband yet, Amastan ag Moussa. And I do not believe for one moment that you fell from your camel, you who are such an expert rider.' Pinning his hand beneath her knee, she started to push up the sleeve of his robe, exposing a bandage beneath. He lay there and let her unwrap it, fold by stiff fold, until the crusted dark wound was exposed, the blood rendered black by the starlight. 'And that looks nothing like a wound caused by falling off a camel.'

'I gave my word I would tell you nothing.'

'Because the Kel Ahaggar are traitors?'

Shock stirred him into action. He struggled up on to his elbows, dislodging her. 'Why do you say that?'

'Where did you get the guns, Amastan?'

'I think you must be one of the Kel Asuf. Did you transform yourself into an eagle-owl and glide unseen overhead? Did you send your spirit-self seething up through the rocks in the form of a hyrax? Are you a shape-shifter? Will they open up our tent on the third night of our wedding and find nothing but my chewed-over bones?' He regarded her with wary respect; or was it fear?

'Never mind all that nonsense,' she said impatiently. 'I heard it all; I know what it means. If there is danger coming, as Tana says, I want to be ready for it. The women of the Tuareg have always been as fierce and bold as their menfolk. Teach me to use one of your stolen guns, Amastan, and when the time comes I will prove that the Kel Taitok are neither collaborators nor cowards!'

Amastan looked at her in amazement. Then he laughed. 'Kalashnikovs are not weapons for women! I hardly know how to shoot one myself, though when my arm is healed, Azelouane says he will teach me. But when my arm is healed, if you still wish it, I will teach you how to use a rifle.' He sobered abruptly. 'But, Mariata, I cannot tell you how it is that we came by the guns: it is too dangerous. If the information fell into the wrong hands it would be disastrous, for all of us. Trust me in this one thing, will you?'

She held his gaze steadily. 'I will.'

*   *   *

Mariata felt the tension building in her like a thunderhead as her wedding day drew near. She wanted to have it over and done with, to make her union with Amastan public and blessed, as if the legitimizing of it would ward off the evil influences she felt circling. Her impatience was palpable: her muscles twitched and she could not keep still, even when they draped gorgeous fabrics over her to choose for her marriage robe. 'This indigo cloth came from the market at Kano, and this beautiful

299

green too—see how it shimmers!'

'Green is unlucky,' someone said, and they looked to Mariata for her opinion.

Her thoughts were spinning: it took a while before she realized they were all gazing at her, waiting for her answer. They are enjoying this far more than I am, she thought. What is wrong with me? Most girls would be immersing themselves in every tiny detail of the preparations, living every second of the picking over of embroidery styles and jewelled slippers, of bracelets and earrings and henna patterns, with the knowledge that they would treasure these moments for the rest of their life, would look back on them when their own daughters were married; their granddaughters too . . . But she could not shake off the sense of impending gloom that enveloped her, that made her want to run headlong into her wedding there and then wearing whatever robe she had on, without all this fuss and nonsense. But looking around at the expectant faces, at the eyes brimming with benevolence and delight, it occurred to her that weddings might be more for the benefit of the whole tribe than for the couple who were to be married, that it was an event that brought everyone together in joyful purpose, and that she had better play her part.

'Not the green,' she said at last. 'The indigo is lovely.'

'And very traditional,' Rahma added approvingly.

Mariata caught her eye. Well, why not please her mother-to-be? It was a small and easy gift to give her. 'The indigo, then.'

Now it was veils and slippers and bands of

shimmering embroidery, and strings of beads and belts and brooches: an endless succession of little, but crucial, decisions to be made. People argued over minute details; Mariata felt as if she were in a sort of dream, hovering over them all like a shadowy presence, her mind largely elsewhere.

*   *   *

'More kohl. You need more kohl.'

Mariata squinted critically into the mirror. Her eyes were already startling, the whites contrasting brilliantly with the dark irises and the powdered antimony. They looked huge. 'How can I need more? I've never worn so much in my life.'

Nofa shook her head, tutting. 'It's your wedding: everyone will be talking about you. You will be the target for the *tehot*, the evil eye will be upon you wherever you go, so we must apply as much kohl as possible to turn the malign influences aside.' She twisted the silver wand inside the little pot, removed it again and carefully blew off the excess. 'Now close your lids and let me do my job.'

Mariata did as she was told: there was no point in making a fuss about it. She had already spent five hours the day before having her hair rebraided and being adorned with the henna that would protect her hands and feet, with the other girls squabbling and falling out over the designs to be used. She had long given up trying to have a say in the process: she was too happy, too caught up in the dream of marrying Amastan at last, at last. And the day before that? She almost laughed aloud at the thought of it. Such a strange contrast to all this primping and preening, this world of women. The day before, in the hour after the sun rose, she had been in the hills with him, resting the long barrel of a hunter's rifle along a shoulder of rock, learning how to control her breathing so as not to send the shot wide; how to apply gentle pressure to the trigger, how to anticipate the heavy recoil of the weapon when it fired. By the end of the day she had managed to hit two pieces of wood and a shard of pottery that Amastan had set as targets for her; but a moving object was another matter entirely. She had marvelled at Amastan's speed and skill as he brought down a rock pigeon and then a wild boar they had scared out of the bushes. 'What will you do with it?' she had said, gazing down at the strange creature with its wiry-haired hide and its cloven feet. 'Can we carry it back with us?' She had prodded its haunch with a toe: it felt impressively solid. 'There's a lot of meat on it.'

'Little heathen! Half the tribe won't touch it; more than half. Do you not know that pig is forbidden by Islam?'

'That's a pig?' Mariata had never seen one before. She stared wonderingly at its bristly, curled lip, the sharp tusk protruding.

'A fine boar. Don't worry.' He tapped the side of his nose knowingly. 'It'll get eaten.'

'By jackals!'

Amastan laughed. 'You could call them that.'

In the end he had dragged the carcase into the shelter of the rocks and built a cairn of stones over it to keep the scavengers off. 'Can't afford to pass up good meat like that. Don't worry, it'll be used.' And he scraped a series of symbols on to the rock face over the cave wherein the boar lay.

'Amastan welcomes you to feast,' Mariata read the Tifinagh script, smiling. She thought of it now, and her smile broadened.

'See, she is thinking of the third night already,' Bicha said, elbowing Nofa, whose jogged hand drew a long, black line of kohl almost down to Mariata's nose as a result, making all the women laugh and whistle.

*   *   *

People had been arriving for the celebrations all week, some with gifts; most without. Mariata was surprised: she knew none of them. Amastan, however, seemed to know them all. She watched the way he greeted them: a subtle adjustment of the veil to show his respect, the brushing of palm against palm, a light touch of hand to heart. They were mostly men, dressed not in finery but in plain and dusty robes, and they looked too solemn to be musicians, for all that they carried instruments with them.

'Who are they?' she asked Rahma, but the older woman shrugged.

'He says they are friends.'

Her *tisaghsar*, her bride-gifts, were gathered on a wide blue rug in the centre of the dancing field: a carved wooden box filled with spices from the men of the tribe, a robe and an amber necklace with beads as large as bird-eggs, a bag of rice and another of millet, her own mortar and pestle, a bunch of mountain thyme one of the old women had picked that morning, a whetstone, a bone-handled knife, a newly made waterskin, some pots, a blanket, a reed mat and a pair of chickens; and

303

these joined the bolt of pure white cotton Amastan had brought from the market at Kidal and the intricate silver veil-weight, as long as a hand and as heavy as a comb, that she would wear as a wife.

She came out into the bright midday sun at last in her shimmering blue wedding robe, her face painted with ochre and her lips and eyes blackened with kohl, her hands and feet swirling with bright henna, huge triangular earrings weighing down her earlobes, silver amulets pinned all over her robes for luck, and a dozen bright bangles clinking on her arms, to find the women of the tribe erecting a bridal tent for her a discreet distance from the one she had shared with Rahma. There were at least forty goatskins in it: how they had managed to gather so many hides together and stitch them without her seeing them engaged in this secret work touched her to the core. The Kel Teggart were not a rich tribe and did not have forty goats to spare; and that they would do this for her, an outsider without family, was so startling that she surprised herself by bursting into tears.

Tadla came bustling over, her usually dour face transformed by an indulgent smile. She wrapped Mariata in a warm embrace, with the experience of decades managing not to displace the amulets or damage, any more than the tears already had, Nofa's hours of maquillage. 'There, there, sweet one, do not fret: it is your happy day and we are happy for you. You will bring us all great joy and luck, and strong new blood for our tribe; and you are making my dear friend Rahma a proud and happy woman, is she not, my dear?'

Mariata looked up and there was Rahma, wiping her hands on her robe, the sweat glistening on her

304

forehead from the strenuous business of getting the tent up, grinning from ear to ear. 'Now, you know you cannot enter until you are wed: it is the worst luck. Leave it all to us. We will make it beautiful for you: you will want for nothing. We have woven a new rug for your floor: see—' She waved and called to the other women, and they ran off, returning moments later with a long bundle that was proudly unfurled.

'I chose the colours!' called Noura. 'Don't you love them? The lichen for this wonderful green came from up in the hills: it took ages to gather it, but look, it's the Prophet's own colour. And we used indigo for the blue, no expense spared! And the skins of the wolf-onion for this lovely rich red.'

'And I wove the frogs into the border here,' Leïla said, pointing out the geometric triangles and dots that decorated the edge. She gave Mariata a wink and they all chuckled: frogs were well known for their fertility, and were a good luck symbol too, given that they lived in water.

'Make sure the bed is well positioned on this rug and you will give your husband many fine sons!'

There was a great noise of whooping and cheering and suddenly everyone was running. Rahma took Mariata by the elbow. 'It's the sacrifice: come and watch.'

A bull-calf had been led into the festival grounds and the young men of the tribe now ringed it, clutching their best ceremonial lances. The bracelets glittered on their forearms; the sun beat down. The calf backed away from one side of the circle, found its way barred and ran madly around, rolling its eyes and snorting with fear, its long legs awkward and ungainly.

There had been no bull-calf for Kheddou and Leïla's wedding: the expense was too great. Amastan, by contrast, had travelled and traded for years, amassing a tidy sum. The bride-wealth he had offered for Mariata was handsome too, though there had been no one to whom he could offer it and so the *amghrar* of the tribe, the widower Rhissa ag Zeyk, had taken it in trust until such time as it could be passed into the hands of Mariata's family for safekeeping. If anything were to happen to Amastan, or the marriage was dissolved, the money would help towards the raising of their children.

It was Amastan who stepped out of the circle and into the arena, the indigo of his robe glittering with its metallic sheen, the brim of his tagelmust crowned by a diadem of amulets. The lance he carried was generations old, but its head had been honed to a lethal sharpness. The bull-calf stopped before him, jinked and then spun away across the ground, as if seeing its fate in the shining metal. The circle widened to let it run and it drew to a halt on the opposite side, eyeing the figure that paced towards it balefully.

'Can't the smith just take the beast away and cut its throat?' Mariata asked quietly, clutching Rahma's arm.

The older woman laughed. 'I hardly think a year-old bull-calf is likely to do our boy much damage,' she said; but that had not been Mariata's thought. She had never felt particularly squeamish before over the killing of an animal, for food or for luck, but she was gripped by a deep presentiment of dread and the enad's words came back to her forcefully: 'Blood will be spilt . . .' The calf's blood would be spilt one way or another this day; but suddenly she did not want to see it slaughtered in front of her, no matter how fine the spectacle or traditional the ritual.

'No!' she cried out, and people turned, amazed. 'Killing it like this is a bad omen,' she declared. 'I feel it here—' She pressed a palm against her flank, above her liver, that place in the body from which the deepest and most authentic convictions sprang. They stared at her, and for the first time since she had left the Kel Bazgan she felt a wave of hostility envelop her.

Amastan strode across the festival ground. A few paces away from her he rammed the point of the lance deep into the earth. 'If you do not wish to see the animal killed, I will honour your choice.' He turned to address the crowd. 'As you know, Mariata saved me from the Kel Asuf. She hears the spirits. If she says the slaying of the bull-calf is ill-omened, we should respect her instincts.'

People started to mutter; many touched their amulets. It was one thing not to sacrifice a calf at a wedding for lack of funds; quite another to gather for the deed and not see it done. 'No good will come of this,' one said.

'Women should not interfere in a man's ritual,' said another.

'I think we know who will be the master in this marriage,' said another, which made many laugh.

Amastan shook his head ruefully. 'You may tease me all you like, but I value my bride too much to cause her distress on this auspicious day. There's already a fine sheep roasting for the midday *mechoui*, plenty for all to eat and no need to shed more blood. I hereby pardon the beast's

307

life.' He placed his palm on his heart, bowed his head to Mariata, retrieved the lance and walked away to join his companions, leaving the artisans to deal with catching the bull-calf and returning it to the pens.

Rahma patted Mariata on the shoulder. 'I think we'd better get the music started, don't you?' She nodded to the head musician, and the band quickly gathered their instruments and launched into a rendition of 'The Hunter and the Dove', which soon took people's minds off the disquieting matter of the failed sacrifice.

Tana walked across the festival ground and stood before Mariata. 'Bravely done, little one, though it won't make any difference in the end.' She scanned the girl's robe and accoutrements, her head cocked to one side like an eagle surveying prey. 'You'll do,' she pronounced at last. 'Though I see you persist in wearing that damnable amulet.'

Indeed, Amastan's amulet took pride of place in the middle of Mariata's chest. Tana reached out and tapped it lightly but with enough force for it to press hard against Mariata's breastbone; and abruptly the mechanism flipped open. Holding the little hatch open with a finger, the enad pressed a tiny roll of parchment into the revealed compartment, then closed the central boss back over it. 'For luck,' she said. 'For life. It is the charm I should have made for Amastan when once he requested one of me. Perhaps this time it will serve its purpose. But that is not your wedding gift.'

And then she produced, as if from nowhere, the wonderful fringed leather bag in emerald green, scarlet and blue that Mariata had seen her sewing under the tamarisk. She slid the strap over the girl's head and under her arm, positioning it so that it sat in the small of her back, where it fitted so neatly and comfortably it might have been a part of her, for all that it was heavy with contained objects. Even so, curiosity overcame Mariata: at once she twisted so that the bag swung around and, marvelling at the gorgeous clarity of the colours, at the sunburst motifs and minute stitching, she made to open it.

'It is not to be opened now,' Tana said sternly, repositioning the bag. You will know when you will need it most. You will have a choice to make; two lives to save. Choose wisely, no matter how hard it may be.' Then she smiled, the expression in her fierce old eyes softening, and reached out and stroked Mariata's cheek. 'Take care, little one.' And then she walked away, leaving Mariata staring after her, wondering at the strange-sounding finality of this. But there was no time to be lost on pondering Tana's inscrutable pronouncements, for the marabout had arrived to perform the brief marriage service. Their short vows were exchanged, witnesses spoke for each of them, their hands were placed on the Qur'an, gifts were exchanged and in a surreally short passage of time they were man and wife.

After the formalities of the marabout's blessing, the rest of the day was taken up by all the usual delights of a wedding. There was singing and drum-playing, and the sheep that had been turning on its spit since dawn was eaten with much gusto with dates and spice and bread. Camels were raced, sword-dancers showed off their agility and skill; and then the unwed girls danced the beautiful ritual *guedra*, the blessing dance, wearing their cowrie-shelled headdresses and moving their feet in the economic but precise steps of the dance, until the sun went down and the old folk nodded into a trance, lulled by the gentle repetitiveness of the clapped rhythms, until at last the momentum built to a crescendo, heads rocked and braids snapped wildly like striking snakes. The air was full of baraka—you could feel it all around—a great electric cloud of good luck and benefaction. People were gathering it to themselves, touching each other's hands, touching their own stomach, heart and head. Amulets were kissed, children too, to spread the baraka. The women ululated joyfully. Amastan pressed Mariata's hands to his heart: they were married at last.

The feasting and music went on and on. The men heated their drums over the campfires to tighten the skins in readiness for the faster dances. Older people took another glass of fortifying tea and a handful of dates to keep themselves going into the small hours and went off to gossip in clusters, leaving the young ones to flirt and tease one another without the embarrassment of having the married ones watching over them.

The moon was high overhead when some figures appeared on the horizon of boulders to the east of the camp: a large group of riders mounted on camels. It was one of the musicians, taking a walk into the bushes to relieve himself, who raised the alarm. The drummers stopped in mid-beat; the dancers shifted anxiously from foot to foot. Amastan said something quietly to Bazu, who slipped away into the night. Several others followed him.

'Who can they be?' Mariata asked. In the pale

ochre of her face, her kohl-rimmed eyes looked enormous.

'I do not know,' said Amastan, winding his veil tighter. 'They may be late guests delayed on their journey. Or they may not. Go to our new tent, Mariata. Outside it you will find a sword stuck in the ground to ward away the spirits. Fetch it for me now, will you?'

'They do not look much like spirits to me,' she said dubiously, but she went to do his bidding. The antique sword, its hilt and crosspiece bound with copper wire and decorated with bands of coloured leather, had been lent by Azelouane. Mariata grabbed it up and went running back to the festival ground, with Tana's leather bag bumping against her back and the sword banging against her leg all the way; but Amastan was not where she had left him. Instead, she was alarmed to see him far across the encampment running towards the boulders, his hunting rifle slung across his back. She stood there with the ancient sword in her hands, feeling like a fool; then she ran after him. Other men had fetched guns now and were running too; men she had not seen before, or simply did not recognize in this warlike mode. The riders, undeterred, came closer, until a single shot rang out.

'Who are you?' It was the amghrar who cried out, his old voice as reedy as a woman's.

No answer came back, but perhaps they had not heard him.

'They are djenoun,' someone said. 'We should have slaughtered the bull-calf: the spirits are angry and have come to claim the blood they awaited.'

'Announce yourselves or we will shoot!' Amastan cried more loudly.

One of the cameleers advanced. 'My name is Ousman ag Hamid, of the Kel Ahaggar, and my daughter is Mariata ult Yemma. I come with men of the Kel Bazgan and my sons, Azaz and Baye.'

Mariata gasped. She ran to Amastan's side. 'It's my father, my father and brothers!' She gazed into the darkness, trying to make out the features of the three men she had not seen for so long. Would they be much changed by their treks beneath the desert sun? Did they come in joy, to celebrate their union, or under the duress of familial duty? Anxiety gave way to the sudden euphoria of knowing that it no longer mattered whether they came in blessing or not: she and Amastan were lawfully wed and no one could separate them now.

'Welcome!' she cried. 'Welcome one and all to our wedding feast!'

Word soon spread: people began to laugh, tension dissipated; the musicians were reassembled. Someone was dispatched to slaughter a goat and rekindle the cook-fire, someone else set pots of tea to brewing: the visitors must have travelled far and hard to arrive so late, and there was no easy way across the Tamesna.

The riders were almost upon the festival grounds when one of them rode free of the group, into the jumping light of the fires.

'Before you celebrate any more there is a debt to be settled!' cried a harsh voice.

Mariata stared. Dread clutched at her with its chilly hand. She knew before the firelight fell upon his face that it was Rhossi ag Bahedi.

'This woman is a thief!' Rhossi called loudly. 'She stole two camels from me; but, worse than that, she stole my heart!'

People looked at one another in confusion. Was this a jest, or a serious complaint?

Rhossi drew himself up in his high saddle till he towered over them all. 'Mariata ult Yemma took from me two fine Tibesti camels without prior arrangement; and, as everyone amongst the Bazgan knows, she was betrothed to me. Why she left so precipitously is a mystery now revealed: I see she was stolen away by one of the Kel Teggart. So there is a debt of honour to be paid. I carry the word of the amenokal of the Aïr drum-groups, Moussa ag Iba. He has declared that it is a simple enough matter and does not need to get out of hand. Give me back the camels, and the girl and I will be on my way with no hard feelings.'

It was Ousman who intervened, swerving his camel in front of the speaker. In a low but urgent voice he said, 'You never mentioned a word of this "betrothal" to me before we set off for this gathering.'

'If I had, would you have guided me across the Tamesna?'

The look Mariata's father gave him was answer enough. Rhossi laughed. 'Exactly so. Let us say I omitted that detail. But I did discuss it with my uncle, and as you know he is dying. And you know what that means, for you, and your sister, and nephews, and cousins.'

Ousman gave Rhossi a hard stare until the younger man looked away. Then he said, very quietly but firmly, 'I have travelled a long way to find my daughter, hoping to arrive in time to dissuade her from this wedding. Had you not fallen from your camel as we crossed into the Doum, we should have been here yesterday; had you not

313

complained constantly of the discomfort and the need for rest stop after stop as you eased your sore arse with useless unguents and more saddle-padding than any woman would use, we would have arrived the day before. Now you tell me of some "betrothal", of which I knew nothing. As to the camels, that is a matter easily resolved and hardly worth a trip across the Tamesna. You may represent Moussa in making this claim; you may even be the next chief of the Bazgan; but Mariata is my daughter and if you have any care for her at all, you will let me handle this as is fitting.' He clipped his camel's poll and it obediently went to its knees; he dismounted and strode to where Amastan and Mariata stood together watching silently, Amastan with his rifle in his hand, Mariata with the ancient sword in hers.

A few paces away, Ousman inclined his head. 'Daughter.'

'Father.'

They did not embrace.

'I thought I had left you safe with your Aunt Dassine, but it seems you have taken matters into your own hands. Word reached the Bazgan only a week ago of your impending wedding, and I must say your aunt is much displeased.'

Mariata's jaw jutted. 'There was no safety to be had amongst the Kel Bazgan, Father. I decided to leave them and come here instead.'

'As to the matter of safety, we will come to that later. It does seem that you stole away from the Bazgan like a thief in the night, leaving no word of where you were going; and I gather two camels went missing at the same time. What have you to say to that?'

Mariata folded her lips. 'Now is not the time to talk of such things. I had my reasons, and if you hear them you will be angry, though not with me. Let me say only that you and my brothers and the men you have with you are welcome to join our wedding celebration; but Rhossi ag Bahedi is not welcome here, nor anywhere I am present.'

At this, Amastan's head jerked towards her. 'Rhossi?' His knuckles whitened on the rifle.

Mariata put a hand on his arm. 'Now is not the time.' She turned back to Ousman. 'Father, this is Amastan ag Moussa, who is the amenokal's son and a fine, upstanding man, so I cannot understand why my aunt should be displeased about my choice, apart from the fact that I did not consult her about it. But we did send messengers out across the trade routes to try to make contact with you and my brothers, my nearest kin; no word came back, and so I made my own decision to marry Amastan, as was my right.'

Ousman nodded slowly. 'That was always the old way, I know. But things are changing in our world too quickly for the old ways to adapt. Let me speak plainly, Mariata. I have nothing against the man you have chosen, but I wish you would put off your wedding and come with me: our people are in danger, more so here than elsewhere, and that is why I have come to take you away with me to a place where you will be settled and safe.'

Mariata stared at him. 'Settled?'

'I have taken a new wife. She lives in a town in the Tafilalt, in the south-east of Morocco. I am giving up the desert roads and settling there with her. Her father and I have established a business together. You and your brothers will come with me and make a new and better life.'

'Morocco?' Mariata stared at him in horror, but Amastan took a step forward. 'I understand your concern for your daughter's welfare, but I can assure you her safety is the dearest thing to my heart, now that we are wed.'

'But this is the first night of your wedding?' It was Rhossi who interrupted. He spoke smoothly enough, but the whites of his eyes were bloodshot and his gaze sparked fire.

Amastan acceded that this was indeed the case.

Rhossi turned to Ousman. 'So it is not too late, then; for everyone knows it is only on the third night that a decent marriage can be consummated! Place the safety of your daughter in my hands, sir, and I will guard her life with the whole might of the Aïr when I am chief.'

Ousman shook his head. 'It is a handsome offer, Rhossi, but I am determined that she shall come with me to the Tafilalt.'

'I am going nowhere, Father, without my husband.'

Another man joined them now: the amghrar, Rhissa ag Zeyk. He and Ousman exchanged the proper greetings, and then the chief of the Kel Teggart said, 'These two young people are properly wed, by a marabout and in the eyes of all the tribe. Amastan is a fine man: I have known him for most of his life and can vouch for him.'

'I knew him for twelve years before he came to this rat-hole, and know him as a feeble worm!' burst out Rhossi.

'And you, you were a bully and a coward, as any child of the Bazgan younger or smaller than you were can testify!' Amastan cried.

Rhossi pushed him then, hard in the chest with both hands; Amastan stumbled and almost fell. Mariata jumped between them. 'Stop this! Shame on you, Rhossi ag Bahedi! This is my wedding, a time for celebration. Anyone who does not wish to share in our joy may leave, right now.'

The amghrar smiled, his wily old eyes glittering in the light of the fires, and, though he seemed to address her, his attention was all on Rhossi ag Bahedi. 'We can hardly turn such weary travellers away without offering our hospitality, no matter that we are poorer in material goods than the mighty Kel Bazgan. I think you will find that our encampment is a place of warmth and comfort, especially on this joyful day. Put aside your differences, I beg you. Ousman ag Hamid, your daughter is lawfully married to this man, and of her own free will: be happy for her. Rhossi ag Bahedi, we will talk about your missing camels tomorrow; but I think you will find that we have no fine Tibesti camels in this "rat-hole". We live on the edge of hardship, and our camels are plain and solid working beasts: we are unable to indulge ourselves with rich men's playthings.'

Rhossi drew himself up. 'My camels were not "playthings": I bought them as breeding stock, with the finest Tibesti lineage. The income I have lost from the sale of the bull-calves sired by the stolen stock is incalculable.'

Amastan shrugged. 'Ah, well, if it is incalculable, there is not much we can do to compensate you for their loss, even if they were stolen, which I very much doubt. Most likely you failed to hobble them properly and they wandered away to find a better home where they would not be kicked in a

317

tantrum.'

'You know full well she stole them!' Rhossi raged. 'She may be your wife in name, but she lay with me first!' And while a horrified silence fell at this outrageous claim, he named a truly extortionate sum for the price of the stolen camels, one he knew could never be paid by any except such as the sultans of the ancient Songhai Empire whose palace walls shone with powdered gold, and everyone who heard it gasped. Rhossi surveyed their appalled faces with satisfaction. 'And if you cannot pay that, I will take no compensation for them other than the woman, married or not!'

Mariata could stand it no longer. 'You are mad! First of all, I never lay with you, as well you know: you tried to force me, and that was one very good reason for leaving the Kel Bazgan as swiftly and secretly as I did. Secondly, when I fought back, I caught you a glancing blow in the face and you cried like a baby. Thirdly, we come to the matter of the camels. It is true that I made use of a pair of animals that I knew to be your own; but I took them in payment for your insult towards my honour, and, by my calculation, for that and the second and worse insult you have just added in public you owe me three camels more! Those I took are no longer here: they were sold at the market at Goulemime. I have the money still: they did not fetch much, by your inflated standards. I think perhaps they were not even male, or had perhaps been gelded, at the very least did not function as an entire bull should function. There are many creatures in the world that look very fine and proud of bearing and boast the finest lineage; but they often turn out to be sadly deficient when it comes to the matter of coupling!'

By now a crowd had gathered; someone burst out laughing and soon all the men of the Kel Teggart were jeering. It did not take much for them to dislike one of the Kel Bazgan: Rahma's ill treatment by the Aïr chieftain had been widely regarded as an insult to the whole tribe.

Infuriated, Rhossi caught Mariata by the arm and twisted viciously. 'Tell the truth, you little bitch. You spread your legs for me and loved every minute of it! You came back for it night after night!'

The next moment, Mariata felt her other hand caught in a hard grip, and then the sword was torn from her grasp and there was a wild scuffle and suddenly she was free and Rhossi was on the ground with Amastan astride him, Azelouane's antique blade pressed hard against his throat.

What happened next was sheer confusion. A shot rang out, splitting the night. No one knew what to do, how to react. They stopped what they were doing and stared around, bemused. Was it just a rock shattering, or had a gun gone off by mistake? A second shot whistled through the air and a man cried out; and then there came a vast wave of noise, a terrifying, unbreakable wall of sound as automatic gunfire took over from the single rifle shots. As if in a nightmare, Mariata saw Amastan hurled backwards, spinning suddenly away from Rhossi's chest. The front of his robe— the lovely, costly indigo fabric with its magpie-sheen—now gave back a different quality of glimmer to the moonlight, as a new black patch of wetness spread slowly across it. He lay unmoving on the ground behind Rhossi ag Bahedi, his hands

319

flung back and the useless antique sword relinquished. Against the hard, dark, dusty surface, the palms of his hands were pale and tender-looking, as light and as soft as oleander blossoms.

A woman screamed his name, over and over and over—*Amastan, Amastan, Amastan!*—and the word reverberated through Mariata's head till it sounded like a nonsense word in a child's rhyme, and only after the longest time did she realize it was her own voice she heard, demented and forlorn.

Then it was swallowed by a great barrage of noise—shouting and wailing and the whine and beat of rapid gunfire, and people were falling down all around them, clutching at themselves, shrieking in agony and shock as if blown by a great wind, their arms cartwheeling, feet scrabbling for stability.

Camels bellowed; someone ran past with their clothes on fire; it was Leïla, Mariata saw in horror. And then there was a man—no, many men, scores of them, hundreds it seemed, swarming like ants around the campground, their faces unveiled and bare, open to the night. She propelled herself forward to the space on the ground where Rhossi had been (where was he now? the question whispered at her but she had no answer for it, and did not care) and caught at Amastan's arm. 'Get up! Get up! We are being attacked!' But the arm was limp between her hands. It lay as limp as the lamb she had delivered stillborn from a dying ewe that spring, shockingly limp and loose and clammy, as if it owned no fibre of working will or muscle. Even so, she shook it hysterically. 'Amastan!'

He was just unconscious: she knew it. Lying

there with his eyes tight shut, asleep in the midst of the mayhem. 'Amastan! Get up!' She managed to get an arm beneath his shoulders and tried to heave him upright, but he was so heavy. So heavy! He was a lightly built man, wiry and quick on his feet: how could he be so hard to move? Her wits felt dulled: she could not understand it. 'Amastan!' she bellowed at him, filled with a fury that was now tinged with terror.

Someone caught hold of her and wrenched her away. 'There is nothing you can do for him!'

She dug her heels in and tightened her grip on her husband's sleeve, her fingers as hard as claws, knowing that if she let go now she would never see him again. 'No!' she wailed. 'No!'

The costly indigo cloth held, rooting the struggling figures in a bizarre tableau; then, with a ripping sound that was audible even amidst the chaos, it suddenly tore apart, leaving only a bloody fragment in her hand. Released at last, Mariata was spun around and bodily lifted, slung over a shoulder and borne away.

From her strange inverted vantage point she saw Rhossi ag Bahedi drag her brother Azaz from his camel so that the boy fell in a crumpled heap on the hard ground, saw her enemy scramble up into the saddle and kick the beast viciously till it took to its heels and fled. She saw Baye lean down and haul Azaz on to his mount; and all she could think was that she did not care, though she knew she should, about the fates of others, even if they were her brothers. None of it seemed real, especially seen upside-down. All that did seem real to her was the still figure lying on the ground behind her, dwindling further and further with each step until, no matter how she twisted her head and craned her neck, she could see it no longer.

She saw Tana flung to the ground by one man while another ripped at her robe; saw the amghrar casually cut down by a pair of dark-faced boys. She saw Azelouane stride through the mêlée, a glinting black Kalashnikov grasped in his hands, the fierce grimace of his face lit by the bright flashes of light that issued from its muzzle. She saw kindly Tadla yelling like a demon as a uniformed man tried to slash at the child that hid behind her. Her last sight was of Rahma bravely wielding a flaming branch against the attacker, who turned and almost negligently rested his black, scorpion-like gun upon his hip and calmly shot her in the face with a burst of gunfire that lit up the night air; then, as she spun and fell, another man caught her by her long braids and decapitated her with one exultant stroke of his moon-bright machete.

CHAPTER TWENTY-FOUR

'Who are you and what are you doing here?'

It was the second time the question had been asked: this time it was in French.

Taïb had his hands in the air. The men who had exited the dusty SUVs were turbaned and veiled, their eyes hidden behind gleaming sunglasses; and they were heavily armed. There were seven of them. The man who had spoken—tall and wiry, his skin weathered to a rich, deep brown—had a semi-automatic rifle levelled at Taïb. Another had his weapon trained on me. I had never seen a gun

322

before: not a real, live, deadly gun held by someone who looked as if he knew exactly how to use it and would have no compunction in putting not one but a dozen rounds in me and leaving me to bleed my life into the sand. Curiously, I felt nothing at all about this prospect, neither fear nor anger: just a sort of detached numbness, as if my brain had slipped into some neutral default gear.

'We just came out to see the desert,' Taïb told him. 'My friend is a tourist: English.'

'No one comes out here! You've crossed the border illegally: that's not something a tourist guide would do. Who are you? Show me her passport, and your identity card.'

His air of easy authority, even without the tangible reinforcement of the weapon, was unquestionable. Taïb complied quickly, rooting out my handbag and handing over his own document. The man turned my bag upside-down: pens, make-up, a hairbrush, notebook, ChapStick, wallet, folded papers, passport—they all tumbled to the ground, sending up little puffs of dust.

The man bent and extracted the passport, flicked through it and then tucked it into his shirt. He picked up my wallet and opened it up, grinned at his companions. 'Plenty euros, and some dirham.' He tossed the wallet to another man, who spirited it away into a pocket. I opened my mouth to complain, then thought better of it. Who were these men? Did policemen steal so blatantly? I had heard many tales about police taking bribes, but had thought that was just *baksheesh*, petty corruption. These men didn't look much like police to me, or any other form of officialdom. In fact, they looked a lot more like the guys from

323

whom Taïb had bought his illicit fuel, with their fatigues and desert boots, to say nothing of their studied anonymity.

A third man was walking towards me. He swaggered from the hip, a loose-limbed confident strut. He walked as if he owned the place—if anyone could own the desert. If he had a weapon I could not see it. 'What's all this?' he gestured towards the scuffed mound of sand topped by the seven flat stones. 'What have you buried here?'

I looked at Taïb, not knowing what to say.

The man prodded the ground with his boot, shifting one of the stones.

For some reason it was this action that brought my emotions back to life. 'Don't!' I cried out sharply.

Taïb shouted out in his native tongue and one of the men hit him hard with the butt of his gun so that he fell backwards to the ground, clutching his head. If I had held any hope of these men leaving us alone and going on their way, it disappeared in that moment.

Now the man who appeared to be their leader walked towards me. I felt my pulse begin to race. 'What have you hidden here—drugs? Or guns?' he asked harshly. 'Tell me or we will shoot your guide.'

I was so shocked I laughed. 'Neither!'

From behind me Taïb shouted, 'Tell him, Isabelle: tell him about Lallawa!'

I looked up at the man looming over me, alien and unknowable in his mixture of modern and ancient garb. 'There's the body of an old woman in there,' I said dully. 'She is called Lallawa, a . . . relative of my friend Taïb. She wanted to see the

324

desert for one last time before she died; we brought her here, she died and we buried her. That's all there is to say.'

The man looked at me for a long time, the glinting black sunglasses rendering his regard inhuman and unsettling. 'I have never heard such an absurd tale,' he said contemptuously at last.

'But it's true!'

He said something to his comrade, who dropped to his knees and started to remove the stones from the grave.

'Have you no respect for the dead?' I said angrily.

No one deigned to respond. I watched as they brought shovels from their vehicles and deliberately and methodically started to open up Lallawa's grave.

'Stop! Stop it!' I looked to Taïb; but he was still sitting on the ground by the SUVs with his head between his hands while another man rummaged through the Touareg, tossing blankets, CDs and drums out on to the sand. 'Can't you stop them?'

He raised his head slowly and looked me in the eye. 'Does it look as if I can stop them?' Both his demeanour and his tone told of a sort of flat acceptance of a situation that could be changed only by God.

I thought they would stop when they saw the old woman's body—but no. It took no time at all for them to find the white-shrouded form. The leader bent down and brushed the sand away from the fabric that covered the head, but even that was not enough proof for him: he pulled the white cotton away to uncover the old woman's dead face. Seeing, perhaps, the richness of the jewellery she wore, he drew the shroud further down, revealing the bright amulets and the rings and bracelets on her crossed hands; he knelt there for so long, looking at Lallawa's jewels, that I thought he was about to rob them. But the rest took a step or two back and muttered nervously, touching necklaces hidden beneath their headscarves or making odd warding-off gestures with their hands. With the light fading from the sky, it was an eerie sight. At last, without touching the jewellery, the leader pulled the shroud back over the old woman, then barked something at his men and they knelt and with evident reluctance lifted Lallawa from the resting place she had occupied so briefly and laid her to one side.

I could not take my eyes off Lallawa's body, so casually rendered up to the air again, the pristine white shroud now dirtied with sand, the fabric that Taïb had arranged so carefully to give the old woman her dignity now rumpled and desecrated by their manhandling. I had barely had time to get used to the idea of her death, let alone my part in the upsettingly bizarre al fresco burial; but to see her disinterred like this, in a manner at once casual and respectful, broke something inside me. I wept and wept, hunched over my own amulet, choking out great rasping sobs that seemed to come from far down in the depths of me; dark places I had deliberately left undiscovered and unexplored, sealed up with all their horrible, morbid treasures intact like an ancient pyramid. The tears came as loud and violent and unlooked for as a desert flood. I could not seem to stop them, had lost, it seemed, all control over myself at last. I did not even know why I cried. It may have been for the disrespect shown to the old woman's corpse, for the shock of seeing Taïb clubbed to the ground, for being in the hands of brutal armed men; or it may have been a culmination of the day's whirlwind of emotions. But a crack in a long-shored-up dam finally gave way once and for all.

No one took the least notice of me, which was I suppose a blessing. The men were too involved in searching for whatever they thought might still be in the grave: they just kept digging and digging. Taïb had his head bowed as if in prayer; his guard was smoking, the smoke curling in a thin grey wisp up into the sunset sky.

At last the leader said something and the men set their shovels aside.

'It seems you were telling the truth,' he said grudgingly to me. His French accent was rough, with a sharp African twang to it that spoke of origins far to the south without the smooth polish of precise Moroccan schooling or family visits to France. 'Get up and go back to the car.'

I staggered to my feet. 'What about Lallawa? Are you just going to leave her lying there for the jackals?'

'We are not savages,' he said sharply and gave the order for his men to bury the old woman once more.

I walked slowly back to the Touareg and sat down beside Taïb. The guard who stood over him watched me through slitted eyes. He couldn't have been more than twenty: his skin was fine, almost downy, though there was a deep crease between his brows and another at the corner of his mouth; when he drew deeply on his cigarette I watched his face settle into these lines like a man settling into a

327

couch. He saw me looking at him, and drew his turban up over his mouth again as if I had caught him doing something shameful.

Taïb took my hand in his, and found the amulet nestled there. I saw him frown. 'If I were you, I'd put that on and cover it up,' he said softly, and I did as he suggested. 'Don't be afraid,' he added.

'Who are they? What do they want with us?'

He gave a barely imperceptible shrug. '*Trabandistes*—smugglers. Maybe something more than that. I imagine we will find that out soon enough.' For a man who had been clubbed over the head with a gun butt he looked remarkably relaxed, I thought, though there was a graze and a swelling on his forehead as if he were about to start growing a horn out of it. I touched it gently. 'Are you OK?'

He nodded. '*Alhamdulillah.*' He ran his hand down his face, touching his fingers to his lips and then on down to his chest.

The young man with the gun said softly, '*Salama.*'

I didn't know what to make of this at all. It should have served to make me feel ever more the outsider, the European intruder into an entirely North African drama, but somehow I found the exchange oddly comforting. I turned my head to watch the other men reinterring poor Lallawa and was surprised to see that they were doing so with considerable care, flattening out the bed of the grave with their shovels, smoothing the sand down with their hands, then handling the body as if the old woman still breathed. It was the leader himself who arranged the folds of cotton much as Taïb had done, so that the shroud lay uncreased and taut around Lallawa's form, all the loose edges tucked firmly beneath the corpse. I saw him bow his head and touch his forehead, then his heart. The murmur of words drifted to me on a sudden cool breeze that suddenly blew up off the sands, stirring the men's scarves, and then they filled in the grave and replaced the stones, leaving Lallawa buried better and deeper than Taïb and I had been able to manage. For several moments they all stood around the grave silently as if in thought or prayer, and I found myself thinking what a strangely dignified honour guard they made and that maybe, after all, Lallawa would not have resented the reburial quite as much as I had imagined she might.

It was almost dark by the time the men turned to walk back to the cars. As they approached, Taïb got to his feet and I noticed with some surprise that in the intervening minutes he had rewound his turban so that it covered most of his face, leaving only his eyes visible. The trabandiste leader regarded him quizzically, then said something that made the other men laugh. Taïb stood straighter and responded, his attitude suggesting that he was defending himself. More words were spoken: they seemed less aggressive. I noticed that the guns were all slung over the men's backs and that no weapons were trained on us. Were they going to let us go? I could hardly breathe for fear of disturbing whatever delicate balance might be in the air. Then someone said something and Taïb responded angrily, his words emerging in a shout. I put a hand on his arm, thinking perhaps to quiet him, but he shook it off as if I wasn't there.

'What is it?' I asked fearfully. 'What are they
329

saying?'

It wasn't Taïb that answered me but the trabandiste. 'You will come with us.'

'Come with you where?'

'To our camp.'

'But why? Can't you just let us go? Who are you, anyway?'

Taïb grimaced at me, a clear indication to shut up.

The trabandiste's gaze was enigmatic, as deep and serene as a pool untouched by light. 'Who we are does not concern you. Who you are concerns us much more, Miss Isabelle Treslove-Fawcett.' The way he said it made the words foreign and barely recognizable. 'Get in the car.' He opened the back door of the Touareg.

I hesitated. 'Where is my passport?' It was a ridiculous thing to say: very British and entirely inadequate to the situation. But no one laughed.

The trabandiste tapped his shirt pocket. Then he gestured to Taïb and barked out a demand, and without a word Taïb surrendered the vehicle's keys to him. 'Get in the car, Izzy,' he said quietly. 'There really is no choice.'

CHAPTER TWENTY-FIVE

Four months had passed since the attack on the encampment. Mariata remembered little of the journey from the Adagh to Imteghren: she hardly noticed anything, so focused was she on the pain that burned inside her. As they crossed the Vallée de l'Azaouagh, entered the Tamesna and headed north, she would not eat, but turned her head away from food. She lay at night on a blanket on the ground with her eyes open, staring at the stars, a small scrap of dried, rusty indigo cloth clutched against her heart. Her brothers found her in the same attitude in the mornings, and it made them afraid. They invoked charms against the evil eye, when they thought their father could not see them and cuff them for it. 'If your stepmother catches you acting like an ignorant baggara, she'll throw us all out of the house. We are going to be modern people now, so you'd better start getting used to it.'

(But as they'd crossed the Great Erg and a sandstorm threatened to swallow them, they'd heard him murmuring all manner of charms to appease the djenoun.)

Mariata did not make a good impression on her new family. Wan and limp, with her black eyes as dull as spent coals, she looked as if she might at any moment pass through death's door, and in truth she would have welcomed it. Everything that made her Mariata had been taken out of her: she went through her days as a living corpse, mourning for Amastan, seeking respite in her dreams.

'What are we going to do with her, Ousman?' his new wife nagged him. 'You said she would be a help to me around the house and look after Mama Erquia, but all she does is sit in the courtyard with her face turned to the wall: I can't get her to come into the house. She seems to be afraid of the stairs. Can you believe such nonsense?! Can you imagine how hard it will be for me to find her a good husband if word goes around that she is mad and sickly into the bargain?'

'I've told you before, my daughter is of noble

blood: she's a princess of the Kel Taitok. I didn't bring her here to be married off but to be safe.'

Aicha gave him a sardonic look, one elegantly pencilled eyebrow raised. She was still getting used to this new husband; she did not know how far she could push him yet. But she would have his measure in time.

When he was out at work, setting up the new shop with his sons and her father, Aicha, her grandmother Mama Erquia and her younger sister Hafida would stand over Mariata in the courtyard and torment her, princess or not.

'Get up, you lazy peasant!' the grandmother would cry, eliciting no response.

'She's like one of those flea-bitten mutts that lie around in the market square, sleeping the day away,' Aicha said, curling her lip.

'The ones they round up from time to time and poison around the back of the abattoir to stop the place being overrun with their hideous offspring,' agreed Hafida. Having never before in her life had the luxury of another human being to bully, she threw her discarded date stones at the seated form and laughed when they stuck to the dusty blue of Mariata's robe.

'I wish someone would take this one around the back of the abattoir. Look at her, the filthy creature, littering up my courtyard!' Mama Erquia complained. She had a wizened brown face, withered and toothless, resembling nothing so much as one of the elderly apes kept caged in the market square. 'Nomads: barbarians, the lot of them!'

'But some of the nomad men are very fine,' Hafida demurred, 'very noble and dramatic, all

332

covered up in their indigo veils.' She was jealous of her sister, for Ousman was very handsome and outlandish, with his Tuareg regalia and his desert manners, and her own fiancé was fat and boorish and twice her age.

'It's true: I have few complaints about Ousman,' said Aicha. 'He has quaint ways, and he treats me like a queen. He could wash more often, I suppose. But the women! They walk around the town as brazen as you like with their hair out on show for every man and his son to see, and with the boldest look in their eyes. I've even seen them accost men and talk to them openly in the streets!'

'They are no better than bitches on heat,' Mama Erquia spat. 'They'll lift up their skirts in an alley for anyone. And the men run after them with their cocks up like dogs. They have no morals whatsoever. I have not seen a single one of them at the mosque.'

'That will change with this one, I can assure you,' Aicha told her, eyeing Mariata significantly. 'I have asked Lalla Zohra to visit next week.'

'The *ma'allema*?' Hafida's eyes were round with awe.

'The girl is in need of instruction. She has to be taught to behave like a proper young woman if she is not to bring shame upon us all.'

*   *   *

Lalla Zohra was an enormous besom of a woman, dressed from top to toe in black. She arrived with her copy of the Qur'an in her right hand; in her left was the long switch that she used to rap the hands of girls who did not pay due attention to their lessons, be they embroidery, scripture or moral training. The girls of Imteghren bore the marks of her chastisement—as pale moon-shaped cicatrices on the backs of their hands, or invisibly, as hard little patches of scar-tissue in the soul.

Residual fear of the ma'allema caused Hafida to invent an errand she simply had to run on the other side of town, leaving Aicha alone, and in a worse mood than usual. Nor was her mood set to improve.

'*Salaam aleikum.*' The ma'allema waited but Mariata made no response. She looked back at Aicha. 'Can she not speak?'

'Not in any civilized manner,' Aicha said, and folded her lips primly.

The ma'allema crossed the courtyard. 'Now then, Mariata, my name is Lalla Zohra and I am here to bring you the words of the Prophet and the light of Allah, so that you may make your peace with him and with your family and behave as you should. Peace be with you.'

The black eyes lifted and glared at the old woman fiercely, full of defiance and despair.

The ma'allema had seen everything in her long life: she was not to be put off by such a show of silent insolence. 'When your elders and betters greet you, my girl, you had best remember your manners,' she said sternly. 'Let's try again. *Salaam aleikum*, Mariata. Come along, after me: *wahai aleikum es salaam.*' Again she waited, but the returning silence was freighted with hostility.

There was a sudden blur of movement and a whistling sound; then the switch landed with an audible snap. Mariata made a sound in the back of her throat like a wolf at bay. Like a wolf, she bared

334

her teeth at the ma'allema.

Lalla Zohra grabbed hold of Mariata's hand and turned it towards Aicha. 'Have you seen the state of her? Shame on you, Aicha Saari. Have you and your sister not impressed on her the need for cleanliness in a proper Muslim house?'

'How can I get her clean? She will not even enter the house,' Aicha said crossly. 'She has only ever lived in tents and is afraid of the roof, and of the stairs.'

'Just because someone behaves like a savage does not mean you should allow them to continue to do so. It is your responsibility—as a good Muslim woman and as this poor girl's new mother—to educate her in the ways of polite, God-fearing folk.'

'Mother! She is barely younger than my sister! I say if she is determined to live like a beast, I shall treat her as such.'

The ma'allema's eyes flashed. She stood foursquare with her hands on her capacious hips. 'The Prophet teaches that whoever is kind to the creatures of God is kind unto himself; and that a good deed done to a beast is as good as doing good to a human being; while an act of cruelty to a beast is as bad as an act of cruelty to a human being. I remember teaching you these *hadiths* myself. But, quite apart from that, I beat into all my students the importance of cleanliness. *Taharah*, Aicha. *Taharah!* Shame on you. Allah loves those who turn to Him constantly and He loves those who keep themselves pure and clean. How could you possibly let her get into such a filthy condition? Now, go and fetch towels and scrubbing cloths and soap. We are going to take her to the *hammam!*'

$$* \qquad * \qquad *$$

Mariata walked sullenly between her two captors from the house to the hammam, relieved at least to be outside. Imteghren was an uninspiring town, drab and dusty. Sand filled its streets and clogged the air. Impossible to believe now that once it had formed part of the great medieval trading town of Sijilmassa, into whose markets ebony, ivory, spices, oils, perfumes, slaves and all the golden treasures of the Songhai Empire had flowed on their way to Marrakech, Meknes and Fez, to the ports of the Mediterranean and the kingdoms of the north. Now, the entire place smelt of goat shit, cooking oil and diesel fumes. Mariata stared at the unfamiliar vehicles grinding their way through the crowded roads with their belching black fumes and grumbling engines and clutched her amulet. Scrawny sheep and goats wandered at will between piles of kitchen waste on the street corners; feral dogs lay in heaps in the shade; wild cats slipped out of the shadows when the dogs weren't looking and snatched scraps from the bins. There were people everywhere: hugely fat women in enveloping robes and veils, swathed from head to toe despite the sweltering heat; thin men in striped robes and yellow sandals, their faces naked to view. To Mariata, they looked stupid and weak, more like boys than grown men. Even the men who had grown beards to cover their faces looked bizarre to her, as if they had been surprised halfway through eating a black sheep. She stared at the men insolently, and they gazed back and smiled with their big, wet mouths and greedy eyes, until she turned her face away, shuddering.

The ancient fortress walls that surrounded the town were pitted with shot from bygone wars, but Mariata could not imagine why anyone would want to take the town or, indeed, defend it. Let the desert swallow it, she thought. Let the desert swallow them all. She did not want to live.

The bathhouse was in the middle of the town, past the souq and the artisan stalls, in the shadow of the tall minaret of the central mosque.

'Off with your clothes!' Lalla Zohra commanded her as soon as they entered the changing room. 'Every stitch—come along.'

Mariata folded her arms and glared. Well versed in all manner of defiant behaviour, the ma'allema beckoned for the bathhouse manager to join her. If Lalla Zohra was a big woman, Khadija Chafni was huge: twice as wide in hip and chest, her wiry hair confined under a coloured cloth and every tooth in her head jutting at a different angle. Taking the desert girl by surprise, they managed to flip the fringed leather bag Tana had made for Mariata over her head, and together wrestled off her robe while Aicha stood aside and watched with a strange little half-smile on her face. Removing the amulet was more of a struggle. By the time they managed to take it from her all three were red and sweating.

'Little heathen!' Lalla Zohra declared, examining a long rip in her *djellaba*.

Aicha, unscathed, swung the talisman from its beaded string. Even in the gloom of the changing room, the red carnelian in the amulet winked with a wicked light. 'I wonder how much Ali would give me for this,' she mused. 'It's solid silver, I do

337

believe.'

Zohra wagged a finger. 'The necklace belongs to the girl, for all her beastly behaviour. And you know what the Holy Qur'an has to say about stealing and thieves.'

Aicha pouted; then she stashed the jewel in the pocket of her own robe along with her own jewellery, 'to keep it safe'. She calmly removed the robe and hung it on her usual peg, while Zohra and Khadija Chafni each took turns to hold Mariata by the arms while the other disrobed. Mariata stared at the three of them in disbelief. She had never seen a woman wholly naked before.

'Come with me, darling girl,' said Khadija Chafni. 'We'll get you so clean it'll be like having a whole new skin.' She turned to Zohra. 'My, but this one smells bad: where did you find her, sleeping in the *funduq* with the camels?'

'Close enough. She's from one of the desert tribes,' Aicha said, sneering. 'A Tuareg princess, or so they say.'

Khadija shook her head and clicked her odd teeth. 'Ah, these desert girls. They never wash: some are even afraid of water. They say there are djenoun in the buckets, can you imagine? The noise they make, it's terrible. Anyone would think it was a torture to be clean, rather than a pleasure.'

'And a duty,' Lalla Zohra reminded sternly. 'A sacred duty.'

They dragged her, stiff-limbed and resisting, into the hot room. There, the noise was raucous, trapped by the shining tiles and stone floor. Mariata stared about her, horrified. Everywhere she looked she glimpsed bare flesh, gleaming with sweat and water, black hair running in rivers down backs and breasts. It was strange to realize that these must be the same women she saw in the town, swathed from top to toe, some with only their eyes visible, who were now brazenly naked in each other's company, blatantly displaying even their most private parts, which she could not help but notice had been stripped of every body-hair. Amongst her own people, although the women walked bare-headed and wore no veil, such unreserved immodesty would be regarded as scandalous.

She was still gaping when Aicha suddenly upended a bucket of steaming water over her head. Gulping for air, Mariata slapped at her and then screamed in horror with all the force of her lungs. As the hammam manager began to apply the thick black soap that had been rendered down from olive pulp and clay, she batted away the woman's huge, invasive hands.

'Stop behaving like a child!' Lalla Zohra growled, imprisoning Mariata's wrists.

'I'm a grown woman: leave me alone!' Mariata's eyes burned with outrage.

It was the first thing any of them had heard her say. For a moment, amazed, they relented in their attentions. Then Lalla Zohra said, 'If you want us to treat you like an adult, you must behave as one. Here, take this and clean yourself. Thoroughly.' She passed Mariata a handful of soap.

Mariata rubbed the black stuff dubiously on to one arm. It felt disgusting, as slippery as frogspawn. How could something so black and foul possibly make you clean? It defied all logic.

'Now rub hard!' Zohra gave her a square of cloth formed of knotted string and watched as

Mariata swept it gingerly over the soaped surfaces. 'Harder!'

'Like this.' Khadija placed her vast hand over Mariata's and applied pressure, rubbing up and down till the skin felt raw. 'You see?' she beamed. 'The dirt is coming off. Look!' She turned and beckoned the women of Imteghren. 'Look! Have you ever seen such filth? See, it is coming off in great rolls of black. Underneath it the child will be as white as an Arab!'

They all laughed and peered, happy at last for their curiosity to be licensed.

Mariata glared at them. 'What are you gawping at? Don't look at me: look at yourselves, all soft and pale and fat as grubs!' She prodded one woman with a considerable belly who had got too close, then bared her teeth at them all and laughed as they drew back into the steam. 'What, afraid I may bite you? Isn't that what the desert people do, the Kel Asuf? Yes, I am one of the People of the Wilderness now, and proud of it!' And with that, she ran from the steam room, grabbed Aicha's robe, her own robe and the fringed bag, and without bothering to dry herself dressed and fled the hammam at a run, her long black braids slapping like wet eels down her back.

*   *   *

It was Ousman who found her as the sun dipped, on the road south, heading for Erfoud and the Sahara beyond. Drawing up beside her camel in a battered jeep, he wound down the dusty window. 'What are you thinking of?'

'I will not stay amongst these people.'

340

'And where did you think you were going?'

'Into the desert.'

'Without supplies?'

'I have water,' she said mulishly, indicating an ancient goatskin *gerber* slung across her back. 'And food.' A sack of stale bread. 'Besides'—she tossed her head and her silver amulet flashed in the failing light—'I do not care any more whether I live or die; but, whichever it is to be, it will not be in this disgusting place.'

Ousman got out of the vehicle and walked slowly around the camel. It was a Mauretanian, big and brown and mangy-looking. He punched its flaccid hump and felt its ribs; then caught hold of its halter and expertly manipulated its lip until its vast and filthy teeth were exposed. The camel bellowed its disapproval at this undignified treatment. Ousman looked it in the eye and it subsided; but when he moved around its shoulder to examine the hide on the back of its neck, its head swung round menacingly, lips curled, to bite. Without looking, Ousman reached back and swiped it smartly across the muzzle, making it gurgle in surprise. He looked up at Mariata, shaking his head. 'Daughter, if you will run away into the desert, at least do so on an animal that does not bring shame to the reputation of the People of the Veil. Its teeth are rotten, its fat-stores diminished, its neck worn bald by riding. It has to be nine years old if it's a day. Who sold you this walking bone-bag?'

Mariata eyed him almost as sullenly as the camel. 'The one-eyed man.'

Ousman shook his head. 'That charlatan! Everyone knows that any camel left at the end of the market is fit only for the pot. What did you give him for it?'

She would not say. Ousman thwacked the beast till it went to its knees, then manhandled his daughter, kicking and shouting, into the jeep. He tied the camel's halter to the back bumper and drove slowly, very slowly, back to Imteghren with the windows up so that Mariata could not escape.

At the house Mariata was confined against her will in a room with an iron grille across its single small window. She heard the key turn in the lock; and running to look out saw her father leave the house with a purposeful stride and the camel in tow. He did not return until the muezzin called the faithful to fifth prayer, without the camel.

Hushed conversation turned to raised voices in the next room. Mariata pressed her ear to the door.

'That hussy!' Aicha's voice was shrill and indignant. 'She did it to spite me. That jewellery was your wedding gift to me, and she knew it. And she left me naked but for my underthings at the hammam. The shame of it! I was forced to borrow Khadija Chafni's djellaba, and now I will owe that great sow a favour that she will take great pleasure in extracting. Ugh. The little bitch, she will rue the day . . .'

Ousman's response was low and even-tempered, too low for Mariata to catch. Even so, she smiled, for the first time since Amastan had died.

CHAPTER TWENTY-SIX

For stealing her stepmother's jewellery, only half of which Ousman had managed to get back from the one-eyed camel trader, Mariata was punished in small ways each and every day. Lalla Zohra came in the mornings to read the Qur'an at her; but after initial resistance Mariata surprised herself by enjoying the stories it contained. Some even made her think about things other than the massacre at the village and the void of loneliness inside her. Almost as if Aicha intuited that this punishment was not sufficiently painful to Mariata, she sent chores at her thick and fast. Mariata was to clean and sweep and wash every item of clothing and every piece of fabric in the house until her knuckles were raw and red and her back ached to the marrow. She washed every item of clothing in the house, or so it seemed: garments that had never before seen the light of day. When she had done that, Aicha brought her armfuls of rugs and blankets, couch covers and cushions, dishrags and dusters and teacloths, and Mariata washed and beat them all, carrying out her tasks mindlessly, in a sort of haze. Physical movement of any kind provided some sort of release from the blackness inside her; and it stopped Aicha's incessant nagging.

Her brother Azaz found her one day in the courtyard bent over a new tub of washing, spitting with fury over the stinging detergent. He watched as she rinsed and wrung out a huge white item and draped it, dripping, over the line.

'What in the world is this?' He took it down and held it up against himself: it was twice his size.

'Mama Erquia's bloomers,' Mariata told him with a sigh. 'She wears them underneath her robe. They do that here, you know.'

Azaz hadn't had the chance to find out such information yet: the girls in Imteghren seemed to want nothing to do with him, had wailed and flapped him away when he tried to court them. They weren't like desert girls at all. He made a face and swiftly slung the bloomers back over the washing line. 'That old witch! Why are you washing her filthy underthings? You're Kel Taitok, it's insulting!'

Mariata gave him a small, exhausted smile. 'You think I don't know that?'

'I'm going to tell Father: they can't treat you like this!'

She looked away. 'It won't do any good.'

But while Aicha and Hafida were out of the house one day and their poisonous grandmother was snoring in her room, Mariata sought out her father. 'They are treating me like a slave,' she said wearily, showing him her cracked and reddened hands.

Ousman looked away, awkward. 'The way of life here in Morocco is different from ours: there are no slaves in this community. Here, everyone has to do their own "work".' For this concept, he used a word unfamiliar to Mariata; in Tamacheq there was no such verb.

'Aicha and Hafida do nothing!'

'They cook, and they cook well—even you have put a little more meat on your bones.'

They had tried to make Mariata cook. It had

344

been an experiment that lasted only a single day.

'I hate them, and I hate their food!' She caught him by the arm. 'Let me go home, Father, back to the Hoggar. I will go with whatever caravan comes through Imteghren; I will have no pride. They can pack me up with the merchandise for all I care: just let me go.'

But he was adamant. 'You will stay. The old way is dying out and we have to adapt to change. Besides, the conflict between Morocco and Algeria means that there are no caravans coming through Imteghren now; there are soldiers enforcing the border.'

'What do I care about their borders and boundaries? We're the People of the Veil. We have no boundaries: our country is wherever we wish it to be, we carry our territory within ourselves.' How many times had she heard Amastan say these things? Her eyes filled with tears. 'How can you bear this dull, settled life, amongst these awful people?'

Her father's jaw set: she could see he would not shift on this matter. And she knew why. Every night, even from the other side of the house, she heard his groans of pleasure and the shrill, birdlike cries of his new wife. It brought back unwelcome memories of her life with Amastan, of the life that had been so brutally wrenched from her. Night after night she dreamt of lying with him down by the river, of how his skin felt beneath the palms of her hands: warm and smooth, the muscles bunching and shifting under her touch, and she would wake with tears still wet on her face and a dull, deep ache in her belly.

Then her father and brothers went on a buying

trip to fetch supplies for the new shop in Marrakech, and Mariata found herself fully at Aicha's mercy. With no one to intervene, Aicha treated her with sneering disdain, observing her as she went about her tasks, making comments all the while to her sister.

'See how clumsy she is with the dishes, Hafida. In the desert they eat off stones. Even she couldn't break those.'

'Are those rat-tails growing out of her head, do you think? Perhaps she has a rat's nest for a brain.'

'It does not look much like hair to me, sister.'

'And that great piece of tin she wears around her neck: I have never seen a necklace so badly made. Poor thing, she probably thinks it is worth something.'

'I expect she thinks a spirit lives in it: an afrit or a djinn!'

'They are a backward people, the nomads, old-fashioned and barbaric. What do they know of the modern world? They don't even have houses, Hafida: can you imagine? They live in houses made of goatskins, with their goats.'

'That will be why she smells as she does.'

'Don't worry, sister, it's her bath-day tomorrow.'

'Imagine living without electricity or running water.' The sisters were very proud to inhabit one of the first houses in the town to own such amenities.

'No showers.'

'No cars.'

'No market, and only one smelly old dress.'

'Did her father lie with a goat to get her, do you think?'

There was a pause, and a slap, followed by a cry,

and then Aicha said icily, 'Do not speak of my husband so.'

*　　　*　　　*

The next day at the hammam Aicha regarded Mariata critically as she got undressed. 'You've put on weight, daughter. It suits you.'

'My mother was a Tuareg princess, and she is dead,' Mariata replied sullenly. 'Do not call me daughter.'

Aicha shrugged. 'Like it or not, I stand in place of a mother to you now.' She put her head on one side and looked Mariata up and down. Then a line appeared between her brows. She turned to her sister. 'Take hold of her, Hafida.'

'Why?'

'Don't question me, just do as I say.'

Obediently, Hafida took Mariata by the arms. Aicha walked around Mariata, scrutinizing. She frowned as she took in the girl's fuller breasts and rounded contours. 'When was your last period?' she asked sharply.

Mariata stared at her dully. 'What?'

'Your period. Your monthly bleed.'

Mariata flushed to the roots of her hair. 'It is none of your business.'

Aicha was not to be put off. 'I am your stepmother and you will answer me. So think: when was it?'

Silence. Mariata thought about the question, for her own benefit. She could not remember the last time she had bled. Not since leaving the Adagh, that much was certain. She had not given it a thought: there had been too much else to think

347

about, to mourn. But now that Aicha had called her attention to it, she turned her mind inward to examine herself as she had not done in a long, long time; and then she knew. Just like that, she *knew*. The realization was world-changing, immense. A spark of warmth flickered in the core of her, flowing up from her belly and around her ribs, engulfing her heart until she felt as if she were on fire—on fire with hope. *Amastan, oh, Amastan . . .*

She must have smiled to herself, because when she focused on Aicha again, the older woman was staring at her in rising fury. Gathering herself, she said, 'I really have no idea.'

'Insolent brat!' Aicha took her by the upper arms and shook her till her head flopped this way and that. 'Think, damn you! Think. When did you bleed? You have been here for three months now: have you not bled during all that time? Are you ill? You don't look ill.' She thrust her face aggressively at Mariata. 'Have you somehow managed to sneak out of the house and sell yourself to men?'

The whites of Mariata's eyes showed all around her dark pupils. Unable to fight free of Hafida, she spat at Aicha, who slapped her hard across the face, so hard that the sound ricocheted off the tiles.

Mariata's shriek of rage drew Khadija Chafni from the hammam's antechamber. 'What is going on here? Are you having trouble with the Tuareg girl again? People will talk!'

'They certainly will.' Aicha shoved Mariata's robe at her. 'Put that on: we're going home before anyone guesses your shame.'

But Mariata felt no shame: only a glorious, rising triumph.

Back within the safe walls of the house, Aicha was inexorable. She consulted feverishly with Mama Erquia, as the resident expert on such matters, and the old woman sent a boy and a donkey to fetch a healer from an outlying village. It took several long hours for this person to arrive, by which time Aicha had worked herself into a froth of rage and Mariata had settled herself comfortably in the knowledge of her changed state.

The healer was not from Imteghren but was of the Aït Khabbash, a semi-nomadic tribe living on the fringe of the desert. She wore a blue robe pinned with huge silver fibulae and had a sigil tattooed uncompromisingly on her forehead: two diagonal lines crossing at the top with a triangle of three dots seated above the intersection. A huge, colourful scarf enveloped her head and draped down her back. Ushered into the room in which Mariata had been shut, she removed this with a flourish.

After a few minutes of prodding the healer declared the Tuareg girl four months pregnant; maybe more. Aicha paled. Her hands flew to her mouth. 'Oh my God,' she muttered. 'My God, what will we do? Such shame it will bring down on us all. It will destroy our reputation.' She turned to the healing woman. 'What can you do about it?'

The Aït Khabbashi considered Mariata with her head on one side, her eye as bright as a bird's. 'I can attend the birth when it comes.'

Aicha glared at her. 'No, no, you've misunderstood. I want you to get rid of it.'

349

'No one is getting rid of my baby,' Mariata said quietly, but nobody paid her any attention.

The healer regarded Aicha steadily. 'She's too far along for me to do anything other than that.' Out of Aicha's sight, the woman looked Mariata briefly in the eye. One lid dropped swiftly, then she turned back to Aicha. 'I'm afraid I can't help you.'

Aicha let out a wail. 'Are you quite sure?'

'Quite sure. I'm sorry.'

'A lot of use you are as a healer, you old charlatan!'

The Aït Khabbashi shook her head in mock sadness. 'What will people say when I tell them? Great goodness, they'll be surprised to hear the Tuareg's daughter will be beating you to the first birth in this house.' She rubbed her hands in glee.

Aicha pursed her lips. Then she took off one of her gold bangles and thrust it at the woman. 'Take that and stop your mouth. If I hear one whisper of this I will send someone to come and find you. In the night. Do you hear me?'

The healer regarded her with loathing. Then she turned to Mariata and said something to her in the old language. Mariata caught her hands and kissed them, smiling, then kissed her own hands and pressed them to her heart. 'Thank you,' she replied in the same tongue. 'Thank you.'

'Get out!' Aicha caught the healer by the arm, digging her nails in hard, and propelled her towards the door.

The woman did not flinch. At the door she disengaged herself from Aicha's grip and made a complicated gesture in the air, chanting as she did so. 'And that is no more than you deserve!'

*   *   *

The next day they found strange symbols chalked on the door. When she saw them, Mama Erquia almost swooned in horror. She subsided against the door with her head in her hands. '*Sehura*,' she kept saying, '*sehura, sehura* . . . It is my fault: I knew she was a sorceress. I have brought woe upon our house!' and no one could get anything more out of her for the rest of the morning. Mariata noticed when they went to the souq to buy vegetables that people who had most likely passed their door on the way regarded them curiously and no one greeted Aicha with their usual warmth, keeping their distance as if she carried some contagious disease.

By the time they got back to the house, Aicha was in a foul temper. She marched into the old woman's quarters and switched on the electric light, flooding the room with its harsh glare. 'Put it off, put it off!' Mama Erquia covered her head with her hands, moaning that now the djenoun would come for her.

Mariata smiled to herself. Today she could hardly keep from smiling. She felt as if she carried a furnace within her, as if the world was being remade in her own belly. It was just as she had suspected: the healing woman had cursed the house and placed a waymarker on the front door to attract any passing djinn. But before leaving the house she had blessed Mariata, and the baby she was carrying, to exempt them from this curse. 'May you have a fine son,' she had told Mariata. 'As fine and strong as his father.' For that, Mariata had kissed her hands.

351

Ousman had barely set foot inside the house on his return from Marrakech before Aicha was upon him. 'She is pregnant!'

'Who is pregnant?'

'Your daughter! Your stupid, stupid daughter!' And when he threw his hands up as if to deflect her words, she rounded on him accusingly. 'Did you know?'

Ousman sighed. Then he said, 'It is no shame for a woman to bear her husband's child.'

'What husband? There *is* no husband!' Aicha stormed, hands on hips.

'Not now, no: he is dead.'

'No one will believe that tale for a moment. Well, she had better *have* a husband, and soon: I will not have her dragging my family's reputation through the streets.'

'She is still in mourning for his death. And our women have always made their own decisions about whom, and whether or not, they marry. I cannot force Mariata to marry if she does not wish it.'

'What nonsense! What sort of man are you if you cannot even command your own daughter?'

'It is not our way.'

'You're not living in a tent any more like an animal, and your daughter cannot just spread her legs for anyone she chooses. We have standards, and I'll not have a bastard under this roof!'

Another man might have struck her, but Ousman was a Tuareg, bred to respect women no matter how annoying they might be. Instead, he turned and stalked off into the gathering night and did not return while any of the inhabitants were awake. Mariata found him the next morning when

352

she rose early to have some time to herself before the inevitable chores started, rolled in a blanket in the salon. At first she thought there was a stranger in the house, a wandering man who had come in off the streets, for she had never seen her father without his veil before. And he had a beard! Such a thing was rare amongst their people. But when he opened his eyes she knew him.

She folded her arms, uncomfortable. 'So, has she told you?'

Ousman uncoiled himself from the floor, retrieved his tagelmust and wound it slowly and neatly until he was decently covered once more. Only then, it seemed, did he feel able to address the subject. 'Felicitations, Daughter.' He inclined his head.

'You do not seem overly happy about it.'

'I am neither happy nor unhappy. But I worry for you.'

'As well you might, since your new wife is intent on finding someone to destroy my baby!'

Ousman looked pained. 'It would be better if you were to take a husband, Mariata. A man from the region, to take care of you and the child, when it comes.'

Mariata recoiled. 'Never! How can you even think of it?'

'Aicha will not let you live under this roof with an illegitimate baby.'

'It is not illegitimate!'

'Even so: there is no husband here to claim the baby as his own. No husband to protect you. And this house is not mine to rule over. I am in business with Aicha's father, and I have my sons to think about as well as you. The best thing you can do for

353

yourself would be to take a husband, to protect you in the eyes of this society.'

'I don't care what these people think of me—I despise the lot of them! Do you really think I would take as a husband one of these bare-faced men, who have no respect, no heritage and no code of *asshak*?'

'Hush. These folk may have different ways to our own now, it's true, but once, a long time ago, we were the same people. Our own founder came from this very region in the time of the Romans: your own ancestor, Tin Hinan. Your bloodline began here, in the soil of this place.'

Mariata stared at him in disbelief. 'From here? No wonder she left: I would walk a thousand miles out into the desert to escape Imteghren!'

Her father sighed. 'Mariata, there is no dishonour in marrying a man from Imteghren.'

'I would not pass this child off as some other man's. I had rather live on the streets.'

Ousman made the sign against the evil eye. 'Be careful what you wish for, Daughter.'

*   *   *

Ousman and his new wife were reconciled: once more the quiet night air of the house was disturbed by their cries. And somehow a compromise was reached. Aicha would make it known that her stepdaughter was to be offered on the marriage market; but in the proper Tuareg tradition Mariata would be allowed to have the final say in choosing her husband from the young men put forward.

'There is no time to waste,' she told Hafida grimly. 'If she's already starting to show, how will a

354

man accept the baby as his own if it comes too soon?'

'Best not to choose a man who can count,' was Hafida's only advice.

For some reason there were far more unwed men than women in Imteghren. No one knew why exactly there should be such a shortage of girls of marriageable age, but that was how it was. In addition, the word appeared to have gone around the town that although something of a firebrand Mariata was a beauty; and men were intrigued by the possibility of taking a fiery young Tuareg girl to wife. They had heard that nomad girls were wild in more ways than one, not as shy and buttoned-up as the local girls, and Mariata's reputation (no doubt earned by her scenes in the hammam) bore this out, and so they begged their mothers and aunts to pay their suit. Rather to her horror, Mariata found herself in some demand. Rigged out in one of Aicha's second-best robes in pastel colours that flattered her skin colour, and a headscarf that hid her tribal braids, she gazed at her reflection in the big mirror in Hafida's room. With kohl painted around her eyes and the creamy rouge that Hafida had rubbed into her pale cheeks, she thought she looked like one of the ugly plastic dolls she had seen in the souq: make-believe mannequins like fake miniature human beings. Her spirit rebelled at such treatment but she quelled it. 'It is not you they are seeing,' she told herself fiercely, 'but only a mask.'

Besides, she would soon see off any suitors and their crow-like mothers. Of that she had no doubt. And the longer she played along with Aicha's ridiculous scheme, the longer her baby would be

355

safe.

Her brothers found the whole idea of their sister being paraded for sale offensive and demeaning, and for a short time Mariata's hopes were raised that Azaz and Baye might talk their father round; but they were soon to find that Aicha had a greater hold over Ousman than his own kin.

It was not long before the mothers and aunts and cousins of certain young men of the town came calling. They would spend an hour or so sitting in the salon with Aicha and her grandmother, sipping mint tea and extolling the virtues of their sons and nephews—so handsome, so hard-working, the eldest of ten, or eight, or seven; such a good man, so pious and good with children, and with his hands, and able to pay three thousand dirham and some goats for the right bride. And then Mariata, in her alien disguise, would be trotted out and made to sit hemmed in by her hated new family, nodding and smiling and inwardly seething as the women asked Aicha about her skills. Could Mariata make good bread? And keep a clean house? Did she rise before cockcrow: was she a hard worker? Could she make goat's cheese and card wool? Did she embroider and sew clothes? Could she make a proper couscous and did she know the secret of *harissa* paste? Could she recite the Qur'an and observe Ramadan and the prayer times like a proper Muslim? And, with lowered voices as if she had no ears or wasn't even there, was she a clean girl, and possessed of an unbroken hymen? To all these questions, Aicha looked them in the eye and answered yes, and yes, and yes, while Mariata flushed to the roots of her hair and dreamt of flinging off her borrowed robes and

356

setting about the lot of them with a large stick, whooping Tuareg war-cries all the while. But for her child's sake she endured the shame and the fury: now let the young men come.

*   *   *

A few days later, the first suitor—Hassan Boufouss—turned up in his best white going-to-mosque robe and skullcap, accompanied by his two grandmothers, father and three sisters. In the guest salon Hassan's large lugubrious eyes roamed in panic over the smooth-plastered walls, the shelf of plates and ornaments, the coloured rug and fretted windows, and returned constantly to the open door as if he might at any moment bolt out of it.

Aicha ushered Mariata in ahead of her. The Tuareg girl's headwrap was askew and her cheeks were flushed, as if there had been a tussle preceding this entrance. She cast a contemptuous gaze over the gathered crowd and turned to Aicha. 'Who are all these people?' She folded her arms. 'I'm not going to do this with all of them staring at me.'

The old women exchanged glances.

'Forgive the girl: she's shy and not used to our ways,' explained Aicha, pushing Mariata in the back.

'I am certainly not shy!' Mariata tore off the offending scarf, uncovering her tribal braids.

The throng gazed on, frozen by shock. Then one of the grandmothers grabbed Hassan by the arm. 'She has no modesty, this one,' she declared, and dragged him to his feet.

Mariata smiled and stood aside to let them pass.

Led by his grandmother, Hassan went like a docile calf, though his gaze flickered wonderingly over the Tuareg girl as he left, as if she represented to him a glimpse of a forbidden world; a world from which he would ever be excluded.

The next day, undeterred by the whispers that at once circulated throughout the town following Mariata's untoward conduct, Bachir Ben Hamdu and his parents arrived. Bachir was a very different proposition to his cousin, Hassan. Mariata was shocked by the immodesty of his clothing. Not only did he bare his face in the way of all the men here, but the garment on his lower half would normally be worn only as underclothing amongst her people, clinging as it did in a shamelessly revealing manner to every part of him. She stared at him, stone-faced, keeping her eyes fixed carefully on a point between his chin and his waist as he stood under the gaze of the portrait of King Hassan II, making his greetings. He told her his name and that he was delighted to make her acquaintance and hoped soon to know her better. He did not wink or in any other way accompany this last remark with a salacious gesture, but she felt his palm, hot and sweaty, as he touched her hand, and went rigid with disgust.

Aicha was delighted. 'That went very well,' she declared after he had gone. 'I think he will offer for you.'

'Offer? For me? What, am I a camel to be bought and sold?'

Aicha laughed mirthlessly. 'Sadly, nothing so useful.'

*   *   *

358

One day a man knocked at the door. No one was in but Mariata and Mama Erquia, who was asleep. Mariata peered through the window grille beside the door. Outside stood a thickset man wearing a frayed brown robe, a bloodstained apron and a knitted hat pulled down low over his ears. His sleeves were too short, stopping three or four inches above the wrist to reveal large, hairy forearms; his hands looked filthy.

Not liking the look of him, Mariata called through the grille, 'Who are you and what do you want?'

'My name is Mbarek Aït Ali,' the man replied gruffly, 'and I have some business with the lady of the house.'

'Aicha Saari is not here at present, but she'll be back later,' Mariata told him sharply, hoping he would go away. There was a musty scent to him, deep and animal, that was wafting through the window. She wrinkled her nose.

'I'll wait for her.'

'You can do what you like,' Mariata said curtly.

The man cocked his head. 'To whom do I have the pleasure of speaking?' His accent was rough: the polite phrasing sounded sarcastic.

Mariata drew herself up. 'I am Mariata ult Yemma of the Kel Taitok.'

The man took a step closer and applied an eye to the grille. Affronted, Mariata took a step back. 'I see they do not lie,' he said after a moment, and went away, laughing to himself.

When Aicha returned, Mariata said, 'There was a man here looking for you. He said his name was Mbarek Aït Ali.'

Aicha looked surprised. 'But he knew I would not be at home: I passed his shop on the edge of the souq an hour ago and he asked how Mama Erquia was.' Her eyes narrowed. 'Did you let him in?'

'He smelt disgusting,' Mariata said, 'and he was wearing a bloodied apron; of course I didn't let him in.'

A little while later there came another knock at the door and Aicha bustled off to answer it. Curious, Mariata slipped into the side room to see who it might be. It was a man with a deep voice that she thought she recognized. The usual greetings were exchanged and then Aicha said, 'Mariata told me you had called by.'

'Yes,' said the man. 'I came to make you a proposition.' He sounded very pleased with himself.

'A proposition?'

'An important proposition.'

'Are you sure it is not my husband you want to see?'

'I believe these matters are usually brokered by the women of the house. Unfortunately, I have no female intermediaries I can ask to act for me since Mother died.'

'Well,' said Aicha, sounding perplexed, 'I suppose you had better come in, then.' But, after a look at his grubby shoes and frayed robe, she ushered him into the utility room rather than the guest salon, Mariata following at a safe distance.

Mbarek cast a sardonic glance around the shabby room. 'Is this where you conduct all your marriage discussions, Mistress Saari?' he asked, amused.

'Marriage?' Aicha sounded surprised. 'I thought you'd come to sell me meat.'

At her listening post, Mariata gasped. A butcher? A butcher had the gall to come and offer for a princess descended from Tin Hinan? She remembered the bull-necked man in the bloody apron and laughed aloud.

The sound alerted Aicha. 'One moment,' she told the butcher. 'Go through to the salon and I'll bring us some tea.'

In the kitchen Aicha caught Mariata trying to escape into the courtyard. 'Come with me,' she said sternly. 'And be civil.'

'You expect me to be civil to a man like that? A common butcher, with animal blood on his hands and slaves' blood in his veins?' Outrage drew out of her generations of Tuareg snobbery.

'Beggars can't be choosers!' Aicha snapped. 'Now, go and fetch a headscarf to hide those wretched rat-tails!'

*   *   *

'I realize it is not the done thing for a man to come into a house of women or to press his own suit,' the butcher said, draining his glass of mint tea in a single mighty slurp, 'but I have no female relatives I can call on to carry out such sensitive business. You must excuse my plain appearance and my plain words. I like to run all my own affairs, and in the same straightforward way.' He placed the tea glass back on the tray and leant forward, hands clasped.

Mariata could not help but notice the caked black blood beneath his fingernails. At least, she

361

thought contemptuously, seeing the balled-up cloth between his dusty naked feet—which looked huge and monstrous and yellow-taloned against the delicate colours of the best rug—he had taken off his bloodstained apron before coming in.

'So, in the spirit of honourable business, I have come to make you a good offer for the girl.' He nodded towards Mariata, but kept his eyes on Aicha. 'She's a nomad, I know, but I won't hold that against her. I'm sure I can soon civilize her, eh?' He spread his hands apologetically. 'Not that you haven't already done a fine job of that, I'm sure.'

'An offer for the girl?' Aicha echoed, sounding rather cowed.

'I find myself in need of a second wife.'

'A *second* wife?'

'The first one is ill; and besides she has got too fat to run around after the children—'

'Perhaps you would be better off employing a servant than seeking another wife,' Aicha said acidly.

'Ah, well I would, but a man has certain . . . needs. Besides, we've only girls, and I'll need sons to run the business.' Mbarek stared frankly at Mariata and wet his mouth.

Repulsed by the thick lips that now glistened like entrails, Mariata cried, 'I wouldn't be the second wife to a king, let alone a butcher!'

Aicha shot her a furious look, but the butcher only laughed. 'No need to chastise the girl on my behalf. I like a woman with spirit. I'll pay you good bride-wealth for this one.'

And he named, right out in the open and quite without shame, a sum that made Aicha's jaw drop.

362

'Goodness,' she said weakly. 'Goodness me.' Then she just stared at him as if she had run out of words.

Mariata took her opportunity. 'You cannot buy a princess of the Kel Taitok,' she said scathingly. 'I suggest you go down to the livestock market and purchase yourself a nice fat ewe to fulfil your . . . needs.'

She allowed herself the satisfaction of watching his slab of a face turn from ruddy brown to an unhealthy shade of puce before sweeping up the tea tray and marching from the room.

*   *   *

The next week brought Omar Agueram and his sisters. Omar was a pleasant man, tall and well-enough made to remind Mariata somewhat of Amastan. When he smiled at her, she burst into tears, surprising herself and everyone present. The sisters bustled around, dabbing at her eyes so as not to smudge her kohl, patting her shoulder. When everything had calmed down, Omar started again. 'I have a little carpentry business,' he explained. 'By the kasbah wall. I inherited it from my father, who died last year. Since then I've been working hard to get the customers back; he was ill for a long time and fell behind with the orders, so I didn't have time to think about myself. But now the business is doing well, very well. I've got more work than I can handle and I've just taken on two assistants. I'm ready to settle down and take a wife. And I'd like children, lots of children.'

Mariata felt the tears welling again. Another woman in her circumstances might well settle for

363

this kind man and the life he had to offer, but her dreams still hung in rags around her. Forcing back the tears, she reminded herself of her Kel Taitok heritage and summoned her most haughty demeanour. 'I'd prefer to raise goats,' she said coldly.

Omar looked taken aback; but she was a nomad girl and their ways were different, so he tried again. Leaning forward earnestly on the couch, he said, 'We can have goats, if you like; and perhaps we'll come to children later.'

It was no good: he was too kind. Fearing she might suddenly lose control and accept his suit, Mariata ran from the room.

*   *   *

The weeks went by, and one by one they still continued to make their way to the Saari house, even though reports of the 'Tuareg princess' were less than inviting. There was a little round mechanic whose fingers bore the saffron stain of nicotine; an elderly schoolteacher whose wife had passed away; a bus driver with sunken cheeks and a greying moustache. Mariata was paraded in front of them like a prize mare; but even if she managed to keep a civil tongue, her eyes were insolent and it was not long before some of the sharper-eyed female relatives began to distinguish a swelling beneath even the most voluminous robe in which she was dressed. Aicha was beside herself. She cornered Mariata one morning in the courtyard. 'You have to marry! You cannot bear a child without a husband in this town!'

'I have a husband,' Mariata answered dully.

364

'He is dead! Dead, dead, dead!' Aicha punctuated each word with a dig of a painted nail into her stepdaughter's growing chest. 'He's dead and gone and he's not coming back! Get that into your stupid, ignorant head.'

Again and again Mariata saw Amastan fall back lifeless into the dust, the black stain spreading across his wedding robe. The loss of him and of their future together cut through her like the chillest desert wind. 'He may be dead,' she said bleakly, though even to admit this to Aicha felt like a defeat, 'but this is his child and I will not let any other man claim it as his own.'

'If you give birth to a bastard, it will shame the entire community!' Aicha shrilled.

'They will be talking of it from here to Ouarzazate!' Mama Erquia added, grinning horribly.

'Let me tell you this.' Aicha wagged a finger in Mariata's face. 'If you do not take a husband I will have you thrown out into the street and proclaim that any man in the town may take you as his whore.'

'My father will not let you treat me so.'

'Ousman? Ousman will do the best thing for this family. How will his business thrive or his sons find themselves decent wives if everyone knows you to be a whore? I tell you this,' she said, leaning closer, 'if you have this baby, I will take it from you while you lie weak in the birthing bed and I will kill it with my own hands. I will wring its neck as easily as a chicken's and take its wretched, stinking little body out to the abattoir where the wild dogs wait for bones.'

Preposterous though this was, of all the things

Aicha had threatened it rang most true to Mariata. She closed her eyes. 'I will take Omar,' she heard herself say faintly. 'I will take the carpenter, Omar Agueram.'

The old woman cocked an eye at her and then cackled. 'You may wish with one hand and crap in the other,' she cackled. 'See which hand fills up first.'

*   *   *

But the news when it came back was not good: Omar, under the urging of his family, who had heard the rumours of Mariata's condition, had retracted the marriage offer. He sent his uncle to make his apologies to Ousman. 'Omar regrets very much having placed the young lady in a false position, but it seems he is not in a situation to marry at this precise moment after all.' The uncle, a dapper man in his fifties who worked for the *caïd* in the local administration, had a firm manner. He shook Ousman by the hand, turned on his heel and left.

Aicha, who had been listening on the other side of the door, flew into a rage. At last, unable to bear her tears and fury and screeching voice, Ousman gave up his daughter's right to choose. The next day Aicha sold her to the butcher.

CHAPTER TWENTY-SEVEN

That night Mariata dreamt.

She dreamt of another woman, in another time. Even in profile the woman was tall and imposing, long-nosed and with an imperious air. She was dressed in a long dark robe, but her head was uncovered: long black braids streamed down her back to her waist. Emerald earrings dangled from her lobes. Nine gold bracelets decorated one slim arm; eight silver bracelets the other. Great strings of beads were draped around her neck and waist, beads of carnelian, agate and amazonite. Then she turned. Her bright black gaze, vivid in the luminous paleness of her skin, drilled into Mariata.

'They tried to sell me too,' she said. Her Tamacheq was oddly accented, lilting, but it was still clearly recognizable as the language of the People of the Veil. 'They tried to make me marry against my will. To a son of the Roman governor: can you imagine? They wanted me to take a foreigner to my bed: it would be an honour for our family, they said, to ally themselves with the Romans. With the oppressors!' She tossed her head and her black hair flew out like snakes. 'I refused: they punished me. They locked me away until I told them I would marry him. I made it seem as if they had finally worn me down and won the argument.'

'What did you do?' asked Mariata in her dream; but she knew the answer already. The stranger's face was blurring now, fading in and out of focus. One moment the brow became more pronounced and she saw her mother's features imposed over those of the woman; then the nose and chin lengthened and wrinkles wreathed the skin, and there was her grandmother, with her eagle's beak and her sharp eyes. A succession of other women's features flowed across the stranger's face, one after another, faster and faster, young and old; and yet always there remained certain constants: the imperious eyes, the fierce brows, the strong bones that Mariata also shared.

'I walked away from Imteghren,' said Tin Hinan. 'I walked into the wilds. I walked through the fields and into the savannah and across the desert, until I came to the mountains. It took me months but I made the journey, and at the end of that journey, in the foothills of the great Hoggar, I set down my tent. And where I stopped, I founded a people: the Imazighen, the Free People. Your people. *Our* people. Stay free, Mariata: do not let them sell you into a shameful marriage, do not give your child into their hands. Be proud; be strong. You are my kin, my blood. I am in you; you carry me within you, as do all the women of our line—my words, my power, my strength. It is time for you to follow in my footsteps, to make the same journey I once made. It will be harder now, for you. The desert has spread her robes out far and wide; and the child you carry will sometimes feel more like a burden than a blessing. But I will be with you every step of the way.'

*   *   *

The dream of Tin Hinan hung around Mariata like a nagging grandmother. For days it wagged its

368

finger at her, reminding her constantly of her dire situation, goading her to action. In truth, Mariata needed no goad. She knew well enough that she would have to leave the Saari house, Imteghren, and the whole civilized world; and that she would have to do it before they married her to the butcher. But, while her instinct was to pack up her few possessions and simply walk out early one morning before the family was awake, she knew this would not do. She had made that mistake the first time she had headed for the desert and she would not make the same mistake again. This time there would be stealth; there would be planning.

The decision—huge and immanent—sat sturdy and reassuring inside her like an invisible twin to Amastan's amulet: it acted as a prophylactic against the horror of the future that awaited her with the butcher in the same way that the amulet warded off the negative influences of the universe.

A date was set for the wedding, and in this Mariata had an initial small gift of luck, for the butcher's cousins had to travel from Casablanca, and his aunt from Marseilles. She would not fly (it was not natural) and boats took time. Aicha was angry and tried to persuade the butcher to have the wedding first, followed by a separate celebration for the relatives, but he was surprised and affronted by the suggestion.

'Why would you say such a thing?' He puffed out his cheeks, then let the air out in a rush. 'Is there some reason for the haste?'

Aicha assured him there was not, only that the weather was so fine at this time of year that it would surely be more conducive to those relatives, especially the elderly, who would find the sudden

369

drop in night temperatures the next month a severe shock to the system; then she marched straight down to the souq in search of cotton bark root. The old medicine trader she found there pretended not to hear her request and tried instead to sell her snakeskins—to guard against disease—dried chameleons and lizard's feet to combat the evil eye, hawk root and wolf onion. When she pressed him again for the cotton bark root, he sent her away angrily. 'Such things are against the will of God!'

For her part, whenever Mariata had a chance to visit the souq she searched out travellers in the funduq, telling them her brothers were about to make a desert crossing and that she was worried for them and listened attentively to their stories of drifted-in wells and sick camels, storms and swallowing sands. Another woman might have been daunted by these tales of doom, but Mariata was fierce in her determination and the confidence of her ancestry and kept asking questions and taking careful note of their answers. From one she found out the points to look for in a riding camel; from another the likely price she would have to pay for a good example. It was, of course, more than she could possibly lay hands on; but she refused to give up on that account. Something would turn up. She walked from camel to camel, looking them up and down, comparing them; and one day one of the veiled men came up to her as she was examining his beast. 'Do you like her?' he asked.

Mariata was taken aback. 'She seems . . . nice.'

'She has a filthy temperament and hates all humankind. She has a hideous bellow and a poisonous bite and will take little or no instruction.

In short, she is just like every woman I have ever known.'

Mariata laughed. 'A fine independent creature she sounds.'

There was a pause. Then the trader said, 'I've seen you in the funduq before. Why do you come here?'

Mariata reeled off the usual story about her brothers' planned long journey, but the man's regard was sceptical. 'You must care very deeply for your brothers,' he said at last.

'I do.' Mariata felt herself colouring. Quickly she embroidered her tale, adding that her brothers might be in need of another riding camel for their caravan, but she could tell halfway through her overlong explanation that the old trader was not fooled. His eyes bored into her. 'Don't do it,' he said.

Mariata took a step back. 'Do what?'

'What I can see in your eyes.'

'What can you see in my eyes?'

'The desert.'

'I . . . ah . . .' She made to leave, but the man touched her arm.

'Forgive me. Too much time spent in the empty place makes my senses too acute. With that complexion and those eyes you must be Kel Taitok, no? It is rare to see one of such lineage in this place.'

Mariata was surprised to see him adjust his veil upwards to cover even more of his face than he had before. It was a gesture of great respect, one she had not seen for a long time.

'I am travelling north from here and have no further need for this camel, or for my desert gear.

371

Take it with my blessing.'

She stared at him, lost for words. At last she said, 'I cannot just . . . take it.'

'Think about it overnight. I will still be here tomorrow.'

*   *   *

Mariata ran back to the Saari house, filled with equal measures of terror and excitement. Was this the miracle she had hoped for, or was it too good to be true? But when she got there, it was to find that the hand of fate had made another intervention. Mama Erquia had fallen suddenly and gravely ill, so ill that Aicha was rushing around the house, gathering the necessary items they would need to take with them to the hospital in Meknes.

'There you are!' her stepmother exclaimed angrily. 'Get your things: quickly!'

Mariata stared at her. 'Me?'

'We will choose a dress for your wedding in Meknes.'

It was the last thing Mariata wanted to do, but she tried not to make her panic too obvious. 'No, no,' she said. 'Meknes is a big town: I would be frightened to go there. Surely you and Hafida would make a better decision when it comes to a dress for me.' She waited, her heart banging.

Aicha sucked her teeth. 'You are right,' she declared at last. 'You must stay here and cook for the men: lunch every day, and a meal when they close the shop each night. We will be back in a week, *insh'allah*. Mama Erquia would hate to miss the wedding.'

372

And indeed, though she could not speak, the old woman gave Mariata the evil eye when she walked past.

*   *   *

The women left the next day on the dawn bus for Meknes with old Mama Erquia wrapped in blankets; and the men left the house not long afterwards to open their grocery, leaving Mariata on her own. It was the first time she had ever been alone in the house. The silence was strangely oppressive, as if something waited its moment to burst out of one of the empty rooms and prevent her escape. She fairly ran about the place, gathering the things she would need, which included a roll of notes she had one day found inside an ornamental jar when cleaning a high shelf in the guest salon. The roll had lost weight since the last time she had seen it, and from this she conjectured that Aicha had taken some money with her to the city, but there was still a considerable sum left. She tucked the notes into the fringed leather bag she had brought out of the Adagh, the one Tana had made for her, which contained a small knife, its haft inscribed with Tifinagh symbols; a whetstone; two flints; a skein of cord; three candles; several small bundles of herbs; a Cross of Agadez; a shiny metal cylinder for which she knew no use; and the scrap of Amastan's indigo wedding robe, with his blood dried hard upon it.

She arrived at the grocery just before noon, wearing her most distinctive robe. Azaz and Baye sat outside playing cards on the dusty pavement.

Just inside, watched by three or four customers who were clearly in no hurry to go back out into the baking heat of the day, Ousman and his father-in-law, Brahim, were pouring rice from a sack into a rat-proof plastic drum. They all regarded her with curiosity as she had appeared so unexpectedly, bearing a large tajine between her hands and a bag of flatbreads over her arm. She beamed at them, placed the tajine and bread on the counter and drew off the lid with a flourish. A fragrant cloud of lamb-and-spice-flavoured steam at once enveloped everyone in range and all the customers craned their necks and sniffed appreciatively. Ousman stared at his daughter in wonder. 'It seems you have been hiding your light under a barrel, Mariata. Or,' he said, regarding her shrewdly, 'perhaps you have been playing up your stepmother all this time on purpose?'

Mariata returned his scrutiny with wide-eyed innocence, the very picture of daughterly duty, and then ran back to the house safe in the knowledge that no one was going to miss her for some time. There, she changed her clothes, retrieved her travelling gear and wrapped her head in a veil that hid her identity from all. She ran down through the souq into the warren of dusty streets that led to the funduq with her heart jumping. What if the trader and his camel had gone? What if he had not meant what he said?

And, indeed, when she arrived at the reed-roofed place in which all the passing travellers stabled their animals and slept rolled in their blankets in the little walled enclosures around the sides, there was no sign of the man. She walked around in a daze, staring at one prone figure after

374

another as they took their afternoon naps, trying to remember what had made the trader so distinctive. She did not even know his name . . .

'Daughter of the Hoggar, are you looking for me?'

The relief almost made her buckle at the knees. There he was, tall and straight despite his age, his canny eyes taking in her thick travelling robes, sturdy footwear and the fringed bag slung across her back.

'I have come to take you up on your word.'

He could tell that she wanted to be on her way, but he made her sit and take tea with him anyway in a quiet corner of the funduq where they would not be overheard. There, he boiled water over a small brazier and brewed, slowly and meticulously and with full Tuareg ceremony, a small silver pot of *terghele* tea, while Mariata fizzed and bubbled with impatience. At last, over the second glass, he said solemnly, 'If I give you my Moushi, it must be as a loan.'

Mariata was affronted. 'You said it was a gift!'

'Moushi is a she, not an it.' He leant closer. 'Do you have a route planned out? Do you know where the hidden wells are, and where you will find enough pasturage to keep my camel alive? It is a long way from here to your ancestral home: over a thousand miles as the crow flies, and you are no crow. The terrain you must cross is amongst the cruellest on earth. She is not a young animal, and has already endured much: I would not have her expire on her way.'

'You sound more concerned about your camel's welfare than mine.'

The old trader's eyes crinkled. 'She and I have

passed five good years together and I am very fond of her. I have spent more time in her company than that of my wife.' He paused. 'In addition, she does not answer back.'

Mariata reminded him of the hard words he had given her about his camel when they had last met.

He thought about this for a long moment. 'Ah, well, it is true that I said that about her. We had just finished a taxing journey and she was being . . . recalcitrant. Again, I believe I may have misspoken myself. Now, the fear of losing her reminds me of her good qualities . . .'

Mariata glared at him. 'I know what you are doing!' she burst out. 'You lead me to believe one thing, then introduce a problem in order to bargain up your price, just like all the faithless people in this place.' She had just experienced the same situation with the neighbour who had cooked the tajine for her and ended up having to double her price.

The trader did not seem to take offence at this diatribe but merely continued mildly, 'Also, in the time we have been here she appears to have formed a tender attachment to two other camels in the funduq, and it seems to me it would be cruel to separate them.'

This beggared belief. Mariata scrambled to her feet, reaching into her robe as she did so. A moment later the roll of notes lay in the dust on the ground between them. 'There! Take that for your wretched, ugly, bad-tempered, moth-eaten animal!'

The old man's shoulders shook and a peculiar wheezing sound escaped his tagelmust. He made no move to pick up the money. Instead, he said,

'Wait here.'

Half an hour passed. Mariata paced. Forty minutes went by. She watched the sun creep gradually across the reed-roof, the striped shadows subtly elongating themselves across the courtyard like tabby cats stretching. She left the funduq and stared up and down the streets surrounding it, but there was no sign of the trader, or the camels. She went back in again and sat in the shadows once more and waited, brooding. He must have left her, embarrassed by his change of mind, shamed that he had broken his word. More likely he had never meant a word of it in the first place. Gloom settled over her, weighted her to the ground, sapped her resolution. The idea of returning to spend yet another night in the house while maintaining an apparent equanimity was horrible, but soon she would have no choice but to admit defeat, go back, stash her collection and meet the suspicious eyes of her family as she failed to produce a meal that matched her noon tour de force. And then the next day she would have to steel herself once more to repeat the ruse, return to the souq to find, haggle for and buy another camel and equip herself for the journey and start out once more. Sighing, she levered herself to her feet. And just at that moment the man reappeared in the doorway. Not caring now that she drew attention to herself, Mariata ran across the funduq to meet him.

'I thought you had gone . . .' she started, but the trader put a finger to the cloth that veiled his mouth and motioned for her to follow him outside into the hot, unshaded street.

There she found not one camel, or even two, but three: his Moushi, another animal of fair appearance and a third scruffy Mauretanian. With a clicking of his tongue he brought the leading two camels to their knees, mounted up on the one he had called Moushi and waited expectantly. Mariata stared at him. 'What are you doing?'

'Moushi will not go into the desert without me or her beloveds. So it seems that you will have company on your journey to the Hoggar.'

This was not at all what she had planned and she could not understand his motive in offering to accompany her. It could not be to rob her, since he had spurned the offer of the money. Would he sell her to slavers or, worse, to the French? It was easy to conjure any number of lurid possibilities. She looked at him closely. 'Why are you doing this?'

'If you are going to spend all that remains of the day asking questions, perhaps I will reconsider.'

But Mariata stood her ground, chin tilted pugnaciously. 'I need to know your reasons.'

The trader said nothing, but his eyes dropped eloquently to her belly. 'I am no expert in the world of women, but to cross the desert alone in your . . . condition . . . would surely result in not one death but two.' He paused.

Mariata flushed. 'I see that you have an eagle's gaze.' She bit her lip, caught between her pride and her need. At last she said, 'My father has remarried with a settled woman; she has been trying to rid herself of the embarrassment of a pregnant stepdaughter ever since. At last she managed to sell me to a butcher.'

The old trader sucked in his breath. 'And your father allows this?'

'He is in thrall to his new wife.'

'Will they come after you?'

Mariata had not even considered this possibility. Would they? She could not imagine that her father would do so, for Aicha would be delighted by her disappearance, but what about the butcher? Having his soon-to-be wife run away would surely make a fool of him, and she could not imagine he would bear that lightly. 'Someone might.'

The old man thought for a while, then gave a nod. 'The women of our people are proud and hardy, but even for Tin Hinan herself the journey would be arduous and fraught with unusual dangers. A vicious border dispute has broken out between Morocco and Algeria: they are calling it the War of the Sands. You will need to know where best to cross between the two territories if you want to avoid soldiers, and in my opinion soldiers are always best avoided, especially for a woman travelling alone. And unfortunately they are not confined only to the border region: their vehicles are to be found along all the main routes to Tindouf. It is necessary to know the less-well-travelled roads and the hidden wells if one is to travel with any degree of safety.'

Mariata digested this silently, remembering: she had heard people talking about the conflict these past weeks but simply hadn't paid any attention to their chatter. 'It seems much to ask of one who has only just finished a long journey out of the desert, to accompany an unknown woman back into that wilderness again.'

'To let you go alone into the Sah'ra would weigh heavy on my conscience till Allah calls me home.'

'But why would you do such a thing for a stranger?' Mariata persisted.

The old man smiled. 'The People of the Veil are

379

one people, for all their age-old tribal rivalries. Besides, if you were to tell me your name, and I were to tell you mine, we would be strangers no longer. I am Atisi ag Baye, of the Kel Rela.'

The Kel Rela. Some called them the People of the Goats and looked down on them because of their lowly descent. Mariata pressed a palm against her heart. 'I am Mariata ult Yemma, daughter of Tofenat, thousandth daughter of the Mother of Us All. I have heard tell in one version of my ancestor's history that Tin Hinan made her journey to the Hoggar with her servant Takama, from whom the Kel Rela trace their ancestry. I have also heard that history may repeat itself in unlooked for ways. And that the hand of fate has sleight and craft to match that of any magician.'

For a moment a glint lit the old trader's eye. Then he nodded his head slowly as if considering the all-confounding mysteries of the universe.

*   *   *

Night falls swiftly in the south of Morocco. One moment the landscape is filled with scarlet light, each rock, bush and undulation bathed by its lambent fire; the next the sun's baleful eye blinks and is gone, leaching all colour from the scene, leaving it bleak and grey.

Mariata rocked and swayed on the back of her docile mount, her back aching from the unaccustomed motion, her tailbone jolting against the hard pack on which she was perched, her knuckles white from gripping the crosspiece of the old-fashioned wooden saddle tree. Ahead of her Atisi ag Baye sat tall and straight, at one with his camel and the rest of the world. But every time the discomfort assaulted her she reminded herself of the fate that lay behind her back in Imteghren, and as if by magic her spine would straighten and the aches would disappear, for a while at least.

They had been riding like this, slowly and methodically, without pause, for five hours through the low sandy hills, dusty *palmeraies* and scrubby vegetation that lay south of the Tafilalt plateau. Eventually they moved into a valley through which caravans had passed for a thousand years on their way from the desert to the sea. The corridor cut through the surrounding limestone was wide and deep; moonlight glimmered on the pockets of water in the bottom of the valley and was glimpsed through the waving fronds of the palms. They passed a myriad of little settlements whose golden lights punctuated the gloom, and saw huddled beneath the walls of a ruined kasbah a group of men who had lit a small brazier and were cooking their evening's meal. The scent of it drifted up to Mariata, reminding her of her own hunger. Atisi made a quiet greeting to the men, who returned the greeting and watched them pass, their eyes scanning the pale oval of Mariata's uncovered face with interest, before turning back to their tajine.

She heard her own voice, plaintive as an owl's call: 'Can we not rest for a while?'

There was a long pause in which the silence hung heavy. Then the old trader said, 'Information has a way of finding those who seek it; and if you would not be found and returned to Imteghren, we must put as much distance between ourselves and the Tafilalt as we can.'

When at last they made camp for the night, Mariata found it hard to sleep, though she was bone-weary. She lay on her back on a coarse camel-hair blanket and stared at the sky. Somewhere up there, Amastan was looking down on her, his spirit wandering the distant black sky. She searched each cluster of stars for some sign of him, but they gave nothing back but a cold and pitiless regard. She must have slept a little, for when she was aware of herself again, the stars had moved position and a portion of sky was paling. A short distance away the camels shifted and snorted; one of them lumbered to its feet as the sun showed its gold rim over the eastern horizon, as if it knew there would be no more rest, that the journey must be continued.

Atisi surprised her by making porridge over a small fire and bringing a bowl of it to her and then moving away so that she could eat in privacy. Even on the road it did not do for men and women to eat together or to see one another eating. It tasted far better than she had expected, hot and savoury with the aroma of pepper, and she ate quickly, her hunger sharpened by the chilly dawn air.

Vehicles passed them early in the morning on the road to Merzouga. They were commercial lorries, painted in red and blue, hugely overloaded and festooned with charms and plastic flowers, and with amulets and Qur'anic verses dangling from their rear-view mirrors. Their drivers regarded the pair with greater than usual curiosity, and after the third of these passed them Atisi drew the camels off the road. 'Now we must deviate from the usual route. There is an oasis at Tahani. We will make our way towards it and take a pause there till darkness comes. It will be easier to cross the border when night falls. Then we will head into the Hamada du Guir and let the camels graze there overnight. It'll be the last good pasturage they get before the sands. And after that'—he spread his hands—'our lives will be in God's hands.'

* * *

In the heat of midday Mariata swayed with the gait of her camel, oblivious to the monotony of dried watercourses and parched hills through which they moved. The sun was like a hammer on the top of her head, beating incessantly, making her temples throb. Trickles of sweat ran from the nape of her neck and down her back. The weight of her growing belly dragged at her spine, making it ache, but she did not have the energy to shift position in the hard saddle and rode as if in a stupor, mesmerized by the motion of the animal beneath her. They saw no one but a herder tending a flock of scrawny-looking black goats that scavenged for the last morsels of vegetation in the unpromising landscape. The herd's ram was thin and wild-looking; it turned its yellow slotted eyes upon them balefully as they passed, as if it knew that its herd was on a doomed journey to death by starvation. She could not help but wonder whether her own journey was equally doomed.

Have courage, she told herself. This was only the beginning of her journey: a few meagre hours out of the weeks that lay ahead. Could she survive such a journey, through terrain that would soon become far crueller and more hostile than the dull rock-strewn wastes they had thus far traversed?

383

Was it mad to think she could make such a perilous journey? Was it dangerously selfish even to try? Already she was plagued with doubt and they had hardly made a start. Mariata touched her amulet to ward away these bad thoughts, and as she did so they crested a rocky rise and saw the green palms of Tahani in the distance.

*   *   *

Lying in the shade of the oasis trees while the hobbled camels methodically chewed their way through what vegetation they could find, and Atisi ag Baye sat on an outcrop keeping watch for bandits or rogue troops, Mariata dozed. And as she dozed she dreamt. She was back in the Adagh and the rhythmic sound of the breeze that rattled the palm fronds above her transformed itself magically into the distant tap of drums and the singing of wedding songs, and she was lying not on the hard ground wrapped in a smelly camel-hair blanket but on a soft bed in her own bridal tent, with fragrant incense burning in a dish, wrapped in the arms of her husband, breathing in his warm and vital scent as they lay skin to skin beneath a cover embroidered with rows of geometric red camels that marched across a background of gold. By the light of the candle-lantern she saw over Amastan's burnished shoulder how the stylized flowers sewn into the coverlet's borders made pretty star shapes just like one of the mosaic tileworks she had seen in the mosque at Tamanrassett, and she sighed contentedly. Could any person be so happy? She did not think so. They were married at last and no one could ever separate them now: they were one flesh; man and woman brought together to be each other's eyes and ears and hearts. They would be together for ever; they would have a dozen children and establish a new dynasty, honouring the name of Tin Hinan. And with their flocks and their camels they would travel the salt road for the rest of their lives, moving from one fertile oasis to the next, free from constraints, living lightly on the land, at one with the spirits. Warmth cocooned her, hazing her thoughts. She drifted contentedly, half aware of the distant drumming and of the regularity of Amastan's breathing as his chest rose and fell against her own.

After the longest time she heard a voice. Amastan was talking to her, whispering in her ear. She struggled up through the heavy waves of sleep that had engulfed her, trying to break the surface of consciousness. What was he saying? Something important, something crucial . . . She fought for clarity, strained to listen.

'Lady . . .'

A hand on her shoulder. A chill on her face.

With a start, she jolted upright. But the hand that had touched her was not Amastan's but an old man's, his face seamed and weathered by passing decades, and the chill she had felt was his shadow falling across her. Who was he? For many seconds she did not know, could not think because of the panicked batter of her heart. Then the man withdrew and hot light fell on her once more, so that she blinked and squinted at the dazzle of sun through the palm branches overhead, branches that replaced the dark and comforting cocoon of her marriage tent. Bewildered, she closed her eyes

385

and reached after the dream, trying to focus on the material details that would bring it back to her, wrap its alternative reality around her and comfort her. Tatters of its gorgeous imagery trailed away like mist burned off by the rising sun. The coverlet, she thought wildly, clutching to herself the marching camels and the star-like flowers. For a moment she could feel the cool cotton beneath her fingers and the raised texture of the stitching. And then she remembered where last she had seen that lush embroidery: in her Aunt Dassine's tent in the Aïr Mountains, on the night Rhossi ag Bahedi had tried to force himself upon her. Where it likely still lay. She had never taken it with her to the Adagh, had hardly taken anything of her own on her flight through the Tamesna with Rahma, the mother of Amastan.

Amastan . . .

The loss of him struck her anew and she gave a ragged cry and then began to weep bitterly, broken once more by the loss of all hope.

Atisi ag Baye drew back. Despite the long years of his life, his experience with women was limited. Their volcanic emotions he found far stranger and more confusing than the simple exigencies of the desert. And so he walked a discreet distance away and set up his little brazier to make some tea. In his experience, a glass of sweet green tea made everyone feel better: it was one of Allah's gifts to man.

By the time he came back, Mariata's sobbing had quietened, though the tracks of her tears still stained her cheeks. He handed the glass to her without a word and she took it with a slight inclination of her head to indicate her appreciation

386

of the gesture, then drank the contents while staring morosely at the ground. After a long while she said, 'I have something to tell you. It is not pretty or pleasant, and my circumstances are such that you may reconsider your offer to guide me through the desert.' Her voice was hoarse; she paused, gathering herself.

Atisi sat quietly waiting. He had learnt his patience from his long dealing with camels, which after women were surely the most intractable creatures God ever made. Besides, he sensed a story in the air and he knew that all stories have their own way of being told and can never be hurried.

And so at last Mariata told the old trader her tale. When she described Amastan's affliction being a sickness brought upon him by the Kel Asuf, Atisi ag Baye's grizzled eyebrows rose high into the brim of his turban and one hand touched covertly the small leather amulets he wore on a string around his neck, and when she came to the ritual that had drawn the spirits out of him she was careful to assure him that she did not think it had been her doing, but more likely the magical intervention of the village enad.

'An enad? Ah, the inadan are men of great power.' Atisi nodded thoughtfully. 'It is true that they can manipulate the spirits.'

'Ah, the enad was not a man,' Mariata said.

'A female enad?' He sounded incredulous. Women could not work with iron: it was taboo. To work with iron meant commanding the spirits that lived in fire, and that could cause irreparable damage to a woman's ability to bear children. Besides, anything they touched would surely fail: a

387

key would not turn in a lock, or would stick fast and never come free; a tool would crack in two, the head of an adze fly off and harm an animal or a child; a sword or spear-head break at the most crucial moment. Everyone knew that.

Mariata looked uncomfortable. 'Not . . . really.'

'Neither a man nor a woman?' He sat back suddenly, comprehension dawning. 'I recall an enad and his wife who had a child once, a child that was neither boy nor girl, but both at the same time. They travelled with the Kel Tedele. Is it possible, I wonder . . .'

'She—I always called her "she"—was called Tana and was one of the most remarkable people I ever knew. But she lived amongst the Kel Teggart.'

Now the old trader gave her a direct look. 'You lived amongst the Kel Teggart?'

She nodded.

'I heard something . . . terrible had happened to that tribe.'

Mariata opened her mouth to speak; but her torrent of words had dried up. She felt as if there was a boulder in her throat and that her feelings battered themselves against it in an attempt to get out. Instead, water welled from her eyes again.

Atisi looked away. 'I will go and see to the camels,' he said gruffly.

At last as twilight obscured her face she went to find him. 'You are a man of few words,' she said, 'and I am a proud woman, so do not ask me more than I tell you. The child I carry is no child of shame but the child of my husband, son of the amenokal of the Aïr, late of the Kel Teggart. His name was Amastan ag Moussa and he was my moon and stars.' Her voice caught: it was the first

388

time she had spoken his true name since she had seen him die and somehow saying it aloud made it all the more real. 'I will not have his child raised in ignominy by a butcher. There, I have told you all there is to tell.'

Atisi said nothing for a very long time. Then he sighed. 'Truly, you must have excited much envy for the evil eye to have been cast upon you thus. I hope that with every step into the desert you take the distance between you and your misfortunes will be lengthened. *Insh'allah.*'

*　　*　　*

As they waited for full night to fall, Mariata opened Amastan's amulet for the first time since her wedding and shook the roll of paper it contained into the palm of her hand. By the light of the rising moon she read the charm that Tana had made for her, but the lighter downstrokes were hard to read and all she could make out was her own name and Amastan's. At last she gave up: whatever magic it contained had failed to save Amastan's life, and so was meaningless. Feeling more bereft than ever, she was about to throw the useless scroll away. Then she closed her fist over it: to do so, here, in the realm and the time of the Kel Asuf, was likely to attract even worse luck, so she rolled the parchment back into its hidden compartment and closed the central boss over it again.

*　　*　　*

With a thin crescent moon rising slowly overhead,

389

they picked their way down through the rocky darkness towards the road that crossed the disputed territory. To Mariata it was just a dead strip of nothingness, slightly paler than the surrounding ground, artificially flattened and smoothed, an imposition on the face of the wild. Nothing moved upon it as far as she could see, but, as they reached the last tumble of rocks before the road, headlights showed in the distance. The sudden light caught the side of Atisi's face, and she saw something unreadable flare in his eyes. Then he turned his camel's head towards her. 'Get behind the boulders, quickly. There is cover there for one animal but not for three. If they stop I will talk to them. Keep Moushi quiet and whatever happens do not show yourself.'

Moushi was unwilling to leave her master: it took all of Mariata's strength to urge her into the cover of the rocks. And only just in time, for the vehicles came roaring over the rise and bore down upon them at terrifying speed. Peering out, Mariata saw how the old trader got down from his camel and loosened his veil. Was it out of disrespect for the soldiers that he did this, she wondered, or so that they would not fear him?

For a moment it seemed that they had not seen the man and the two camels, or that they were not concerned by his presence. Then the leading jeep screamed to a halt.

'Who are you and what are you doing here?' a man shouted, levelling a gun at Atisi. 'Show me your papers!'

Atisi gaped. 'Papers?' he asked, thickening his accent to a raw peasant twang.

The man motioned two others out of the jeep.

'Get his papers.'

The two soldiers approached, laughing. 'He's just an old man, lost in the desert.'

'No one passes without papers. How do we know he's not a Moroccan spy? And, while you're at it, search his baggage. We don't want a repeat of last week's fiasco.'

The soldiers dutifully poked and prodded the bags. 'No guns,' one of them said at last.

'Idiot,' said the other, taking the rifle slung over the side of Atisi's camel. 'There's this gun.'

Moonlight glinted on the antique stock, on the chased silver and the charms etched into it by an ancient smith. The soldiers passed it between each other, laughing. 'That knackered old thing,' one said, 'hardly qualifies as a gun. It'd probably blow your head right off if you tried to fire it.'

A muscle twitched in Atisi's jaw, but he said nothing and kept his eyes firmly on the ground.

'So what about it, old man? Where are your documents?'

'I have no documents.' He stumbled over the word deliberately.

'Everyone has documents.'

Atisi shrugged. 'I don't. I am just a poor old man separated from his caravan. One of my camels fell ill and they left me behind.'

'On your own?'

Atisi met his gaze unwaveringly. 'Alone.'

'With friends like that!' one soldier laughed.

'Just let him go, Ibrahim. If you don't we'll have to file a report: it'll take all night.'

'What's he got in those packs, anyway? Anything . . . useful?'

The other soldier grimaced. 'Barley, bit of dried

391

meat, dates and stuff. Miserable rations.'

'No beer?'

Atisi shot him a contemptuous glance. 'No beer.'

Ibrahim glared at him. 'You're a very lucky man. We don't have time to waste on threadbare old nomads.' He looked towards his two subordinates. 'Take his gun, though.'

'No!' Atisi's cry was fierce. 'It was my grandfather's.'

As he grabbed for the rifle the soldier who had hold of it swung it around with casual but deliberate force. It struck the old trader hard across the temple and he fell down with a groan.

At that moment Moushi let forth a bellow that split the night air: 'A-wa-aaaagh!' She lunged forward and Mariata was suddenly flung to the ground, catching her foot awkwardly in the saddlecloth and landing in a tangle of fabric, losing the reins. Thus freed, Moushi ran headlong towards her master, while the third camel, unnerved by this untoward turn of events, wrenched its head back and managed to free itself from the lead rope. Off it went across the road, lit garishly by the headlights of the jeeps, its legs splaying out at all angles.

Shots rang out.

For a moment she lay there, stunned, in the shadow of the rocks before a great fear gripped her. Images from the attack on her village, images that she had successfully fought down once that evening, now assailed her. She saw again the sudden invasion of the uniformed men, the flash of their gunfire ripping the night apart; Rahma with her robes on fire, the soldiers forcing Tana to the ground, lust and hatred painted on their dark faces by the leaping flames. Again and again she saw the dark stain spreading across Amastan's beautiful wedding robe, and the mysterious wet darkness on her own hands as her father dragged her away from her husband's body. Terror galvanized her. She crabbed sideways into a gap between the rocks, making herself impossibly small, and listened to the shouts of the soldiers and the bellowing of Atisi's camels, the sounds melding into a single, incomprehensible noise that spoke only of violence and brutality. A scream began to well up inside her. Some part of her—the rational part that urged survival at all costs—knew she could not let it out; but another, wilder part was trying to prevail. Her eyes bulged with the effort not to cry out; she stuffed the corner of her headscarf into her mouth to stop the howl escaping. What was happening to the old man? Had they shot him? She did not dare look for fear of being seen. If they would do such a thing to a defenceless old man, what would they do to her?

Footsteps came closer, crunching on the loose stones; she heard voices just feet away.

'What's that over there?'

Mariata closed her eyes. But there was no escape inside her head. She saw Tana's robe being torn apart by the soldiers, their hands grabbing at her breasts . . . Perhaps they would kill her, if she was lucky. The amulet pulsed between her fingers, hot in her palms, as if the little discs of red were burning into her skin. *Don't let them see me . . .*

A leg came into view, then a hand and a head with a cap on it. The figure bent and a hand reached out and picked something up. 'An old leather bag. Must have fallen off the camel that ran away.' The sound of objects falling to the ground. The boot pushed them around.

'What's in it?'

'Just the usual worthless old rubbish these people carry with them. Some candles, a bit of string, a couple of stones, a filthy old rag, a cigarette lighter and an old knife.'

'A knife? Any good to us?'

'It's covered in their magical symbols.'

'It's just words, you superstitious fool. Words aren't magic.'

'Even so, I'm not picking it up. I've heard about Tuareg knives with curses carved on them. Knives that have come alive in an enemy's hand and slit his throat before he could even blink.'

'For God's sake. Here, let me see.' A second figure came into view. He bent, his back to Mariata. There was a pause as he examined the spoils. 'It's blunt. What a piece of shit.' The knife clattered to the ground again. 'Seems he was alone, after all.'

'Why'd the second camel have a saddle on it, then? Tell me that if you're so clever.'

A pause. 'You've seen how these camels behave. How'd you like to be left in the desert without another saddled mount if your own got spooked and bolted?'

His companion's acknowledgement of this logic was grudging. 'Let's get back. This place is enough to spook anyone. Could have sworn I heard something breathing a minute ago.'

Mariata held her breath.

'Everyone knows the desert makes odd noises. Rocks get hot during the day and cold at night: they break apart, shed their skins. That's probably what you heard.'

The other man contested the point, but the voices were moving away, and soon she could not make out their words. A few minutes later the jeeps roared to life again, the beams of their headlights slid away, and an eerie silence descended. After a very long time Mariata extracted herself from her hiding place and crawled out into the open, dreading what she might find.

Moushi lay bloodstained and unmoving by the side of the road, but there was no trace at all of Atisi ag Baye, nor of the other two camels. It was as if the djenoun had swallowed them whole. Mariata stared around, but in every direction she saw the same thing: emptiness. Empty darkness, barely touched by a moon that had drifted behind a curtain of cloud.

Why had she done nothing to help the old man? Now he was gone, possibly dead, and she had done nothing but hide herself like a craven coward. He told you to stay hidden, a voice reminded her, but still she felt ashamed. Numbly, she picked up the fringed leather bag that Tana had given her, the last vestige of her previous life. It was empty, its contents thoughtlessly scattered by the soldiers, but after a few moments of frenzied search she retrieved the whetstones, the skein of cord, the three candles and the knife that had placed such superstitious fear in the heart of the soldier. A glint of moonlight a little way away led her to the Cross of Agadez. She found the bundles of herbs scattered here and there, and at last what she thought might be the flints: but how to tell, amidst a million other sharp-edged stones? She was mildly surprised to find the silver cylinder the soldiers had called a cigarette lighter lying in the dirt. She dropped it back into the bag and it fell with an audible clunk that sounded unnaturally loud in the silent darkness. But where was the scrap of indigo cloth? Suddenly it became vitally important that she find it. She ran her hands through the dust, amongst the stones, without a thought for the creeping scorpions that lurked there, as if her whole life, and that of the life growing inside her, depended on her finding it. It took many long minutes, but at last she found it impaled on a thorn bush. She pressed it to her face, taking in its faint, musty, unmistakable scent, and then she kissed it and stowed it carefully away.

Then, sitting back on her heels, she stared bleakly out over the road towards the south. Out there lay the Tinariwen, the many deserts, a thousand miles of the primal unknown: a wilderness of rock and dust offering neither shelter nor sustenance; sands studded with the bones of the long-dead—the lost legions, the ancestors, the unwary invaders; wave upon wave of dune-seas and mighty ergs; wells known only to the expert *madugus* who led the caravans; rivers that ran so far below the surface that no trace of their waters showed themselves to men. And all this belonged to no one but the demons of the wastes: the Kel Asuf. There was now nothing to act as a buffer between her and the desolation: she had no guide, no camel, no supplies. Out there lay only madness and despair.

Behind her, however, lay the known. Even on foot and alone it would be relatively easy to retrace the journey she had made thus far with Atisi from

Imteghren. Once back there in the hands of her stepmother she would be forced to marry the damned butcher, be his second wife and slave; but she would live and so would her child. There was no choice.

Mariata stood up and slung the leather bag over her shoulder. Then she set her face resolutely to the south and started to walk into the unknown.

CHAPTER TWENTY-EIGHT

Outside the off-roader the world rattled by at a speed I would never have thought possible in such a rough wilderness. I pressed my face to the cold glass of the passenger window and stared out into a deep, uncompromising darkness. Only the pale beams of the dipped headlights sliced through the blackness, illuminating the immediate shapes of humps and hillocks of sand, strange giant plants, scatters of rock. Sometimes the wheels slipped sideways as if glissading on snow and the driver casually corrected them; but for the most part he kept a straight course, foot down on the accelerator as if he knew each metre of desert intimately, which I decided he probably did. It was the leader of the trabandistes who drove; in the back sat two of his men. They had taken Taïb in the second vehicle, which followed us at a distance.

Now that he wasn't wearing his sunglasses, I could make a more accurate guess at the age of this man. There were lines deeply incised around his eyes, and his eyebrows were shot through with grey. I estimated him to be anywhere between fifty-five and a very well-preserved sixty-five. Despite this, he looked fit and hard, a man at one with his environment, like a piece of wood long seasoned by the desert, every vital juice and drop of sap taken by the sun, forged in the heat till it was like iron. He also looked like a man to be feared: his gaze when he turned it upon me was as piercing and direct as that of a bird of prey.

'Are you a rich woman, Isabelle?'

I stared at him, taken aback by such a direct question. 'Why do you want to know?'

He smothered a joyless laugh. 'I wish to know if your family will pay good money to get you back.'

'Get me back?' I echoed stupidly. 'What do you mean?'

'If they are to have you back safely, maybe your family must pay a ransom for you.'

A ransom? The very thought seemed absurd, something from a fairytale. Who on earth would want to pay a ransom for me? But what had I thought was happening here, bundled into a car in the middle of nowhere by armed men, driven ever deeper into the desert at speed to some unnamed camp? Of course, my brain accepted dully, we were being abducted. Kidnapped. Held for ransom. 'You mean we're hostages?'

The trabandiste smiled thinly. 'You could say that. I have not yet decided. And you have not yet answered my question. Isabelle Treslove-Fawcett. Forgive me—I am not entirely *au fait* with the nuances of British society—but does not a double family name like yours indicate that you come from . . . shall we say a higher echelon? From the richest level of that society?'

Now it was my turn to laugh bitterly. 'I am very

much afraid that you are out of luck. All my family are dead.'

'All?'

He turned a curious face to me and for a moment I had the bizarre thought that I had seen those eyes somewhere before, and had to look away. There was something about the set of them that was strikingly familiar. A shiver ran through me. Might it be fear? Under the circumstances it seemed the most appropriate response, but if this was fear it was not the same sensation I had experienced at those times of my life when dread had gripped me: at the crux point on a tough climb; before an exam; or earlier in my life, waiting for the footsteps on the stairs . . . I pushed that thought away quickly: even in this clear and present peril it was the memory of those times that brought the sweat pricking on my palms.

'There is no one who will pay to get *me* back.'

'I cannot believe that, Isabelle. Not for a moment.'

'My mother died of cancer when I was at university. My father a few weeks ago. I have no brothers and sisters.'

'To lose a mother at such a tender age is always hard, and I am sorry for your latest bereavement.' He paused, but, just as I thought he would leave the matter there, added, 'But there is always someone who will pay. Are you not married?'

I turned away to stare out of the window. Somehow that vast and empty space outside the car was a lot less disturbing to me than the charged space within. Perhaps, I thought wildly, I should start lying if I were to save my skin. If there really was no one who could be coerced into paying a ransom for me, they would simply shoot me in the head and dump my body in the desert like so much ballast. But somehow I just couldn't seem to lie. 'No,' I said flatly after a while. 'I am not married.'

'Your husband is dead too?' he persisted.

'I have never had a husband.'

He raised an eyebrow at me. 'Such a handsome woman unmarried? That is a surprise.'

Handsome? It was not a term I'd ever associated with myself. 'I've never chosen to take the opportunity.'

'An unplucked rose,' he said musingly. I hoped fervently he was not thinking what I thought he was thinking.

'Well, I wouldn't say that exactly,' I said in my most clipped English accent.

'No matter. The British government will pay for you, I am sure.'

'My mother was French. I hold dual nationality, so both countries will probably wash their hands of me. Besides, the European governments tend to maintain a very strong stance when it comes to kidnappers and criminals. They can't be seen to give way to blackmail, can they?'

I saw a muscle twitch in his cheek, but whether the reflex was caused by a scowl or a smile I could not tell.

'Miss Fawcett, I think you will find there can be a considerable gap between what the officials of any government profess to the public and what they do in secret.' He sounded amused. 'Though I must admit that the British are a harder nut to crack than, say, the French. Publically they will declare they will never treat with terrorists, as they like to call us; but there is usually a deal to be done, as we say, under the sleeve. A little *baksheesh* passing hands.'

Terrorists? The very word chilled me. These men did not strike me as religious fundamentalists, but I realized my understanding of the term was no doubt fatally coloured by my culture's view of events since 9/11, by bearded, AK47-toting Taliban militants and young British Pakistanis brainwashed by renegade imams preaching very unIslamic lessons. Or were they political terrorists like the FARC in Colombia, who had kept Ingrid Betancourt a prisoner for six long years and subjected her and her fellow hostages to terrible cruelties? My heart began to beat fast. 'And if there is no deal to be done?' I said lightly, but the tremor in my voice gave me away.

He shot me a look. 'That would be . . . most unfortunate for you.'

So if no one paid up they would kill me, I thought, quite matter-of-factly. It seemed so surreal I almost laughed aloud. 'You sound as if you make quite a habit of abducting people.'

'Money is very important to our cause.'

'Your cause?' The laugh escaped me. 'You make it seem like a charity rather than a crime.'

'You may use whatever words you like to describe what we do, what we are: it is of no matter to me. My people have often been referred to as pirates of the desert. Separating the rich from their undeserved wealth has long been a favourite occupation of ours.'

I was about to respond to this curious pronouncement when one of the men behind me said something and the driver snapped back a reply, going in a moment from urbane and relaxed to tense and aggressive. I heard a phone call being made and then no one said anything for a long time and the silence in the car felt as spiky as barbed wire. A long time later the headlamps showed the indistinct shapes of a number of low-slung tents gathered in a hollow amongst the dunes and the car slewed to a halt.

As soon as we arrived dark-clad figures swarmed out of the camp. The trabandiste issued a series of sharp orders, and two of them took me away to one of the tents. I had to duck almost double in order to enter; once inside there was nothing for it but to sit on the reed matting and stare out at my captors.

'Could you at least bring me my bag, and some water?' I asked, but they just stared uncomprehendingly back at me. I was ashamed of the tremor in my voice, ashamed of the terror I felt creeping over me as the reality of the situation impressed itself upon me.

For the next hour I tried hard to keep that terror at bay. I occupied myself in the realms of my small prison, gathering the rugs and blankets I found piled at one end and fashioning a nest of a bed to keep out the chill of the desert night. I stared at the innumerable stars shining white and cold in the slice of velvet sky framed by the tent's opening and tried to make out the constellations from amidst their unfamiliar abundance, but to no avail. In my life I had only ever been able to recognize Orion's distinctive three-starred belt, the wavy line of the Plough and the winking Pleiades; but outside were thousands, maybe millions, of pinprick lights, more than I was used to seeing; and this merely served to make me feel more alienated and lost to the world.

Beyond, all was hugeness, and I a tiny insignificant thing, a minute and pointless speck of life in a vast universe that would go on for ever, uncaring around me. There was nothing to identify me as me any more: I was adrift in the dark continent, light years away from everything that had defined me as Isabelle Treslove-Fawcett: my lovely tranquil house filled with its tasteful expensive furniture and carefully chosen paintings, my smart suits and high heels, my job inside the financial fortress, the money and respect that it won me. Now I had nothing but the clothes on my back, and they stank of sweat.

I tried to sleep, but the blankets smelt of goats and were scratchy against my skin, and the ground was hard under my hip. Thoughts tumbled through my head, a jumble of images from the past few days: the main street running through Tafraout filled with wandering robed men walking hand in hand; the women carrying their great loads of animal fodder; Lallawa lying slowly dying on the floor of the house in Tiouada, watched over by the dark eyes of the crow-women; the dancing children at the party; the way Taïb had held me, the sensation of the muscles of his arms tightening beneath my fingers . . . I was just drifting into a light doze when I recalled the fall from the Lion's Face and saw the red ground rushing up to meet me, and then I was wide awake, my heart thudding in my chest like a rubber ball bouncing down concrete steps.

It was then that the real fear set in, hijacking me before I had time to shield myself from the truth. I was utterly alone in some nameless part of the world's greatest wilderness, taken prisoner by men

403

who spoke the most foreign language I had ever heard, who hid their identities behind swathes of cloth, who carried semi-automatic weapons as casually as sticks and termed themselves pirates and did not cavil at the name of terrorist. No one knew where I was, and in truth no one cared, with the possible exception of Taïb, and he was a captive too. They would demand money for my release from the British government, which would refuse to pay, and some weeks or months hence after all diplomatic efforts had failed (if they ever even started) I would most likely be raped and then killed and no one would give me even the basic burial we had given to Lallawa. How had such a thing happened to me? I had always lived my life within well-defined boundaries, seeking the safest and most conservative path, taking only those risks most approved of in my own society, or those bound by well-established rules and codes of conduct. If only I had not taken my father's bait, I thought bitterly. If I had not opened that wretched Pandora's box in the attic, none of this would have happened. I would be the Isabelle I had been for the past twenty years: self-sufficient, successful and assured, relying on no one else in order to avoid being disappointed in others.

Except, a small voice reminded me, all you have been doing all this time is running from your memories, burying everything that ever made you Izzy. You turned yourself into a corporate automaton: you buried your individuality, your spark and your conscience. You lost your wildness, lost the person you should have been. And now, just as you have found a man who might help you to become Izzy again, you are going to be snuffed

404

out of existence altogether and probably so is he.

Tears began to leak down my cheeks: tears of self-pity and fear, for myself and for Taïb; tears of regret for all that might have been. I was surprised to find I did not want to die, that I should suddenly care so much about staying alive, and for some reason that made me cry all the more. I took the amulet out from under my shirt and pressed it to my cheek and wailed like a lost child. I was still snuffling noisily and pathetically into the smelly blanket when someone put their hand on my shoulder and almost made me leap out of my skin.

'Izzy.'

I looked up. It was Taïb, his face indistinct in the shadow of the tent. Relief flooded through me. 'You're alive!' I blurted out.

His teeth gleamed in the darkness. 'Did you think I was dead?'

I wiped my nose on my hand and it came away slick with snot. I had never felt so comprehensively lost in all my life. Where was stiff-upper-lipped Isabelle Treslove-Fawcett when I needed her most? 'Yes . . . no. I . . . I don't know what I thought.' I pushed myself upright, ran a hand through the haystack of my hair. 'Are you all right? Have they hurt you?'

'They roughed me up a bit; nothing terrible. I think they accept we are who we say we are. I'm sorry, Isabelle: this is my fault. I should never have brought you with me: it was stupid; naive.'

'I wanted to come,' I said quietly. 'I took the risk.'

'Without knowing the odds. I should have warned you, instead of showing off.'

'Showing off?'

405

'The petrol at the oasis. It was a bit showy: making you think we were heading into the wilderness with no fuel, then producing the smugglers like a magician conjuring genies. You forget when you deal with contrabandiers that their network is so wide-reaching.'

'I don't know what you mean.'

He sighed. 'Despite the appearance of ease, stolen oil doesn't just appear out of thin air. It requires a highly organized and committed operation to extract it, smuggle and sell it. I vaguely knew the guys at the oasis: I've dealt with them before. They obviously have some connection with the group who've taken us captive and must have reported in our details and where we were heading. If you hadn't been with us, this wouldn't have happened. You're a prize, Izzy: a rich European woman, represented by a rich European government. You're a useful pawn in the game.'

How ironic, I thought. I had never felt less useful, or less European.

A match flared in the gloom. I turned away to compose myself, but he caught hold of my chin and turned my face back towards him. In the light of the small candle-lantern he placed on the matting between us, Taïb leant forward and wordlessly rubbed away the traces of my tears. Then he ran a finger across my forehead. 'What gave you this line, Izzy?' he asked gently. The finger moved horizontally again, its touch like sudden fire on my skin. 'And what about this one? It is as deep as the furrow of a plough.' Soft as a feather, he traced the deep incision that ran from my nose to the corner of my mouth. 'Or this? Now, this one is a very sad line. Let me see if I can make it go away.' And he moved in to kiss me.

I could not help myself: I flinched. Taïb sat back on his heels, looking affronted. 'I am sorry,' he said quietly. 'I forgot myself. I shouldn't have done that. You hardly know me, and here we are in this bad situation, and I am thoughtless, stupid . . .'

'No, it's me who should be sorry. It's just . . .' I shook my head. 'I can't forget myself. That's the problem. I wish I could. But I can't. I can't . . .'

The absurd tears started again, hot and insistent. I rubbed savagely at my eyes as if I could somehow bully them back in again.

As if to stop this self-violence, Taïb imprisoned my hand in his. 'It will be OK, Izzy. It will. They are not bad men, however they may seem. They are rough and harsh and driven by their beliefs, but they will not hurt you, I am sure of it. Don't cry: please don't cry. I cannot bear to see you like this. You are a lioness: you are strong. I saw you climb a mountain; I saw you fall and almost die and you never once cried. You buried an old woman and you did not flinch from it. You are strong, and you do not know it.' He turned my hand palm-up and brushed it with his lips.

At another time in my life—at every other time in my life—I would have snatched it away as if he had tried to burn me, but perhaps because I felt guilty at my previous flinch I let him do it. I could not think of anyone who had ever kissed the palm of my hand, or anyone who had ever touched me so tenderly. I had spent my entire adult life avoiding intimacy with men: if I were honest with myself, they frightened me. I looked down now at Taïb's close-cropped head, the cap of hair so black

407

against his coffee skin, and felt . . . what? It was not fear, exactly, but it was not a comfortable sensation. I started to pull my hand away.

'No,' he said, holding on to it. 'Look: you have a water-diviner's hand.'

I stared at him as if he was mad. 'What?'

'You see this line here?' He traced the line that ran horizontally across my palm, bisecting it neatly.

'Yes?' I frowned.

'Have you ever seen a line like that on anyone else's hand?'

'I don't make a habit of grabbing people's hands and examining their palms,' I said. The conversation was becoming surreal.

'The water-diviner's line is almost always inherited. In our culture it is highly prized, thought of as tremendously lucky.'

'Lucky?' I laughed bitterly. I thought of my mother's hands, so small and neat. Mine, darker and broad as a spade, looked nothing like hers. My father's . . . An image, unbidden, of his hand pale against my stomach, reaching down. I almost gagged, the memory was so strong. I pushed it away, as I always did when such recollections surfaced, but this one was stronger than most; or perhaps I was weak. I closed my eyes and was fourteen again. I was wearing shorts and a T-shirt I had rolled up and tied under my breasts like a pop star I had seen in *Jackie* magazine. I had been outside sunbathing and had come in, hot and damp with sweat and sticky with Ambre Solaire, to get some orange squash and a little shade. There, in the kitchen, my father had pressed himself against my back, imprisoning me against the sink as the tap poured out an unending stream of water diluting the brightly coloured soda till the glass overflowed and ran clear. Some part of him as hard as rock pushed itself insistently against my buttocks as he pressed his hand against my stomach and down into my shorts. 'Oh, Izzy,' he breathed into my ear. 'You are so beautiful.' And then he had led me up to the attic . . .

Fighting to stop myself retching, I pulled away from Taïb. But he would not let me go. 'What is it?' he said. 'You look as if you are terrified of me.'

I shook my head, inarticulate with remembered horror. 'Not you,' I forced out at last. 'Not you, never you.'

'Then what?'

'I can't tell you.' I pulled away again. 'Don't. Don't look at me, please.'

'I love to look at you, Isabelle. You are so beautiful.'

The howl that broke from me was that of an injured animal. And, like an injured animal, I wanted to run out into the desert with my wounds wide open and lie down and let my lifeblood seep into the sand and just . . . stop . . . existing. But Taïb wouldn't let me.

'Tell me, Isabelle. What is it that hurts you so? I cannot bear to see you like this.'

'I cannot tell you. I have never told anyone.' I gave a small, bitter laugh. 'There was never anyone to tell. There never is, when you need it most: I learnt that lesson young. And anyway, I was too ashamed.'

'There is nothing you could say that would shock me or make me think less of you.'

'You do not know me. You do not know anything about me. If you knew me, the real me,

409

you wouldn't say this. You would despise me. You wouldn't want to be anywhere near me.' The words were tumbling out, tumbling over themselves in a dangerous, exuberant stream. I tried to hold them in, but they kept on coming, pushed up out of the roots of me by some terrible, unknown force.

And then I told him what I had never told another soul: the dark and shameful secret that I had buried so deep since my awful fourteenth summer when my life had split in two. Before that summer there had just been Izzy: little wild, innocent Izzy who laughed and shouted and did not think before she spoke, who climbed trees and jumped off walls and threw herself into life with delighted abandon, knowing that she was indestructible; after that summer there had only been Isabelle, broken, terrified Isabelle, abandoned by one parent to the untender mercies of another, who could never talk, even with her best friend, about what was going on in her life, who had learnt to present a quiet, bland, industrious mask to the world, a mask that had fused itself on to the woman everyone now knew. Disgusted with myself, I had rooted out of my life everything that had made me the wild little creature that had driven my father to behave in such an unnatural fashion and then walk away for ever, terrified by what he had done. I had become half the person I might have been: buttoned down, emotionally repressed, fearful of intimacy and risk, and closed off from joy and release.

Throughout it all Taïb's solemn dark gaze never left my face. He did not grimace or show disgust, nor did he interrupt or try to touch me. He just listened, as no one had listened to me before.

410

At last the well of words ran dry, leaving me as hollow as a gourd, my skin stretched as tight as a drum over the void my bones contained.

Taïb looked away from me and was silent for a long, long time, his eyes downcast, until I was sure I had shamed him as well as myself by my vile confession. Then he said gently, 'Poor Isabelle; poor Izzy. Such a terrible betrayal of trust and innocence, such an abuse of power. How could anyone do such a thing to any child, let alone his own?' His eyes met mine and I saw the candle flame dancing in them. 'And you have blamed and hated yourself for what he did to you.'

'Oh, I have blamed him too, believe me,' I said sourly. 'Blamed him, and hated him for it.'

'But you have blamed and hated yourself at the same time.'

And even as he said it, I knew it to be true. All this time I had been punishing myself, caging the wildness in me, netting it down. I had conformed to the social norm, allowed the middle-class world to straitjacket me within its uniform and economic structure and sought to regulate every aspect of the world around me. And I had been remarkably successful in doing so. I had been so afraid of everything beyond my own control; and, most of all, I had been afraid of myself.

I nodded slowly. 'You are right,' I acknowledged. 'But I do not know how to change that.'

'My people have a saying: time only moves forward, yesterday is gone. Turn your face to the future, Izzy; the past is behind you.'

I gave him a shaky smile. 'I wish it were so easy.'

'Things are hard only if you make them hard.'

411

'Sometimes things just happen to you and you have no control over them.'

'Now you're talking like my aunt! She would fall ill and claim it was the will of God, *insh'allah*, and she could do nothing but put up with it, and as a result would get sicker and sicker. My grandmother, whom you met, used to be driven mad by this *insh'allah* attitude of her sister, as she called it. "We are not puppets!" she would cry. "Get up and walk, instead of complaining about the stoppage in your guts. Drink water; eat figs!"'

I could not help myself: I laughed aloud. I had just unburdened myself of my worst and darkest secret, the thing that had poisoned my entire adult life; and he had raised the subject of his aunt's constipation. When I looked back again, there was a twinkle in Taïb's eye and I knew that he had deliberately lightened the mood.

He gave me the smallest nod and became solemn again. 'It is true that in Islam we are taught that the path of our life is written for us by God, who is all-knowing and all-powerful. But that does not mean that we have no freedom to act and react. We each have responsibility for how we live, how we deal with the circumstances we are handed. We are free for all practical purposes, and claiming the omniscience of destiny is no excuse for making the wrong choices in our lives. We must always strive to be the best version of ourselves we can be, in this life and the next. Who knows what is written for your future, Isabelle? The future could be wonderful.'

'Or it could be very short.' Despite this doomy pronouncement, I smiled, and Taïb smiled back and I felt a vast weight lift from me.

412

I looked past his shoulder. Outside, the sun was coming up: a pale band of numinous light showed in the glimpse of desert afforded me by a gap in the circle of dark tents. I crawled out into the cool sand and stood to watch the glowing rim break over the distant dunes, transforming their weary grey to rich creams and burnished golds, the hollows in between filling up with colour as the sunrise poured its light down into them. It was the most beautiful thing I had ever seen. I felt my mind emptying itself, all the old fears and memories flowing out of me, until I was as light as the glowing air, and there was nothing between me and the sky and sand.

CHAPTER TWENTY-NINE

Mariata walked all night. The moon was kind to her, but sometimes she stumbled; and once she fell down and skinned her knees even through the thick fabric of her robe, the scattered rocks were so sharp. She walked as if in a dream; she walked as if she had no idea in her head except that of walking. In fact, she tried not to think at all and every time a doubt crept up on her, she pushed it away, allowing her body to take over and keep on moving. Despite this, it was not true to say she had no idea where she was or in which direction she was heading, because as the constellations moved overhead a voice inside urged her to take note of the alignment of the Scorpion's Tail and unconsciously she found herself adjusting her course to follow it as it inexorably lowered its sting towards the south and east.

As she walked she recited silently to herself folk songs from her childhood that her grandmother and aunts had told to her, songs heard around the fires when the caravanners returned from their journeys or the warriors from their raids; little bits of long-buried nonsense that surfaced from the depths of her memory:

> *Two little birds sitting in a tree*
> *One like you and one like me*
> *Black his wing and bright his eye*
> *Throw a stone and see him fly . . .*

The stones were horribly sharp underfoot. She wished she had not worn the sandals she had brought with her from the Adagh but had invested in the solid red leather boots favoured by the Aït Khabbashi women, boots soled with Goodyear rubber; boots that covered the ankles and were laced tight to the shin. That was the right sort of footwear for hard walking like this, where each step was uneven and the ground crunched and grated underfoot like cinders. Up a rise she toiled, and down the other side, sliding one foot after the other, feeling the gravel and scree pour away beneath her weight.

> *Oh, my camel, so mighty and strong*
> *With your fine hump so heavy with fat,*
> *Ride along now, my dear one, ride along—*

No, that wouldn't do. She tried not to think about camels, for with that thought came panic and the memory of Atisi being beaten by the soldiers. Who knew what had happened to him down there on the road? Had they beaten him senseless and taken him prisoner? Or had they killed him and removed his body? The sight of Moushi dead by the side of the road, and the pack animal kicking up its heels as it vanished into the darkness, came back to her again and with it the knowledge of the stupidity of being out here alone, with nothing, not even a cup of water, to sustain her. The knowledge pushed at her, insistent. It poked insinuating fingers into the spaces between the songs and rhymes with which she tried to smother it. It whispered *you will die* into the gaps between words. *You will die and no one will mark your grave.*

Mariata gritted her teeth. *Shut up*, she told it. *We have only just started and there is a long, long way to go. If you threaten me with death on the very first night, what will you have left to frighten me with in three days, or five, or twelve?*

Hours passed and the stars wheeled through the black night and still she walked, a monotonous trudge through an unendingly flat region, studded with the ever-present clinker that battered her sandals and turned her ankles and made her calf muscles ache and protest. The Scorpion scuttled off the edge of the world and disappeared into the void. One by one the stars began to lose their clarity and eventually the moon gave up its dominion over the sky. When the sun finally made an appearance, it was to a grey and weary world. Colourless and pale, the land stretched itself out in front of Mariata, bleak and unfriendly. Things that until now had been formless revealed their grim monotony of shape: mile after mile of stone-

415

scattered plateau, grey turning to dun and then, as the sun rose higher, to a dead and dusty brown. Her heart sank. This must be the Hamada du Guir, the vast barren plain that stretched for hundreds of miles between the great ergs, the seas of sand that lay to east and west. And everywhere she looked it was as dry as week-old bread. There was no sign anywhere of the oases the caravanners spoke of; there was no splash of green at all.

She closed her eyes and tried to remember what she had heard from the traders in the funduq, sifting through the information she had stored away for just such a journey. Words came back to her in little bursts, like underground streams surfacing through the desert of her mind. *The rock desert is the one that will kill you. If you miss a waterhole, you are dead. Igli and Mazzer and Tamtert are good places for camels. The sun will come up over your left shoulder. Find the two-horned peak and walk between the horns. They say a man can survive for a week without food or water. But only if the weather is cold and God smiles upon you.*

But it was another voice, distant, female, that reminded her: *In the Hamada du Guir the dried riverbeds run north-west to south-east: follow their line and at last you will come to the Valley of the Oases.*

Mariata opened her eyes, turned her face to the sun and began to walk.

*　　　*　　　*

Hours later nothing in the landscape had changed significantly. Even though she ploughed on determinedly, the horizons remained as distant

416

and unchangeable as they had seemed at first light. The oueds she had followed were just indentations in the dusty ground, jagged and crumbling, floored with jumbles of stones smoothed by a river that had flowed and disappeared long ago, leaving only dry boulders in its wake, and even these dead watercourses faded out after a mile or two of hard walking. Once she found an area of spiky green plants and quickened her pace towards it; but the ground surrounding the vegetation was just as dry and dusty as every other part of this grim wilderness, and she cut her fingers when she tried to take some of the leaves. On she went, her back aching, her belly feeling heavier with each step she took, trying not to think of disaster. It was only half a day since she had eaten, she told herself, just half a day since she had drunk liquid. She could survive: she was a daughter of the desert. *A man can survive for a week without food or water,* she told herself over and over, her mind conveniently slipping past the dread provisos to recall the tales men told around the campfires, amazing feats of survival and perseverance when camels had died under them or been stolen in the night, leaving them with nothing, and she believed with all of her will that she was as determined as any man and that determination would give her hardiness, even though she carried a child. *A pregnant lioness is the most dangerous animal of all*, she remembered one of the hunters saying. But then she remembered that men said that this was because the female would rather turn on her pursuer and die in the process than save herself and her unborn cub. A few steps later she also recalled that they had laughed when they said this and joked about Ali's pregnant wife, Hennu, who had become so bad-tempered with him of late that she had beaten him over the head with her shoe when he had come into her tent one night. Disheartened, she eased herself into the shadowy lee of a boulder and drowsed for a while, but her sleep was fitful and her dreams disturbing, so she pushed herself upright and kept on walking, even though the afternoon sun burned like a fire and beat down on her like a hammer.

*   *   *

She did not know what it was that caught her eye—whether it was the distant flicker of movement or a new colour that entered the spectrum of duns and greys—but when she saw the camel it was as if a lightning bolt had pinned her to the spot. She stared and stared, unable to believe her eyes, thinking it a trick of the heat-haze, a deceit of light and shadow. But yes, there it was, a camel-coloured object moving slowly, its head down as if it were searching in vain for something to graze on. And not just camel-coloured, either, for as she drew closer she began to make out other details: the red and blue of a distinctive striped blanket; black waterskins; white sacks of rice and flour; bundles of straw. It was the pack animal belonging to Atisi ag Baye. She almost cried out in shock, for to come all this way across the barren *hamada* and to find in the midst of nothing the very camel that had escaped you the day before was surely a miracle! She touched her amulet to her lips. *Thank you*, she whispered, though whom she thanked she was not sure. Whether it was Tin Hinan or the

418

spirits who were responsible, or whether quite unwittingly she had followed the animal's trail all this way, or whether they had both been channelled unerringly along the same route—none of it mattered. She was a daughter of the desert and the desert had provided.

Filled with a surge of energy, Mariata girded her robe and started to walk quickly towards it, keeping always out of the animal's line of sight. She was no more than a hundred yards away when she saw that there was a second figure with the camel: a man; no, a boy. Her skin shivered, despite the heat. Then she marched determinedly towards them. 'Hey, you!'

The boy was thin, his eyes large in his head. He looked appalled to see her. She could see the whites of them all around the pupil. His skin was as dark as the rocks.

'That's my camel you have there!'

Quicker than a rat up a rock, the boy scuttled up the camel's neck, settled himself amongst the provisions and urged the beast away.

'No!' Mariata started to go after him, but her speed of movement was hampered by her pregnancy, and the scattered rocks bruised the soles of her feet and turned her ankles. 'Come back!'

But the camel took off as if pursued by afrits, its great feet flailing, its neck swinging from side to side.

Mariata shrieked till her throat was raw but to no effect. Soon the camel and the boy were no more than a speck in the distance, though a miasma of dust hung in the air and marked their passage. Mariata sighed with frustration. She felt

419

like an elephant, slow and lumbering, and now they had got away. Furious at herself as much as at the thief, Mariata marched on in their wake. They would have to stop somewhere: there must be a camp. The boy had a look of the harratin, or of an iklan child, avoiding its chores. If the camp was not too far away she would be magnanimous, would not demand restitution for the theft and the inconvenience of walking the extra mile or two. After all, she could afford to be generous, for hospitality surely awaited her: tea, and a good meal. When they knew whose camel it was, when they heard of her prestigious bloodline, they would probably slaughter a goat, or even a sheep, to honour her. In better spirits now, Mariata walked with her head high and a good long stride. Each time a crest of rock scored the horizon she climbed it with the expectation of finding an encampment on the other side, an oasis and fresh water, smiling women and respectful, veiled men. Perhaps they would even be heading south as far as the Hoggar and she could join their entourage.

Hours passed with these pleasant thoughts rolling through her mind and still there was no sign of the boy and the camel, except for tracts of churned-up ground where stones had been displaced, the sand between them imprinted with the split-toed impression of the beast's feet. The terrain no longer seemed so hostile: she managed to find a certain bleak beauty in the cratered, rock-strewn landscape and to marvel at the changes the sun falling lower in the sky wrought upon the scene, transforming the ground from a pale and powdery dun to the ochre of a gazelle's hide and finally to the rich purple-red of blood. By the time the setting sun cast long fingers of shadow between the rocks, she was parched and exhausted—so when she topped out on a rise and saw below her three tents of black hide pegged low to the ground, she almost cried out for joy. She began to run down the slope, letting gravity guide her steps, before realizing that three tents were all there were. Where was the rest of the tribe? Screwing her eyes up against the falling darkness, she made out only a handful of goats rather than the herds that would be necessary to support a proper encampment. A handful of goats, and a solitary camel. Were these people outriders, or outcasts? She slowed, unsure.

Then dogs began to bark. There were half a dozen of them, rangy mutts whose ribs showed through their coats. Years of miscegenation and poor diet had not improved their tempers, or their welcome to visitors. Mariata drew back, nervous. Her own tribe had hunting dogs: sleek, elegant animals that ran obediently at their masters' heels; and the Kel Teggart could barely support themselves, let alone a pack of wild dogs. The dogs advanced, running low to the ground. Mariata stood rooted to the spot. Then she bent, picked up a stone and threw it at the nearest dog. It caught the animal on the shoulder and the dog fell back with a yelp. Mariata gathered more missiles and sent another spinning down amongst them. The dogs danced, outraged. Their barking redoubled in noise, but they did not advance.

At last a man came out of one of the tents. He was tall and thin and as black as night. *Iklan*, was Mariata's first, relieved, thought. 'Call your dogs off!' she cried imperiously. Where there were

421

slaves there were always masters.

The man stared at her suspiciously. He called out and the dogs circled back towards him, turning warily as they went, as if expecting her to throw more stones. The noise of the dogs had brought the rest of the tent-dwellers out. No masters here: they were a motley collection, none veiled. These were baggara, wandering beggars: ragged nomads who scraped a living outside society. It did not look as if they were making much of a success of it. Amongst them she recognized the boy she had seen with the pack camel. The man who had brought the dogs to order ducked back into the tent and a few moments later another man came out, followed by a woman cradling a small child. They all looked towards where Mariata stood silhouetted on the rocks. For a moment Mariata's eyes locked with those of the woman and she experienced a jolt of pure sympathy, almost tangible, as if her soul was a bead running down a string stretched taut between them.

Then the woman began to shriek, 'It is a spirit! It is the spirit that took my boy!' She came rushing out of the enclosure, her face a mask of fury and pain. Mariata saw that the child's limbs flopped limply with the impact of the woman's steps and it came to her in a sudden unwelcome rush of understanding that the child was dead and that, appearing out of the wilderness in the fey twilight—just when the Kel Asuf began to walk abroad—the woman had taken her for a djinn.

The men caught up with the grieving mother before she came close to Mariata. One of them pulled the body of the child from her and stalked back towards the tents and, as if she could not bear to be separated from it, she followed, arms outstretched. The second man stood still, watching Mariata.

'I am not a djinn!' she called out; but her throat was parched and the words came out in an unearthly rasping whisper that had him reaching for his amulets. She swallowed and licked her lips with a dry tongue and tried again. 'I am not a djinn,' she repeated, walking towards him. 'I am a flesh and blood woman, a woman of the Kel Taitok. Do not be frightened. My camel ran away last night. I have been following it all day. That boy there'—she pointed beyond him—'he took it. Maybe he thought it was a stray, or that its owner was dead; maybe he took it to care for it. Whatever his reason I have come to claim my camel and the pack-goods that were on it, and I would be grateful if you would let me have some water and shelter for the night. Then I will take my camel and be on my way.'

The man said nothing; then he went down on his haunches. It was an odd gesture and she did not know what to make of it until she saw him stand up again and let fly the first stone. It whizzed harmlessly past her shoulder, clattering against the rocks behind her. The second caught her a glancing blow on the arm, the shock of it rather than the pain making her cry out.

'What are you doing? I have done nothing to you!'

The man hefted another stone. 'The camel is ours now: go away.'

'You are thieves!'

'Go away or we will kill you.'

'Have you no honour? Do you have no respect

423

for the code of the desert?'

'The only code in this desert is death.'

'May the spirits curse you if you drive me away!'
Mariata waved the amulet at them. 'I will call down
the evil eye upon you: you will all die.'

The man's eyes were dull. 'We are dying anyway.
Go away.'

The third stone he threw lost its force in the
folds of her robe; but he was already gathering
more and the dogs were barking, bouncing stiff-
legged with pent-up aggression. Mariata turned
her back on them and walked away.

*   *   *

She lay in the lee of some boulders for long hours
pondering what to do. The idea of her camel so
close at hand and yet so unattainable gnawed at
her. She could not simply leave it with the baggara
family, but she did not know how she might steal it
back. All through the night she thought about it,
anger boiling away inside her, concocting and
dismissing dozens of foolish schemes. She could
have been using the cool darkness to walk on to
better fortune, but the knowledge that her pack-
goods, water and supplies were just a few hundred
yards away held her prisoner. Something in her
knew that if she allowed the opportunity to regain
the camel to slip away she would die, and
deservedly so. The People of the Veil valued
cunning, resourcefulness and stealth as highly as
their honour; to be so feeble as to allow such low
vagrants to get the better of her would be an
admission of defeat, a shameful act. Had the
Mother of All ever suffered such indignity? She

found it hard to believe. What would her esteemed ancestress have done? 'Tin Hinan,' she said softly into the darkness, 'guide me now with your wisdom and strength.' She pressed the amulet to her forehead and felt its metal cold against her skin.

How long she stayed in this attitude she did not know, but after a time she became aware of a small sound in the rocks to her left. She stilled her breathing, suddenly terrified. Had they tracked her down: would they carry out their threat to kill her? Silently, she reached into the fringed leather bag and drew out the little knife and waited.

The noise was soft, barely audible, like something brushed against the rocks; a tap, a scuffle. It came closer. Mariata readied herself, teeth clenched. She would not go without drawing blood; they would not take her easily.

When the hare appeared she stared at it, bemused. It stared back at her, frozen in surprise, its ears held rigid, every muscle poised for sudden flight. She caught it before she knew consciously what she was doing, felt its strong back legs kicking out at her as she buried her hands in its fur. It felt so warm and determined, so shockingly vital and alive, that she almost relented and let it go, but some more primal instinct prevailed. A few moments later she looked down to find it lying limp, its blood black against her hands.

It was a large animal, sturdily built and well muscled. Examining its body by the pale moonlight, Mariata found herself blinking back tears at its beauty: the cool silk of its coat, the long limbs and huge ears. Then she mastered herself and did what she had to do.

Mariata watched the sun come up from the back of the camel many miles from the nomad camp. The beast was sweating, despite the chill of the dawn, and so was she. But elation banished exhaustion. She had risked everything and she had triumphed. She shuddered, remembering how the dogs had torn into the pieces of the dismembered hare that she had flung far and wide, how their jaws had crunched down on its fragile bones; how a fight had broken out between them for the last and best morsel, the head, and how the men had had to come out of the tents and beat them with sticks to make them stop their noise. In the midst of all this she had slipped into the enclosure and been surprised to find the camel clumsily hobbled and the pack-goods stacked haphazardly to one side, along with the saddle and the blanket. Only the sack of flour and the old bread were missing, she saw, amazed at her own good fortune. The rice sack stood to one side, a little of its contents spilling out into the sand, the tiny white grains rendered pearly and luminescent by the moon's light. Mariata stoppered the hole in the sack with some of the fodder straw, checked that the waterskins were full and slung them over her back.

The camel regarded her sulkily and, when she came near, threw its head up and rolled its eyes. I have walked far enough, those eyes told her, quite clearly: do not think to make me walk more. Mariata knew camels to be obdurate beasts; but she also knew a firm hand and a determined attitude would usually prevail. She marched up to it and, remembering how Rahma had bound the

426

muzzle of the camels they had ridden across the Tamesna when the soldiers had come to the oasis, used her veil to gag it before it had a chance to bellow its dismay. This took the beast so much by surprise that Mariata was able to sling her pack-goods aboard, and then haul herself up with them. The camel swung its head to regard her with an aggrieved look and Mariata glared back at it grimly, then wrenched it to its feet by sheer force of will and urged it into a lumbering gallop.

Now she laughed aloud and patted her belly. 'You are the son of Tuaregs, and do not ever forget it! What an adventurer you will be, inheriting the best of your mother and your father. No ragged baggara shall trick you or steal from you, for between the goodwill of the spirits and the power of your own resources you shall always triumph!'

She tapped the camel peremptorily upon its poll. Grumbling, it folded its knees and let her down and in the rosy light of the desert dawn she undid the knotted veil and carefully hobbled the animal so that it could not escape again; and then they feasted and refreshed themselves before seeking a well-earned rest in the shade of the spreading branches of a solitary acacia.

CHAPTER THIRTY

Mariata's fierce optimism did not last. For days, her instinct had been urging her to move eastwards, but she ignored it because not to keep moving south seemed plainly wrong; and so it was that when she passed between the oases at Ougarta and Aguedal she did not even realize it, for by seeking the shadow of the Jebel el-Kabla she took a col that led only into yet another long arm of the bone-dry Hamada du Guir by mistake. The terrain through which she travelled alternated between crumbling towers of red rock and areas in which a strange dark patina lay plastered against the ground, a brittle glaze that shone dully in the sun and cracked beneath the pressure of the camel's wide pads. Not a plant grew here, not even the hardiest cactus or euphorbia, and the camel bellowed his displeasure whenever they stopped, twisting his head tortuously to try to steal the ever-diminishing bundle of fodder strapped to his back. He was starving, she knew: the usually solid hump was collapsed and soft, its fat reserves almost gone.

'No, Acacia!' she told him fiercely. She had not meant to form a bond with the camel—he was a pack animal, as functional as her own feet—but, after being all day and night in his company and sharing his trials, she had been ambushed by an unexpected affection for the smelly, bad-tempered, recalcitrant beast. The name had offered itself easily: the animal shared the tree's spiky hardiness. If one of those tough and thorny trees were able to express itself, she was sure that it would roar and grumble and gargle and spit in just the same way as its namesake. 'If you eat it all now there will be nothing left and then you will regret your greed. Be strong and patient and bear your troubles without complaint and you will be rewarded.'

Strength and patience and obduracy: these were the values her people most valued. No man ever complained about the hardships he had faced in the desert; his pride would not let him, for to complain rendered him less than a man. Instead, they vied with one another to recount the worst trials they had faced: the sand beetles they had cracked with their teeth and chewed to a bitter paste; the vipers they had eaten raw; the urine drunk at the worst of times. She remembered the near-legendary tale of the trader separated from his caravan on his way to Sijilmassa, who had wandered without food and was down to his last mouthful of water when a caravan of merchants from a rival tribe had happened upon him. As is the way of the desert, they had offered him their hospitality: some dried camel meat and water from their gerbers; but he had merely smiled and patted his pack and told them he had all he needed and offered to prepare tea for all of them instead. The situation was quite clear to both sides; but no one would shame the lone traveller by calling his bluff, and so the merchants had gone their way and the trader had died a day later. His story lived on, five hundred years later. And is that not a better legacy, the men of the Kel Ahaggar said, to die nobly and with your pride intact than to have survived by taking sustenance from your enemy?

Mariata was not sure her own resolve would hold quite as firm: even if Rhossi ag Bahedi himself were to suddenly appear bearing fragrant lamb and apricots, she would probably fall upon the food and devour every last morsel before remembering that she had such a luxurious thing as pride, so she could hardly blame the camel for his attempted thievery. She felt the saliva glands in the corners of her jaw twitch and clench, but she was so dry her mouth could not even water. She had not taken a drink since the sun went down.

One waterskin hung slack and useless, slowly baking to a crisp; what was left in the other furry black gerber tasted warm and brackish, as if the liquid in the goatskin had transmuted back to blood. And as if it too were complaining at the lack of nutrition, the baby kicked out hard, once, twice. She placed her hand over her belly, fingers spread. 'Quiet in there, little man. Kicking your mama won't make it any better.'

By the thirteenth day all the fodder was gone and there was so little water to spare that she had enough only with which to wet Acacia's nostrils, and when she did so the ungrateful beast did his best to bite her. He nosed at her sandals, but these were too precious to be eaten, so she let him eat the reed mat that she slept on, and he chewed slowly and with painful effort, grinding the mat to a dry cud with a determined back and forth sawing of his long jaw. For herself, she tried to eat the rice uncooked and all but cracked her teeth, and even grinding it between stones just reduced it to a flour-like powder that coated the inside of the mouth and was impossible to swallow without water to mix it with. Now she realized why Atisi had brought two female camels with him: their milk would have sustained them in such hard circumstances, and she remembered poor Moushi lying dead by the roadside and cursed her luck that the only mount left to her was male. She had heard of traders reduced to tapping the blood from their camel's neck; but when she approached Acacia with the little knife from Tana's bag he peeled his lips from his long yellow teeth and pronounced he would bite her arm off if she came a step closer; or at least that was what she imputed to his bellow of rage, and so she persuaded herself that things were not yet so desperate.

Even so, when they stopped on the thirteenth day, she tipped the bag upside down for the hundredth time and interrogated its contents in the vain hope that she had missed something useful. She pushed the objects around in a desultory manner as the camel chewed the handful of fodder, seeing nothing new. Just as she was about to scoop the items back into the bag, a small, striped pebble caught her eye. It was a bluish-green with a single white horizontal band running around its centre: quite different to the ambient red and dun. Mariata picked it up. It sat smooth and tiny in her hand, as smooth and tiny as a songbird's egg. She brushed grains of sand from its surface and then, without a single conscious thought, placed the pebble under her tongue, where it fitted with perfect comfort. Within moments saliva had flooded her mouth, trickling over her teeth, and she swallowed gratefully. She kept sucking at the pebble and moving it around with her tongue and found for the rest of the day that it kept her mouth moistened and took the edge off her thirst; but it was the smallest of aids and at best a temporary measure.

They kept out of the sun when they could, moving around the leeside of rock towers till dusk, then walked by the light of the waxing moon. South and east they went across the dry, rock-strewn plateaus and found only dried-up watercourses and hardly a leaf or plant that was not withered almost to dust. Acacia walked with his head down, slower and slower, until at last he sat down and simply refused to get up. Mariata waited, but he would not even look at her. She tried to cajole him with the last of the fodder, but he gave her the briefest glance of reproach and turned his head away as if to say: too late! Now you will be sorry for your meanness. She dragged on his halter, but obstinacy made him strong. She sat down beside him and sighed. She sang to him, a song her grandmother used to sing to her when she was little: he snorted and gargled raspily in his throat and just sat there, flicking sand spitefully with his tail.

Mariata got up and stood in front of him with her hands on her hips. Acacia pretended she wasn't there. Mariata moved into his eyeline so that he would have to make an effort to ignore her. The camel looked at her with dull eyes. 'You need a rest. I understand. I need a rest too. But we cannot stop here: we have to keep moving till we find an oasis or a well. Then we will rest, and you can dip your head into the cool water and drink to your heart's content and feed on palms and dates. But you have to get up, get on your feet. Because if you don't, you will die. And if you die, I will die.' She paused and touched her swelling abdomen. 'And so will my child.'

Eventually, unable to evade her penetrating gaze, Acacia struggled painfully to his feet once more; and Mariata walked beside him, shuffling one foot in front of the other. It was impossible to avoid the thought of death. Her mind kept circling around the idea like a hawk gyring around its prey. They came down into a valley in which the desert sands had been blown in a smooth, pale carpet, but down in the soft hollow something was sticking up through the sand. As soon as it saw what it was, the camel jinked sideways and began to bellow

432

piteously. Mariata stared at the bones, bleached white by the sun, polished to a fine sheen by the windborne sand, and her heart thudded dully inside her own bones. Was this all that was left of the last traveller who had passed this way? Would she and Acacia be prey to the same fate? A terrible image drifted through her mind then, of a skeleton curled upon its side, lapped by waves of sand, its knees drawn up to protect the tiny skeleton cradled beneath its ribs.

The image filled her with determination. 'Damn you!' she told the camel. 'Pick your feet up. We *will* survive!'

It was an instruction to herself as much as to the exhausted animal. Jaw out-thrust, Mariata drove them both on, though she was tired, so tired, setting a course directly east. Why she changed direction she did not know, but her hand itched and burned and her skull buzzed with hidden knowledge. Somewhere out there was the Valley of the Oases the traders in the funduq had spoken of, the long valley that ran from north to south, studded with ancient wells and oases, through which the trade route that had been followed for thousands of years wound its way. She would find it or die.

The hamada gave way to erg—a great sea of dunes, sweeping and sickle-shaped, their long crests carved to a pitiless knife-edge by the wind. She stood on a rock and looked out across the dunes that rolled away from her, their bright ridges alternating with their shady troughs, striping the ground like the barring on a falcon's wing, and knew they were on the edge of the Grand Occidental Erg, and that if they did not find a well soon, they had no chance of survival at all.

Acacia collapsed the next day. His knees folded under him and he fell in a heap, a great huff of foul-smelling air rushing at the same time out of his mouth and his rectum. After this, he sat staring into space as if he could see his own death, a speck on the far horizon, advancing step by inexorable step. Mariata cried out and then threw her arms around his neck, burying her face in his burning hide. 'Get up!' she urged him. 'Get to your feet!'

Panic made her harsh. She pummelled the camel with her fists; but he bore the assault without reaction. She kicked him and sobbed drily as she did so; but he did not move. And so at last she lay down beside him, in the shadow his form made, and waited until he stopped breathing. Even then, he did not fall, but sat there as unmoving as a sphinx, alive one second, gone the next. It was impossible to judge the exact moment of his passing, for nothing essential appeared to have changed in him. Mariata put her hand to the camel's mouth and felt no breath there. She laid her cheek against the hollow ribs and heard no heartbeat. She pulled at his long eyelashes: he did not even twitch. At last she had to admit the terrible truth: that he was dead and she was alone, and too far now from anywhere to turn back and seek help. She did not imagine that she could survive in such a place, with nothing but her own feet to bear her. She sat with her back propped against the camel's corpse and stared deadly out into the sands. So this was how it would end for her and her unborn child. It would be a bleak ending, but at least they would die as People of the Veil, in the desert where they belonged.

That night the djenoun came for her soul. She heard them on the wind as it picked up at nightfall, whipping streamers of sand off the peaks of the dunes. Their song was faint at first, a sort of dull hum that thrummed through her bones, making her ribs vibrate; and then it was all about her, in the air, in the ground beneath her feet: a slow drumbeat of life, a drumbeat that had always existed, had been here before the dunes formed, before the grasslands that came before the sands, when the gazelles and the giraffes ran here and the world was lush and green; when God formed the djenoun from smokeless fire. The song became a roar and then a howl. Mariata let the sound flow through her, by turns terrified and fascinated. The Kel Asuf, the People of the Wilderness: they were singing to her because they recognized her as one of their own, one of those who speak with no one, who travel through the empty places. They had come for her. In some ways this was a relief: she would not have to battle on towards her doom, and her death would be taken out of her own hands. She stood up and let the wind and sand batter her.

*   *   *

She awoke the next morning with her face buried against the belly of the dead camel. A blanket of sand encased them both, trapping a large pocket of foul but breathable air: there was no doubt that Acacia, in death, had saved her life. Pushing herself to her feet through the tide of sand, Mariata stared around her, marvelling at the pale bright blue of the sky, the gleaming gold of the dunes. The wind in the night had been so strong

435

that the landscape she awoke to was pristine and unfamiliar, as if its hollows and curves had all been rearranged by a giant hand. For a brief moment she felt a keen disappointment that her trials in this world were not over; but then the life inside her delivered a powerful kick. Despite her desperate situation, Mariata laughed aloud. 'Hello, little one! Did you think I needed to be reminded that you were in there?'

Charged with new energy, Mariata took Tana's knife from the fringed bag strapped across her back, sharpened it with the whetstone until its edge was as thin as a sickle moon, and set about butchering the dead camel. She tapped its blood into one of the gerbers and dressed the corpse: flayed off its skin, cut out the last of the fat reserves, set aside long strips of meat from its flanks and shoulders for drying. Soon poor Acacia was reduced to nothing more than bones and hooves and his big, sad head. Many would have chided her for leaving the skull intact, with its nutritious brain and its juice-filled eyes untouched, but an unwonted sentimentality came upon her, by which it seemed wrong to defile the head of a friend, particularly one whose great efforts had saved her life, and so she patted it uncomfortably on the poll, smoothed a patch of sand beside it and with the blade inscribed a prayer: *May your spirit wander cool gueltas and rich pasturage; may cool shadows ease your soul. Mariata ult Yemma thanks you. The child of Amastan ag Moussa thanks you.* No breath of wind disturbed the stark Tifinagh symbols.

Using the coarse hair of the camel's tail as tinder and the last of its dried droppings as fuel, she made an acrid fire and cooked and ate the heart and liver. Having eaten so little for so long, this task alone took her a vast time. It felt strange to force food into herself in this way, but she knew that the more she could eat, the better prepared she would be to carry on her journey. The blanket was gone, taken by the desert winds, so that night she lay beneath a cover made from the flayed and bloody hide. Her practicality in arranging such things surprised her: she had not before been known for her capability, but then never before had she needed to rely entirely on her own resources.

For two more days she stayed with the corpse of poor Acacia, cooking and eating what she could of the flesh and drinking the blood before it congealed. The herbs that Tana had included in the wedding bag enabled her to eat when she thought she could eat no more and warded off any sickness or discomfort that eating so much meat might otherwise have brought about. As the sun fell on the third day she gathered the cured jerky into a bag fashioned from the camel's stomach, which she fastened across her back with strips of hide. It was heavy and uncomfortable, but it represented survival. Now I shall bear Acacia's hump and it will lend me its strength, she told herself fiercely, slinging the gerbers across her front.

She stumbled south and east, following the passage of the stars. She walked through a region of flat, compacted sand that the wind had left striated in thousands upon thousands of tiny wavelets. The patterns, so elegant in their perfect regularity, distracted her mind and soothed her eye; she was sorry when the sands rose again and she found herself wading ankle-deep through their soft tide, but soon the dunes flattened out once more and before long she found herself in an area of perfect camel-dun as far as the eye could see, a dun unspoilt except for an irregular studding of dark stones, each the size of a child's fist. When she sat to rest she picked up one of these stones and felt how it gave weight and meaning to her hand. It seemed far heavier than any ordinary stone should seem: she examined it curiously. Flecked with brown and pitted as if by fire, the stone seemed more like metal than rock, and it was then that she recalled how Amastan had told her of the thunderstones that fell from the skies. They had been sitting on one of the tall sentinel rocks that guarded the way into the tribe's grounds from the Tamesna, watching falling stars blaze a silver trail through the night. 'I walked in a place where the hearts of such stars had fallen in their hundreds,' he had told her, and she had made a face at him, her expression eloquent with disbelief.

'Another of your wild tales!' she chided him, though she loved to listen to the cadence of his voice no matter how absurd the subject.

'*Insh'allah* you will never be in such a place. Many have tried to cross that plain, but Al Djumsjab, the glooming breath of the erg, who separates companions and devastates caravans, has devoured them all. Now all that is left of them is their bones parching white in the sun while their spirits wander the wastes with the Kel Asuf, playing ball with the iron hearts that have fallen from the skies.'

She had thought it one of his poetic fancies, but

now she remembered how he had at another time asked if she thought that the stars that shone above might be the souls of the dead, and she threw the stone away from her and got to her feet and walked as quickly as she could manage through the field of thunderstones, itching with dread every step of the way.

The next day while negotiating a steep dune she slipped and fell and rolled to the bottom and lay there, panting. Her left hand ached and burned. She turned it over and examined it. Right in the centre, where a long, straight line bisected the palm, a thorn had lodged itself so deeply that no part of it protruded. Dark blood lay stoppered around the thorn. Wincing, Mariata squeezed and pressed the flesh around it, to no avail. She tried to dig it out with the blade of the little knife, but the thorn buried itself more deeply. Had she been able to, she would have wept with pain and frustration, but there was nothing behind her eyes but a hot ache.

The next day her hand was swollen; pads of reddened flesh pushed up around the wound like pillows. It throbbed with every step she took and felt as heavy as if she were carrying a thunderstone. Before long it felt as if the wound was at the very centre of her, a raw and pulsing other heart, and the rest of her as insubstantial as smokeless fire, trapped by some magic in human form but ready to fly up into the air if the spell somehow broke. She was almost delirious by the time the oasis came into view and stumbled towards it thinking it a trick of the desert, a mirage of heat-haze sent to taunt her, even though it was barely dawn. The closer she got, though, the clearer it became, the green of the palm trees an assault to the eyes after the unending duns and reds. The water shone the sky back at her like a mirror, so still as to seem a solid mass. Suddenly, with a clarity so intense it was like hallucination, she saw herself immerse the burning hand, saw the water closing over it so that there was nothing but wrist; felt the coolness with a piercing bliss that rivalled the sweetest moment in Amastan's arms. She imagined it so clearly that dream and reality merged into one long swooning fall. It was when she started to drink that she came back to herself, for that was not bliss but a raw and fiery sensation. Her throat was so dry and closed that she almost could not swallow; instead she choked and rasped and retched. At last she managed to get some water down; then like a dying thing she shouldered her bundles, crawled in amongst the shady roots and fell asleep in the cool darkness there.

She awoke to the sound of voices and sat up suddenly, terrified. Three camels were drinking at the waterhole, legs splayed as they craned their necks; three men sat at the other end of the oasis, refilling their waterskins. They did not seem to have noticed her. With her dark and dusty clothing and black gerbers she was well camouflaged in the shadows. Part of her wanted to call out to them and ask their help; but another, warier instinct prevailed. She settled back against the palms and watched and waited. She watched as two of the men settled themselves on the ground beneath the palms and rested, while the third stamped impatiently around and tried to get them moving, without success. At last he too sat down with his back against a tree and appeared to sleep, but still

440

Mariata dared not move.

As night fell the men made a camp fire and gathered around it to prepare tea and food. The smell of their preparations wafted across the still pool towards her so that her stomach clenched and growled. She drew a piece of camel meat from the stomach-bag and chewed on it, all the while yearning for the taste of green tea and sugar. The jumping firelight lit their forms: Mariata saw that two of them were veiled, and in Hoggar fashion, and this gave her the heart she needed to move closer. Treading softly through the fallen branches with their crisped brown fronds, she reached the edge of her cover, and there she squatted down and listened.

The man who wore only a loose head-covering seemed unhappy. He could not sit still, and appeared infuriated by his companions' equanimity. 'I do not understand why we are stopping here!' he said again. 'After all, it is I who am paying you: you should do what I say!'

The taller of the two veiled men gave him a level look. 'The camels are exhausted, and so are we.'

Mariata's heart stilled in her chest. She knew that voice: it was her brother, Azaz.

'She may yet be ahead of us; she may have taken a faster route!'

Azaz sighed. 'There is no faster route. All travellers know the Valley of the Oases is the only safe way through this part of the desert. Deviate from it and all you will find is a swift death.'

The butcher, Mbarek Aït Ali, threw up his hands as if to ward off evil. 'I pray to Allah she did not, it would be a waste of such a juicy peach.'

At this, the second veiled figure got up and

kicked sand over the fire in a gesture that spoke of repressed violence. 'This is no more than a wild hare chase.' Mariata heard how his voice broke like that of a boy on the threshold of manhood. It was her young brother, Baye.

'The storm must have covered her traces; or she has used some sort of magic to hide them,' the butcher said.

'My sister is no sorceress: you should not listen to my father's wife.'

'Then where is she? Has she vanished into thin air, or taken to flight? No one has seen her since Douira, in the company of that raggedy old trader.'

'They may have parted company.'

'Or they have made better time than us,' the butcher persisted. 'Whatever the way of it, I am determined to find her. I cannot go back without her: I will be a laughing-stock. Another day or two, I tell you. We will continue into the desert.'

Azaz and Baye exchanged glances but said nothing. At last Baye clicked his tongue. 'My sister has lived a pampered life: she is not made for tramping deserts. She's probably back in Imteghren by now, feasting on couscous and laughing up her sleeve. We should give this up as a bad job.'

'We have gone further than expected, and further than you have paid for. As it is, if we're caught by the Algerian Army it will not go well for us,' Azaz added.

'I thought you nomads didn't give a pig's arse for borders!' the butcher sneered.

'I care about my neck,' Azaz replied levelly.

The butcher slapped one massive fist into his other palm. 'Perhaps if I raise the price by another hundred dirhams you may find a tad more courage.'

Azaz shook his head. 'It's not just the money. We simply do not have the supplies to go any further.' The expression with which he regarded the butcher was one that Mariata recognized. Even as a child of three Azaz had been strong-willed, his wails of fury heard far from their camp when he was forced to wear even a scrap of clothing.

The two men locked eyes, but it was the butcher who looked away first. 'I would have thought you would wish to save your sister from a hard journey, and probably death.'

Azaz turned his back on the man, rudely. 'There are worse things in the world than death in the desert,' he said softly, but only Mariata heard him.

That night as the men slept she stole past them and grabbed up one of the *tassoufras*, delved into it and discovered a skin of dates. They tasted impossibly sweet, and the corners of her jaws sent shooting pangs through her bones at the first bite. She could not help herself: she ate them all, gathering the sticky stones up in her skirt to hide amongst the roots of the palms. She considered, briefly, stealing one of the camels, but her brothers were expert trackers and would soon find her, and no matter what sympathy they might have for her plight, they were duty-bound to carry out the job the butcher was paying them for. Nor would they shame their father by going against his word. Besides, this reminder of her suitor's bull-like features and his overbearing temperament steeled her resolve: she would let them go where they would without her. Close to death she might be, but it was still better than being close to the butcher.

The next morning the light seeped slowly over the horizon, a dull grey-blue to start with, followed by a burnt-orange glow that gradually lightened and spread itself like a flood into the night sky, so that the stars were put out one by one. Azaz was the first to rise. He uncoiled himself from his blanket and went straight to the foodsacks. He lifted the tassoufra that had contained the dates and weighed it contemplatively. Baye came to stand at his shoulder. He bent down and examined the gritty sand, then looked back up at his older brother. Azaz nodded once, then put a finger to his lips. They both glanced around to where Mbarek lay snoring. Then Azaz scuffed the sand as if erasing something. He picked up one of the other tassoufras, walked into the shade of the nearest palms and hung it up out of sight, looking around all the while as he did so. Then he walked to where the camels sat couched and unhobbled the smallest of them. 'When he wakes tell him one of the camels wandered off in the night,' he told his brother quietly, 'and that I have gone to look for it and when I find it I will catch you up. Break camp quickly and head back on the same path on which we arrived. Wait for me in the hills by the oued with the blue stones in its bed; I will be there by noon.' He pulled the camel's head around by its lip, threw a leg over and urged it to its feet. 'If I am not, do not wait for me.' Moments later both man and camel had vanished from sight.

Baye scratched his head, then went to brew tea.

The butcher grumbled mightily about having to turn back, and one camel light at that, but an hour later he and Baye were gone, and Mariata was left alone at the oasis. But she was not alone for long. A lone figure on a camel came slowly into view.

'Mariata!' he called.

She did not answer; nor did she show herself.

Azaz rode right up to the water's edge and allowed the camel to drink. He filled his own waterskin and took a mighty swig from it. 'I know you are there,' he said softly. 'Your footprints were by our stores this morning and the dates were gone—unless a monkey has stolen my sister's red leather sandals with the carved instep . . .'

Mariata stood up and walked out into the sunlight. 'I will not go back with you, so do not try to make me.' Her voice, which had once been so mellifluous that grown men had wept when she sang, sounded now as harsh as a crow's.

Azaz regarded the ragged figure before him. 'The desert has not been kind to you, sister.'

'It is kinder to me than a butcher might be.'

'What about the baby?'

It was the first time either of her brothers had acknowledged her condition: back in Imteghren they had averted their eyes and said not a word on the matter.

Mariata put her hands over her belly, and, as if on cue, the baby kicked not once but twice. She smiled and looked down, and was at once struck by how thin her wrists were, how the bones showed through the tops of her hands. She knew that beneath her robe her ribs and pelvis would be equally prominent. What would Amastan say if he saw her now, he who had peeled away her clothing under the indulgent eye of the moon and run his hands over her sleek, opulent curves? The desert was paring her away, layer by layer, like a healer

445

peeling a wolf onion. Soon she would be down to the thin green quick. 'We are both fine,' she said.

'And where will you go?'

'Home. Home to have my child in the lands of the Kel Ahaggar.'

'It is a long way to the Hoggar, sister, and you are alone. Perhaps two would stand more chance than one?'

'We are already two,' she smiled at him, touched by this oblique offer. 'Go back to the others and say nothing about me.'

Azaz caught the camel's halter and held it out. 'For you. And there is food, up there in the palm. Our father would wish it, if he were here. No one should force a woman of the Veil to marry against her will.'

Mariata's eyes filled with tears. She bowed her head so that he would not see her cry. 'Won't you be punished for the loss of the camel?'

She heard the smile in his voice. 'It is a small price to pay. Just east of here there is a road. Do not go on to that road: there are military vehicles patrolling on their way to Timimoun and Tindouf. Try to keep its position clear in mind as you go. Cross the road at night on to the Tidikelt Plain, where you will see the three-horned hill; then keep moving east for three days. When the wind begins to pick up as the sun goes down, set your face into it and keep walking. The Guide will appear over your left shoulder and keep travelling around in front of you. In the hours when he has disappeared beneath the earth's rim, keep the North Star at your back and the Daughters in front of you. There are waterholes along the way, but they are few and far between. The land rises steadily: follow the contours and they will take you to Abalessa. The camel is called Takama. She is generally sweet-natured, but can be headstrong. She should suit you well.'

Takama was the name of the servant who had walked out into the desert with their ancestress. Mariata looked up, surprised by both the grim irony of this and by the gift of her brother's sudden invention, and tears spilt down her cheeks. 'Tin Hinan should be proud of the men of her line.' She took the halter as if it tethered her to life itself; the plaited rope felt at once massive and fine against her skin.

'And of the women too.'

They touched hands; then Azaz turned and walked away, his back very straight, his arms swinging freely. Moments later he was gone, a diminishing figure running swiftly across the sands.

CHAPTER THIRTY-ONE

We stayed in the camp for three days while a sandstorm whistled around us, making it impossible to move anywhere else. Bizarre to relate, they were amongst the best days I had ever spent. Taïb and I were left in one another's company, a situation I would have found claustrophobic and intrusive at any other time in my life; but the weight of fear and reserve that had been pressing down on me all my adult life seemed to have been lifted. And perhaps the semi-darkness of the tent helped: it provided the perfect venue for confession and discovery. We lay there

447

on our backs, staring up into the gloom, asking one another the sort of questions you wanted to ask someone you knew was going to play an important part in your life, a sublime mixture of the profound and the absurd. I asked Taïb why he had never married, how many times he had been in love and what had gone wrong; whether he believed in an afterlife, if he had ever wanted children; what he had learnt from the mistakes he had made in his life; the music he liked; his favourite meal; the best memories he had; the funniest joke he could remember. We lay there close but not touching and laughed and murmured and dozed. At last, he asked me about my life in London and about my childhood, and I told him about my tent in the garden and the war-games my friends and I had played, and how we had run about half naked, hitting one another with sticks.

'What a wild little thing you were,' he said, smiling.

'I was,' I said softly. 'It was a long time ago.'

'But wild calls to wild, Izzy. I can see it in your eyes when you look at the desert: the wild part of you still loves wild places. Isn't that why you climb; isn't that why you came to Morocco?'

I had never thought about it quite like that; but he was right, in his way. 'It was the box that brought me here.'

'The box?'

I explained about my father's legacy to me: the box in the attic and what it had contained when Eve and I had opened it up. Then I sat bolt upright. 'Eve!'

He turned towards me, his eyes wide. 'What? What is it?'

448

'Eve: she'll be worried sick. She'll have the entire Moroccan police force looking for me!' I burrowed in my bag for my mobile phone, found it and pressed buttons frantically. 'Shit!' The battery was dead. I hurled it furiously across the tent, all self-control lost, and it hit the canvas wall with a most unsatisfying soft thump.

Without a word, Taïb dug in a pocket, then handed me his phone. Amazingly, even here, in the greatest wilderness on earth, there was a signal, though it was weak. It took me three attempts to compose Eve's number, and then it rang and rang. At last a distant voice said, 'Who is this?'

'It's me, Eve: Izzy.'

'Iz! Where the hell are you?'

At the time it had amazed me that our captors had not confiscated our mobiles, but it was at this point that I realized there really wasn't any point in their doing so. What could I say? 'Good question. I haven't the faintest idea. In the middle of the Sahara somewhere.'

Her cry of surprise was audible even to Taïb. I held the phone away from my ear till she calmed down, then told her as quickly and simply as I could what had happened to us.

'Kidnapped? Jesus, Izzy. What shall I do, shall I call the embassy?'

I was struggling for an answer to this when a man ducked inside the tent and, seeing me speaking on the phone, snatched it out of my hand and broke the connection. He barked something at me in his aggressive-sounding language but all I caught was the *veck moi*; however, the gesture he made with the gun was unmistakable. I turned helplessly to Taïb. 'Go with him,' was all he said and the look in his eyes was enough to warm me to the pit of my stomach.

Outside, the storm seemed to have abated. The air was still grey-yellow with a suspension of sand, and banks of it had drifted up against the sides of the tents like snow, but, even though it was gritty in my mouth, I found it was possible to breathe. I followed the guard to the largest tent, which was black and low-slung, and had to duck almost double to enter. Inside, the leader of the trabandistes lounged full length on a reed mat, propped up on one elbow. If it were not for the sparseness of his surroundings, he would have resembled some ancient emperor or war-chief, for such was his demeanour. He had changed from the dusty fatigues he had worn on the day he had taken us captive into a long dark robe and a pair of loose cotton trousers with an intricate white design embroidered down the side; his brown feet were bare, showing long bony toes and the wide, tough soles of a child that had rarely worn shoes; and his head remained swathed in his tribal veil so that only his dark, glittering eyes showed. On the floor in front of him a small round table bore a pair of steaming glasses, a dented blue tin teapot, a pile of flatbreads and a bowl of oil. He gestured for me to sit, and I crumpled gracelessly to my knees.

'So, it seems the British are saying you are a French citizen, and the French say you are British.' He seemed highly amused by this. With his free hand, he pushed one of the glasses of tea towards me, and it was only then that I realized that in his other hand he held, of all things, a state-of-the-art satellite phone. 'It seems no one wishes to claim you, Isabelle Treslove-Fawcett.' So saying, he tossed my passport back to me, a gesture of utmost contempt, as if to say, see how much good *that* does you here.

I tucked it away in a pocket, though I could hardly think of an object less useful in this desolate place. Not knowing what to say, I picked up the tea glass and concentrated my attention on it, but the liquid was so sweet and strong I almost recoiled.

'No matter. It is all part of the game. I advance my piece, they parry with some time-wasting move while they try to work out where we are and what to do next . . . it is an old pattern. They pretend disinterest, but you can be sure they are scurrying about in some panic, hoping that we do not decide to speak to the media.'

He pushed the basket of bread towards me and did not speak again until we had both eaten for several minutes. I was fascinated to see how he passed the bread up under his veil and turned his head aside from me as he ate, as if there was something too intimate in the act for me to witness.

The satellite phone pealed suddenly into life and he pressed a button and listened intently, then growled something fast in response, finished the call and sprang to his feet, shouting to his guards. Suddenly, where all had been peace and order there was noise and urgent movement. In a great and organized whirlwind of activity, men took down the tents and stowed them on the roof-racks of the vehicles. I was bundled into the Touareg with such force that I did not have a chance to see where Taïb might be, and suddenly we were bumping across the rutted desert tracks at speed, and all in different directions.

Fiercely shepherding the car over the vicious terrain with one hand on the wheel, the trabandiste shouted orders into his phone. A great cloud of dust engulfed us as we fishtailed through soft sand, then we were out the other side and banging across a gravel-strewn plain, loose stones clanging and thudding against the floor and body of the vehicle as if we were being strafed by small-arms fire. Taïb's poor car, I found my Western brain thinking: its once sheeny black paintwork would be utterly ruined by such treatment. For a small, mean moment I was glad it wasn't mine. This thought was interrupted by a high-pitched roar overhead: a military jet with a pale belly and camouflaged wings arced swiftly away from us and in an eyeblink vanished into the distance.

The trabandiste grinned with grim delight, the fan of wrinkles beside his eyes deepening to crevasses. 'Ha! They think we are worried by their spycraft? While we have you with us, no one will dare to attack us. Imagine what bad publicity it would make for them!'

He paused as if to allow me to assimilate the fact that he, a rough desert man, should understand the concept of publicity, then threw the car into four-wheel drive. He took it crawling up a steep dried riverbed, topped out and gunned it off on to a harder track bordered by feathery tamarisk trees.

'Of course, if anything were to happen to you they would simply blame us. "Brutally murdered by her terrorist captors", that's what they'd say. But we have our own sympathizers amongst the world's media.' He flicked a sly glance at me. 'Do you know any journalists, Isabelle?'

452

I stared at him. 'Me? No.'

'No one at the London *Times*, or the BBC? No one at *Le Monde*?' he persisted.

I made a helpless gesture. 'I move in different circles.'

'It's of no consequence. You can post something yourself on the BBC website: we can upload photos of you at the next camp.'

He sounded so sure of himself it made me obstinate 'You've kidnapped my friend and me, you've stolen his car, you're driving us God knows where—why on earth should I help you?'

'When you see what I am going to show you, you will want to do whatever you can to help our cause.' For him it was simply a statement of fact; I shook my head and stared out of the window at the jolting scenery, trying not to laugh, all my outrage seeming to have fled away. As the desert swallowed us, I found I hardly cared any more about where I was being taken or what was going to happen to me. It was out of my hands; it was not my fault. I did not feel threatened or even upset any more; forces more powerful than I was had me in their grip, and I just accepted it. Surrendering myself to any eventuality, I felt a sensation of calm I had never before experienced in my life creep over me. How very odd: was the *insh'allah* attitude catching? If it was, I seemed to have got a good dose of it. Taïb's grandmother would be furious with me. Taïb: even the least thought of him made me smile inside. Now, why was that?

After a time we found ourselves on a flat, sandy plain dotted sparsely with round black stones and the occasional solitary tree that spread its branches wide. The trabandiste drew the car to a halt under

453

one of these and we got out into stifling heat. The two guards in the back went off to relieve themselves, and I followed their example, picking a good-sized acacia tree at a discreet distance from the car. When I came back, the leader of the group had picked up one of the stones. He tossed it to me nonchalantly, as if playing ball with a child, and I caught it and almost at once dropped it, for it was much heavier than I had been expecting. I turned it over and examined its rusty, pitted surface.

'It's a meteorite, but my people call them thunderstones,' he told me. 'They are considered very lucky.'

'Not so lucky if you're hit by one,' I said sourly, and he burst out laughing.

'Ha, Isabelle Treslove-Fawcett, you have a properly Tuareg attitude! Even in the worst of circumstances you can still show humour.'

Tuareg. Why hadn't it occurred to me? I don't know what I had been thinking all this time; I had thought he maintained the veil as a disguise, rather than for cultural reasons, that he was simply a criminal who wished to hide his identity. I regarded him with renewed interest, although a chill began to spread through me. When Taïb had mentioned his Tuareg ancestry, I had been charmed by the exoticism of it all, but now my mother's bloody history lessons came flooding back. A French column under the command of Colonel Flatters, making an expedition into the Algerian Hoggar in 1881 to map out the route of a possible Trans-Saharan railway, had been brutally slaughtered, lured by the Tuaregs into an ambush in the hills, and between the tribesmen and the desert wiped out to a man. Four hundred camel-

454

mounted Tuaregs had launched a reckless charge against the later, better-prepared Lamy-Foureau Expedition and were cut down by grapeshot till not a single camel or warrior was left standing. As a child I had always pictured them to be like the Cherokee or the Sioux, bravely battling against the impossible odds of modernity and 'progress'; and, as I had always sided with the Red Indians against the cowboys in the films, so I had inwardly cheered the Tuaregs on against the stiff-necked French, intent on netting down and taming the wild world much as Mother was intent on doing to me. But in hindsight I had to admit there had always been a more sinister side to these desert warriors: a cool ruthlessness that cared for nothing but their own concept of honour and freedom. And now I was caught up in that age-old conflict of the ancient world against the new, a pawn caught neatly in the middle. The *insh'allah* feeling I'd had an hour or so before soon began to ebb away.

'You know my name,' I said after a pause, 'but you have not given me yours. Will you not do me that courtesy?'

'Some call me the Fennec, for the desert fox; others the Tachelt, the horned viper,' he said, which did nothing to ease my growing fears.

'Don't you have a more personal name?' I asked, remembering that I had read somewhere how important it was for hostages to make some form of emotional contact with their captors so that they were seen not simply as prisoners but as human beings, and were thus less likely to be murdered in cold blood.

'I do not give out my Kel Tamacheq name; I have had no use for it in a long time now.'

'You sound ashamed of it,' I said boldly; maybe too boldly, for I saw him bristle and his chin came up sharply.

'Ashamed? Never. A Targui's pride in his ancestry is unassailable: and we carry our ancestry in our names. My pride is intact, no matter the indignities that have assailed our people, but I will keep my name and my heritage to myself. My tribe has suffered enough; I would not have them persecuted further because of my association with them.'

I had obviously touched a raw nerve. 'Persecuted?' I wondered in my naivety—who could possibly persecute a nomadic desert race, never in one place for any length of time, providing, one would have thought, an impossibly moving target? I looked to him for clarification, but his eyes seemed distant, pained and bitter, and then he turned away from me and called out to his men to bring me some water.

A few minutes later we were back in the car and shortly after this were joined by two other vehicles with which we drove in convoy, flying over the sands like ships in full sail, their path bounded on all sides by towering waves.

It was nightfall before we stopped again. I had been dozing with my head pressed awkwardly against the window; when I came properly awake it was to the sight of full darkness punctuated at intervals by small glowing fires. This seemed to be an entirely different sort of camp to the one we had left that morning. Dogs ran towards me barking cheerfully, and there were people everywhere, especially, it seemed, children, still up and running about at what felt like a late hour.

456

There were women too, I noticed curiously, though they kept their distance. I heard the plaintive sound of baby goats calling out for the mothers from whom they had been separated in order to conserve their milk. How I knew this—which I did with utmost certainty—I had no idea, but it sent a shiver up my spine.

The Fennec's guards shepherded me into an outlying tent and at its entrance exchanged greetings with the inhabitants; then they stepped away and ushered me inside. I went in almost on hands and knees, not the most dignified way to meet the first Tuareg women I had ever encountered. I stared at them and they stared at me, each taking in the strange appearance of the other. I had become used to seeing the women of Tafraout wound in their black robes from head to toe, coyly hiding their faces from strangers, never looking me in the eye. But these women regarded me with frank curiosity, and when I caught them staring grinned and chattered so that their jewellery swung and caught the candlelight. They sat in a row like figures representing the Three Ages of Man in a medieval painting: one young and strikingly pretty, one comfortably middle aged and a crone with the beaked face of a grand hawk. I wondered if they were related, as they seemed so relaxed in one another's company; I wondered what they made of me, in my creased and no doubt filthy linen shirt, designer jeans, expensive sandals, Longines watch and discreet-to-the-point-of-invisibility earrings. Their own earrings were vast and impressive, great chunks of silver in uncompromising geometric shapes that looked extremely uncomfortable to wear; yet the women carried them as though they were as light as feathers. And all of them wore, in a dozen variations, amulets like my own: pinned on their dark robes, on their bright, embroidered blouses, on their elaborate head-wraps, or, like mine, around their necks on strings or plaited thongs.

My hand went to my own necklace, safely tucked away under my shirt. I could feel my heart beating beneath my fingers as if something inside me knew before my conscious brain did that I had stumbled on something truly significant, something that was going to change my entire life. I had the ineffable sense of having been brought by a conspiracy of fate and circumstances to a crux point, to the heart of the mystery; and yet now that it trembled on the brink of revealing itself I found I was afraid to know what it was. Part of me wanted to take my amulet out there and then and show it to these iconic women, but something made me hesitate. It would have been a graceless gesture, too sudden and abrupt, for this first meeting, at this late hour. Instead, I let them make room for me on a rope-strung bed raised a few inches off the ground and mattressed with colourful woollen blankets, and before I knew it I was under the covers. I was slipping over into sleep almost before my head came to rest, my mind going fluid and my muscles melting, leaving me with just that quiescent perceptiveness that is sometimes the most acute of all. For a moment I was aware only of their lowered voices like whispers of sound carried on the wind, a susurration of leaves or of wavelets lapping on a beach, and then the sounds seemed to coalesce and I heard the word *Lallawa*, over and over.

CHAPTER THIRTY-TWO

When next my eyes opened the air was full of light and I was alone in the tent. I stretched luxuriously, feeling a strange languor in my limbs. I could not remember having slept so well in years. I went outside and stared around. We were in a dry valley in which the non-existent river had carved a wide plain and everywhere on this plain were people and tents; dozens of tents, and maybe hundreds of people. Old men whose billowing robes and swathed turbans did little to disguise their stick-thin ankles or the stretch of thin skin over prominent bone. Children with swollen stomachs and huge eyes, their heads shaved except for one or two long pigtails. A group of old women tending cooking pots over open fires; younger women rhythmically pounding something in large wooden mortars.

I heard a rumbling sound behind me and saw a line of dust-shrouded trucks come into view. As they drew up, the women threw down their pestles, gathered up their robes and walked towards them, very slender and straight of back, dignified in their refusal to run. Men handed sacks of food down to them—grain and rice, it looked like; a sack of vegetables; cooking oil; dates—and the women waited their turn for their share.

'Good morning, Miss Fawcett. I hope you slept well.'

I looked around to find the Tuareg chief beside me, and with him Taïb, his eyes locking immediately on to mine and shining like stars.

'How are you, Izzy?'

I was so happy and relieved to see him I could hardly speak. I found I wanted to touch him to reassure myself he was really there, but the presence of the Fennec restrained me. I hoped what I felt was in my smile. 'I'm fine, thanks.' Our eyes lingered on one another's faces. At last I dragged my gaze away and composed myself. I turned to the Tuareg chief. 'What is this place?' I asked him. 'It looks like some sort of refugee camp.'

'You could call it that. These people are certainly in need of refuge.'

'They have lost their homes?'

'They have lost everything. Everything, that is, except their lives and their dignity; but famine and drought threaten even those. Come, there are people I wish you to meet.'

He took us to one side of the camp where a woman of maybe my own age sat carding wool, using one hand and one foot. Her other hand ended in a stump, the brown skin there rendered down to an obscene and shiny purple. Puckered scars seamed what I could see of her face and neck; one eye was squeezed closed. The Fennec knelt and exchanged greetings with her and she lay down the wool and extended her one hand and they touched fingers to one another's palm, a gesture both formal and tender. Then she gestured to Taïb and me to sit down with a sweep of her hand, a queen accepting court.

'Kella will tell you her own story,' the Fennec told me. 'Our people are raised never to complain or to display weakness, so she will not elaborate. I will leave it to you to read between the lines.'

460

Kella began to recite in long rhythmic sentences that sounded close to song, her single hand tapping the ground for emphasis as her voice rose and fell, and the Fennec's voice made a low counterpoint to her fluting words. 'I come from a tribe that has ancestral pasturage rights around the area of Tamazalak. The soldiers came one day and took all our camels. They said they had papers that gave them the right to requisition them. Some of the young men protested; so they took them away in their trucks. We never saw them again. When the soldiers came back, there were only the women, the children and the old men who were left, but that didn't stop them beating us. They said rebels bred like scorpions in our village, and they threw two of the children down the well. They were the sons of my cousin Mina. We heard their cries as their bones broke; I hear them still when I go to sleep. Those of us who survived this attack fled into the desert with the animals that were left. But there was drought, and the animals died one by one. At last I came here; *alhamdulillah*.'

I sat there stunned as the Fennec thanked her and Taïb touched her hand, obviously moved by her story. 'Thank you,' I said. '*Merci bien*, and *shokran*,' and she smiled serenely, nodded once as if dismissing us and went back to carding her wool.

He took us next to meet a young woman in a bright head-wrap, amongst a group of other women in dark robes. Greetings were exchanged, and then the Fennec translated as she told how her husband had been taken away from their camp and killed on suspicion of being a member of the rebels. 'It is happening all the time,' she finished with the hint of a shrug, but for all her assumed

461

nonchalance I could see the pain in her dark eyes as she spoke of her dead husband, left hanging from a tree in the shadow of Mount Tamjak.

We made our farewells and the Fennec led us away. 'C'est l'enfer,' said Taïb, his face taut with repressed emotion. As we walked behind the Tuareg chief, he reached out and brushed the tips of his fingers against the back of my hand. It was the slightest, most surreptitious of touches, but my whole arm felt as if it was on fire.

As we crossed the encampment the Fennec pointed out others as we passed: 'Khabte is an orphan—his family was killed in the Adagh des Iforas; Nama was taken by soldiers and raped at their barracks—she was in a coma for three weeks. They dumped her in the desert, but the desert took care of its own; we found her and brought her here. Moktar is a member of a tribe whose ancestral grounds were taken over by the French when they found uranium at Arlit; that tribe has dispersed far and wide, unable to support itself. Some fled into Algeria and were later expelled from there; now they beg on the streets of Bamako. Many people there hate us. They say their ancestors were our slaves and that now that they are running things the boot is on the other foot. And they are using that boot with unbelievable malice.'

On the other side of the trucks he pointed out a one-eyed man in dusty combat fatigues and a black turban. 'Elaga was a survivor of the massacre of Tchin-Tabaradène.' He turned to us, his eyes gimlets. 'Do you know about Tchin-Tabaradène?'

Taïb looked sick. 'I know a little,' he said in a low voice. 'But I never before met anyone who was there.'

I shook my head and leant up against one of the vehicles, feeling both hot and cold at the same time.

'If you are to write an article for us, Isabelle, you had better know the history,' the Fennec said, looking not at me but at the line of women with their arms outstretched for food. He took a deep breath. 'We used to be the freest people to walk the face of the earth; now we are amongst the poorest and most oppressed. Our pasturage has been taken from us and we have been driven from pillar to post. When famine and drought ravaged our people, the food that aid organizations sent to save us was stolen and sold on the black market by the authorities. So now I prefer to provide my own aid. Uranium and oil have been mined all over our ancestral lands, the desert raped for her riches, and yet we have been given no compensation for this hurt; instead foreign guards patrol the boundaries of the Arlit mines and shoot anyone who comes near. And out of all the vast profits that have been made by this exploitation of our lands, has any money come in our direction? Not one sou. No schools or hospitals have been built for our people; no jobs made available to us; we had no representation in the governments of either Mali or Niger. Our young men were either interned or went into self-exile, so that whatever there was to eat went to the old and the children. Elaga and I became *ishumar*, the unemployed and unwanted: the uprooted. Ill advisedly we took up Gadhafi's invitation to go to Libya to prepare for the future of "the Tuareg republic". This was in the 1980s: Elaga was still young then; I was old

463

enough to have known better. But I harboured a dream, the dream of my forebear Kaocen: that one day all our tribes would unite and create the Azaouad—a republic in which all could roam freely and follow the Tuareg life. Gadhafi's promises were no more than illusions; but for a time I believed in those illusions. To earn my keep I fought in his army in the Western Sahara; in Chad; in Lebanon—I was so angry with the world I would have fought anyone. It was nothing but vanity on his part: he liked the idea of sending his private army off to aid his Arab cousins in their struggle, but in the end it all came down to money and favours, neither one of which was coming back to the Tuareg. The promises evaporated into thin air, which was no surprise. I should have remembered that Kaocen always said the Tuareg have no allies in this world.

'We were expelled from Algeria in 1990, along with the rest of our people; but no one else wanted us. Mali claimed the problem was Niger's, Niger that it was Mali's. In the end a deal was done and Niger was prevailed upon to take eighteen thousand of its people back. We thought we would return to our homelands in the Aïr and the Tamesna, but instead we were interned at Tchin-Tabaradène.

'It was a terrible place: filthy, crowded, full of disease and brutal treatment. The military loved having the famous, feared Tuareg at their mercy at long last. There were many beatings, rapes and ritual humiliations: old men stripped naked in the streets, their veils removed for the first time in their lives; adolescents made to crawl like dogs for the amusement of the soldiers.'

464

He looked me in the eye. 'When I hear the outcry in the West about the atrocities at Abu Ghraib or Guantánamo, I laugh. If the West had witnessed one tenth of what happened to us at Tchin-Tabaradène, it would have wept for shame that such a thing should happen in the so-called civilized world. But Africa is the forgotten continent, and we are amongst the forgotten people.'

I found myself clutching the amulet beneath my shirt, feeling as if I had stepped into some sort of minefield, words exploding around me with the power to kill and maim.

'They would not let us leave the camp or school our children. At last, some of the younger men protested outside the police station. A soldier was killed with his own gun. It was just the excuse the authorities had been waiting for. We were unarmed, exhausted, dying of disease and malnutrition: but for the death of one soldier they called down the might of the entire army upon us, declared a national emergency, sent in battalions, tear gas, parachutists. Camps were annihilated; wells were poisoned or blocked up. They came in the night with machetes and cans of petrol . . .'

His voice hitched suddenly and I saw with a quick sideways glance that his eyes were glittering with anger. Taïb stood like a statue, waiting to hear what came next.

'I escaped, along with some others. I feel guilty to this day that I did not stay; but I had seen such scenes before and I knew what was coming. Elaga stayed: he had a wife and three children. I had no one: it was easy for me to run. Fight like jackals: that was what Kaocen always said, and it was what

465

I urged them to do. It is better to attack and run than to fight like lions, face to face; but some of our people have trouble with this concept. To them it represents cowardice, not pragmatism; but these were the men who revered those who rode their camels against the tanks of the Malian Army in 1963 and were cut down like corn. It was a magnificent gesture; but a gesture only: doomed and pointless. I was not thanked for saying as much. Those who stayed died or were grievously wounded. Elaga lost his family, his eye—and very nearly his life. Many were killed in the initial outbreak of violence; then the formal extermination began. They even talked of a final solution—yes, they used those very words—the need to cull the Tuareg, to expunge us from society. Hundreds of us were loaded on to trucks and driven into the desert towards Bilma. We knew this route well: in the old days we called it "the salt road". Most of those who took the old caravan route as prisoners in their military vehicles were never seen again.'

'My God,' Taïb said in a whisper. 'I never knew.' He wiped a hand across his face and I saw the sun catch the sheen on his fingers as they came away wet.

'We lost nearly two thousand people, but the authorities claimed the number was only sixty. Those of us who escaped formed a coalition. We made a formal protest to the old colonial powers, but France turned its face away from us. They were in too deep with the providers of oil and uranium to want to involve themselves in the mêlée, even when the UN took our part. Under some diplomatic pressure, the Niger government staged a trial, but it was no more than a sham. When the chief torturer at Tchin-Tabaradène took the stand he boasted of how he had strangled one old man to death with his bare hands, and the onlookers in the courthouse cheered. We have tried to use diplomacy but to no avail. Direct action became our last and final hope. For some years I led a rebel faction in the mountains, but our raids had no more effect on our enemies than mosquito bites.' He took a long, deep breath. 'Since then there have been uneasy truces and ceasefires, attempts at assimilation, but in essence nothing has changed. Now I try to do what little I can to aid my people and bring their plight to the attention of the world.'

He turned towards me again and gave me a steady look. 'So perhaps now you will begin to understand why I do what I do, Isabelle Treslove-Fawcett, and forgive my rough methods a little.'

I burst into sudden tears, overwhelmed by a combination of what he had told me and the tensions that pulled me in different directions. By comparison with the grim recent history of the Tuareg people my own woes were tiny; but at the same time somehow they felt huge and world-swallowing, as if something inside me had risen up in a great tide of fellow-feeling.

The Fennec half turned away from me, embarrassed by my outburst. Then he turned back, staring. Not at my face, but lower down. I realized suddenly that the button of my shirt had come undone beneath the compulsive working of my fingers. Just as I was about to do the button up again to maintain my modesty, he caught me by the shoulder with one hand and caught hold of the amulet with the other.

'Where did you get this?' His eyes blazed at me; then he turned to Taïb. 'Did you take this from the old woman you buried?'

'No, no, of course not!' Taïb looked horrified at the suggestion, as well he might. 'It is Isabelle's own. Tell him, Izzy.'

The Fennec pulled the necklace out into full view just as I took a step backwards. In an instant, the leather thong—the thong that had held a huge fall and saved my life on the Lion's Head—snapped and the amulet tumbled into the dust at our feet. Despite his age, the Tuareg chief was faster than me. Like a striking snake he was upon it, flipping it up into his hand, where he turned it over and over. Then he flicked open the hidden compartment behind the central boss as if he had some magical prior knowledge of its workings. The little roll of parchment fell out into his hand.

'Tell me how you came by this thing!' he demanded hoarsely.

'My . . . my father,' I stuttered. 'My father left it to me in his will.' And I told him about the box in the attic and its strange contents. 'He was an archaeologist, my father, you see. In my handbag you'll find the papers he left in the box for me.'

He glowered at me but only briefly: it was as if now he had seen the amulet and its contents he could not take his eyes off them. After a long moment of contemplation he started to walk away from us with long, urgent strides. 'Come with me,' he called back over his shoulder, as if it was an afterthought.

I trotted after him, feeling oddly naked without the amulet; light too, as if I might float away like a seedhead.

Inside the Fennec's tent—the same one that I had been in the morning before, miraculously re-erected in this place as if teleported there in exact and minute detail—he gestured for us to sit down while he rooted through a box, at last emerging with my handbag. He thrust it at me. 'Show me,' he said. He seemed almost feverish, frequently rubbing his hand across his face, all composure lost.

I dug out the folded papers and handed them to him. When he opened them out, the illegible green form fell to the floor. He snatched it up and scrutinized it. 'What is this?'

'I've really no idea,' I said truthfully.

The Fennec tossed it away and turned his attention to the typed foolscap page, which he pored over for an interminable amount of time. At last he thrust it at me, pointing to two words with an accusatory finger. 'Tin Hinan! What does it say here about Tin Hinan?'

I realized these were the only words he'd recognized, and these with difficulty, so I translated my father's paper roughly for him, stumbling over my lack of French for the words 'bier' and 'carnelian' and 'amazonite', which remarkably Taïb appeared to know.

'So the amulet was found at the tomb of Tin Hinan?'

'That's what it says here.' I was feeling distinctly uncomfortable now. My father had evidently stolen an important historical artefact from the tomb of the Tuareg queen. He was no more than a grave-robber, and I a grave-robber's daughter. 'I'm sorry,' I said. 'I have no idea why he left it for me.

469

He loved puzzles, my father; he loved to mystify people, tease them with his superior knowledge.' And I told them about the letter he had written to me, the final bullying manipulation. 'He knew I would never be able to simply let it lie.' I paused, then leant forward. 'Can you read the inscription? Do you read Tifinagh?'

He was outraged. 'Of course. All children raised as true Tuaregs learn the Tifinagh at their mother's knee.' He and Taïb exchanged a combative glance. Then the Fennec went outside and squatted down in front of the tent, brushing a square of sand smooth with his hand. With a car key he inscribed a series of symbols, checking them back and forth against the parchment. Then he shook his head, muttered something to himself and erased what he had written. He turned the scrap of paper on its side, examined it carefully and began again. After several false starts he gave an exclamation full of frustration, sprang to his feet and kicked over the sand. 'Follow me!' he ordered us imperiously and once more we trailed him across the encampment like dogs walking to heel. In the shade of a tree he found the crone who had been in the tent in which I had slept the night before. They went through a prolonged series of ritual greetings until I felt like wrenching the necklace and the parchment from him and thrusting it in her face. Luckily, English reserve and good manners prevailed, and I managed to confine myself to shifting impatiently from foot to foot. At last the Fennec got around to the matter of the amulet and we then had to endure a long pantomime as the old woman examined in minute detail its etched designs and discs of red, the raised central boss and intricately knotted leather thong, now broken in two. When the Fennec showed her the workings of the hidden compartment she chattered like a child, held it close to her eye and moved the boss back and forth with gleeful delight. They then started to share a discussion of its artful craftsmanship and the amulet's provenance, and then at long last he flattened the inscription on the palm of his hand and held it out for her inspection. She clicked her tongue and swivelled her head to one side, then another, all the while muttering away. She poked a finger at one of the lines of symbols that ran from bottom to top of the paper. There were three of these lines, but another three lines ran across them.

'Mariata,' she said; and the Fennec gave out a great sigh of air, as if he had been holding his breath for an eternity. She touched the second line. 'Amastan,' she said.

Neither of these words meant anything to me, but the air was so charged with emotional electricity that I felt the hairs prickle and stir on the back of my neck, and suddenly I knew what the third vertical line signified. 'Lallawa,' I whispered; and they all stared at me. I went hot, then cold; I began to sway.

'*Ey-yey*,' said the old woman, her voice sounding as if it came from a long, long way away. 'Lallawa.'

Taïb steadied me with an arm around the waist and I felt his breath warm against my neck, which very nearly had the opposite effect. 'Did you just read that? Lallawa? Or did you guess it?'

I shook my head, wordless. I had no idea.

The Fennec was trembling now. I could see his hand shaking as the old woman turned the parchment ninety degrees. But no matter which way she looked at it, it seemed to fox her. At last she threw her hands up in the universal gesture of defeat and rattled out a long complaint. The Fennec tried to roll the parchment up again, but his hands were shaking too much. In the end, the crone took it from him and neatly folded it back into its nest, then slid the central boss over its abiding mystery.

We went back across the camp at such speed that I was out of breath by the time we got back to the Fennec's tent. 'What, or who, is Mariata?' I asked.

I watched the older man's grizzled brows knit hard over his eyes as if to shut out the question, then he turned away from us and put his head in his hands. And then this man—trabandiste, rebel leader, veteran fighter, Tuareg chief, whatever he was, who had just related the most harrowing stories of persecution and atrocity to me without a trace of emotion in his voice—broke into racking sobs. Awful sounds escaped his splayed fingers, filling the small space of the tent with an immensity of pain.

I was appalled, frightened even, to be trapped in this claustrophobic place with such raw feelings. I wanted to run outside and keep on running, but something kept me rooted there. I remembered how he had told me that his people were raised never to complain or to show weakness, and I wondered how on earth a pretty tribal necklace and its hidden charm could have had such an effect on this tough, fierce man. But even as I wondered this, I knew what I had always known: that my amulet was a powerful object, charged with magic and freighted with its own deep and tragic history.

CHAPTER THIRTY-THREE

The skin of my beloved shines like rain on high rocks

Like rain on high rocks
When the swollen clouds open themselves
Amongst lightning and the roar of thunder
The skin of my beloved is as bright as copper
As bright as copper
Beaten by the inadan over the fire
Ah! I love the sheen of his cheekbone
Sharp as a knife's edge in the evening light
When he unveils himself, only for me.

Mariata's voice caught on the last line, remembering, and tears threatened. *A waste of water*, she told herself fiercely, and started it again. Besides, she must not show weakness to her son. He was always with her now: she could feel him moving all the time, as if he were eager to escape the annoying prison of her womb. She sang the verse over and over, at first at a whisper, then like a chant, until it lulled them both almost to a trance. Beside her, the camel's feet beat out the rhythm, slow and stately: The *skin* of my *beloved* shines like *rain* on high *rocks.*

She had made the song for Amastan as they lay in the moonlight by the side of the water, when the frogs were singing at their loudest. On the night when the baby was made. How she knew this to be a fact she did not know; she just knew. Her eyes pricked, but they were too hot and dry to contain tears; instead they ached, though not as painfully as her heart.

'Enough!' she told herself fiercely and aloud, and started another, different song:

> *Let us away from the abodes of men*
> *Even though there be water in plenty*
> *For water makes slaves of the wisest of men*
> *And I am but one and twenty.*

Those words stopped her in her tracks. *One and twenty.* How old was she? Now that she thought about it she was not sure. The women of her tribe usually commemorated the passing of each new summer with a border added to a handmade rug, a new carving or amulet, but Mariata had not been in the same place for long enough to have done the things that girls usually did to mark the turning of each new year, and now she realized she no longer knew her own age. Suddenly, it mattered to her terribly that she did not know. It was like having no real sense of herself, no identity. It was easy to lose a sense of identity in this immense place. At night under the stars she felt like the tiniest creature on the face of the earth, creeping and crawling along like one of the little long-legged desert beetles she saw climbing the dunes, their feet barely touching the hot ground as they scurried away, leaving their feathery traces in the sand. And even those tracks blew away at the sign of the first breeze. That was how she felt now, as if all trace of her existence on the earth might as easily be erased.

To restate her identity, if only to herself, Mariata dug deep in her memories. First, she

474

brought out the summer when she had turned seven: watching frogs hatch in the guelta near their summer pasturage; then at eight, being shown the stars by her grandmother's sister as they sat together on the nose of the Wolf, which projected out over the Outoul Valley. At twelve, winning the poetry challenge against a rival tribe, using words some of them had never heard of, making prettier transitions and buried insults that made the people of her own tribe shout with delight. More childhood images fleeted by as they walked on and on; once she even laughed aloud at the memory of teaching her little cousin Alina to catch figs, throwing them high in the air, so high that she was almost blinded by the sun as she followed their flight, catching them purely by instinct as they came down again. How Alina had laughed; and then, naughty five-year-old that she was, how she had run off giggling with a fig in her hand and eaten it whole to stop Mariata taking it back, and almost choked. Figs . . . She experienced a sudden, painful jet of saliva into the back of her mouth, and abruptly was so filled with desire to eat one that she almost fainted clean away. She must have figs, now; at once! She had not eaten a fig since she had left the Hoggar; and then only when they had passed through the harratin-tended gardens where the silver-barked trees grew in shady abundance.

But there were no figs. Not here, not for hundreds of miles in all likelihood. She knew that to be an objective fact; but something inside her— maybe her son, unreasonable and demanding as only babies can be—could not accept the logic at all. Figs: she must eat them at all cost, no matter what she had to do to get them. If it was the baby's demand, then not to give it what it craved was to risk the dark mark of the fruit appearing on its back or, worse, its face. There were always children in the encampment with such marks upon them, marks that spoilt their beauty; and mothers-to-be knew well that the only way to avoid their unborn being touched in the same way was to eat the thing their child demanded: whether it be ashes, or salt, or even camel dung.

Taking down the bag that Azaz had left her, she burrowed to the bottom and took out the last handful of dates, the ones she had been saving these past several days. All else was eaten, except the strips of poor Acacia, now so sun-hardened that she feared for her teeth to attempt them. Pretend the date is a fig, she told herself fiercely, and if you imagine it hard enough perhaps you can fool your son into accepting that a date is a fig. Remember what a fig tastes like, remember how the skin resists your teeth at first, before the sugared fruit fills your mouth; remember the gush of juice, the soft seeds between your teeth . . .

'Don't ask me for figs again,' she told the baby quietly a little while later. 'They are all gone now.'

They had been lucky thus far: they had found pasturage on the lee side of a dune untouched by other passing travellers, and there Takama had spent a day of grazing, burbling contentedly to herself, her jaw working from side to side as she masticated the hard, dry grass into an evil green cud. They had found water too: even those wells that were no more than holes in the ground, almost hidden from view, drifted in and lost to any but those who stumbled right upon them. She had followed her brother's instructions—she had been guided by the stars and turned her face to the wind—but she had also followed her instinct, and let her feet take them where the line on her palm dictated. Even so, there was only so much water that a small female camel and one very pregnant woman could carry between them, and although Takama's hump stood proud and firm, Mariata worried constantly about the camel's well-being—more than she worried about her own, if truth be told. In the heat of the sun, when they took their rest, she would lie there, feeling her belly with the flats of her hands; feeling how it swelled and pushed out the little knot of flesh that was normally hidden from view—'your little desert well', Amastan had called it, licking her flanks so that the night air felt chilly on the tracks he left, before pressing his tongue deep into the spot and making her writhe with laughter. 'One day,' he had said, 'there will be a child attached to you here the way you were attached here to your mother; and that child will be mine and there will never be a child so beautiful or so loved in any corner of the world.'

She wondered what he would think of her body as it was now, huge and swollen to bursting, the skin stretched as tight as a drum; her breasts, once so prettily tip-tilted, now as heavy and engorged as a ewe's udders; her legs like palm-trunks, her ankles like sacks . . . There was no profit to be had from such thoughts: wearily she drove herself on, one foot shuffling before the other, with Takama following serenely.

Planes flew overhead more than once, so fast that their noise preceded them and was left behind in their wake. The camel seemed unconcerned by

477

their presence, but to Mariata they seemed ominous, belonging neither to the earth nor the sky. She crossed the road Azaz had told her about in the early hours of a moonless night when the whole world was black and not a headlight could be seen in any direction. Leaving the Tanezrouft at her back and setting her sights on the stars, they crossed the Erg el-Agueïba, though she had no name for it; all she knew was that when the sun finally rose it was upon the most forsaken place she had ever seen, an endless sandflat punctuated with hard brown saltpans and the sort of thorny vegetation even Takama, who had thus far showed none of the characteristic neuroticism of other camels, would not go near.

Some days south of the plain of salt, they came upon a huge dry riverbed and this they followed for three days, until Mariata's sandals finally fell apart and they were forced to stop. Mariata sat on a rock in the bed of the river, inspecting her callused feet. She had been proud, once upon a time, of her pretty feet; they were dainty and long-boned, and when adorned with henna for her wedding everyone had exclaimed at their elegance. Since then the desert had taken a heavy toll. In the early days blisters had given way to sores, which had finally healed over, only to blister again. Now scar tissue lay over scar tissue and a great thick pad of hard skin had pushed the delicate lines of the sandals to a broader profile, pressing the seams outwards until at last they had simply given way. She bound them quickly with strips of cloth torn from her robe, before the ugly details made too much impression, and thought she would not be dancing barefoot for a long time to come. Her lips curled up in a brief sardonic smile.

As they walked now, she kept an eye on the weather, for clouds had been building these past days and she knew that the rainy season was almost upon them. 'More people die from drowning in the desert than from thirst,' Amastan had once told her, and she had laughed at him and called him a fool for expecting her to believe such nonsense. 'You'll see,' was all he would say. The next day he had gone across the camp and fetched old Azelouane, who had confirmed the unlikely tale to her. 'When the rain falls in the desert, it comes with thunder and downpour,' he said. 'It falls too hard and too fast for the sand to absorb it, and so it gathers in the oueds and becomes a torrent. When the clouds loom, we make for higher ground.'

She still had not quite believed him, and thought Amastan had persuaded the old cameleer to spin her this yarn; but even so the words came back to her now and as the day darkened she led Takama up on to the slopes of the rocky valley. The going here was harder and slower as they picked their way through rocks and between boulders; but she soon found that Takama had a knack for finding the best path, and at last got up on to the camel and rested her weary bones. They had walked side by side for the last weeks—she was simply too cumbersome to haul herself upon it—and now Mariata was glad that she had been sparing of the beast, for Takama moved with a care and intelligence that reassured her that the camel was in good fettle. Her intuition was good: towards dawn the first drops came pattering down, staining the dusty rocks with their black splashes, and soon they had to take cover as the water fell in sheets.

From her vantage point on the hillside Mariata watched in amazement as a wall of water came tumbling down the oued: a great, churning bore of brown water, sand and soil suspended in a thick veil inside its ruthless cascade. If they had been walking down there, both she and Takama would have been swept away in an instant. Soon she was shuddering from top to toe; but whether it was because of the drop in temperature or the shock of imagining what might have happened had they kept to the oued, she did not know.

The coming of the rains was a catalyst for an intense burgeoning of life: plants sprang up in every nook and crevice, pushing their heads out into the world, only for Takama to greedily nip them off. Surrounded by this sudden abundance and vigour, all of Mariata's energy seemed to be absorbed by the growing child, for her belly swelled like rising dough, though it seemed quite impossible it could grow any more. Exactly when had it been planted inside her, this giant child, she asked herself, and could not muster the energy to count back through the weeks and months to Amastan's death and beyond. Exhausted, she slumped in the saddle, gripping its carved wooden fork with both hands, swaying with the movement of the camel. Suddenly, she had never felt so tired in her life.

Then one day as they walked on she felt a gush of wetness beneath her robes. For a moment she thought it was urine, even though she had hardly been producing any these past weeks; then a pain spasmed through her abdomen that made her bend double, gasping. A minute later it eased, but it was not long before another seized her; then another and another.

*   *   *

In the hills of the Adrar n'Ahnet, Mariata had her child. She was very matter-of-fact about the birth, willing herself not to panic. What was the point? There was no one who could help her. She stripped herself and chanted the words that would keep the djenoun away from her vulnerable places. In a sandy hollow between crumbling red rocks, alone but for her patient camel, naked to the single, boiling eye of the sun, Mariata squatted and pushed and prayed and sweated, and as the moon rose over Mount Tinnîret, the baby at last came slithering into the world while the jackals called to one another in the night.

Shaking with weariness, Mariata knotted and cut the cord as she had seen women do in her own tribe. The cord was as long and thick as a snake: she hung it over a bush to dry. The afterbirth she buried to stop the scent reaching the jackals, all except for a small piece that she ate so that a part of the baby would always be in her and she could fight the Kel Asuf for its soul.

The baby was strong but quiet. It lay on the sand, squirming as if it wanted to be up and walking there and then. Mariata brushed her hand over its tiny, swollen face and squeezed-shut eyelids, its mass of black hair, already drying in the cool night breeze. She cleaned it with sand and placed it on the soft leather bag that the enad had made for her. The knife, she thrust into the ground beside it to keep the spirits away. Until it was protected by the ritual on its naming day, six days hence, it would be at great risk from the djenoun. Next she cleaned herself as best she could and kicked fresh sand over the place of the birth. And then she dressed herself in her ragged robe, lay down and curled herself around the new life that she and Amastan had made.

The baby fed quickly and easily and never once complained, getting on with the task of living as if it knew the dire circumstances they faced and had no wish to draw the attention of the evil eye. Over the next couple of days Mariata rested and regained her strength. She could not stop looking at the child. She cooed over it and sang to it, every song she could remember from her childhood in the Hoggar, even the sad ones; even the war songs. When the baby opened its eyes they were as dark as shadows, and for a moment Mariata was afraid, but whether she was afraid of the child or for it, she did not know.

On the third day, when Mariata stirred in the afternoon heat to fetch some water from the gerber that hung from the bush where the afterbirth was curing, she disturbed something that shattered white and translucent into a hundred different pieces, exploding out into the light of the blue sky. She stared at them for a few seconds before realizing they were butterflies, tiny and fragile, their pale wings made translucent by the sun, and then she smiled to herself. 'If you can survive in this place, so can we,' she whispered.

On the evening of the sixth day Mariata got up and walked solemnly three times around the baby and the camel, the nearest thing she had to a tent. There was no ram, and no member of the inadan to sacrifice it for a feast, so Mariata begged

Takama for just a little blood from her neck. She was careful not to make too deep an incision. She gave the baby a taste of it from her finger, but it twisted its face away, hands batting the air at the salty scent of it. Mariata sighed and persisted until it took a little to keep the Kel Asuf out of its mouth. Then with a fine twig she drew the patterns of goose feet at the corners of its eyes and across its forehead so that its eyes and its mind would be strong. When the blood was dry there, she turned it over and marked patterns down its back and legs, for strength and protection. She wrote its name over its liver and proclaimed it six times to the world, so that all would know it for itself, its parentage and tribe, as part of the matriline of Tin Hinan. Then she took off her amulet, removed the scroll inside and painstakingly, with her tongue clamped between her teeth for steadiness, wrote in tiny letters the name of the new life beside the names of the two who had made it.

Then she took down the cured umbilical cord and with great concentration beat it flat upon the rocks and cut it into three thin strings, which she then braided so finely that Tana herself would have praised her handiwork. She removed the pretty beaded string that had held the amulet till now, reknotted that and placed it back around her neck; then she rethreaded the amulet upon the braided thong, and wound it around the baby and put them together into the bag. It was now the most powerful amulet that could be made, and if that couldn't keep her baby safe, nothing could.

On the seventh day she unhobbled the camel and led it down the long, dry watercourse that ran down to the plain. In a valley at its base they came upon the well of Azib Amelloul and some nomads who called out, '*Isalan?* What news?' and praised the beauty of her child. They were kind, simple people, but although they were as poor as mice they insisted on killing one of their goats for her. For two days Takama shared the good pasture with their animals, and Mariata was treated like visiting royalty. The women spoke a different dialect of Tamacheq to the one Mariata was used to: their intonation was harsh and nasal, the vowels drawn out at great length. They were curious as to why she was alone and where she was going.

'I came out into the desert to have my child,' she told them, and they nodded approvingly: it was the old way.

They asked her to stay with them—a newborn always brought good luck—but they were travelling north to the Adrar Tissellîlîne. 'It is not good for a woman to be travelling on her own,' they told her. 'There are many bandits and soldiers about, travelling between Tamanrassett and In Salah. If you must continue alone, be sure to avoid the road. They do not follow our code: they have no respect for women.'

Mariata thanked them, but the next day they parted company. She watched them until the last goat was no more than a speck in the distance, then she slung the baby across her back and took Takama's halter to load her up. The nomads had cleaned and mended her robe as well as could be done, replacing the ragged edges with a bright new border. They had given her a clean, fresh swaddling cloth for the infant, a new veil and a pair of old shoes that almost fitted her. They had given her millet and dates and goat's milk and cheese. At

each gift, tears had sprung to her eyes: people—
and strangers at that—were so kind. She kept
trying to refuse, knowing how little they could
spare these things, but they acted as if she gave
offence by her refusal, and so she came away
feeling as rich as a princess.

Mounted up on Takama, she travelled south and
east for two days until the mountains of the
Hoggar loomed on the horizon, their spiky,
volcanic peaks unmistakable against the setting
sun. Mariata laughed out loud. She had done it!
She had come home, against all the odds. She took
the baby in her arms and turned its face to the
hills. 'There lies your homeland, my little lamb, my
sweet figlet, my love.' As they went, she told it the
legends of the Ahaggar: of the Sanoussi revolt,
when the Kel Taitok rose up against the foreign
invaders; of the legendary beauty and poet
Dassine, courted by nobles far and wide, who
imperiously turned down the suit of the most
powerful chieftain of them all, because she said he
was ugly; of the massacre at Tit; of the cunning of
raiders and the courage of warriors. She told it of
the paintings of Touhogine and Mertoutek, where
elegant gazelles danced across the rocks, and of
the Mountain of Spirits, the Garet el-Djenoun.

'Soon we will be amongst our own people and
you will be fêted and adored by all the women as
the only baby who has traversed the Great Desert.'

But by the end of the following day the massif
seemed no closer. They crossed the Oued Tirahart
and took on water at the well of Anou in Arabit,
and there marvelled at all the prints in the ground
that surrounded it: not just goats and sheep and
camels but also donkeys and mules. 'If there are

485

donkeys here, we are almost home,' she reassured herself by way of the child. Takama gave a great gurgling bellow and shook her neck out, tilting her chin skywards as if in assent.

They crossed the streams that ran below the isolated peak of Ti-n-Adjar. Beyond lay Abalessa and the valley of Outoul; above lay the hills of her people. The land rose steadily, giving rise to strange and magnificent rock formations that changed colour dramatically through the course of the day, going from a pale, sandy ochre at the height of noon to a glowing umber and then a flaming scarlet as the sun dipped behind her. Mariata touched them with wonder, her heart filled with joy. They seemed full of energy, these rocks; and so did she.

As dawn came the next day it brought with it a lowering cloud billowing in from the south, and Mariata groaned. There was precious little cover here, little that would protect them from a major sandstorm. Best to press on. She got Takama down on her knees and made the baby safe aboard before hooking a leg over and climbing up the camel's neck and into the saddle. Despite the approaching storm she laughed: it was good to be nimble again after feeling like a pregnant ewe these past weeks. They made some progress but soon the leading edge of the storm was upon them, lashing them with sand so that even swathed in a veil Mariata felt the grit between her teeth. Harder it came, and thicker. At last it was clear there was no advantage in going on: they had to find shelter and take cover until the storm passed. Through the stinging waves, Mariata made out a hillock with what looked to be a cave in its side. She urged

Takama towards it and tapped her on the head till she couched. Then she crawled up the crumbling side of the hill. It was a cave: thanks be! She placed the baby inside the opening, then went back down to hobble the camel, the sand stinging her face and hands. But Takama had already seated herself with her hindquarters determinedly set against the storm.

Inside the cave, Mariata hugged her baby close and lifted a milk-heavy breast towards its small, seeking mouth. They had had such luck thus far it was as if Tin Hinan herself kept watch over them. Outside, the storm howled and shrieked like a thousand hungry djenoun, but inside they were safe and well. Mariata lit one of the candles from Tana's bag. She melted the end of the second candle with the flame of the first and stood it on a stone. Then she did the same with the other. The twin candles lit the cave, only to reveal it as something else entirely, and not any natural formation. Mariata stared around, amazed. She was in a chamber of stone, stone shaped unmistakably by human hands. A chill crept over her. She was in a tomb, or the entrance to a tomb, for there seemed to be what looked like doorways leading off from the antechamber where she crouched. As soon as the realization struck her, she wanted nothing more than to be out of it, even if it meant running out into the teeth of the storm. It was the child that kept her there: it gave a small, inarticulate cry and reached its hands up, grasping at the air as if at something unseen. Mariata immediately became convinced that a djenoun had entered the tomb, or more likely had been lying in wait there for unwary travellers. 'Keep off! Stay away!' she yelled; but her voice was lost in the howling of the storm. At last she burned the remains of the herbs Tana had given her, and, mixing their ashes with drops of blood from one finger, she made a paste and used it to inscribe a charm: first on the wall of the chamber; then in the amulet, so that each line of names took in a symbol from each of the other three lines, a complex, dense weaving. Satisfied, she replaced the parchment in the amulet's compartment and placed the necklace on the infant's chest. 'This amulet will surely protect you against the worst of the worst,' she promised. And then she cried, because no charm in the world had been able to save her Amastan.

* * *

The next morning there was a lull in the storm, though the sky remained a louring, heavy yellow, hanging low over the Hoggar, obscuring its famous peaks. There would be a reprise soon, she was sure: there was no time to be wasted. But the baby was uncharacteristically obstructive and uncooperative today. It twisted in her hands like a mountain hare and would not take milk. At last, Mariata lost patience. 'Well, if you won't eat, you will go hungry!' She swaddled it fiercely in the cloth so that it could not kick any more. Then she went out to see to the camel.

But of Takama there was no sign. Mariata shouted and interrogated the landscape, but to no avail. There were not even tracks in the sand: everything had been scoured clean by the passage of the storm. She sighed. So be it: she had walked further distances than that which remained; it was no great way and no doubt she would find Takama as she went. But her heart was heavy: the two of them had shared so much that to lose the camel now was painful.

She picked up the baby and the enad's bag, took off her veil and was about to make the sling in which she would place the child as she walked when she heard the sound of someone approaching. She whirled around to see three men on camels leading a fourth animal. It was Takama! She was about to run down the mound towards them before remembering herself. They were Kel Tamacheq: they wore the veil. It would not do to go running at them like a mad beggar woman. And no ordinary Tuaregs either, for they rode on big white mehari and carried guns, as well as their traditional *takoubas*, strapped to the sides of their camels. What a fine sight they made, coming out of the sun towards her. So she sat there on the edge of the grave mound, watching and waiting.

The leader rode forward and sat looking up at this woman whose face shone with light in the bright air, at this mother with a baby in her arms. He looked at her for a long, long time. Then he said, 'One miserable Mauretanian is hardly a recompense for the two meharis you stole from me, but I will take it as down-payment on your debt. And I know very well how you can make up the rest.'

Mariata felt as though someone had slipped an icy knife into her gut. Then her heart began to beat painfully and arrhythmically. She could not breathe, let alone speak.

The three riders dismounted and came towards

her. The tallest of them stared with distaste at the swaddled baby. 'You can put that grub down into the dirt where it belongs,' said Rhossi ag Bahedi. 'You won't be needing it any more.'

* * *

She fought: she wailed; she bit and scratched—but they were too strong for her. They dragged her out of the tomb; she'd tried to resist them but they trussed her up like a shot gazelle, slung her over Takama and took her away with them. For three hundred yards Mariata screamed for her baby; but when it became clear they had no intention of turning around, she mastered herself and made herself concentrate very, very hard, memorizing every step of the way they took, every stone and plant they passed. She took note of each change in direction, of the patterns in the sand made by the prevailing wind and the positioning of shadows. Months in the desert had taught her many things; but most of all they had taught her fortitude.

* * *

Just outside the encampment Rhossi threw her down to the ground like a sack of rice and stood over her contemplatively. Then he smiled. 'Scream or struggle and you will be made very sorry for it later. You are a poor, lone traveller whom we have rescued. I am taking you as a second wife for your own protection and out of the goodness of my heart.'

These words washed over Mariata. They were meaningless: all she cared about was the baby. She had a plan, but she would have to be patient. Whatever happened in between did not matter. Uncharacteristically docile, she let them lead her into the camp. They passed a group of hobbled camels, a knot of men, smoking; they passed two battered khaki jeeps and some people in European dress.

'Do not look to them,' Rhossi told her quietly. 'They care nothing for people like you. All they care about is dust and bones, not about the living.'

There were tents beyond, and more people; women mainly, a few children. They all stared incuriously at her, but Mariata kept her eyes averted. Behind her, she heard the jeeps start up and rumble away; people seemed more interested in their departure than in her arrival. Until she was pushed into a long, low black tent, that is. In there was a plump, dark woman with a small, mean mouth and the receding chin of a rabbit. Her dark eyes took in Mariata's ragged appearance and the proprietary hand of the man on her, then she launched into a blast of invective. 'What are you doing, bringing a baggara into my tent? She will be vermin-infested, one look could tell you that. Get her out of here before she ruins all my good things!'

Rhossi just laughed and pushed Mariata hard so that she sprawled over the other woman. 'Calm down, wife; or should I call you "first wife" now? This is . . . Mina.' It was the first name that came into his head. It would do. Better not let word travel that a member of the powerful Kel Taitok had strayed into his path. 'She will be my second wife, since you have so far failed to give me sons, and I know this one to be fertile!' How he knew, he

491

did not specify, but this alone was enough to cause the woman to shoot a look of utter loathing at the newcomer, even as she kicked her away. 'Make sure she is clean and presentable for me by sunset or it will be the worse for you.' He gave her a sweet smile, but she quailed: she knew all too well what that meant.

The first wife, whose name was Hana, took out her frustrations on 'Mina', though she never once addressed her directly. Instead, she spoke to the air, as in: 'Have you ever seen hair so matted and foul? We should cut it all off and have done,' and 'What he sees in her, I can't imagine: she is thin as a stick and she stinks like a he-goat.' For her part, Mariata let her do what she would, making no sound even though the combing and the scrubbing and the hair removal was as painful as Hana could make it. Nothing mattered but the rescue of her child: it became a chant in her head through the short ceremony in front of the marabout, through the cursory 'celebrations', which were in any case both muted and curtailed. No one much liked Rhossi ag Bahedi, it seemed, and many of those present appeared to be related to the first wife and took the arrival of an unknown second as an insult to their clan. Besides, it was all very unusual, people agreed, for a chieftain to take a second wife, especially at such speed. But the normal codes of conduct were all at odds now, with troubles everywhere and no one safe from day to day. The men agreed it was necessary to take your pleasures where you could and make the most of them: you might be dead tomorrow. And you had to admit that the woman was striking, now that she was clean and well robed and decked out in

492

wedding finery, even if it was borrowed; much more interesting to look at than poor Hana. But she was thin: much too thin, they all agreed on that. Still, she'd soon put some flesh on those elegant bones and then she'd be a real beauty. And no bride-price to pay either: what a bargain!

The women thought none of this, though not one said a word. Better the desert than to be Rhossi's second wife. Or even his first. They'd seen the bruises on Hana, though she tried to hide them. They'd seen the harratin girls Rhossi had used too. And so, though they all loved a good wedding better than most things, their heart was not really in the singing and drumming that night, and as soon as Rhossi took the new wife to bed, they dispersed.

When Rhossi disrobed her and stood staring down at her half-starved body, with its milk-full breasts and slack stomach and skinny limbs, Mariata willed herself elsewhere. When he laughed at her and reminisced delightedly about the attack that had taken his cousin Amastan from her even as he forced himself deep into her secret places, she stared fixedly up into the dark eaves of the tent as if she could see through it to the stars. An hour later when he was snoring heavily, she threw on her clothes, slipped outside, found Takama and disappeared into a night that was peculiarly moonless.

How she found her way she did not know: everything looked so different under the blanket of darkness, but, as the sun came up over the hills in front of her, Mariata saw the piled earth and rock of the tomb ahead. She did not wait for Takama to couch, but hurled herself off the camel and hit the

493

ground running, her bare feet slapping the ground. 'I am here! I have come for you!' she cried, but no baby's cry responded. She ran up the hillock and threw herself into the entrance of the tomb, but the interior was empty. She wailed, and the sound flooded in echoes through the chamber, bounding and rebounding off the stones. Out she went, scrambling on all fours, all around the tomb, until her hands and knees were bloody and raw. But there could be no mistake: the baby was gone.

CHAPTER THIRTY-FOUR

For three days and nights the Fennec had driven like a man possessed, hurling the Touareg across the desert pistes and stone-studded plains. The world passed by in a blur, landscape spun out into separated strands of colour like something in a centrifuge. Part of the journey was along a tarmacked road, but this was even more unnerving than the rough tracks. The Fennec had a habit of tailgating lorries and then overtaking them and cutting back in again in such a reckless fashion that my right leg was going like a piston on the phantom brake pedal. Which would not, I realized after some time, have done me much good, since we were in a left-hand-drive car.

Back on the pistes, we were jolted once again, up and down and sideways, and the amulet banged against my collarbone and the vehicle's suspension groaned and clanged. I turned to look back at Taïb after one particularly vicious impact, but he was as impassive as ever, as if this top-of-the-range SUV hadn't cost him the best part of two years' work. Hard come, easy go. Beside him, the Fennec's lieutenant looked rather less nonchalant as he watched the ground go past at this unnatural velocity, his eyes as big as dinner plates.

'Can you tell me where you're taking us?' I had asked on the first day. It had been an effort even to speak, since I risked smashing my teeth together just by opening my mouth.

'To see someone I know.'

Was it necessary to be quite so cryptic? 'Perhaps you could tell me why?'

'You'll find out when we get there.' And that was all the Fennec would say until he slewed the car to a halt beneath a big acacia, got out and made two phone calls. I had got the gist of the one in French, though it involved much swearing and many colloquialisms I could only guess at, but it seemed to have something to do with a payment that would be made by somebody else. The other was in a language so impenetrable I didn't even try to understand it. I turned to Taïb. 'Any idea what all that was about?' I had asked quietly.

'He maintains the camp we were at by paying a *pourboire* to the commander of the local garrison. He was checking there wasn't going to be any unexpected change of personnel for the next few days and assuring him the money was on its way. As to the other call, I only caught a word here and there: something to do with checkpoints and police stops.' He shrugged.

Which did little to settle my nerves.

But in the end we saw no checkpoints and were stopped by no soldiers or police, and I gave myself up to the flow of events and the weariness that engulfed me. Forcing myself to embrace my inner *insh'allah*, after a while I fell asleep.

When I awoke, the world had stopped rushing by outside and a pale and tranquil sun was showing its face over a cliff topped by boulders in all sorts of fantastical shapes. With very little imagination I could make out a crouched rabbit there, an eagle here; a sitting man, a giant mushroom, a long dog's snout.

'Where are we?' I asked Taïb. Of course, he had absolutely no idea. We left the car parked in the shade of the rocks and started to walk. The Fennec strode out ahead as if determined to eat up the ground with his boots. I could imagine how fierce this man must be in combat, how obdurate and focused. I was glad those fierce hawk-eyes of his were trained on the way ahead and not on me; as it was, I was having trouble keeping up with my injured ankle and was having to follow at a half-run, half-hobble. Beside me, Taïb loped along as if he could keep up this punishing pace all day, but the poor lieutenant was suffering: I could hear the soughing of air in and out of his smoker's lungs, saddled as he was with the semi-automatic and a canteen of water.

The Tuareg chief clearly knew where he was and where he was going: each time a myriad of possible pathways fanned out between the rocks, he selected his route unhesitatingly. After an hour's hard walking, largely uphill, we came out on to a rocky escarpment. Down below us was a glint of water, sparkling between boulders, a sandy enclosure, a dozen or so low black tents and a small hut with smoke rising from its fire.

The Fennec took the slope towards this small

settlement at a run, scree skittering downhill in his wake. I had made hundreds of descents from cliffs and tors in my time and thought myself reasonably sure-footed, but I had never seen anyone move with such nimble, goat-like feet. By the time we reached the bottom he was nowhere to be seen. But a lot of other people came out to stare curiously at us. Fearless children with fearless eyes and gap-toothed smiles who ran after us, touching our clothing or arms as if on a dare, running away again giggling behind their friends. They pointed at my jeans, which they seemed to find inordinately amusing; they set about Taïb, climbing up his leg and demanding a ride. They laughed a lot at the poor, sweating lieutenant with the 'Kalach' and some of the boys picked up sticks and pretended to engage him in battle. One little girl with vast eyes and two dancing braids took a fierce interest in my watch and would not let go of my wrist, so fascinated was she by the way the second hand ticked around and the diamond in its face glinted in the sun. In another time and place it had cost me the best part of two grand. A ridiculous amount of money for an object that would tell the time of day and nothing more, when all you ever had to do was look at the sun or the length of its shadows on the ground. I could hardly imagine anything less useful in this place, except perhaps the paper money that had bought it. With a smile, I unbuckled the leather strap and let her run away with it, pursued by her friends.

Taïb raised a quizzical eyebrow. 'That was Longines, wasn't it?'

The outraged face of the lieutenant was a picture. I took one look at him and burst out laughing. It was the reappearance of the Fennec that stopped the laughter turning hysterical. *'Venez avec moi,'* he said abruptly and turned on his heel.

We passed all the tents with their bright rugs airing outside, the women preparing food or weaving, the men plaiting and sewing coloured leather. At the far side of the enclosure we came to the hut with the smoking fire. Inside, it became clear that it was some sort of forge. There were blacksmith's tools everywhere, hammers of all sizes, a stone anvil, a brightly decorated bellows. The child who was manning this watched us with large eyes, then went running outside, revealing a figure crouched before the fire. Its leaping flames showed skin wreathed with lines, bright eyes and a cap of close-cropped white hair, a shocking contrast to the blackness of the face beneath. When this person rose, he was almost as tall as the Fennec, and almost as imposing: his handshake was crushing, for such an old man.

The lieutenant and his weapon were sent outside and the rest of us were beckoned out of the smoke and darkness into a courtyard beyond that was bright with flowers and vegetation. At a glance I could make out tomato, pepper and chilli plants, fennel, oranges, marigolds and bougainvillea. It was a veritable miracle, an oasis of plenty.

'I see you like my garden,' the blacksmith said in a small and delicate voice that was completely at odds with his stature. 'Forgive me that I wear no veil: it is not out of disrespect but because I would be entitled to only half a veil in any case.' The Fennec seemed to find this amusing, but my blank expression must have given me away, for the blacksmith smiled. 'My name is Tana and they call me an *homme-femme*, but I prefer to be known by the feminine article,' she told me in perfect French.

I'm sure my mouth was a perfect O of surprise, and not just because I had never, knowingly, met an *homme-femme* before. 'Your French is remarkable,' I said, grasping for something to say that did not completely give away my discomposure. 'How do you know it so well?'

'I know many things. I know a little Songhai too: I find that dealing with the local authorities and aid agencies in their own languages can have more positive results.'

She gestured us towards a bright blanket spread upon the ground with a small round silver table at its centre; a silver teapot was already heating over a charcoal brazier a little distance away. The table was beautifully and minutely patterned and tooled; at its centre sat four tea glasses, as if she had known we were coming. Or perhaps she had only four glasses and they sat there always. Tea was made and poured out most ceremoniously, and no one spoke through the entire procedure, as if to do so would be to interrupt a sacred ritual.

At last, Tana leant forward. 'I'm told you have a certain amulet in your possession.'

I looked at the Fennec and he gave me a sharp nod. 'It has a scroll written in Tifinagh inside.'

'Ah, yes, the scroll.' The blacksmith regarded me steadily. 'What do you know of the Tifinagh?'

I had to admit I knew very little.

She pulled back a corner of the blanket and made some marks in the sand underneath. 'Our language is all about the world we live in. It's the same for all cultures, of course, but ours represents

499

the fundamentals of our life more directly than most. You see all the straight lines we have? These are the sticks: they represent the legs of men and animals, whose lives are entwined in permanent interdependence—the goats and sheep and camels, the gazelles and jackals and lions. The crosses indicate the roads we must choose from, the paths we take through the desert of our lives, the road along which the sun and moon and stars guide us. There is a saying amongst our people that all important things start from the heart and move wider and wider still into the Circle of Life, just as the world's horizon circles around the tribe and the herd. But it always comes back to the heart, you know. Love is the strongest force in the world.' She opened the amulet's hidden compartment, shook the parchment out into her hand and gazed at it for a long time. Then she gave a long, slow smile and put it back, closing the central boss with a very final-sounding snap. 'This was something I never expected to see again. But I am glad to hold it in my hand, for all the ill luck it has witnessed.' Her dark eyes seemed to pierce right through me. Then she turned to the Fennec. 'Poor soul. Forty years in the wilderness; forty years of turning your face away from love, from the things that hurt most; forty years denying that the heart is at the centre of the world. You never found her, did you? And that is why you are back here with this thing after all this time. Oh, don't get me wrong: we have been grateful for all that you have done for us, for the gifts of money and aid. But it would have been good to see your face, once in a while. And if you'd kept in better touch, I could maybe have saved you two years of misery.' She gave a small, strangled laugh. 'Why is it always poor old Tana who holds all the threads in her hand? Ah, well, we shall weave the tale soon, strange though it is.' She patted my hand. 'This is all very strange for you, child, I can see. Stay here: I'm afraid it will get stranger.' Like a much younger person, she uncoiled herself from the ground and ducked back into the hut.

'What does she mean?' I asked the Fennec. He was staring into the glowing coals of the brazier as if all the necessary information might be read there. And he was shaking.

I looked at Taïb: he ran a finger across the top of my hand. 'There is a great mystery here, but I think it's about to reveal itself. Have patience, Izzy.'

There was a disturbance at the door and then Tana reappeared, followed by a shorter woman whose long black hair was shot through with streaks of white and braided in elaborate tails and coils. Long silver earrings dangled from her ears, reaching almost to her shoulders, alternating pieces of silver shaped into hollow circles and inverted triangles. More silver shone upon her fingers and arms; long silver weights held down the corners of the scarf she wore over her head, and a dozen decorative pins adorned her dark blue robe. Her hands were hennaed to a deep rich brown; her lips too, so that they stood out sharply against her pale skin. I thought I had never seen such a stately woman. She looked as I had imagined the desert queen might have looked in all her finery. But the desert queen was long, long dead and this woman was very much alive. The eyes with which she regarded us were the colour of a storm cloud,

501

though there was a gleam of humour there and a deep intelligence that spoke of hard-won lessons. Her nose was long and straight, her brows were thick, and her chin told of a determination that ran to wilfulness. No one had ever called this woman pretty, I thought: she was too striking for that. Handsome: the word slipped into my mind. Handsome: she defined the term.

Her bold, black gaze fell upon me first of all and lingered for several moments, and I thought I saw that strong chin tremble; then she looked to Taïb, gave an approving nod, and finally allowed her eyes to rest on the Fennec.

'Amastan,' she said, quite clearly.

'Ah, Mariata . . .' It came out as hardly more than a sigh.

The names in the amulet. I stared from one to the other, trying to make some sense of all this. Tana leant towards me and touched me on the shoulder. 'They haven't seen one another in forty years, and each thought the other dead. Forty years is a long time to hold another deep in your heart but never in your arms. Come with me. They have eyes only for each other, but perhaps we shouldn't eavesdrop.'

We walked out of the garden through an archway of flowers that droned with the sound of bees. Beyond it, we came to a deep, largely dry river in which pockets of water glinted between the smooth white boulders of the bed. 'In my youth there was always flowing water here,' Tana said sadly. 'There were reeds and frogs and birds singing always; and oleanders with beautiful pink flowers. The number of children I've fed charcoal to because of oleander poisoning . . .' She shook her head. 'Life can be like that: the most beautiful things are often the most lethal. Take those two back there: you never saw two more handsome young people in your life. Amastan, he was straight and tall—well, he still is—with the most eloquent eyes, poet's eyes, I called them; but you've seen what he became when life turned bitter on him. It's not surprising he chose the course he took: he'd seen too much already by the time he first came here as a child. Then to lose your first love by nineteen; and your second by twenty-three: that does things to a man's soul. Now he's fought his way from here to the Levant, and what good has it done him?'

It was a rhetorical question. Taïb squeezed my hand and I curled my fingers around his—we were transfixed.

'And Mariata, well . . . She was a proper little princess, that one, when she arrived here, claimed to be descended from Tin Hinan herself, but who knows the truth of that? The Kel Taitok love to boast of such things. I say it's better to be yourself than to carry a thousand ancestors around on your back, but that's how our culture always has been. It can hold you back.' She considered this with her head on one side like an intelligent blackbird interrogating a worm. 'But then of course it can give you the backbone and the pride you need to carry you through tough situations. You can look at it both ways. It was Amastan's mother who brought her here.' And then she told us about the woman she called Rahma and how she had been happily married to a great chieftain, until he had taken a second wife. 'That's a rare thing amongst our people,' she said to me gently. 'Polygamy. One

503

man, one wife: each for the other their heart and eyes and soul. That's how it usually works in Tuareg society and it's always the best way. The many-wives custom came in from the east and caused nothing but trouble. Women hate to share their men and men can't understand it. Anyway: Rahma, she had nothing left after she divorced Moussa except for Amastan, her only surviving child. She loved that boy: loved him too much for sense. So when he lost his mind, I had to do something or she'd have lost hers too. I sent her off to the Aïr to fetch Mariata. She needed something to do, and I thought it might serve. You hear things in the inadan community that others don't hear; and you read signs others can't read. None of the girls here was pretty enough or sharp enough to attract Amastan's eye, not after what he'd gone through. And she was something special—she still is, you've seen for yourselves. A beauty: not pretty, mind you, but properly handsome, which is much more enduring than prettiness anyway. A strong, strong face, and a strong will to go with it. How could he resist? I wish now that I'd read the rest of the signs around that union; but I did what I thought was right at the time. I didn't look far enough forward, and by the time I did they were inseparable. Love is stronger than fate, isn't that remarkable? Some say it's stronger than death, but bless my stars I haven't had the chance to find out *that* yet.'

And then she told us about the extraordinary events that had separated the man I knew as the Fennec, whom she called Amastan almost with a mother's fondness, and the desert woman, Mariata.

504

'When the soldiers came it was on their wedding night. Of course, they'd been lying together for weeks—months, probably—not that any would think the less of them for it. The People of the Veil turn a blind eye to things like that. Try not to get caught, is what we say, and if you do you'd better come up with a good story to entertain us with. She was already pregnant by the time they married. Married and widowed on the same day: at least, that's what she thought, for years. Poor Mariata. Poor Amastan! It wasn't the soldier's bullet that nearly killed him, it was the blow to his head. The bullet struck him here'—she pressed her hand just above her heart—'but he hit his skull so hard when he went down that that might as easily have done for him. He was unconscious for weeks: God at his most merciful. He'd already seen the aftermath of a massacre once, he had no need to see one again, to see what I saw . . .' She shuddered. 'It was a terrible night.'

'How did you survive?' Taïb's eyes searched her face.

The blacksmith's mouth twisted into a grimace. 'They raped and killed just about every woman they could lay hands on. But when they came to me—' She paused. 'Well, let's just say they'd never seen anything quite like *that* before. Terrified, they were. Ran off. Never was so happy to be born different in all my life.'

'So it was you who saved the Fennec's life, was it?' I asked.

She scoffed at the name. 'Always the romantic, that one. Couldn't bear to use his own name any more after she was gone. I thought he'd find her and bring her back, but life isn't like water, it

505

doesn't follow the line of least resistance, does it? It took him a long time to recuperate after that wound and the head blow; months. By the time he was able to walk, let alone think straight, she'd already gone; first of all taken by her father into the Tafilalt, and then setting off on her own into the desert. She trekked all the way from the south of Morocco back to the edge of the Hoggar, over a thousand miles. A feat for anyone, let alone a pregnant woman.'

I stared at her in disbelief. 'She crossed the desert? Alone?'

'And pregnant.' Tana gave a decisive nod. 'As I said, she's a remarkably strong-willed woman. Anyway, by the time Amastan found out where she'd been taken and made it to Imteghren, she was gone. He found the house she'd lived at, knocked at the door and it was opened by the woman Mariata's father had married, no one else there. Well, she took one look at him, this ragged nomad asking awkward questions, and got the measure of him at once. Told him the girl was dead, just like that. Dead of a sickness, she said, and shut the door in his face. He asked around, but no one told him any different. What was left of his heart was broken. He came back here, couldn't settle, and went off into the hills; got swallowed up by the rebel cause.'

'So when did you find out she was still alive?' Taïb asked.

'A couple of years ago, that's all. She too had changed her name. It's hard enough to keep track of people in the desert at the best of times; but when they change the names they were given at birth?' She clicked her tongue, shook her head. 'I knew she wasn't dead. I knew it here . . .' She touched a finger to her heart. 'And I read it in the bones too: but what was the point in telling him that? He'd never have listened to me.'

'Why did she change her name?' I asked, curious.

Tana sat back, closed her eyes. 'Fate is mischievous, sometimes positively malign. At the end of her long desert trek she was taken captive by the very man she hated most in all the world: Rhossi ag Bahedi, the heir to the Aïr drum-group. It is sometimes whispered that it was Rhossi who brought the soldiers down on our tribe: whispered, but never confirmed. It must be said that Rhossi managed to escape more easily than one might expect in such circumstances . . .' She sighed. 'Well, escape he did, and almost a year later he got exactly what he wanted: Mariata, to do with what he would. He took her to wife, as his second wife, to be precise. Poor dear: she held her lineage in such high esteem, such a fall must have been hard to bear, and Rhossi would never have allowed her to forget it. You can see why she might have decided to change her name. She got her own back, in her way: he never managed to get a child on her, so he bore his own measure of ridicule.'

'And the baby? Did she have the baby? Did it survive?' Taïb's expression was avid. He seemed to be enjoying this little game of revelations more than I was. Something was gnawing at me, deep inside, something I didn't have a name for and wasn't sure I wanted to face.

Tana weighed the amulet in her hand. 'There are three names inside: Amastan, who had it first; Mariata, to whom he gave it . . .'

'And Lallawa.'

She gave me an approving nod. 'Good girl. And Lallawa. Yes, Mariata had her child: a girl, which came as a surprise to her. It had been such an active baby she'd been sure it was a boy, had even named it Amastan in her own mind. But, clear as day, no boy-parts, just girl-parts. And so she named it Lallawa, spirit of freedom. Lallawa ult Mariata ult Yemma ult Tofenat. All the way back to Tin Hinan. She wrote the name in the amulet to protect her newborn; and she bound it up with the best protective charm I've ever seen, binding the spirits of the parents to take care of the child, weaving the words in and out of one another, drawing a web of safety, a net that would draw those three souls together. She thought it would never be in this world but only in the stars, but sometimes fate makes up for its mischief and writes its own pretty *conte de fée*.'

She leant forward. 'Tell me, child, how did you come by the amulet?'

I told her, and watched her smile, a long, satisfied smile.

'So that's the story you were spun, was it? Well, let me give you an alternative version. Mariata had her child, and it was a girl, and she wrote its name in the amulet and tied the talisman around it for luck. Rhossi, he wanted sons. But the baby, someone else's baby, he didn't want that. He left it to die. She went back, though, ran away on the wedding night to where she'd left the child. In the tomb of Tin Hinan—ah, the patterns of life and death, they're elegant and ineluctable. But there was no baby when she got there; just tyre tracks and the imprint of feet. Feet wearing shoes such as

508

you'd not find in all of Mali or Niger. One man and one woman, she told me; and he was much bigger and heavier than the woman, whose feet were hardly larger than a child's.'

I could not take my eyes off her, but all the time my heart was racing and my mind was thinking ridiculous things like 'My mother's feet were tiny, she was a size 3 . . .' And knowing there was something wrong with this sentence.

Tana touched me on the forehead. 'You have that serious look she used to get when she was concentrating on something. Except that her brows used to meet; I see you shape yours to prevent that. Yes, my dear, no matter what they told you, you did not belong to them. They did not make you. They found you in a desert tomb and they stole you away.'

I felt the world spin. I blinked and swallowed and tried to focus.

'You say the woman was French, yes?'

I nodded.

'They must have smuggled you out somehow,' Tana mused. 'I'm sure there are ways of doing these things, especially for rich Europeans . . . War of the Sands notwithstanding, such things never really touch Europeans: they live in a different world to the rest of us.'

'The birth certificate, Izzy,' Taïb said suddenly, his warm brown eyes filled with wonder. He dug in his pocket and drew out a piece of folded green paper. I stared at it: the last time I had seen it was when the Fennec had thrown it across his tent in frustration. 'I knew as soon as I saw it that it was a Moroccan birth certificate. You see the stamp?' He indicated the faded rectangle at the bottom of the faded green paper. 'That's Hassan II—our old king. It's very faint, but show that image to any Moroccan and he'll recognize it in an instant.' He laughed. 'You've got a Moroccan birth certificate!'

A fake birth certificate, prepared and stamped by some corrupt official for a bit of baksheesh. 'No, it's not,' I said so faintly it was almost a whisper. 'It's not my birth certificate. I don't have one.' But I could feel the joy slowly overcoming my confusion, seeing off my doubts, gradually, inexorably rising up inside me, like water drawn up into the light from the depths of a dark well.

*   *   *

'Tana told me you would come.'

'How could she know that?'

'You know Tana: better than I do. She knows so much.' A pause. 'Do you know, I have carried you with me all these years, in my heart, over my heart.' She unpinned a silver brooch that was fastened to the centre of her chest and unwound the leather binding that held it closed. From within she took a scrap of indigo cloth tinged with rusty brown, folded small. She gazed at it fondly for a moment, then let it flutter to the ground between them. 'That came from your sleeve, when they tore me away from you. I thought it bore the last of your lifeblood, until I realized I carried your child inside me.' The smile she turned on him was luminous. 'Did you not recognize our girl when first you met?' She chuckled. 'Fancy abducting your own daughter!'

He shook his head. 'How could I know? I did not even know there *was* a child, and making a

510

connection like that, in such circumstances . . .' He let the sentence trail off. It was absurd. 'Of course not.' He paused, thinking. 'And yet, you know, there was something about her. Something of you.'

'I knew her at once. I would have known her amongst a thousand women. She has your eyes.'

Amastan felt moisture gather in his own. He dashed it away with the back of his hand: the asshak demanded that you did not show weakness, even to your wife. But the tears were too strong for him, and at last he let them run down his face, into the cotton of the tagelmust. 'She has your chin,' he managed at last.

Mariata reached a hand to his cheek. 'Let me see you. Let me see your beautiful face.' She drew the veil down and gazed at him, taking in greedily every muscle and pore of him, every line and wrinkle. 'I do not care about the time that has passed between us: it means nothing. You are the same as ever. You are my Amastan; and I am your Mariata. Never leave me again. Promise me.'

He found he could not say anything, so instead he simply nodded, and folded her hands against his heart.

TWO YEARS LATER

The desert sun, striking down out of the pale blaze of the sky, cast its light upon a group of figures in an encampment set at the foot of the mountain. The scenery was spectacular: on one side jagged, volcanic peaks rose to pierce the horizon; on the other a dramatic sea of sand lay unmoving, its crests and troughs caught as if frozen in a moment of time. In a pasture near by—vivid emerald against all the red—camels grazed or sat staring patiently into space, their jaws shuttling contentedly from side to side. Down by the silver strip of river a herd of black goats tumbled neatly from rock to rock. Play-fights broke out between some of the young males, and the bellows of the rams upbraiding this precocious behaviour echoed off the red walls. Across an enclosure on the far side of the camp, beyond a number of dusty vehicles, a knot of children had gathered outside one of the long, low-slung tents, listening intently to two men who were robed and veiled in the traditional fashion. The older man had a strong, craggy profile and watchful eyes. At present these were trained on the younger man, who gestured enthusiastically, and then bent and traced great looping lines in the sand at his feet with the aid of a pointed stick. He stood back to survey his handiwork, then walked quickly away and came back some moments later with the skirt of his robe full of stones. Beneath the robe he was wearing jeans, well cut and narrow-legged in the French style. He cast the stones down and a great cloud of dust rose up and made the nearest children sneeze and shout. The older man said something and they all laughed, so that even the harsh planes of his face for a moment gave themselves up to a less fearsome expression. The young man placed one round, red stone upon the path of one of the ellipses he had drawn, then another, larger and lighter in colour, a little further away. More stones were set amidst the whirling, concentric lines. The children looked on fascinated but bemused. He talked with great animation, pointing first to the stones, then up to the sky, then to the desert, and finally made a grand, expansive sweep of the arm that drew them all into the pattern he had made.

Two women sat apart from all this lively education, looking on with a mixture of tenderness, pride and amusement. In profile they could be mirror images of one another, for the sun's lavish attentions had erased the wrinkles on the face of one and hazed the detail of the other. If it were not for the contrasting colours—silver and black—of their braided hair, they might have been sisters, or maybe cousins. They both wore blue robes, loosely draped, cool in this heat, coloured head-wraps, silver jewellery and kohl that outlined their dark, expressive eyes; one wore a watch, but it was no kind of status symbol, being plastic, digital, uncompromisingly cheap and functional. She consulted it, stood up, pressed her hands into the small of her back and stretched as luxuriously as a cat, then walked towards the class. The other woman patted an amulet—a massive, four-square chunk of etched silver embellished with glowing red discs—that was displayed proudly upon her breast, then pushed herself to her feet, threw the long tail of her head-wrap back over one shoulder and followed.

'And what is this?' The young man pointed to a white pebble and the children craned their necks.

'*Tellit?*' one of them questioned, turning to the older man and regarding him solemnly.

Amastan beamed. '*Tellit*,' he confirmed.

'The moon,' echoed Taïb. '*La lune.*' He touched a piece of rose granite sitting on the next of the elliptical rings he had inscribed in the sand. 'And can any of you remember what this is?'

A girl with her hair in half a dozen braids said something in little more than a whisper. Taïb cupped his hand to his ear and she repeated it timidly.

'The red star, yes, exactly that: Mars. Well done, Tarichat.'

He got them tracing their own ellipses and placing planets and their attendant moons in suitable positions, asking and answering questions in a mixture of English, French and Tamacheq. And then someone trod on Venus, fell over and knocked Earth out of its orbit, and suddenly everyone was laughing and adding new stars and asteroids where there had never been any before. At that moment a great shadow fell across the sand, and they all turned to see what had caused this phenomenon.

One of the boys laughed and shouted something out and Amastan grinned, his teeth startling white in the tan that showed between the black folds of his tagelmust. 'He says you have caused a solar eclipse!'

Taïb walked over and placed an arm around the newcomer's expanded waist. 'How are we to teach

514

them their place in the universe when my giant wife comes and bestrides an entire solar system?'

Izzy punched him affectionately on the arm, which for some reason the children found hilarious.

Mariata shook her head. 'You men, always so concerned about your place in the world. We women have other things to concern ourselves with.' Her bright black eyes sparked an affectionate challenge; Amastan gave her his little half-smile. She held his gaze for a long heartbeat, then leant over and placed a hand on her daughter's bump. 'So, have you decided yet?'

Izzy flashed warning eyes at her mother, but Mariata carried on regardless.

'Where you will give birth?'

'There is no question. She will go back to Paris to have it,' said Amastan, all smiles gone. 'My daughter will give birth in a clean, modern clinic where there can be no mistakes.'

Beside him, Taïb looked equally fierce. 'Absolutely. Izzy, we talked about this! You can't have the baby here, it would be madness.'

'Madness!' echoed Amastan.

They stood shoulder to shoulder: two halves of the same bean. Izzy caught the phrase in her head, turned it over and examined it, amused. Didn't she mean 'two peas in a pod'? Sometimes she found herself using sayings she'd never used before, knowing things she shouldn't have known, given her upbringing. It was weird; but at the same time quite normal. She was almost getting used to it.

'Look, I know all the arguments, I'm aware of the dangers; but you know women have been having babies in the desert for thousands of years!

No—don't say any more: I haven't decided yet. But don't forget that Jean and Anne-Marie will be here.' These were the two French travelling doctors paid for by the trust Taïb and Isabelle had set up with Izzy's redundancy payment and the money from the sale of the two London houses. Taïb's thriving trade in commissioned artefacts for the American and European collectors' market was also a source of revenue; Tana had passed many of her inadan skills on to the younger generation, though not without keeping many of her secrets back, and the results were striking and much in demand.

Mariata gave her daughter one of her looks out of the corner of her bright black eyes, sly and amused at the same time. Izzy knew what it meant: it meant, make your own mind up and take no notice of the men—what do they know of these things? We are desert women and we take our chances with the desert. Knowing the argument would eventually be won, she cunningly changed the subject. 'And what will you call her, have you decided on a name?'

'Are you so sure she'll be a she?' asked Amastan, only slightly belligerent.

Mariata's lips curved beatifically. 'Oh, yes, I have no doubt of that. I've read the signs.'

Taïb shook his head. 'You always know without us saying a word. I don't know why you ask. Izzy and I discussed it and came to an agreement last night.'

'No matter how long I live, women will always remain a mystery to me.' Amastan gave a mock-sigh. He regarded his wife solemnly, perhaps even a little reverentially; a lingering glance passed between them.

Forty years, thought Izzy. Even after two years she had not got used to the idea of finding herself the daughter of such parents. It was like borrowing someone else's life, stepping into a world of fairytale—though a fairytale from a far more benevolent universe than that of Perrault or the Brothers Grimm. Would she and Taïb still be so vitally connected, so alive to one another, after such a time, she wondered. The concept was unreal, absurd, but at the same time quite delightful. *Think how old we will be then!* She laughed at the image thus conjured and looked up to find her husband watching her in an intent way that caused a warm flutter in her abdomen. Or perhaps it was just the baby kicking. Yet again.

'Lallawa,' she said softly, laying her hand across the swell of her belly. 'I feel I owe the world a Lallawa: for the old one who gave her life to the desert; and for the girl who never had a chance to grow up with that name.'

GLOSSARY

adhan	the Muslim call to prayer
afrit	a malevolent spirit
ag	son of
ahal	a Tuareg celebration
Amazigh (pl. *Imazighen*)	Berber, the Free People
amenokal	the chieftain of a drum-group of tribes
amghrar	a tribal chief
anet ma	the maternal uncle, more important than a parent
asfar	Tamacheq word for 'pale-skinned'
asshak	the Tuareg code of honour and mutual respect
azalay	salt trading expedition or caravan
babouches	handmade leather slippers
baggara	a wanderer, a beggar
baraka	the force of good luck
barchan	a curved, crescent dune
bokaye	a sorcerer or manipulator of spirits, West Africa
djellaba	a hooded robe
djinn (pl. *djenoun*)	a spirit, often malevolent
enad (pl. *inadan*)	a Tuareg blacksmith, often skilled in magic and ritual
erg	a sand-sea
fesh-fesh	quicksand
fichta	a Berber celebration
funduq	a shelter for camels and

518

	travellers
ghûl	a malevolent spirit
guedra	a ritual women's dance
guelta	pools of standing water
haik	a traditional women's robe
hamada	a rocky plain
harratin	agricultural workers
Iboglan	Tuareg aristocrats
iklan	tent-slaves
kasbah	a fortress or fortification
Kel Asuf	the spirits of the wilderness
kohl	a dark eyeliner made from antimony
ma'allema	a teacher of religion and such skills as embroidery
madugu	a leader of a camel train or caravan
marabout	a wandering holy man or religious teacher
mechoui	spit-roasted lamb
mehari	a fine quality white camel often used for racing
m'smen	Berber pancakes
oued	a dried riverbed or wadi
qareen	a personal demon
redjem	a tumulus or burial mound
Sah'ra	Arab word meaning 'dun' or 'mouse-coloured'
sehura	a sorceress
sif	a long, blade-like dune
souq	the market
tagelmust	the veil worn by Tuareg men
tajine	an earthenware cookpot, and the dish cooked in it
takouba	a Tuareg sword

519

Tamacheq	the spoken language of the Tuareg
tamerwelt	a hare
tassoufra	a food bag
tcherot	an amulet
tefok	the sun
tehot	the evil eye
Tifinagh	the ancient written alphabet of the Tuareg
ult	daughter of

AUTHOR'S NOTE

This novel came out of the conjunction of two inspiring stories. The first was the discovery that my husband's family roots lie amongst the nomads of Mauretania who brought silver, spices and salt from sub-Saharan Africa through the desert by camel caravan to trade in the markets of Morocco.

The second was meeting a Frenchwoman who had come to the remote Berber village in which we live seeking her father: a Tuareg trader with whom her Parisian mother had had an affair in the 1960s. She had discovered the truth of her paternity only on her mother's death-bed: all her life it had been a mystery, a shameful secret. In contrast to Abdellatif, she had spent her life feeling rootless and confused about her identity, existing as only half a person, never really fitting into the world in which she lived. The rest of her story is not mine to tell; but I must thank her for the inspiration, because without it I would never have written this book.

SOURCES AND BIBLIOGRAPHY

Enfants des sables, Moussa Ag Assarid and Ibrahim Ag Assarid (Presses de la Renaissance, 2008)

Amazigh Arts in Morocco, Cynthia J. Becker (University of Texas Press, 2006)

Art of Being Tuareg, T.R. Seligman and Krystine Loughran, eds. (University of Washington Press, 2006)

Men of Salt, Michael Benanav (Lyons Press, 2006)

Those Who Touch: Tuareg Medicine Women in Anthropological Perspective, Susan J. Rasmussen (Northern Illinois University Press, 2006)

Tuareg Jewelry, Helene E. Hagan and Lucile C. Myers (XLibris, 2006)

Call of the Desert, Philippe Bourseiller (Harry N. Abrams, Inc., 2004)

Tikatoutin, Marceau Gast (Éditions de la Boussole, 2004)

Contes et legends Touaregs du Niger, Laurence Rivaille and Pierre-Marie Decoudras (Karthala, 2003)

In Quest of Lost Worlds, Byron de Prorok (The Narrative Press, 2003)

The Sword and the Cross, Fergus Fleming (Granta, 2003)

Veil: Modesty, Privacy, and Resistance, Fadwa El Guindi (Berg Publishing, 2003)

Civilizations, Felipe Fernandez-Armesto (Free Press, 2002)

Desert Divers, Sven Lindqvist (Granta, 2002)

Sahara, Michael Palin (Weidenfeld & Nicholson, 2002)

Sahara, Marq de Villiers and Sheila Hirtle (Walker, 2002)

Les Touaregs, Edmond Bernus (Éditions Vents de Sables, 2002)

Touaregs, Helene Claudot-Hawad (Gallimard, 2002)

Sahara Man, Jeremy Keenan (John Murray, 2001)

Touareg: la tragédie, Mano Dayak (Hachette, 1998)

The Pastoral Tuareg, Johannes Nicolaison (Thames & Hudson, 1997)

Desert Travels, Chris Scott (Traveller's Bookshop, 1996)

The Blue People, Karl G. Prasse (Museum Tusculanum Press, University of Copenhagen, 1995)

French Lessons in Africa, Peter Biddlecombe (Little, Brown, 1994)

The Tuaregs, Karl G. Prasse (Copenhagen, 1985)

Africa Adorned, Angela Fisher (Harry N. Abrams, Inc., 1984)

The Tuaregs, Kenneth and Julie Slavin (Gentry Books, 1973)

Sahara, Rene Gardi (Harrap, 1970)

The Sheltering Sky, Paul Bowles (Penguin, 1945)

*   *   *

'Unrest in the Sahara: Niger's Nomads Fight for Rights', Alex Sehmer and May Welsh (report, Al Jazeera, 2008)

'Mali's Peace Process: Context, Analysis and Evaluation', Kåre Lode (report, Conciliation Resources, 2002)

'The Rise of Amazigh Nationalism and National Consciousness in North Africa', Dr Larry A.

Barrie (assessment, Strategic Studies
Detachment, 4th Psychological Operations
Group, Airborne, 1998)

*   *   *

www.amazighworld.org

www.mondeberbere.com

*   *   *

Written to a soundtrack of music by Tinariwen,
Tidawt and Etran Finatawa

ACKNOWLEDGEMENTS

Thanks to my husband, Abdel, for helping me to shine a light upon a mysterious culture I would never otherwise have had a chance to comprehend, and for giving me the ancient Tuareg amulet on which the story is based; to Mohamed and the school at Tiouada; to Hassan, our desert guide, and the camels who bore my weight and shocking inexpertise without too much complaint; and to everyone who patiently answered my many dense questions about the nomadic life. To Emma, Karen and Philippa for their support through the writing of this complex book; to Venetia and Jenny at Viking Penguin for their determination and passion; to Danny Baror for his unflagging faith and encouragement.

Being neither an anthropologist nor a linguist, I owe a great debt to my written sources; but any errors of interpretation are almost certainly my own. I've listed my main sources above for any who wish to pursue this fascinating subject further.